THE INFINITE
SEA

Books by Jeffrey A. Carver

The Star Rigger Universe
Panglor
Dragons in the Stars
Dragon Rigger
Star Rigger's Way
Eternity's End
Seas of Ernathe

The Chaos Chronicles
Neptune Crossing
Strange Attractors
The Infinite Sea
Sunborn
*The Reefs of Time**
*Crucible of Time**
(*Pts 1 and 2 of the *Out of Time* sequence)
Masters of Shipworld (planned)

Novels of the Starstream
From a Changeling Star
Down the Stream of Stars

Standalone Novels
The Infinity Link
The Rapture Effect
Roger Zelazny's Alien Speedway: Clypsis
Battlestar Galactica (miniseries novelization)

Omnibus Ebook Editions
Dragon Space: A Star Rigger Omnibus
The Chaos Chronicles: Books 1-3

Short Stories
Reality and Other Fictions
Going Alien

THE
INFINITE SEA

Volume 3 of The Chaos Chronicles

Jeffrey A. Carver

Starstream Publications
in association with Book View Café

THE INFINITE SEA

Copyright © 1996 by Jeffrey A. Carver

Afterword copyright © 2010 by Jeffrey A. Carver

All rights reserved

A Starstream Publications Book
in association with Book View Café

Discover other books by Jeffrey A. Carver at
www.starrigger.net

Starstream/Book View Café print edition: 2019

Edited by James Frenkel for Tor Books

Cover art by Chris Howard
saltwaterwitch.com

Cover design by Maya Kaathryn Bohnhoff
www.mayabohnhoff.com

Ebook ISBN: 978-1-61138-464-2
Paperback ISBN: 978-1-61138-803-9
Audiobook ISBN: 978-1-61138-856-5

To the memory of Gene,
who loved the sea

PRELUDE

Julie Stone

SHE AWOKE TO the sound of the ventilators in her spacesuit. Where am I? Julie thought. And then she remembered: she was in a cavern on Triton, and she'd just made contact with the alien artifact. But what had she—had she lost consciousness? Distant memories jangled in her mind.

Her thoughts were interrupted by a voice in her ear. The helmet comm: "Julie—can you hear me? Ron, I can't get a reading on her monitors, but I think she's alive."

Kim. Her supervisor.

Of course I'm alive. Why wouldn't I be?

"Her eyes are open!" Someone bending over her, hands shading her faceplate to cut the reflection. "She's breathing, I think. Julie, can you hear me?"

Can you hear me? The words drifted back, voices in her head:

Mission yet to fulfill . . . require your assistance, Julie Stone . . .

Assistance? What kind of—?

And as consciousness had slipped away, the voices simply moved farther inside . . .

. . . John Bandicut sacrificed everything to protect Earth . . . saved his homeworld . . . rogue comet . . .

"Julie!"

She started, flinching where she lay on her side, the hard casing of her suit digging into her shoulder and hip. "Yes. Yes!

I'm okay; help me up."

The looming helmet moved away, and hands were lifting her by the arms, helping her to stand. And then she was on her feet, tottering, surrounded by a knot of her crewmates from exoarchaeology. Triton, yes. She was on Triton, in an underground cavern, bluish ice and a bit of rock, halogen lights shining off everything.

And it talked to me. The artifact talked to me. She struggled to remember . . .

. . . stopped the immediate danger . . . but may be other . . .

. . . other . . .

. . . other . . .

. . . require your assistance . . .

What kind of danger—?

"What happened, Julie?" someone was asking.

She shook her head, the bits of memory unraveling and disappearing. "Not sure. What did you see?"

She couldn't quite focus, didn't know who was talking. It was Kim's voice: "The object glowed. It appeared to be engaged in increased activity. You passed out. The activity continued for about ten seconds, then returned to normal. That's when we got to you."

Increased activity? She remembered the appearance of the artifact: a collection of black and silver spheres, seeming to twirl and move through each other, all balanced like an inverted pyramid. "Did you hear anything?"

Through the reflective faceplates, she couldn't see faces, but she could sense the puzzlement in the voices. "We didn't hear anything," Kim answered. "What did you hear?"

She shook her head. "I don't know." She stepped forward through the knot of spacesuited people—then, on a sudden urge, turned to look back at the object, the alien artifact. It had black and iridescent globes, not silver. The translator; that was what John Bandicut had called it. But she thought maybe it had said so, as well.

"Julie?" said Kim. "Can you tell us what happened?"

"I don't—" her voice caught, and she tried to recapture it. "I don't think so. Not just yet. I think I need some quiet to think about it." She turned to her right and was able finally to peer through the faceplate to see the eyes of her coworker. "Can we leave now?"

Kim's eyebrows arched. "All right," he said. "Let's go, everyone! Let's get Julie back to the rover!"

But as she followed Kim, trying to recapture the memories, the words and images could not be formed; thoughts and voices were whirling together like a storm in her mind, in her dreams, in her subconsciousness. So difficult to remember. Except for one phrase that kept recurring:

... *something still out there which is trying to destroy your world* ...

CHAPTER 1

Into an Alien Sea

NOT AGAIN! IK thought. He peered out of the golden bubble into a cerulean sea. Overhead, but receding with each heartbeat, was the rippling mirror of the ocean's surface. Below lay the darkness of the ocean depths, into which they were sinking rapidly — trapped in the forcefield bubble that had swept them across uncounted light-years.

Li-Jared was making frantic bonging sounds. He was terrified of deep water, so this must have been his worst nightmare come true. On Ik's other side the Human, John Bandicut, looked as if he had stopped breathing. He was staring down into the twilit depths, eyes bulging with fear and concentration. He was pointing to something, stuttering incomprehensibly.

It *is* happening again, Ik thought. *Rakh.*

John Bandicut turned around to look at all the others. "Do you see it?" he shouted. "Tell me I'm not crazy! Do you see it?"

Bwong-ng-ng-ng-ng— "See what?" Li-Jared cried, lunging drunkenly from one side of the bubble to the other. "There's no bottom! All I see is water! We're all going to drown!"

But Ik saw now what Bandicut was yelling about. Lights. Below them, and very dim, but growing slowly. Ik bent down to peer through the bottom of the star-spanner bubble. The lights seemed to be globe-shaped. They looked . . . artificial. Like an undersea city.

That was what Bandicut was trying to say. They were plummeting *toward* something, not just sinking to the bottom of an alien sea. Ik didn't know what it was, but he recognized the hand of the Shipworld Masters in it. Someone had aimed them in this direction, and had known there would be something waiting for them in the depths of this sea. Ik found a slight trace of comfort in that knowledge.

Bandicut was trying to calm the terrified Karellian. "Li-Jared, there's something down there! Take a look for yourself!" With that, he plunged his head directly through the side of the bubble, extruding himself into the water without disturbing the bubble at all.

"Hrah—he's right—I see it, too!" Ik said, finding his voice at last. He drew a deep breath and followed Bandicut's example, sticking his head through the bubble wall. The bubble gave and stretched over his skin; he felt a sense of pressure and cold, but no water actually touched him. He held his breath and peered down.

He could see the lights more clearly now. They were definitely drawing closer. Was it really possible that they were bubbles of air? He popped his head back out of the water to take a breath.

Bandicut was looking at him, in the deepening gloom. "My guess is we want to reach those things. Is there some way we can steer?"

A voice from behind Ik said, "Are we certain that we want to?"

Ik turned to the newest member of their party: Antares, the Thespi third-female, Bandicut's acquaintance. Ik barely knew her, but she had helped them all survive their recent battle with the boojum, back on Shipworld. "I'm not sure we have any choice," he said. "It would certainly seem that this place is our intended destination."

The Thespi blinked, her golden eyes wide in the failing light. "So it would seem," she said, stroking the gemlike stones in her throat.

"We're being carried off to one side," Bandicut said, peering outside again. "I think we're going to miss those structures. You don't suppose the star-spanner forgot to allow for currents, do you?"

Ik touched the side of his head, querying his voice-stones. /Can you advise on the guidance of this travel unit?/

There was a short flurry of feedback sensation, before the voice-stones answered:

Guidance negative. Wait for arrival.

Bandicut's gaze had gone blank and unfocused. A moment later it returned to normal. "According to Charlie, my stones say we've been *renormalized* to this environment. Is that supposed to mean we can breathe water?"

"Hrrm, I would not be eager to test such a supposition," Ik said. He caught the eye of Li-Jared, who had stopped panting long enough to stare back at him, the bright blue slits across his eyes wide with fury and panic. "But according to my voice-stones, we cannot steer; we must wait for arrival."

"Arrival?" Antares muttered. "I thought we'd already arrived."

"Yes, well—" Ik rubbed his chest uncertainly. They were sliding farther and farther into the darkness of the depths. The surface was no longer visible, though a blue hue overhead pointed the way back to it. Below, the lights were pulling off to one side. Bandicut was right; they were going to miss them.

Ik felt himself instinctively trying to will the bubble back toward those globes. But it was no use. Soon the lights were level with them, far off to one side. Then they seemed to slide upward and away, as the sea continued darkening. Ik felt the air in the bubble growing thick and dense in his throat.

"Can we do nothing?" Antares murmured.

"Hold on! Look there!" said Bandicut, pointing the other way.

Below, and on the other side, more lights were coming into view. Ik tried to gauge the bubble's movement, and decided that there was at least a chance they would pass close to those lights. And what would they find?

Ik sighed through his ears, touched his forehead, and began preparing himself for whatever world they were about to enter.

Something was moving in those globes of light.

Bandicut was almost certain of it. He strained to see more clearly. The globes were growing larger, but the haze of the water obscured his view. The array had the look of a sunken city; but he hardly dared believe it.

He wondered how much longer the air would last in the star-spanner bubble.

/// Not to worry.
If it can keep us alive halfway across the galaxy,
it can probably give us a few minutes more
underwater. ///

The voice of the quarx in his head was laconic. The alien seemed almost relaxed about their sudden entry into this ocean. Perhaps, lacking a body of his own, he felt less sense of danger.

/// You think I'm too stupid to know danger? ///

Jarred by the remark, Bandicut said, /No . . . I don't think you're stupid./ But this quarx was a very different individual from the last Charlie, whose death was still terribly immediate in his mind.

As the lights drew closer, growing in number, something resembling a landscape began to emerge from their illumination. The globes were gathered in clusters, and they were attached to or suspended from a steep submarine slope that was barely visible now, in shadowy outlines behind and beneath them. Only a few dim, scattered lights were visible in the darkness further below. If they failed to connect with this cluster, they might fall forever.

"Are we going to miss them?" Li-Jared asked, as though reading his mind.

No, Bandicut thought. *Yes.* He couldn't tell.

"Bandie John?" Antares' eyes caught his with sharp intensity.

Was she reading his fear? Feeling it? He hardly knew her. And yet he was unsurprised to sense her empathic awareness. It felt right, somehow.

Before he could answer, though, he felt a vibration under his feet. There was a sound, like a distant murmur. "What the—?"

"Hrahh, it feels like a quake," said Ik. "A distant quake. Do you feel the current, shifting sideways? We *are* going to miss those structures!" Ik's sculpted blue face looked skeletal in the undersea light, as he twisted around to look at them.

"I feel it," Antares said, her eyes glinting.

Bandicut closed his eyes a moment, feeling the movement. Ik was right. If they couldn't reach those structures . . . how deep *was* this ocean, anyway?

He glanced at his companions, their faces dimly lit by a low-level luminosity in the bubble itself. Ik the tall Hraachee'an, his small dark eyes glittering with inner points of light. Li-Jared the simian-looking Karellian, with his narrow, vertical eyes of gold, bisected by electric-blue horizontal slits, wide with fear. Antares, so much like a human woman and yet no such thing, her face delicately angular, her eyes almost Asian-looking, her expressions inscrutable. And the two robots who had traveled so far with him from Triton, dumb machines who had somehow been transformed into sentient beings. Bandicut was grateful for all of them. But he had no wish to die here with them.

"Captain," said the robot Copernicus, "I am uncertain of the medium outside the bubble. But I detect objects or entities moving toward us."

Ik was already looking past the robot. "Someone *is* coming! This way!"

The bubble rocked as they all leaned to see. At first Bandicut could see nothing. And then, like spots before his eyes, he began to focus on very small figures moving through the watery gloom. Moving toward them. Swimming.

For a fleeting moment, he was afraid he was hallucinating.

> /// *After what you've been through,*
> *I'm surprised anything surprises you.* ///

Bandicut grunted. On Shipworld, he had seen everything from fractal beings to sentient ice floes. Why should this—

"They're coming for us," Ik said, interrupting his thought.

He could see five or six figures now—arms and legs moving

rapidly. He thought they looked humanoid, but they were still too far away to tell.

Antares pressed her face to the side of the bubble. "They're bringing lines," she said, her voice muffled.

Bandicut squinted. Indeed, there were long lines trailing behind the swimming figures. They looked less humanoid as they drew closer. They had legs, yes—but with webbed feet. They moved through the water with quick, powerful strokes.

"Captain—over here," said Napoleon, on the other side.

Bandicut turned, and stifled a shout. One of the swimmers had come from a different direction. It was pressing its webbed hands and its face to the bubble wall. Then it pushed its head *through* the bubble and into their midst. It looked like a monstrous apparition: shiny and black, with enormous eyes and pulsing slits along the side of the head, and a mouth slightly open, revealing two rows of sharp teeth. It stared first at Bandicut, then turned to look at Li-Jared.

The Karellian squawked in alarm and backed away. Bandicut could not even find his voice.

Ik spoke up sharply. "Stand back. Don't frighten it!"

Don't frighten *it?* Bandicut felt twin impulses: to flee from the thing, and to kill it.

The sea creature gave a muffled cry that sounded like an animal in pain. Then it popped back out into the sea, leaving the bubble undisturbed, and Bandicut and the others gasping.

*/// I've got this feeling
that these are our new hosts. ///*

"Here are the others." Ik pointed to a cluster of similar creatures gathering on the other side of their bubble. The new arrivals peered in from the near darkness, without poking through.

Bandicut stared out at those toothy, bug-eyed faces. /New hosts—?/

The creatures were working with their lines now, stretching them around the bubble. It took Bandicut a moment to realize what they were doing, and by then the bubble was enclosed in a net. The undersea creatures cinched the lines tight with a jerk that sent Bandicut and the others staggering, and then the creatures began to tow the bubble through the water.

CHAPTER 2

Ocean Rescue

IT WAS LIKE dominoes falling. Ik stumbled into Antares and Li-Jared stumbled into Bandicut, and Bandicut fell against the side of the bubble. His face pressed out of the bubble into the sea, hard against the netting. It took a moment of struggle to get back in. He staggered, gasping, back into the center of the bubble.

They were moving at a surprising rate, under tow. The sea creatures pulling the lines were mere shadows once more, nearly lost in the undersea gloom. "They're taking us toward those structures," Ik said, gazing at the cluster of luminous globes, ahead of and still somewhat below them.

"Are we being rescued or captured?" Antares asked.

Ik hrrm'd and did not answer.

The sea creatures were powerful swimmers. The bubble's motion toward the lights was unmistakable now. But were they actually pulling the bubble themselves? Bandicut thought he could discern a large, round shadow out ahead of them, and thought he heard a hum through the water. He couldn't guess how massive the star-spanner bubble was, but it could not have been an insignificant load.

"Captain," said Copernicus, "I estimate we will intercept those structures in four to eight minutes. Our sink rate has slowed, with the addition of the buoyancy bladders."

"Uh?" Bandicut was startled to see clusters of what looked like grapefruit attached to the net around them. Where had they come from? They seemed to be swelling, as he watched.

"Why are we sinking at all?" Antares asked. "We're in a bubble of air. Why aren't we floating?"

Bandicut blinked, and had no answer.

> /// I wouldn't be surprised
> if we had a supermassive thing or two
> under the hood of this thing, ///

Charlie murmured.

/Ah./ Before Bandicut could voice the thought, Li-Jared did it for him, looking as if he were trying to distract himself from stark terror.

"Star-spanner module—" he gasped. "Micro-singularities—" *bwang* "—for spatial transformation." Trembling, he peered back out.

They were leveling off at the depth of the approaching globes. Habitats. Bandicut could clearly see shadowy figures moving inside them now. Their magnitude was becoming evident as the travelers drew close; the globes were large enough to hold living space for sizable groups of people.

In the pale light of the habitats, he could make out the tow line now. A current of fine, floating particles was jetting backward through the water toward them. And although he couldn't distinguish its form, he was nearly certain that the shadowy object ahead was a submarine, or at least a propulsion unit.

"Hold tight," Copernicus warned. An instant later the bubble jostled and yawed, moving through a change of current. The sea creatures were fanning out with secondary tow lines, probably to steady them in the current. The star-spanner bubble began turning in a slow sweep—past a group of habitats, and on toward a solitary structure that was emerging from the haze ahead of them. They slowed, as they were towed into position beneath the single globe. The mass of the habitat slid over them like a roof. Bandicut felt a moment of dizziness and claustrophobia. Then the tethers pulled tight and the bubble swayed to a stop.

His translator-stones uttered a single word:
Arrival.

Several minutes passed in silence. Four or five of the sea creatures were gathered around them in the gloom, and above them, several more were visible through the transparent underside of the habitat. "What are they waiting for?" Bandicut muttered.

/// Maybe for us to make the first move. ///

/Which would be what? To sprout gills and swim out? I wouldn't even know *how* to get out of this thing. If I wanted to./

/// I suspect that the stones can help.
But I'm not too clear on what you can expect
when you enter the water. ///

/That's something I'd sort of like to know./ Bandicut craned his neck, looking up. The air in that habitat was almost certainly at seawater pressure, and that had to be fifteen or twenty atmospheres at least. He could only guess at their depth here; but with most of the sunlight gone, it was surely close to a couple of hundred meters. What sort of air would they encounter, and would they keel over or go into convulsions from gas toxicity—or fall into a drunken stupor from nitrogen narcosis? For that matter, he wondered what kind of air they had in the star-spanner bubble. He'd done some scuba diving back on Earth, enough to know the heavy sensation of pressurized air. But the air he was breathing right now didn't feel that way. And yet, surely they were at ambient pressure, or how could he have poked his head out into the surrounding water?

Li-Jared was talking, his voice reverberating oddly as he peered up. "I think I see a boundary layer up there—"

The Karellian was talking to Napoleon, the monkey-legged robot from Triton, who was now stretched up and leaning back at an odd angle, pointing his sensory-array overhead. Copernicus, likewise, was whipping his array back and forth, scanning everywhere. "Readings are ambiguous," Napoleon answered with a rasp. "But I believe you are right. There appears to be an air-water interface above us. However, I am unable to obtain spectrographic analysis."

"Nappy," said Bandicut, "can you tell if there's a pressure differential between us and them? Because if there is—"

"Uncertain, Captain." The robot clicked quietly a few times, then said, "I am detecting changes in the membrane layer surrounding us."

Bandicut glanced at his friends in alarm. "Do you mean the *bubble's* membrane?"

"Hrrrrl, we must be prepared for emergency evacuation," Ik muttered, glancing around—wondering, no doubt, what any of them could possibly do, if the bubble failed. Could they bolt straight up, into that habitat? Not likely, if high-pressure water came crushing in.

"Napoleon, is the bubble getting ready to break?" Bandicut demanded.

"Uncertain," said the robot.

Bandicut glanced around anxiously. There were now seven or eight shadowy figures gathered around the bubble. By turns, they pressed their faces to the bubble membrane, peering in, their huge eyes like orbs of darkness. What were they waiting for? Were they hungry for alien blood, or just curious?

"No evidence of hostility yet," Ik said.

Li-Jared bonged suspiciously.

Antares stirred. "Actually, I do sense . . ." She hesitated for a moment, then swung her maned head around to gaze at her companions. "I do sense hostility—*uuhhhl*, suspicion. I am not certain we are going to be welcomed."

"Well," Ik said, "it's likely we were sent here in order to meet these people, or people like them. Some provision must have been made for us to be able to interact with them."

Bandicut stared at him. "Nice of whoever sent us to share that information with us. What are we supposed to do, punch our way out and swim for it? Bye-bye, Napoleon and Copernicus. You two can't survive immersion at these pressures, can you?"

"Doubtful, Captain," said Copernicus.

Bwang. "Aren't there any damn controls on this damn thing?"

"I do not know," said Antares. "But I sense your distress, Li-Jared. Please—we have come so far, and after defeating the boojum. Let us trust that there is a way. Please."

The electric-blue band across Li-Jared's eyes pulsed.

Ik spoke suddenly. "I believe we are pressurizing."

Bandicut listened, and heard a soft but growing sigh. He soon felt the pressure on his ears and sinuses. Pinching his nostrils, he blew gently to equalize. "Where's it coming from?"

Li-Jared was swaying in obvious discomfort. "It's coming from everywhere—through the bubble membrane."

Bandicut held up a hand to the wall of the bubble. It was true; there was a breeze of incoming air from the entire inner surface of the bubble. Pressure was building rapidly on his ears now. He pinched his nostrils again, blowing. "I hope it knows the right gas mixture to use," he muttered.

/// The stones say the renormalization
can handle it, if you're careful—and lucky. ///

If I'm careful—?

"*Uulullululu!*" A cry of pain from Antares interrupted the thought. She was crouching, holding her head in her hands.

Bandicut knelt beside her. "Antares? Is it the pressure?"

"Y-y-y-y-y-y—"

/Charlie! Can our stones talk to her stones? See if they can help?/

/// How would I—hang on. ///

Ik was on Antares' other side, touching her arm, speaking softly. Every few seconds, his own face tightened, and he touched his forehead, then relaxed.

/// Ask her if it's better now. ///

"Antares? Is it easing? Can you equalize pressure?"

Her eyes closed and opened again. "Y-yes. Whatever it—was—my stones have—" She sighed. "Thank you, Bandie John Bandicut. And Ik."

"Hrrm," Ik said. He was already looking up, working on the next problem. The incoming air was starting to taper off. If the pressure was now equalized with the outside, was the bubble about to sprout a door?

Bandicut recalled an old joke about a screen door on a submarine, and shuddered. But what he saw was an opening on the bottom of the habitat above them, dilating like the pupil of an eye. The bubble jostled slightly, pressing against the bottom of the habitat. A soft glow was beginning to form around him, and around each of the others. On an impulse, he touched Copernicus, then Napoleon. A glow formed around each of them, too. "I think," he said, "we're being encouraged to leave the ship. Who's first?"

"Hrah," said Ik.

"Oh hell," said Li-Jared, hopping experimentally up and down. "I'm probably the only one who can get up there." His eyes were like golden, upright almonds, with a slash of electric blue across the centers. "Everyone ready?"

Without waiting for an answer, he sprang up and reached *through* the top of the star-spanner bubble, and caught his hands on the lip of the habitat opening. "Ock," he said. "I think it's going to let me through." The glow from his hands was radiating outward through the bubble membrane. He levered himself up, headfirst, into the opening in the bottom of the habitat. A moment later, he disappeared through the bubble membrane, and was surrounded by several shadowy figures, who pulled him out of sight.

"Li-Jared? Are you all right?" Ik called.

At first there was no answer. Then Li-Jared's head became visible again, above the bubble membrane, which was otherwise undisturbed. If he spoke, his voice was inaudible.

"Hrrm." Ik hefted something in his hand. His rope. He tossed the coil upward, holding one end. The other end flickered through the top of the bubble and disappeared. The sea creatures drew back, startled. A moment later, Li-Jared reappeared holding the rope and apparently making it fast to something above. Ik turned to the others. "Would anyone like to go next?"

Bandicut squinted. "Do you think we should take the robots?"

"If they stay here, what will they do?" Ik asked.

Good question, Bandicut thought. They might be in less danger above. Who knew what was going to happen to this bubble? Would it finally pop, and that would be the end of it? Were they going to live out their (possibly short) lives at the bottom of this alien sea? "All right, let's take them," he said. "Why don't I go last, and help them up?"

Ik's eyes sparkled. "Lady Antares, would you care to wait while I investigate with Li-Jared?"

Antares made a hissy laughing sound. Bandicut did not think that it represented amusement. "Be my guest, if you want to go next," she said. "But don't think I won't be right behind."

Ik made a soft clicking sound, which *was* amusement. He tugged on the rope, then simply held on as it contracted upward, lifting him through the top of the bubble and out of sight. The rope reappeared, followed by his head, upside down. "Come on up," he said, then disappeared again.

Antares glanced at Bandicut. "You will follow, with them?" she asked, indicating the robots.

"We'll be on your heels."

"Safe passage, Lady Antares," said Copernicus. "We'll rejoin you as soon as possible."

Antares dipped her head, and began to climb the rope.

"Just hang on," Bandicut said. "Let the rope do the work."

She glided up and through the bubble membrane.

Bandicut wrapped the rope across Copernicus's back and gave it a tug. The rope contracted and pulled him up out of sight. For a minute or two, nothing happened; the rope did not reappear. Then it did—with Copernicus still attached. He settled back onto the floor of the bubble. "It would seem, Captain," he reported, "that they do not wish me present at this time. I would guess that the same applies to Napoleon."

"Why not?" Bandicut said sharply.

"Unknown, Captain."

Bandicut thought a moment. "All right, you stay here. And watch my backpack, okay? But if anything happens, I want you to give a yell—a loud one. Napoleon, you think you could jump up through that opening if you had to?"

Napoleon flexed his knees slightly. "I think so."

"Okay. I hope you'll be all right here." Bandicut touched a hand to each robot. Then he grabbed the rope and rose, spiraling slowly.

CHAPTER 3

First Contact

BANDICUT FELT A collar of water swirling around him—not quite touching him, because of the protective field of the translator-stone. Then his head popped out of the water, and he found himself floating in a circular basin in an air-filled chamber. Ik reached out to help him climb onto the dry floor. He gasped, as water rolled off the forcefield in rivulets; then he felt the forcefield disappear as he stood, chilly but dry, to one side of the entryway.

He blinked, looking around. To his surprise, he had not stepped out of a well, with sides, as he would have expected in an underwater habitat, but rather out of a round grey patch in the middle of a smooth floor. Aside from the floor, the chamber appeared spheroidal, flattened a bit in the vertical dimension, and glowing faintly from the walls. The air was moist and cool, and it bore the tang of salt and seaweed, and it was perfectly breathable—except that he was quite suddenly holding his breath. He and his friends were surrounded by half a dozen crouching black sea monsters—not quite as large as he was, but with oversized eyes in their glistening, vaguely newtlike heads. Some of their hands and feet seemed webbed, and others didn't. They all wore simple harnesses, with knives and other tools attached. Bandicut tried not to stare. He extended an open palm. "Uh—*hello*," he croaked.

A murmur rippled through the assembly of sea creatures, and they seemed to draw closer together.

Bandicut pulled his hand back. Ik muttered, just audibly, "They may have taken that gesture as a threat."

"They're definitely afraid of us," murmured Antares. "That's why they sent Copernicus back. I think they were afraid he was a weapon."

Bandicut grunted. /Now what?/ he wondered.

/// Go slow, ///

suggested Charlie.

/That much I knew./

The sea creatures were hissing among themselves now, and one of them suddenly moved forward, past Bandicut, and jumped into the entryway. The creature sank through the floor and vanished into the water. The others stared at the visitors, without speaking.

Bandicut wondered if they had just sent someone to get a leader. He raised his eyes to look at the chamber walls, glowing faintly; they looked to be made of some flexible material, plastic-like and yet organic—like some tough, translucent seaweed. Or a material inspired by seaweed. "You guys get the feeling this place is made of plant material?" he murmured. "It almost seems *alive*."

"Hrrm," Ik said softly. "I had a similar impression." As he spoke, the sea creatures stirred, and Ik raised his hands to what looked like a prayerful position, palms together with fingers spread, pointing upward. "We come from a far place," he said slowly. "We mean you no harm. We would like to speak with you." He gradually turned as he spoke, facing first one creature then the next. It was clear they did not understand a word, but he obviously hoped that his voice-stones would translate.

They might have been trying. *Something* was happening, because the sea creatures were starting to become agitated. Ik drew himself up taut, then spread his hands, trying to calm the sea people. "Ik, wait—that's not—" Antares began.

It was too late. Whatever Ik and the stones were trying to do, it was backfiring. The creatures moved in sudden concert. Bandicut felt a quick, strong grip on his shoulder, pulling him back onto a kind of bench seat. Before he could even focus on the webbed hand that was gripping him, he felt loops of rope drop around his chest and cinch tight, pinning his arms to his sides. "Uh—" he grunted, and strained futilely at the bonds.

Each of his companions was caught, as well, and bound with what looked like long, tough strands of an undersea vine. Behind Ik, one of the glistening creatures made a reedy squawking sound, which was answered by the others. A chuckling sound rose in Antares' throat, and it was not a sound of pleasure. Li-Jared was twanging ominously.

Ik, on the other hand, was silent—and nearly motionless. He appeared to be testing the vines for strength. Bandicut wondered what he was thinking. Ik had probably the calmest disposition of anyone in the company, and if Ik got upset you knew it was time for action.

But the best course of action right now was undoubtedly to remain calm.

/// *Agreed.*
What else can you do, anyway? ///

/I don't know, but if the translator-stones have any ideas, I would appreciate hearing them./ Bandicut blinked sweat from his eyes. Strange to be sweating in this chilly air. He studied his captors, and found them studying him. /I seem to remember those stones putting on a pretty good display of power once, when I needed it./ It seemed a long time ago, but wasn't really, since he had fled Triton and Neptune—and ultimately the solar system—in a stolen spacecraft. The black stone in his left wrist had used holograms or forcefields or some goddamn thing to make him look like a terrifying alien, terrifying enough to scare the captain of *Neptune Explorer* off her ship. He wondered if they might want to do something like that now.

/// Where would you go, if you got away? ///

asked the quarx.

/// What would you do? ///

Bandicut was silent a moment. /Yeah,/ he said.

One of the sea creatures was circling behind the members of the company now, examining each one of them. Bandicut took a good look at the creature in return. It was more humanoid than he had realized at first. Its oversized eyes and the general newtlike appearance of its head had distracted him from the rest of its body. But it had a mouth about where he might have expected, and it had nostrils, plus an array of what looked like gills on its neck. It was obvious that the things were amphibious. This bothered him, for reasons he couldn't identify. Did he have some deep-seated aversion to frogs? Or was it the quarx's response, leaking through into his own emotions? Charlie-One had had quite a xenophobic streak . . .

/// And you're so damn perfect—? ///

Before Bandicut could respond, there was a ripple in the center of the floor, and the head of another of the sea beings popped up out of the water. The creature climbed with quick grace into the chamber, and spoke with short mutters and hisses to the others of its kind, while inspecting the captives. It wore a somewhat more elaborate-looking harness than the others.

A leader? Bandicut wondered. He exchanged cautious glances with his friends. Ik was calm, but Ik was always calm. Li-Jared, on the other hand, was barely able to contain his frustration and rage. The new arrival seemed to sense that; its gaze lingered a little longer on the Karellian. Antares' eyes flickered, watching Li-Jared, then meeting Bandicut's gaze. She made a small gesture with her closed right hand, which he did not know how to interpret.

The apparent leader saw the gesture, as well. He raised a half-webbed hand, and pointed at Antares, then Li-Jared.

"*Squee-awwww!*" he called, in a shrill bark. Three of the other creatures responded at once, and moved to separate Antares and Li-Jared from their friends.

"Wait!" Bandicut protested. "We didn't mean anything. What are you doing?"

"*Skaaawwwww!*" cried the creature.

Bandicut felt a sudden backward jerk as the creature behind him yanked on the rope. He had to fight for a moment to keep his balance on the bench. The creature behind him made a warbling sound, probably of anger. Had they interpreted Antares' gesture as a threatening move?

"John Bandicut, I recommend silence, for the moment," Ik said. "Until we can—"

Ik's words were cut off by a yank on the rope binding him.

Bandicut scowled, but did not move, as Li-Jared and Antares were pushed toward the exit spot. Through the translucent floor of the habitat, he could see the faint shadow of the star-spanner bubble being moved to one side. He tensed, thinking about Napoleon and Copernicus.

Bwong. "What are these devils doing?" muttered Li-Jared. He was bending as far forward as the sea creature holding him would allow, peering down through the exit spot.

To Bandicut, what it looked like they were doing was preparing to push Li-Jared and Antares out of the habitat. He flashed on images of terrorists summarily killing hostages, and he strained involuntarily at the ropes. /If they start to push them out of the habitat, I want those stones ready to move fast. Can they make me look intimidating again?/

/// *I have no idea.*
Hey, wait a minute—look. ///

Bandicut squinted. Another shadow was moving into place under the habitat. There was a low rumble, a thump, and a soft hiss. The floor at the exit point turned to a shadowy circle, and then seemed to open—to reveal nothing much but shadow.

"*Skeeekawww.*" The leader of the sea creatures spoke, and

gestured sharply. Li-Jared was shoved forward; he stepped awkwardly, and as he was about to fall, grabbed the edge of the hole and lowered himself indignantly into the well. Antares was pushed after him. One of the sea creatures quickly followed.

"Li-Jared! Antares!" Bandicut shouted, heedless of the ropes cutting into his shoulders. "Are you all right?"

He heard some muffled cursing—and realized that he had heard no splash of water. Then the Karellian's voice twanged, "There's air here. Not much light. Seems to be some kind of submarine."

Antares called, "We are unhar—"

And the opening vanished, cutting off the sound of her voice. The floor was solid again, with only a grey patch where the opening had been.

"Hey!" Bandicut protested to the sea creatures. "Why can't you let us talk to them?"

"*Akka whadeddekka.*" The leader spoke sharply, and Ik and Bandicut were pulled apart from each other, none too gently.

Bandicut glared at the leader. He felt a vibration under his feet, and looked down to see the shadow of the vessel holding Li-Jared and Antares drop away from the habitat, glide forward, and disappear. He looked back up at Ik, feeling his own mouth tighten with anger. Anger and determination. But what was he determined to do? His friends were gone, and he was trapped at the bottom of an alien sea.

"Be patient," Ik counseled, eyes glittering. "Remember the long view."

The long view, he thought sardonically. Even Ik didn't sound all that convinced this time.

———————

/What the hell are we supposed to do now?/ he thought, staring in silence at the sea creatures.

*/// Well, my assumption would be
that these fish-people are as suspicious of you
as you are of them. ///*

/No doubt. So what do we do about it?/ As he spoke to the quarx, he felt a powerful desire to rub his wrists, which was difficult to do with his arms bound to his sides. His translator-stones were itching fiercely, deep in his wrists. Were they working to crack the aliens' language? It seemed an impossible task without meaningful points of reference.

The sea creatures were speaking to each other in soft staccato hisses, their large eyes seeming to revolve like wagon wheels as they peered at Ik and Bandicut—surely an illusion. Four of them remained in the habitat.

Moments later his wrists weren't just itching, but burning. The desire to rub them was almost overpowering. He felt dizzy, his thoughts beginning to blur. If he and Ik could break free, could the two of them overpower their captors? Would they want to? They didn't want to be seen as enemies. They had to let the sea creatures know that.

Ik had been flexing his arms slightly, but gave no indication he intended to do anything. "Ik," Bandicut murmured, "are your stones . . . getting any handle on their language?"

Ik spoke with difficulty. "I sense the voice-stones are working hard. I do not know what they are learning."

"Me neither. My stones are—"

His words were interrupted as two of the sea creatures gripped his arms and lifted him abruptly to his feet. He was startled when they loosened the rope around his arms and chest. "Uhh, that's bet—*ukkhh*—" He choked as they pulled one of the loops tight again—around his neck. It was tight enough to hurt, and to make the threat clear. He stood stock still, breathing with a soft rasp, as they lifted his arms and began prodding at his body and pulling on his jumpsuit.

/// *They're examining you.* ///

/Yah. These guys'd make great proctologists./

When they finished patting him down, the leader of the sea creatures stood in front of him, peering into his face. Its gaze seemed almost cross-eyed, as though focused on a point in front of Bandicut. It spoke to its companions—or possibly to Bandicut—in a guttural hiss. Bandicut returned its stare, trying to memorize its face so that he could recognize this individual again. He studied the horizontal lines in the surface of its glistening ebony face, running from the mouth and flat nostrils back toward what he assumed were gill structures on the sides of the neck. If it had ears, he couldn't see them.

It spoke suddenly. *"Shwaaa-karee-h-h."*

Bandicut felt a sudden shooting pain in his wrists, which the creature was holding in its sharp-fingered hands. For an instant he thought that the creature was causing the pain; then he realized what it was.

/// Whoa—hold tight! ///

He winced at a flash of light on each wrist, and a flaring that was not a pain exactly but more like an explosion waiting to happen—a powerful sneeze—an ejaculation—

Replication complete.

And with that report from the translator-stones, a fiery spark blazed up out of each wrist. Bandicut felt a strange sense of relief, and of time being distorted and twisted. The sparks ballooned to the size of soccer balls—and floated, pulsing with light, one diamond and one dark smoky red, through the air toward the sea creature. It seemed to take seconds, but must have happened in an eyeblink. The balls of light rippled around the creature's head, then shrank back to sparks and vanished into each side of its head. The timeflow distortion vanished, too—as the creature squawked in alarm, dropped Bandicut's wrists, and clapped its webbed hands to its head. A moment later, the creature collapsed to the floor, quivering.

Bandicut was stunned. Before he could react, the noose around his neck was yanked tight and he was pulled over backward. "Stop!" he choked. *"Sto-o-o-p!"* He clawed at the rope. "It's—" His voice cut off with a wheeze. /Charlie—can't the stones do something—?/

/// That took everything they had.
They're still recovering— ///

"*Rakhh!*" Ik was suddenly towering above him, ropes stretching around his arms. The sea creature behind Ik was struggling to pull the Hraachee'an back.

"*Shakka!*" cried the leader, rolling into a crouch on the floor. "*Shakka!*" It had stopped shaking and was blinking its enormous eyes. "*You must . . . stop! Let . . . him go!*"

Bandicut heard a hiss, which matched his own astonishment. The rope around his neck loosened, and he drew in a ragged breath. He pulled the rope away from his windpipe, and got back to his feet and crouched down in front of the sea creatures' leader. "You—understand now—?" he gasped.

The being rubbed the sides of his head, where the two tiny sparks were just visible, glittering beneath the skin. "Under . . . stand?" he hissed—and Bandicut somehow sensed, through his translators, that the being was indeed a *he*. "No—understand, no." He rose, together with Bandicut, each of them peering into the other's eyes. "But—your words, yes. I—what has happened? How do I—?"

Bandicut swallowed. "I—it's hard to explain, I—didn't do it myself, really." And he closed his eyes, thinking. /What *did* happen? Did the stones reproduce? I still have my own, right?/ He realized he was rubbing his wrists, and now he looked down and saw that yes, indeed, he still had his own stones.

/// They reproduced, yes.
It took quite a bit out of them, too. ///

"What . . . have you done to me?" the sea creature repeated, more forcefully. "Who *are* you?"

Bandicut struggled to answer. How could he possibly explain the translator-stones? How could he explain that a mechanism from beyond the stars was enabling each of them to hear the other's words in his own language?

"John Bandicut!" Ik cried, interrupting. "Are you all right?" Ik was looking from Bandicut to the sea creature in astonishment.

"Yah," Bandicut said. "And yes—you just saw my stones dividing." He took a breath and shook his head, then spoke to the sea being. "I am . . . *we* have . . . come here from another world." He gestured helplessly toward the ceiling of the habitat. "You can hear my words . . . because of the *translator-stones*." He touched the spots on his wrists where his stones glimmered, then gestured to the being. "I hope they have not hurt you."

The creature rubbed the side of his head with hands that looked as if they were made of black rubber. "I do not . . . know. I do not think so." Pausing, he looked at his fingertips, as if he might have some trace to inspect. Suddenly his gaze turned inward, as if he were listening to something inside his head. Two of his companions started to move toward him; he raised a hand to stop them. His eyes focused again on Bandicut. "Stones of thought . . . and word. They are speaking to me! What are they going to do to me? What is their purpose?"

Bandicut swallowed, remembering clearly how he had felt when the quarx had first appeared, projecting its words silently into his mind. It had been a bewildering and terrifying experience. "Their purpose," he said, "is to assist you. Not to harm you; they will not harm you. They are not . . . well, I do not know *what* they are, exactly. But they can help you to communicate—and perhaps assist you in other ways." Bandicut glanced around at the other sea creatures, who were pacing suspiciously. "May I ask—your name? What I should call you?"

The being hesitated, then answered. "I am called *L'Kell*. And by what are you called?"

"I am John Bandicut. I am a Human." Bandicut gestured to his companion. "My friend is Ik. He is a Hraachee'an. Our other friends, whom you took away, are Antares and Li-Jared." He hoped for some reaction to the mention of the others, but L'Kell's expression remained unchanged. Drawing a breath, Bandicut continued. "We came from beyond your sky. Do you know the sky? Above the water?" He gestured upward, wondering if these people knew anything at all about the world above the ocean.

L'Kell took a step backward, drawing himself into a crouch. It looked like a fighting posture, hands raised with sharp-nailed fingers curved outward. "From—" *graaspaak* "—above? From the land?" He muttered something guttural, which the stones did not catch.

"Not the land—no!" Bandicut said hastily, wondering what bad association he had just triggered. "From *above the sky*." He gestured expansively upward. "From beyond your sun."

L'Kell was silent a moment, absorbing Bandicut's words. "From beyond—our sun—?"

"It is hard . . ." Bandicut thought, struggling to think how to explain. "May I ask—do you live just beneath the sea? Do you know the air?"

"Why are you here?" L'Kell demanded, ignoring the question. He blinked. Why am I here? /Why *am* I here?/

/// The question has occurred to me, also. ///

Bandicut shook his head. /Does any of us have even the slightest idea? Ik?/ He answered the creature finally, "I'm not sure. But it is not . . . our idea. We do not *know* why we are here." He cleared his throat. "However, if there is something we can do . . . to help?" He glanced at Ik and shrugged.

L'Kell's eyes shifted to Ik, then to his fellow sea creatures. Then back to Bandicut. "I tell you this—you will not be permitted to endanger us. However, if you are innocent visitors, we may speak. I have questions I would like to ask you. But our leader will have *many* questions."

Bandicut breathed a little easier. "We can hardly ask any more. We certainly do not wish to endanger or harm anyone." He spoke slowly, pausing to judge whether his words were understood. The translator-stones were doing well, but he feared misinterpretation. L'Kell's gill openings seemed to pulse, and the creature stroked at the spot where one of the stones had lodged. "I know that our arrival must have been very confusing," Bandicut added. "And the stones', as well. The stones . . . perhaps it will help you to understand—"

"Yes?" hissed the creature.

"—if I say that they are not *of* me, not part of my own body—and yet they work *with* me, and I am—" he hesitated "—grateful for their help."

L'Kell stroked again at the stones on either side of his head. It was a gesture that was familiar to Bandicut; he had seen Ik do much the same thing, on many occasions. But it was startling to see the gesture from so different a creature.

"May I ask," Ik interjected, with a glance at Bandicut that indicated that he understood at least some of the conversation, "if it is not too impolite—by what name may we call your people?"

L'Kell was startled by Ik's sudden entry into the conversation. He seemed to understand Ik's words, with perhaps a bit more difficulty. But then, they were Bandicut's stones, and the stones knew Ik's speech. L'Kell seemed to contemplate the question, then said, "We are the—" *graaa* "—people of the sea, the seafolk." And he pronounced a word that sounded through the translator-stone like ". . . Neri."

Bandicut blinked, aware that his stones had searched through his own memories for some associative word. "Neri," he echoed. *Nereids? From mythology?*

"And the Neri," continued L'Kell, "will want to know *why* you are here, *how* you have come here, and what you want of us."

"Yes," Bandicut murmured in reply. He wondered if L'Kell had even a glimmering of an understanding of his statement that they had come from another world—through space, and not just space, but from beyond the stars. Did the Neri even know what stars were? It would be pointless to try to explain their flight here from Shipworld, an enormous artificial world orbiting outside the galaxy. He scarcely believed it himself.

"Hrahh," said Ik, rubbing his own voice-stones in his temples. "For now, we want only to live . . . and to learn about *you.* Perhaps when we know each other, we will understand why we are here—and what it is that you need from us."

L'Kell stared at the Hraachee'an for several long moments. He seemed to have understood the words—and they must have sounded as if they had come from a madman, or a visiting god: "—*what it is that you need from us.*"

Bandicut was taken aback, too. Why had Ik said that—as if he were expecting these people to *need* something from them. Shipworld had needed something from them, without ever quite getting around to explaining what or why. They had had to discover it for themselves, and risk their lives for it. Was that going to happen again here? Did Ik know something he hadn't mentioned?

"How would you know," L'Kell said carefully, "what my people need? And why would we need it from you?"

"I don't," said Ik. "I don't know. But there must be need." He glanced at Bandicut. "Why else would Shipworld have sent us here? It must have been a tremendous expenditure of resources."

Bandicut could not think of an answer.

All the other Neri were watching them closely. They clearly had no idea what was being said. L'Kell turned and spoke for a moment with his fellows. Their conversation was raspy, noisy, and seemingly heated. Bandicut couldn't understand a word. Apparently the stones translated only when the Neri was actually addressing Bandicut or Ik—perhaps as a courtesy to their new host. When L'Kell looked back at Ik and Bandicut, his black, rubbery hands were clenching and unclenching, his great dark eyes inscrutable. "They are right. We must take you to Askelanda. Are you swimmers? Water breathers?"

Bandicut gulped. "Uh—no." The thought of plunging into that watery darkness made him shudder, not from fear of drowning so much as claustrophobia.

L'Kell gestured to one of the Neri. The Neri made a clicking sound, touched the exit spot on the floor, and when the circle turned shadowy, slipped down the well and away into the water.

"We will provide transport," L'Kell said.

"Thank you," said Ik.

L'Kell's eyes gleamed, as though he were trying to judge the tone of Ik's polite remark.

A moment later, Bandicut became aware of a shadow moving under the habitat. He felt a bump, and heard a soft whoosh. The exit darkened again, and a Neri climbed up, the same one who had just disappeared.

L'Kell rasped out a command, and Bandicut was nudged toward the opening. He peered down into the well and saw an air space, in gloom but not total darkness. They were to be taken away as Antares and Li-Jared had been. "Before we go," he said to L'Kell, "can you please tell me—are our friends safe? Where are they?"

"They are safe," said L'Kell. "Board now."

Despite a harder nudge from behind, Bandicut resisted. "What about our vessel? It contains things we may need." Not least of which were his robots.

"It will be kept safe, too," L'Kell said. This time, the Neri behind Bandicut poked him sharply enough to hurt, and with a glance at Ik he climbed over the edge of the opening and dropped, feet first, into darkness.

It was cool but dry in the chamber. Bandicut felt a rounded floor beneath him, and rounded walls beside him. After a moment, his eyes adapted well enough to discern the visual contours of the little chamber. It was indeed a small submarine. He crowded to one side to make room for Ik. "Hrrm," his friend muttered, landing beside him and folding himself with some difficulty into the space.

A few seconds later, a pair of black feet and legs appeared between them, practically invisible in the gloom. One of the Neri dropped into the chamber. It was L'Kell. As Bandicut tried to make room, he banged his elbow against the wall. It echoed with a metallic bong.

"Metals technology," he murmured to Ik.

"Yes," answered Ik. "A submarine."

"What did you think?" asked L'Kell, crouching between them.

"We didn't know what to think. We really know nothing at all of your world," Bandicut said. He glanced up as another Neri dropped down and crouched in the back of the sub.

"Perhaps," said L'Kell, "we can show you a bit on our way in." L'Kell stretched out in a prone position, his head toward the nose of the submarine. Bandicut and Ik followed his example, which was not easy in the confines of the little vessel. There was barely room for three to lie side-by-side, Ik on the far left, and Bandicut in the middle, with the second Neri remaining crouched in back. The sub's nose was a clear window, through which they peered directly out into the sea. What light there was in the cabin came mostly from a small array of instruments and controls just below the window.

"May I ask," Ik said, peering past Bandicut, "where do you make such things as this submarine? Surely you do not make them down here under the sea, do you?"

That drew an indecipherable look from L'Kell.

Ik continued, "Do you have your factories above—on the surface of the water? Or on land?"

Bandicut sensed a reaction of displeasure from the Neri. "That," said L'Kell, touching the curved control panel, "is something I will not discuss now." A series of new lights came on near his fingers, as he peered forward out the window, preparing to pilot the sub. In the close quarters here, the air seemed staler and full of a mixture of metallic tang and organic, almost fishy smell—perhaps the smell of the Neri. L'Kell caught Bandicut's eye for a tense moment, as though to say, *Do not ask too much, yet. We are not certain we are not enemies.*

Bandicut nodded slightly and looked out the window. The underside of the habitat still loomed over them. Some light glowed into the water from the habitat, some from a headlight on the sub, below his view. Bandicut watched several shadowy swimmers move in and out of the region of illumination.

L'Kell called back toward the hatch. He was answered by a soft jolt and a slight change in air pressure. The hatch was closed. L'Kell touched his panel, and with a soft vibration, the sub stirred into motion—first sinking away from the habitat, then driving forward. /Motors,/ Bandicut thought. /*Quiet* motors. Magnetohydrodynamic, maybe? No moving parts? How do you suppose they power them?/

For a moment there was silence in his head. Then:

/// I don't know.
But I do know that this whole damn place
gives me the willies. ///

/Huh? You're the one who's supposed to be used to all these surprises./

/// Your other Charlies maybe.
Not me, guy. ///

/But you said—/ Bandicut swallowed, trying to remember what the quarx had said, back on Shipworld, not long after coming to life following the death of Charlie-Three. /You said you thought it was your destiny, or something like that, to go where the star-spanner wanted you to go. Didn't you say that?/

/// If I did, that was
before I knew I was going to be
on the bottom of some ocean,
on some godforsaken alien world. ///

/Mm./ Bandicut couldn't disagree with the sentiment.

/// I hate water, damn it! ///

/You hate it? You mean you're afraid of it?/ Now, that was an unnerving thought; he had come to count on the quarx for quite a lot of assistance and support.

/// Fuck you. Yes, I'm afraid of it.
I didn't ask to be. ///

/Look, I'm sorry, I didn't mean—/

/// Yes, you did.
The last thing you want is some dickhead
for a sidekick who's more afraid
than you are. ///

Bandicut winced and didn't answer. He couldn't. It was true. Sighing softly, he peered out the nose window and tried to see where they were going. Some distance away, and a little deeper, he saw a much larger cluster of glowing bubbles. Was that the real undersea city? Probably they'd been held temporarily in some sort of outpost, by what amounted to a perimeter guard. Beyond those bubbles, he thought he saw the dark contour of a sloping seafloor. So they really were at the bottom of the ocean. He wondered if this world had continental shelves, like Earth. If so, they were probably beyond the shallow continental shelf waters, on the descending bathyal slope, headed for the abyss. He glanced and saw Ik peering just as intently. He wondered what the Hraachee'an thought. Was this just a new adventure to him? Did he already have some inkling of their purpose here? Was he scared? There was something out there on the slope besides the habitats, though—just coming into view as they approached the outer city. It looked like reefs, illuminated by artificial lights, nestled into the dark, rocky slopes. Ik heard Bandicut's indrawn breath, saw what he was looking at, and remarked, "Artificial habitat for sea life? For food, perhaps?"

L'Kell noted their interest and steered in a slow arc past the reef area, which was framed on the open side by spheroidal and tubular habitats. The reef was swarming with animals that looked surprisingly like Earthly fish. There were long, silver creatures that moved in quick, gliding bursts; and Bandicut saw occasional flashes of bright yellow, crimson, and iridescent blues and greens as other fish swam into the brightest areas of lighting. There were other things besides fish, too: rounded, jetting creatures and floating jellies that looked like flying saucers.

"The reef growth is natural, but transplanted," L'Kell said. "Most of this marine life, including the reef itself, would not survive at this depth if we did not bring light and favorable currents to the area." As they glided past, Bandicut could see a great many light sources shining on the reef. He also saw a number of Neri working near the edge of the reef area, including several who appeared to be harvesting some form of kelp. A few of the Neri were smaller, and were wearing translucent hoods and ungainly back-packs. He pointed, and was about to ask, when L'Kell said, "Our young, learning to work the reefs. Until their—" *hssss* "—gills mature, they must wear breathing apparatus."

Scuba gear? Bandicut thought in wonderment.

"May I ask," said Ik, "how deep do these waters go, if you follow the slope down?"

"How deep?" said L'Kell. "If you go past the drop-off to the abyss, there *is* no bottom, because of—"

Clang-g-g! Clang-g-g!

L'Kell's words were interrupted by a sound like a distant bell, from outside the sub. L'Kell rasped out a sound that left Bandicut's stones buzzing in confusion, then spoke into something on the panel—a comm unit of some kind. A voice spoke, in words Bandicut couldn't understand, and L'Kell touched another control. The sub accelerated downward toward the deeper habi-tats with an abruptness that left Bandicut breathless. He had a feeling their visitor's tour had just been canceled.

CHAPTER 4

Askelanda

"MAY WE ASK what is going on?"Ik said quietly, as the small sub sped through the water.

L'Kell ignored the question, as his hands worked the control surfaces. It seemed to Bandicut, as he watched the Neri, that the controls were awkwardly designed for the Neri's hands; nevertheless, L'Kell was a skilled pilot. He steered the vessel on a breathtaking slalom course among six or seven immense, luminous habitats. Several times, as they passed the glowing walls, Bandicut caught glimpses of shadowy Neri inside the habitats, moving close to the walls, and peering out.

He shivered. For a brief, hallucinatory moment, he felt as if he were gliding through the skyline of an eerie, celestial city—or diving into a virtual reality sim—or anywhere except in the perilous depths of an alien sea. Then he glimpsed the looming blackness of the sea-bottom slope beneath the habitats, and heard a distant rumble of venting air bubbles, and suddenly it all seemed far too real.

The sub dove beneath a large cluster of habitats and slowed. L'Kell pitched the nose up, and Bandicut squinted as they rose toward an oval, mirrored surface which formed the underside of one of the structures. An air-water surface. There were two shadows in the mirror that appeared to be docked vessels. L'Kell steered between them. The sub bobbed, then rocked slightly, as it breached the surface. The top half of the nose window broke out of the water, and light poured in.

There was a whisper of air around Bandicut, and a popping in his ears told him that the cabin pressurization was increasing to match the depth. L'Kell ran his fingers over the controls, and most of the lights went out. Then he turned his head to stare at Bandicut and Ik. "There has been a very bad incident—many Neri hurt. When Askelanda meets you, he will want to know everything that you know about it."

Bandicut's voice caught. "We will speak honestly—but we know *nothing* of what has happened on your world."

There was again that strange illusion that the Neri's eyes were spinning. "I hope that is so. Now follow, and do not stray." Without waiting for a reply, L'Kell drew himself back into a crouch, gestured to the other Neri, then stretched up to open the hatch overhead. A shaft of light shone into the sub. "This way," L'Kell said, and climbed out.

Bandicut had to squirm around to get into the hatch tunnel. The hand and footholds felt awkward in his grip. When he emerged and looked around, squinting in the light of the submersible hangar, he realized that he was standing in a sort of conning tower or sail atop the sub. For the first time, he could see the hull of the vessel they had ridden in. It was about five meters long, metallic grey, with curiously fluted surfaces running along the hull and curling around the tower. Two similar craft floated nearby.

"Interesting," said Ik, poking his head out of the hatch beside him.

"Come," barked L'Kell, from the bow of the sub. Bandicut climbed awkwardly out of the tower and made his way along the narrow topdeck of the sub toward the docking platform. Four Neri stood on a walkway that ringed the open water, and it didn't take long to notice that they were holding pointed objects that looked like spearguns. L'Kell stepped across the gap between the sub and the walkway, and watched as Bandicut hesitated. It wasn't a difficult gap to jump across; what bothered him was the feeling of stepping over a glowing invitation to a bottomless grave.

As he crossed, he thought he saw a flickering of slightly brighter illumination below, and felt a faint rumble through his feet.

The Neri guards stirred. *"Geesh-kah!"* one of them muttered, glancing down. L'Kell answered in a more subdued voice. Bandicut could not understand the words, but the tone seemed clear: suspicion, as the guards stared at Bandicut and Ik . . . and unease. But was the unease due to them, or to the rumbling from below?

/I wonder what they've done with Antares and Li-Jared and the robots,/ Bandicut thought, following L'Kell into a tubelike passageway that led from the submarine hangar to another habitat bubble.

> /// Yes, well, I'm wondering
> what this terrible incident was
> that has them all so suspicious, ///

the quarx said moodily.

> /// Do you suppose our arrival on the planet
> had anything to do with it? ///

Bandicut frowned at the thought. /I hope not. Do the translators know anything about it?/

> /// They say they don't.
> I'm not sure whether I believe them. ///

There was something in the quarx's voice that worried Bandicut. Since when did Charlie doubt the word of the translators? This incarnation was starting to seem like a genuinely depressive personality, contrary to his cavalier initial appearance. /Why don't you believe them, Charlie? Is there something wrong?/

> /// Something wrong?
> Are you kidding, Bandicut?

Everything is wrong.
This whole damned thing is wrong.
I can't imagine why we're here. ///

Bandicut absorbed the quarx's words in silence. Whatever else he had to adapt to here, the newest quarx was going to be high on the list.

A sharp command from one of the Neri made him move a little faster. They were crawling more than walking now, up a sloping tube that was set at close to a forty-five-degree angle. The shoeless Neri, with the webbings retracted on their hands and feet, seemed to have little trouble negotiating the slope; but Bandicut, with his bare hands and rubber-soled shoes, was finding it difficult. Ik hissed and hrrmed behind him, apparently having some trouble, too.

The connecting tube finally came to an end, and they stepped out into a large chamber—a room—that for the first time looked like something that people might actually live in. Its walls were roughly spherical, but it was broken up by partitions into a variety of open spaces and alcoves, with overlooks and stairlike segments, and variously shaped pieces of furniture. After a moment, he became aware of the voices—a choir of hissing, murmuring voices. It was a choir without melody, though, almost like a rainfall over an irregular surface. Was it his imagination, or were the voices taut with urgency? All through the chamber, Neri seemed to be moving about, as though pacing.

L'Kell led them to a spot overlooking the open center of the room. Neri all around were turning or looking up at them, or peering down from higher balconies. Though he was unbound, he felt like a prisoner in chains. "Here we will wait," said L'Kell.

They did not have to wait long. There was a sigh of air pressure equalizing from somewhere, and an echoing gurgle of water. This seemed to cause a commotion among the Neri, and Bandicut tensed. The Neri below began moving toward the far side of the room. Bandicut instinctively leaned over the balcony and said, "What's this?"

Ik turned to look cautiously over his shoulder. Three or four spears were pointed at their backs. "I think," he said, in a droll tone, "that it is time to stay put."

Bandicut grunted, and wondered what Charlie was thinking. But from the quarx he heard only silence. Gloomy silence. /You there?/ More silence. And then:

/// Yeah. ///

Okay, he thought. He focused back on the Neri, who were gathering into something like a receiving line at an entrance. "L'Kell," he murmured, "what is this—someone arriving? A leader, or dignitary? Everyone seems—" L'Kell looked at him sharply, without speaking, and he fell silent.

A murmur rose, and two new Neri appeared at the edge of the room, walking through an opening in the crowd. At first Bandicut thought they were the ones being greeted. Then he realized that they were simply leading the arrival. Behind them, a Neri appeared who was clearly injured, or very ill, or old. It walked bent over, with an obvious limp. When it finally looked up, its face was covered with lesions and sores. It took a few steps into the room, then turned to look back.

Behind it, two more Neri were bearing a third on a litter. This one was not moving. Was it dead? Bandicut wondered. The voices fell silent. Another litter appeared. This victim was stirring, but only weakly. Finally, a fourth appeared, leaning on the arm of an escort. It appeared in a condition similar to the first.

The greeting Neri closed ranks behind them, as they moved toward the center of the room. Some of the Neri glanced up at the alien visitors—or prisoners—with an intensity that made Bandicut uneasy.

A taller Neri stepped out now from below the balcony on which Bandicut stood. The room fell silent. The tall Neri, who wore something around his neck that looked like a stole made of collected leaves and shells, spoke to the new arrivals in a voice that was a combination of whistle and bark. He stepped slowly among the new arrivals, touching each with a bony hand. Then he stepped back again, and turned the other way. Bandicut finally got a look at his face. His complexion was a dusty charcoal gray, rather than black. He appeared very old. Was he the leader?

A glance at L'Kell seemed to confirm that thought. L'Kell nudged Bandicut and Ik to attention. "Askelanda!" L'Kell called. "I have the—" *hssss* "—intruders here. Do you wish to question them?"

"*Hockkk!*" said Askelanda, raising one hand.

"This way," said L'Kell. Ik and Bandicut followed him down a half-stair, half-ramp, and approached Askelanda. The tall Neri studied them in silence, then made a gesture to L'Kell, who did the speaking. "Look before you at the latest casualties of the—" *hssss* "—death—poison—madness from ashore. Look at them and answer truthfully. Do you know what has caused this? Do you know the people—" he sputtered that last word, as if it caused a bad taste in his mouth "—who have caused this?"

Bandicut started to open his mouth, then closed it. From where he stood now, he could see little more of the injured Neri—except the pain on their faces. Even on their dark, alien faces, he could see the pain. A Neri wearing a harness with many pockets was moving among them, looking closely at each in turn. A healer? Bandicut swallowed, and glanced into the dusty-seeming eyes of Askelanda, and finally answered L'Kell. "I am sorry. I know nothing of this. We have only just arrived in this place, in this sea, on this world. We know nothing of what, or who, caused this."

L'Kell spoke to the leader.

Askelanda turned and issued several brief orders. The injured Neri were helped out of the room, and Askelanda turned back to L'Kell, who translated. "These brave swimmers have been stricken by an invisible blight—a blight from the landers, who poison even abandoned wrecks. They will die soon, all of them, unless Corono finds a way to heal them." Askelanda gestured toward the Neri Bandicut had noticed moving among the sick. Then he studied Bandicut and Ik for a moment, before continuing, through

L'Kell. "We would like to know about you. L'Kell has passed on strange reports. But know that if you are in any way responsible for the sickness that you have just seen, then you too will die."

L'Kell interrupted the leader, and there were some words back and forth before L'Kell continued the translation. "I do not mean this as a threat but as a statement of fact, since you have said that you come from above the water, where this madness, this sickness comes from." More words between them. "It is possible that you are innocent. If you are, then help us." Askelanda fell silent and waited expectantly.

Bandicut held out his hands in helpless puzzlement. As his wrists were momentarily exposed, a murmur arose from the Neri standing nearby. It was the stones, of course, twinkling beneath his skin. He wondered if they had noticed the stones yet in the side of L'Kell's head.

As if hearing his thought, L'Kell spoke above the murmurs so that the other Neri could hear him. "Do you want to know how I can speak to, and understand, the intruders? This is how." He turned his head, and a fold in the skin rippled, and the stone on that side of his head flickered, visible just for a moment. The other Neri hissed and muttered, more loudly still when L'Kell pointed to Ik, and Ik turned his head to expose *his* stones.

Askelanda whistled for silence. Bandicut was aware of the sharp-tipped spears still at his back. Askelanda took a step toward L'Kell and spoke sharply. L'Kell dutifully translated, "Are you still L'Kell of the Neri? Still yourself?" And with only a moment's pause, L'Kell answered the question. "I am, Askelanda. I am unchanged—except that I can speak with our guests." And with pointed hand gestures, he added, "These are John Bandicut the Human, and Ik the Hraachee'an."

Askelanda murmured softly. He turned and spoke directly to Bandicut. His words were an untranslated rasp.

Bandicut felt a sting in his wrists.

Raise your wrists, toward L'Kell.

/Uh?/ He blinked at the sudden instruction from his stones. Then he understood. He raised his hands, palms out.

L'Kell peered at him, uncomprehending. He touched his own stones for a moment, then stepped forward slowly. "I feel that we should . . . though I do not understand . . ." He took Bandicut's wrists in his hands and raised them to the sides of his head. His eyes seemed to lose focus.

Bandicut suppressed a shudder at the Neri's touch. L'Kell's skin felt dry and rubbery; there were folds and tucks along the fingers, where the swimmer's webbing had drawn back out of the way. Bandicut's stones began to tingle almost effervescently as L'Kell drew them close to his. Bandicut felt a flush of nervous energy as something passed out of him, through him, back into him. /What are we doing?/ he whispered.

He expected the quarx to answer, but instead the nervous rush peaked, causing him to shiver involuntarily. And then the stones answered:

Exchanging linguistic information.

The feelings ebbed away. He drew a slow, deep breath, and lowered his hands. "Can you . . . understand me better now?" he asked the Neri.

L'Kell's huge, black eyes blinked. "I can hear you clearly. But what just happened?"

Bandicut closed his eyes, trying to capture the precise answer to that question. He glimpsed a fleeting image of swirling clouds of knowledge, similar to what he had seen in the inner world of the ice caverns of Shipworld. He felt dizzy for a moment, and had to open his eyes to remain standing. "I think . . . I have just been given knowledge of your language, L'Kell. Your stones, which came from mine, have settled in—and have adapted, and learned. And now they have shared what they have learned, at least of your language." He touched his brow with one hand, still feeling some of the dizziness.

"This is extraordinary." The words were spoken flatly. He was startled to realize that they were not L'Kell's words. They were Askelanda's. Translated by his stones alone.

Bandicut bowed. "Askelanda?" he said softly. "Do you understand my words?" There was a reverberation around him as he spoke, an echo following his words. Were his translator-stones actually translating his words, audibly, to the Neri? Usually it took two sets of stones, communicating with each other. And yet, he recalled—a lifetime ago, when he was seizing *Neptune Explorer* for his comet-stopping journey—that the stones had turned his words into an audible alien tongue.

"It would seem so," said Askelanda, drawing himself a little straighter. "Astonishing!" He turned to the other Neri, and from the murmuring, it was clear that he was not alone in understanding the human's words. Bandicut was startled to realize that he, in turn, understood many of the expressions of surprise and suspicion around him.

Askelanda moved around him in a slow circle, studying him. "Who are you, really?" the Neri leader asked.

Bandicut touched his palms together in what he now knew to be a Neri sign of respect. "I am John Bandicut, Human, of the planet Earth. It is exactly as L'Kell said." He glanced at Ik, and realized that Ik was following his words, but not necessarily Askelanda's. "My companion is Ik, of the planet Hraachee'a. We are truly new arrivals to your world, and know only what we have learned here, from your people. We wish—"

"Then how," interrupted Askelanda, "is it that with no knowledge of our people, you have the power to do this?" He gestured to L'Kell. "What power *do* you have in these . . . stones? The power to make my leader your servant? Your slave?"

Bandicut started to shake his head, saying, "No. No." Then he sighed, realizing that he would have asked the same question. "Askelanda," he said, trying hard to get the pronunciation of the leader's name right, "I do not control L'Kell in any way, or wish to. This power—of words, of thought—is not even from me, really, but rather is—" and he hesitated, thinking, *is a gift of . . . the Shipworld Masters?* and finally said "—a gift of the translator."

"And who," said Askelanda, "is the translator?"

"Well—" Bandicut swallowed; this was no time to tell the whole story. "The translator is . . . the machine that gave birth to these stones." He rubbed his wrists. "Daughter-stones, they are called, daughters of the translator. We do not control each other, the stones and I. But by agreement, we often help each other."

Askelanda eyed him for a moment, then stepped away, motioning several of the Neri, including L'Kell, to walk with him. Moving away from Bandicut and Ik, they spoke in low voices for a minute. Finally they returned to face Bandicut.

"These stones of yours—they are very powerful. Can they help our dying friends?" Askelanda barked, his voice startlingly harsh.

"I don't know," Bandicut said, taken aback. He half closed his eyes and turn the question inward. /Can we help them?/

There was no reply from the stones, and the quarx was slow in answering. The first sound was a quarxian sigh. Then:

/// What am I, a miracle worker? ///

Bandicut drew a measured breath. /Well . . . your predecessors helped heal me of serious injuries, on two different occasions. I thought there might be a way. For the stones, maybe./

/// I can ask. ///

/But you know—/ he hesitated, stung by the quarx's sullen response /—it wasn't really the stones that did the healing. It was you—the Charlies before you. I guess it took some knowledge of my physiology . . ./

/// Well, I know nuts about Neri physiology.
So I guess the answer's no. ///

Bandicut exhaled, nodding. To L'Kell and Askelanda, he said, "I don't think so. Not without knowing more, anyway. Perhaps if we knew what happened to your friends—"

Askelanda silenced him with a raised hand. "We have much to learn, all of us. But there is no time; we must see to our people. There may be time for your questions later." He turned to L'Kell. "Take them to the—" *rrrzzz*

The final word was too much for the translators. But Bandicut thought he had a pretty good idea what it meant. "Have you ever been in jail, Ik?" he murmured under his breath.

"Hrah," was all the Hraachee'an said.

CHAPTER 5

Deep-sea Prison

THEY WERE SEPARATED from L'Kell and escorted out of the chamber by three untalkative guards. The first guard led them across the room while the others followed. They entered a transparent access tube that stretched horizontally toward another habitat. It felt as if they were walking underwater, surrounded by the deep-sea gloom, and the occasional movement of lights or fish. Bandicut glanced up, and could see no lightening of the ocean overhead. He suppressed a shudder, and wondered if it was nighttime on this side of this world.

The next "habitat" turned out to be a gourd-shaped structure whose primary purpose was apparently to be a juncture point among a number of other passageways. The guard leading them touched a spot on the wall, and an entryway opened to a narrower tube that slanted downward and curved away to the right out of sight. It was as steep and twisty as a child's slide; there was no way they could walk, or even crawl, down it without sliding out of control. The guard pointed in. "Go!" he said, waving his speargun.

Bandicut looked at Ik and shrugged. He sat carefully on the threshold of the tube. It creaked as it flexed under his weight, a low sound like a thumb rubbing tightly against a bass drum head. He took a deep breath. He pushed off—and slid feetfirst, completely in the blind. He felt a whoosh of air; he hit the curve with a jar, then the slope flattened out a bit. He sensed a barrier ahead, and an instant later his feet hit it and popped through. It slipped up over his body and his face, like nylon fabric whisking over his skin.

The pressure hit him in the ears, and he grunted, wiggling his jaw. He'd just gone down a slope, and thus a little deeper in the sea. He was also flat on his back on the floor of a habitat only a few meters across. There were lights around him in the darkness, and he slowly realized that the bubble was transparent, and he was looking out at the lights of the undersea city. He sat up, looking around. Was Ik coming?

Behind him, on the curved wall, a translucent pressure seal marked the attachment point of the tube. He could see the outside of the tube through the wall, curving upward and away. He also saw a shadow moving fast through the tube. He jumped out of the way—and Ik burst through the translucent seal and landed on the floor beside him.

"Ik, are you okay?"

The Hraachee'an didn't answer for a moment. When he sat up, he murmured, "Hrah, look at that. It would seem that we are to be imprisoned in a—" *rasp* "—fish bowl. Eh?"

Bandicut grunted. He looked up to see if anyone was following them into the bubble. What he saw made him curse. A ripple passed across the pressure-seal membrane, and the tube pulled free of the bubble. It drew upward and away from their prison cell. "Well, I guess we can forget about escaping."

"Urrr?" Ik followed the direction of Bandicut's gaze. "Urr."

Getting to their feet, they started examining the bubble, top to bottom. They were completely isolated. The bubble was tethered beneath the floor by a cable or rope. Around the attachment point were clustered some solid objects which Bandicut suspected were ballast. The bubble was definitely buoyant, though; as they walked around, it jostled and bobbed slightly. The tether, visible through the floor, disappeared down into the haze of the water. Bandicut could not see where it was attached; but in trying, he gave himself a rush of dizziness and claustrophobia, as he sought to follow it down toward what looked vaguely like a sloping bottom. He shut his eyes and waited for the feeling to pass.

Ik steadied him with a hand. "Are you unwell?"

"I'm okay. Just shouldn't have looked down there. Does that tether look awfully . . . *tenuous* . . . to you?"

Ik peered down, seemingly untroubled by the depths below. "Perhaps," he said. He looked up, his eyes glittering. "But look at it this way. If it breaks, we'll get to the surface quickly. We'll see the sun. Find out what color the sky is here."

"Yeah," Bandicut grunted, imagining the bubble rocketing to the surface. "Boom!" he said, pantomiming the decompressive explosion that would follow.

"Boom," Ik echoed, hissing with laughter. He folded his legs into the familiar lotuslike position that was his rest pose, and added, "I guess it would be better if we didn't."

"It would be better," Bandicut agreed.

"Take the long view, my friend John Bandicut. Take the long view," Ik said in a voice that was somehow, in spite of everything, reassuring.

Ik didn't mind too much the darkness or murkiness of the depths. What bothered him was the continual creaking and groaning of these frail-seeming underwater structures. He didn't suffer from claustrophobia, but he was constantly aware of the crushing pressure that surrounded them, and the thickness of the air with its metallic tang and organic richness; and every creak triggered a little spark of tension in his chest, a heightened awareness of the fragility of life here.

Partly to keep his mind occupied, he began a methodical study of all the lights that he could see from their bubble. In his view, it was always helpful to gather knowledge—anywhere, anytime, but especially in strange surroundings. He started piecing together a mental map of the undersea city, as far as he could make it out. There was just enough light cast through the water from various sources that he could identify several distinct clusters of interconnected bubbles, and perhaps a dozen more that appeared to float in isolation. He could just glimpse, past the edge of one of the nearer habitats, the artificial reef they had passed on their way in. Twice he spotted small submersibles similar to the one they had ridden in, but most of the activity he saw was individual Neri swimming around and among the habitats. Ik found himself envying their adaptation to this environment, and their ability to move with ease through both air and water.

He wondered if he would still envy them once he knew what was wrong here. He had just seen the dreadfully injured or sick Neri who had been brought in. But brought in from where? And why were they so badly hurt? There was no question in his mind that something serious was going on. Why else would Shipworld have hurled them across the galaxy to this place? Presumably some care had been taken to give them a fighting chance to survive, if for no other reason than that they were expected to accomplish something useful. Not that he didn't share John Bandicut's concern about their safety here—it would be idiotic not to. Especially given his previous experiences.

Before he'd met Bandicut, before he'd met Li-Jared, he'd been dropped by star-spanner onto a world in crisis, a world torn by strife. The people on that world called themselves the *Pelli*, meaning "as one, from the soil." But their society was broken into fractious elements, and their knowledge of the life sciences was great enough to permit deadly biological warfare. They had experienced alien contact before—which was probably the only thing that kept them from killing Ik outright, as an invader—but though they could accept outsiders to their world, they could not accept their own people. Despite Ik's efforts to act as peacemaker, in the end the factions would not come to terms. Ik was forced to flee, carried back to Shipworld by the star-spanner even as a cloud of airborne toxins was killing most of the population of the planet. He didn't know, even now, if anyone had survived.

And yet, despite that, he had to presume that there was hope in this situation. *The long view*, he thought, in his private inner refrain. *Keep taking the long view.*

A dim flicker of light caught his eye, and he peered off to his left, searching out its source. There it was again—not like a head-light or habitat light, but dimmer and more diffuse, like distant heat lightning in a stormy sky. He was about to call Bandicut's attention to it, when it faded from view.

Before he could describe it, his human friend asked, "What do you suppose they've done with Antares and Li-Jared?"

Ik sighed through his ears and turned, facing his friend. "I suspect they're probably in a jail just like this one, somewhere out there. I trust they're being treated fairly."

"Mm." Bandicut was walking around the bubble now, pressing his hands to the walls. "Well . . . the air here seems okay, anyway. It hasn't gotten stale yet." He paused and visibly drew a deep breath. "They must have some way of renewing it that we can't see."

Ik murmured agreement. "Perhaps some sort of osmotic or chemosynthetic process through the walls." He recalled their earlier observation that the translucent chamber walls looked al-most as if they were made of plant material. But he wondered now, having seen some of the Neri's remarkably versatile mem-branes at work, if this clear material were not simply a variation on the theme.

His friend nodded, but still looked worried as he touched the walls. "Are you afraid that the walls might fail?" Ik asked.

Bandicut raised his shoulders momentarily in that human up-and-down motion that indicated uncertainty. "There's no moisture condensation," he said, not answering the question.

Ik touched the wall. It was smooth and cool to the touch. "It must breathe somehow."

A movement outside caught his eye, and he peered out and glimpsed some small fish flashing by, their long slender bodies a muted quicksilver. "John," he murmured, pointing.

"I see them," said Bandicut. "It's incredible." There was a tone in his voice that Ik was able to recognize as strong emo-tion—though he couldn't say precisely which emotion.

"Why 'incredible'?" Ik asked. "Did you not expect to see ma-rine life here, because of the depth? Or is it something else?"

Bandicut shook his head, walking slowly as if to follow the silver school as they swerved away into the darkness. "No," he said, and his voice seemed on the verge of failure. "Not that."

"Then—"

"It's just that they look *so much* like the fish back home on Earth," Bandicut whispered. "I feel as if I could *be* on Earth." He gazed at Ik, and it was finally clear what he was feeling. Homesickness.

"Is this world . . . like your Earth in other ways, too?" Ik asked, feeling a sharp reminder of his own loss of a homeworld. "Do the Neri look as if they could be from your world?"

Bandicut shook his head no, peering outside again. "But who knows what's happened since I left? Millions of years could have passed."

"Well, we don't really know that, John Bandicut. My impression is—"

"That's just it! We have nothing but impressions!" the human cried. "How can we know?"

"We can't," Ik admitted, hearing in his friend's voice the anguish of someone who's left behind everyone he has ever known, to be thrown in among alien strangers. And to be put repeatedly into danger, for reasons unexplained. Ik understood his anguish very precisely. But though he, like Bandicut, felt driven to find answers, he was more able to accept the short-term ambiguities. To Bandicut he said, "I believe that the star-spanners complete their transits in outward time intervals not greatly different from the inner, subjective time." He clacked his mouth shut for a moment before admitting, "I do not know if the same applies to the means by which you or I were brought to Shipworld."

Bandicut stared at him, pinching his lower lip. Contemplating the spatial transformation that had carried him out of the galaxy? Bandicut made a gesture of uncertainty. "I know the quarx spent *eons* inside the moon Triton, traveling to my solar system after it was knocked out of another system by a terrible war." Bandicut's eyes went out of focus for a moment, but if the quarx was imparting any further information to him, he didn't speak of it.

"Hrrm," Ik murmured, following another school of fish swerving by—shorter, striped ones. "John Bandicut," he said, "if you are suffering with the thought that your world has died and vanished eons ago, you must not be so sure." He clacked his mouth shut then, and stood, seeing nothing, as he rubbed his fingers on his chest and wept silently for his own world—destroyed, not by the passing of eons, but by an exploding sun.

He finally faced Bandicut again and found his friend watching him. "Ik, have you been through the star-spanner before? You've never talked about it."

Ik found himself hissing with sad laughter. "You and I have done enough together to fill a turn of seasons—and yet, we have not been together so long. We have had so much to talk about—and so little time in which to talk." Though in truth, he had not been eager to speak of such difficult memories.

"What happened? Can you tell me now?"

Ik closed his eyes, remembering the pain. When he spoke, his voice was dry and hollow. "I was sent alone to a world at war, where I tried to bring peace. And I failed . . . I could not do it by myself . . ."

"That's terrible," Bandicut whispered, as he listened to the end of Ik's story. He guessed that Charlie must have felt a deep sadness, too, if he was listening—or at least the earlier Charlies would have. The quarx had tried and failed in more than one effort to help a world find its way to peace and survival. Bandicut couldn't tell what the present Charlie was thinking; the quarx wasn't talking.

When Ik fell silent, Bandicut asked softly, "Had you made *friends* there?"

Ik rocked his right hand in a side to side motion. "I tried. But in the end, there was no one I could trust, or who fully trusted me. And that was one of the things I thought, afterward—that I needed friends, partners, people I could trust to work with me, and whom I could trust with my life."

Bandicut nodded slowly. He did, in fact, trust his companions with his life. They had already saved each other several times over.

"When I met Li-Jared, and again when I met you, I felt that I had met such a person. And perhaps—who can say yet?—Antares." Ik hesitated, then hissed with laughter. "I wasn't so sure that I wanted to put it straightaway to the test, though."

Bandicut stared at him, unable to believe that Ik could laugh about it, until finally the absurdity of their situation began to bring laughter welling up in him, too. Ik's laughter stopped first; he slapped his side with a loud clapping sound.

"You okay?" Bandicut asked. He thought the Hraachee'an looked distressed.

Ik peered around in apparent befuddlement. "I was just wondering, hrrm, what one uses for a relief station around here."

They had to wait a while to learn the answer to that question. Bandicut was about ready to give up and go to sleep to postpone the issue, when a Neri swimmer appeared at the bottom of the bubble. He appeared to be towing something. The Neri made a wiping motion across the underside of the floor, and a shadowy circle appeared. A moment later, he pushed his head up through the floor, looked from Ik to Bandicut, and lifted himself into the bubble. He reached back down through the floor and pulled in two boxlike objects on tethers, one large and one small. He set the smaller one aside, and tilted the larger one. Water poured out of the box and drained out through the membrane in the bottom of the habitat, as if by magic.

Bandicut watched in amazement, wondering if Earth's technology could ever have done that.

The Neri opened the box's lid and indicated a round opening. He pointed, squawked briefly at Ik and Bandicut, and set it down on the floor of the habitat. Bandicut stared at the box, then at the Neri. "What the hell is that?" he said. "A portajohn?"

The Neri didn't answer, but made a hand gesture from below its waist into the box. Apparently that was exactly what it was.

Bandicut scowled, but had to admit that it was a lot better than going for a swim to relieve himself.

The Neri turned to the other box. It opened with a hiss; it had been sealed. He took out several smaller objects wrapped in what looked like large leaves. With a glance at his prisoners, the Neri unwrapped the objects. They appeared to be fruit: yellow, translucent, crescent-shaped wedges like waxy, oversized orange segments.

Bandicut felt his eyes widening with hunger, and unease. He wondered if he dared try it.

/// What th'hell, ///

murmured the quarx, speaking up for the first time in a while.

/You know what this is?/

/// Naw, but what do you want to do?
Starve? ///

Bandicut blinked. He looked at the Neri and made a hand-to-mouth gesture. "Food? To eat?" he asked. When the Neri merely stared at him, he asked, "What is your name?"

The Neri stood straighter, and as if he had finally gained the self-assurance to try speaking to aliens, said in a voice that had a gargling resonance, "I am Hargel. I will provide for your needs, for now."

"Hargel," Bandicut said. "Pleased to meet you. How long are we to be kept here?"

Hargel rubbed his thumbs and fingers together, in what seemed a nervous gesture. "This . . . food . . . should meet your needs. Please tell me if your needs are different." He handed one fruit to Bandicut, and another to Ik. He drew his hands back as if afraid to touch the visitors.

Bandicut accepted the offering, hoping that Hargel would answer his question. But the Neri simply turned away. Then, as though in afterthought, he brought one more thing out of the smaller box. It was a convex disk about the size of Bandicut's hand, balanced on a small base. He set it down, removed a small hammer from the base, and struck the disk. A bonging sound rang through the bubble.

"If you need assistance," said Hargel, "ring three times."

Ik spoke, haltingly, giving Bandicut the sense that the Hraachee'an's stones were working hard to produce Neri speech. "You . . . will . . . hear?"

"We will hear," Hargel said. He bent and touched the floor, and with one smooth movement plunged headfirst through the membrane and into the water. There was no splash, and almost no sound.

Ik and Bandicut looked at each other.

"I guess I'll try the fruit," Bandicut said.

"Hrah. I guess I'll try the portable—"

"Right," said Bandicut.

The fruit tasted like a combination of lime, mango, and a third taste he could not identify. Bandicut nibbled, his back turned to Ik, and peered out at the Neri city. He was finally beginning to relax enough to absorb the sight. He saw Neri moving through the water, but mostly at the limits of visibility. He thought he saw some smaller figures and he wondered, were those the young, the females, or someone else altogether?

"Hrrm," said Ik, joining him. "It works fine."

Bandicut looked up. "Glad to hear it. Are you going to try some of this fruit?"

Ik eyed the piece that Hargel had given him.

"It tastes pretty good, and I haven't keeled over yet."

"Hrah. That is encouraging." Ik nibbled at the fruit, then took larger bites.

"Ik, do you think we should put our stones together and let them do a linguistic exchange? It might help you talk to the Neri a little more easily."

"Yes," Ik said. "That is a good idea." He took another bite. His fruit was nearly gone.

"You must have been hungry." Bandicut set his own aside to finish later; it was only half eaten, but it had satisfied his appetite.

Ik finished his fruit, then sat, and Bandicut crouched before him and raised his hands. Ik pressed Bandicut's wrists close to his temples. The four stones pulsed. Bandicut felt a buzzing sensation in his mind, now familiar, as his stones joined with Ik's, transferring knowledge . . .

———

A wave of dizziness came over Bandicut, as the link dissolved. He swayed, feeling a great heaviness, then sank to the floor. He was nearly overcome with fatigue.

"John Bandicut, are you—?"

He gave a hand gesture to wave off Ik's concern. But he couldn't answer. He felt a strong, tingling preoccupation among his stones, a feeling that they were working hard to assimilate the information they had just received. They had been through a lot today, and they didn't want to have to explain just now. /Did we just download a lot of Hraachee'an background?/

/// Yep. Ik can speak Neri now,
and you're going to know what makes
Ik tick. ///

Bandicut blinked, trying to clear his mind. /I am?/

/// Well, the stones will.
Close enough. ///

Bandicut sighed. He wanted desperately to close his eyes and put all of this out of his head for a while.

"Hrah," Ik murmured. "If it is all the same with you, I would like to meditate in sleep now. Will that disturb you?"

"Only in my dreams, Ik. Only in my dreams."

As Ik sat motionless, Bandicut stretched out on the floor of the bubble. It gave slightly under his weight, and was actually fairly comfortable. In due course he fell into a sound sleep.

CHAPTER 6

Powers Within

BANDICUT AWOKE TO a rumbling sort of bark from the far side of the bubble. In the moment it took him to remember where he was, the sound became more like a groan. Then he recognized its source. It was Ik, and he was in distress.

"Ik, what's wrong?" he called hoarsely, peering through the gloom at his friend. It seemed darker than it had been before; many of the Neri habitats were dimmer, casting less light.

It was several seconds before Ik could speak. The words were nearly indecipherable. "Hurt . . . ball . . . center . . ." But where words failed, the translator-stones seemed to grasp the Hraachee'an's tones. Bandicut realized that Ik was suffering from terrible . . . *kairenkroff* pain. Stomach pain.

Illness? Bandicut wondered. Or food poisoning?

Bandicut felt his own stomach knot with worry. He took a quick internal inventory to see if he felt any symptoms himself. As far as he could tell, he felt fine. But Ik had eaten more, and faster.

The quarx stirred.

/// What is it? The fruit? ///

/I don't know. We're supposed to be normalized. We're supposed to be able to eat the food here./

/// Maybe his normalization was faulty. ///

Bandicut crouched close to Ik. "Is it the food you ate? Are you having a bad reaction?"

Ik's eyes flickered, but their internal light was dim, like fading embers. "Hrrrrrr, yes," he managed finally. He was holding himself with both hands, right about where a human's diaphragm would have been.

/What can we do? If it were me, I'd have you trying to fix it./

/// If I knew how, you mean. ///

That stopped him for a moment. /If your predecessors could, you should be able to./

/// Maybe. But that was them.
This is me. ///

Bandicut watched Ik, jarred by what seemed indifference in the quarx's voice. /Well, would you mind trying to learn what the other Charlies learned? It could mean the difference between life and death—for Ik now, for us maybe later./

/// Lemme ask the stones. ///

Bandicut waited, reaching out to touch Ik's arm. The Hraachee'an was shivering violently. /What do they say?/ he asked impatiently.

Before Charlie could answer, something else interrupted Bandicut's thoughts—a shadow moving under the bubble. The membrane-circle appeared in the floor, and a Neri poked his head up into the bubble. In the gloom, he couldn't tell who it was. Then the Neri lifted himself into the habitat, and Bandicut saw the flicker on the side of his head. "Am I disturbing your rest?"

"L'Kell! No—but my friend Ik is not well."

"Volll?" said L'Kell, turning to look. "Why did you not ring the gong?"

"I just woke up and found him this way. I think it was the food—I'm not sure what's wrong—but I don't think he can eat it." Bandicut turned, squinting. He thought his friend looked worse than he had a moment ago, greyer in the dim light.

L'Kell muttered in puzzlement, "If you come from another world, do you not have ways to cope with such difficulties?"

Bandicut felt helpless to explain. He didn't understand it himself; all he knew about normalization was that it worked. Usually.

Ik spoke with great difficulty. "Something . . . about your world . . . or me . . . that the transformational field got wrong." He gasped air through his ears and rocked, holding his abdomen.

Bandicut scowled with frustration and fear. /Charlie? Have you found out anything?/

> /// Well, the stones say they learned a lot about him.
> But they didn't cover Hraachee'an physiology. ///

/But—damn it—can't they talk to Ik's stones?/

Charlie seemed to go away again, and came back a few moments later.

> /// You've got to touch Ik's stones. ///

Bandicut let out a slow breath. "Ik, my stones might be able to do something to help. Or the quarx." No point just now in trying to explain the quarx to L'Kell, who stirred with interest at that statement. "But they need to make contact again, to learn some things. Do you mind?"

Ik's voice was a gasp. "What do *you* think, John Bandicut?"

Bandicut managed a smile as he raised his wrists to Ik's head.

The link was broken after just a few seconds. By Charlie. Bandicut knew that *something* had been exchanged which his stones found helpful—and which made Charlie extremely uncomfortable. /What?/ he asked, rocking back on his haunches.

> /// What do you think?
> Now we've got the info, you're going to want me
> to go in and do the work.
> Right? ///

/Well—/

>>> */// Of course you are.*
The stones can manipulate forcefields and
all sorts of fancy things,
but they're not experienced with low-level
biological functions.
That's why Ik's stones aren't healing him.
You were just lucky. ///

Bandicut blinked, wishing he could see better in the dark.
L'Kell was watching him; Ik was in too much pain.

>>> */// Lucky to have me.*
I can mediate with the nervous system
and shit like that,
as long as the stones have the
basic knowledge. ///

Bandicut tried to suppress his annoyance. Nervous system
and shit. /I'm glad you're willing to do it,/ he answered.

>>> */// I didn't say I was willing.*
I hate the whole idea. ///

Bandicut closed his eyes. /So what are you saying?/

>>> */// Well . . .*
I guess I can't refuse, but— ///

/But what?/

>>> */// Never mind.*
I guess we should just do it
and be done with it. ///

Bandicut hesitated. If Charlie felt a sense of revulsion at
making intimate contact with another lifeform—even though he
was already inside a human who was an alien . . .

>>> */// Look, let's get it over with, all right? ///*

Bandicut nodded and spoke to Ik. "Charlie thinks he can help you. If you're willing to try." Ik flicked his fingers in something like a shrug of helplessness. "Okay." Bandicut glanced at L'Kell. "This might take a little while. I don't know if it's going to work."

The Neri said nothing, but crouched down to watch.

Bandicut carefully touched the side of Ik's head with his fingertips. The curves of the alien's head felt bony and smooth, like ivory. Bandicut felt a tingle, and a slight rush . . .

. . . and then a sudden wave of nausea . . .

Pulsing of blood, murmur of hydraulics, roar of bubbling air and roiling chemicals. The stench of activity was overwhelming . . .

He moved on, somehow, without moving at all. He had to pick his way through a vast and convoluted system, peering out from his virtual presence in the alien nervous system to locate leverage points from which the changes could be introduced into the system. It felt like an invasion of Ik's privacy; he had no real idea what he was doing at all. Guided by the unseen influence of the stones, he/Charlie found their way to a deeper place, where spasming nerve endings were triggering great rushes of inflammatory chemicals. And there they found a promontory and stood fast as waves of pain rose up from a sea of mingling ions and dashed over him like breakers on a restless ocean. And the breakers seemed to be growing stronger, threatening to consume them, threatening to consume their host, Ik, and drown him forever.

Bandicut/Charlie stood there in jangling confusion, listening as wordless voices carried messages up and down the surrounding array. Somewhere within, they were listening and measuring, assessing the hidden causes of this maelstrom, searching out solutions, balancing risk against possible benefits. At last, without conscious thought or understanding, they stretched out both hands—like a wizard from an old tale, raising a staff in incantation. Fire flashed from his hands, flickering, then brightening into two shafts of steady luminescence playing over the troubled sea below. It was the sea of Ik's neurotransmitters, the sea of chemicals that surged within his body, the sea of impulses that merged to become his body's responses to its environment. The shafts of light carried information and instructions down into the sea, and the sea began to change, but slowly. He sensed it in the air: a shift in the salt breeze from a bitter, metallic tang to something sweeter and more aromatic. The sea began to grow quieter.

He knew that everything he saw here was not a view but a metaphor, an interpretation; but it was no less real for that. They were making changes in Ik's digestive subsystems—programming changes, fine-tuning something that the normalization had altered but not gotten quite right. He had enough comprehension to be grateful that the changes required were small. And even if he did not understand them, his stones—and Ik's stones—were beginning to. Even so, they labored a long time, weaving their changes, coaxing the system to correct itself. And then he watched, Charlie watched, the stones watched as the seas began to glow from within and turned into a gently rippling, clear lake.

And then he felt the nausea of disorientation once more, and his foothold slipping away . . . and felt himself spinning back into his own body.

He sat back with a lurch, struggling for breath.

"Hrrraahhh—" gasped Ik, drawing his own breath with a sharp rasp. "What did you do, I feel—I am much more—"

                    /// Don't thank me, but don't ever ask me
                    to do something like that again, ///

Charlie wheezed, interrupting.

Bandicut drew in a ragged lungful of air and tried to bring his reeling thoughts into focus. He blinked, and forced a grin. Ik was sitting upright, touching his abdomen with murmurs of wonderment. "John Bandicut—I am—"

"Did it work? Are you better?" he whispered.

"You have done it!" the Hraachee'an marveled. "My pain is nearly gone."

Beside him, L'Kell was rising and turning. "You do have the power to heal, then! Why did you say—?"

But the rest of L'Kell's words were lost as a wave of fatigue came over Bandicut and he fell over in a dead faint.

"I don't think there's any way to know."

"Then we must talk when he awakes."

It was the sound of Ik's and L'Kell's voices that brought him back to consciousness. He opened his eyes, struck by Ik's calm. He pushed himself upright.

"John Bandicut!" cried Ik. "Are you all right?"

He grunted, remembering what he had just been through.

/// Remember it well, ///

Charlie whispered ominously, deep inside him.

/// And understand why
you should never expect me to do that again. ///

Bandicut groped for understanding. Why was the quarx so determinedly unhappy about this? He had helped save Ik, possibly from a fatal poisoning. All Bandicut could capture was a maelstrom of unidentifiable feelings in Charlie which seemed in the aggregate to amount to a combination of revulsion and . . . unworthiness. What the hell? Why would Charlie feel unworthy?

"John Bandicut. Was it you, or your quarx, that I sensed—?" Ik gestured vaguely with one hand.

Bandicut answered with a hoarse voice. "I'm not sure, to be honest. Charlie was there, along with the stones. But I was there, too." As he focused on the memories, he realized that while the quarx had reacted with revulsion, his own reaction was a deepened sense of empathy with his friend, as a result of sharing his pain.

Ik sighed through his ears. "Well, I thank you. But what did you do?"

Bandicut opened his mouth, but found it hard to answer. Finally he mumbled, "Well, we . . . readjusted something in your inner control system. Somehow."

"Is this becoming a specialty of yours?" Ik asked, and Bandicut heard the silent chuckle. "I did not know you could do it in people as well as machines."

"Neither did I," Bandicut admitted.

L'Kell made a husky sound. Bandicut knew exactly what the Neri was thinking. "You want to know if I can do the same thing with your people."

"You said earlier that you could not," L'Kell answered. "I believed you then."

"And I thought it was true. But now—I am not so sure. You must understand, it is not just me. It is—"

"I know of the second one within you," said L'Kell. "Ik explained, as you rested."

"Ah. You know of my . . . companion." He almost said *friend.* But the word caught in his throat. He wasn't really sure it was true, with this Charlie.

/// *Same to you, buddy.* ///

He felt a sting of shame. But the fact remained. This Charlie was so dark, so moody. Did he trust Charlie-Four the way he had trusted the others? He wasn't sure.

/// *I saved your friend's ass, didn't I?* ///

/Yes. And I am grateful,/ he murmured, and meant it, even as he wished that he could keep some thoughts to himself.

"John Bandicut, my people are dying."

He blinked his eyes open with a start.

L'Kell leaned forward and spoke slowly and precisely. "You must understand. I know you are weary, and perhaps uncertain. But you have shown yourself capable of healing." The Neri's eyes seemed to grow larger. "Healing someone not of your own kind."

"Yes, but it's not just—"

"Not just you."

"But not just the quarx, either. I do not think I could have healed Ik without *his* stones assisting." Bandicut nodded toward his friend.

"My people are dying," repeated L'Kell. "In the eyes of my people, and Askelanda, if you are unwilling to at least *try* to use this power to heal—"

Bandicut exhaled. "We will be considered enemies. Yes?"

"Yes."

Bandicut closed his eyes. /Charlie? Did you hear that?/ There was no answer from the quarx. "I am very tired," he said at last, not knowing what else to say. "I know that without rest, I can do nothing more."

L'Kell gave a slow nod of his head. "If you must take rest, then take it. But we cannot wait long for your answer."

As if in reply to his words, a low rumbling sound began to vibrate through the walls and floor of the habitat. Bandicut thought, but wasn't sure, that he saw a faint glimmer of light far off in the distance. He rubbed his eyes. It was gone now—if it had been there at all. But when he looked back at the Neri, he saw L'Kell peering worriedly out into the deep, dark night of the sea.

CHAPTER 7

The Obliq

THEY HAD BEEN sitting a long time in the dark, watching and waiting. Suddenly Antares stirred. "I feel someone coming."

"Where? Are they hostile?" asked Li-Jared, an arm's length away.

"They are—" she paused, concentrating "—determined, I think. And uncertain."

"Confused? We could put that to use, perhaps."

"Not confused, exactly. More like *cautious*." She gazed at her companion, wary of the rising and falling tide of fear within the Karellian. Poor Li-Jared; he was terrified of being underwater, and no amount of rationality could take away that base, primal instinct.

The Karellian rubbed his fingertips together nervously, and finally made a clicking sound. "Can we explain? Communicate somehow? What about those telepathic senses of yours?"

Antares pushed her hair back. "I can only sense feelings, not thoughts. And I have never tried to *send*, not with an alien being." It seemed a risky thing, fraught with hazards, not least of which was exposing her own inner feelings to others, perhaps the wrong emotion at the wrong time. On the Thespi homeworld, her role had been to facilitate communion among others, and to keep her own feelings to herself.

"Perhaps," said Li-Jared, "the time has come to try."

Antares didn't answer.

A light was approaching—a vehicle, perhaps, or a torch-carrying sea-person. It hovered a short distance away. She thought she could discern shadowy movement in the dark. Still, she was startled when a circle appeared in the floor, and a black, bug-eyed face peered up at her through rippling water. Antares felt Li-Jared recoiling, and suppressed an urge to do the same. Then she focused; and she found fear, but not animosity.

The creature climbed, dripping, onto the floor. The circle-opening disappeared. "*Rakkagrrrreee,*" it said.

Antares listened carefully, her knowing-stones tickling her throat. So far they'd produced nothing like a translation of the aliens' words. Surely there was a way; and in fact, she felt an image rising in her mind of how it might be done. It was a startling thought. Not something to risk casually.

"*Frikkatagaasss,*" said the sea-being, studying her.

It seemed interested in communicating. "Can you hear me?" she asked, raising a finger to one ear.

The being froze, then cocked its head.

"Can you—" she opened her hand slowly "—*feel* what I am feeling?" She had no reason to fear this being, or dislike it, she told herself. She wanted to convey a sense of . . . not trust, exactly, because that was premature, but perhaps quiet confidence. And curiosity. They were curious about her, and it might help them to know that she was curious about them.

The being shifted its position, and seemed to relax slightly. Beside her, Li-Jared was jittering inwardly, trying to calm himself with the knowledge that he was still, so far, safe. It was odd, she thought. Li-Jared seemed one of the smartest beings she had ever met—and also one of the most excitable. She sent a silent breath of calm in his direction.

She turned her attention back to the sea-creature, and wondered, with slow thoughtfulness, *Is there someone in command, with whom I might exchange confidences?* She lingered on the thought, not because she expected the being to understand the words, but in hopes that something of the spirit, the longing, would come through.

"*Hyahh,*" said the being, stirring and gesturing toward itself. "*Haleekah.*"

What did that mean? Was it offering itself as a possibility? She would have to respond carefully. Quite possibly this was an individual worthy of trust. But she sensed that there was a hierarchy of power here, and she needed to aim higher. "I must," she said deliberately, "speak with one of *eminence.*" She folded her arms across her chest, then unfolded them again with a gesture of reverence.

"*Hah-ruum?*"

She repeated her words, aimed her fingertips inward to herself, then outward.

The sea-being touched his sides with both hands, pointed toward the place in the floor where he had entered, and made a sweeping gesture away, hands together. "*Corri-kaola?*"

Antares inclined her head in a bow.

The sea-being touched the floor. When a circle of water appeared, he slipped into it and vanished.

"Is that good, what just happened?" Li-Jared asked, crouching nearby.

"I'm not sure," Antares admitted. "We'll have to wait and see, I guess." She studied her companion. It was hard to call him a friend yet; she had only known him for a few days, despite having traveled light-years together. But she liked the Karellian and hoped she could depend on him.

They sat quietly, until there was movement again outside. This time as the lights drew closer, they revealed a small submersible. It slid beneath the little habitat and stopped with a shudder and a momentary rush of air bubbles. When the floor opened, it was to a shaft of air. She caught Li-Jared's steely bright gaze, sensing eagerness and apprehension.

The same sea-person emerged. "*Squeee-quaa,*" it said, making quick hand movements down toward the sub.

"Want to go for another ride?" Antares asked Li-Jared.

The Karellian rubbed his thumbs and fingers together and stepped close to the hatch. "I'll take a look first," he muttered.

"You don't have to—" she began, and then realized that he was fighting to overcome his fear. "Good. Thank you."

The Karellian dropped out of sight, then called up, "It's roomier than the last one. Come on down."

She followed quickly. Their guide secured the hatch and took his place at the controls. The sub dropped away from the habitat, then glided through the undersea settlement, climbing slowly but steadily toward the upper levels of the city.

It felt as if they were seeing everything, and nothing: lights glowing greenly in the distance, and shapes that Antares could not quite visually resolve. She saw dark sea-people swimming through the water, singly and in groups, and flashes of what she took to be animal life, swerving and darting. One moment, the bottom slope was a looming, angling presence before them; the next, they were turning and climbing between luminous habitats with shadowy beings inside.

Antares had never been underwater before. It wasn't frightening to her in a visceral way, as it was to Li-Jared; but it was confusing and mysterious, and some of the long, silver creatures that swam through the water might have been alarming if she hadn't been surrounded by a hull of metal. Where were Ik and Bandicut? she wondered. Where were the two norgs, Bandicut's robots? And where was the star-spanner bubble, which she presumed was their only hope—if there was hope—of ever leaving this place?

"Up there," said Li-Jared, pointing—referring to their apparent destination.

A wide habitat was emerging from the undersea haze. This one was flatter than most they had seen; it was shaped like a broad tree-fungus, flat on the bottom, with a drooping overhang around the outer edges, and a top surface shaped with an undulating curve. It was wider than it was high, but still tall enough to have at least a couple of living levels stacked on top of each other. It was shimmeringly transparent.

Antares felt a growing sense of expectation from their pilot, but an expectation mixed with uncertainty. He (she was almost certain it was a *he*) was taking them to meet someone, and worried that he might be making a mistake. They came in under the habitat, docked, and climbed up through the hatch. They were met in a small room by a group of sea-beings, including three who were taller and more slender than the others, with skin of a dark greenish cast. These three seemed more graceful in their carriage and movements; and Antares decided that she was in the presence of females.

"*Olla compollay?*" said the nearest one at last. Antares caught a hint of the being's curiosity—a tentative mixture of fear and welcome. She found herself drawn toward these three, perhaps in response to their less hard-edged emotions.

"Yes," she answered, referring not to the words spoken but the feelings sensed. She extended a hand toward Li-Jared and made an ushering motion, hoping to emphasize that they were to be considered a team. Li-Jared made a soft bonging sound which she interpreted as a greeting.

The seafolk twittered among themselves, then herded them into the habitat, through several small chambers and a wider area that seemed less spartan and more like a gathering place. A number of females were in evidence, some busy in corners of the room with much smaller (juvenile?) sea-creatures. Antares paused, watching them curiously, wondering if the rearing of the young was a primarily female function here. There were no males around, except as part of their escort.

The floor of the room undulated, with a slow, up-and-down rolling movement like the surface of a tranquil sea. The juvenile seafolk were bouncing and swaying on the floor, and apparently enjoying it. Was that the ocean directly beneath her feet? It was; she could feel her feet sinking slightly into the flexible material that kept the sea out. She could tell it made Li-Jared uneasy, but she found its give comforting, almost nurturing.

Another female came up and spoke to their escort, and they seemed to decide something among themselves. *"Kaylay, kaylay,"* one of them said, urging Antares and Li-Jared back into motion.

They were led through a passageway that was nothing more than a clear tube passing through the ocean. In the artificial light outside, they saw the occasional finned animal flit by, and once a long, pulsing jet-propelled creature. At the end of the passageway, they stepped through another solid-and-yet-not-solid membrane, and entered a chamber unlike any they had seen before. The walls were opaque and half concealed by dark, hanging curtains of what looked like fabric. It looked like a place of meditation, perhaps. Or even worship. Antares looked around and realized that most of her escorts had stayed outside; just two females stood behind them. They seemed to be waiting for something.

"Ah-ko-bahh," said a voice from beyond the farther curtains.

Antares waited for someone to answer, and finally did so herself. "Hello?" she called. "My name is Antares. My companion's name is Li-Jared. May we speak?"

A figure stepped through the curtains. It was recognizably one of the female seafolk—and yet different. This one seemed to project a sense of age; but it was not necessarily *physical* age, so much as the experience of years. Knowledge. *"Ah-ko-lahh-bah,"* she said, coming more clearly into the light. She wore a kind of shawl over her shoulders, made of interwoven strands of what looked like soft, dry seaweed and threads of copper or gold. Her face seemed slightly luminous, or perhaps that was a trick of the lighting. Her eyes were larger than those of her fellow seafolk, and they moved slowly, almost unblinkingly, studying her visitors.

Antares felt at last that sense she had been waiting for— that she was in the presence of someone in a position of authority. She felt something else, too—in herself—an odd itching on the front of her throat. She resisted an urge to reach up and stroke the spot, but the sea-female's gaze had already alighted on her knowing-stones, imbedded in the same area. Were they glowing?

Antares wondered, wishing for a mirror. /What's happening?/ she murmured silently to the stones.

The stones did not answer at once, but the itch on her throat was becoming sharper and better defined. It was unquestionably coming from the knowing-stones, and was rapidly turning from an itch into a burning sensation.

Please remain still.

She felt the stones' urgency like a physical pressure. They were preparing to establish contact. She wasn't sure how, but she knew she shouldn't interfere. Even so, when the moment came, it took her by surprise.

The flash seemed to come from somewhere behind her. She felt the sparks erupting from her throat . . . and her consciousness wavered just for an instant, not a sense of *un*consciousness, but of consciousness expanded in time and space.

The sensation lasted only a moment, and then she blinked and saw the sea-woman staggering backward, eyes wide, webbed hands pressed to the sides of her head. And through the thin webbing between the sea-woman's fingers, two new stones glimmered.

"Colimay, colimay!"

The two females behind Antares stepped forward as though to help, or protect, but they stopped at the sound of the sea-woman's voice. They stood flanking Antares and Li-Jared; nobody seemed to know quite what to do. Antares was reeling from the splitting of her stones, and trying to remain standing. She felt as though her stones were reeling, too, and trying to regain their equilibrium and control.

The sea-woman took a halting step forward, gazing at Antares. She was clearly astonished and frightened. But the fear was fading. "Kalakala—" she started to say, and Antares felt an inner shifting and heard, "I am . . . Neri . . . what have you . . ."

It was like listening to a comm transmission breaking up, and she cocked her head, and with a whisper of excitement, said, "Again, please. Again?"

The sea-woman seemed wreathed in dismay and delight. The second time her words came out more comprehensibly. "We are the Neri . . . what have you done? . . . who are you? . . . why are you here?"

"Antares," she murmured, and then spoke more distinctly. "Call me Antares. I am a Thespi third-female. And this is my friend Li-Jared." She turned. "He is a Karellian. We are not of your world. Do you understand about the stones?"

"Stones," the Neri woman echoed, her voice husky like a dry leaf fluttering in the air. Her eyes closed, with a slow-motion blink, and opened. "I feel them . . . speaking . . ." And her voice trembled with a fresh rush of fear, tempered by growing comprehension.

Antares worked to maintain a sense of calm, for the sea-woman's benefit as much as her own. It was going to take time to get through the fear and bewilderment. But now the halting progress of words was like a slowly emerging breath of joy.

The sea-woman, whose name was *Kailan*, had a great many questions for Antares.

"And so even though we have landed practically in the middle of your city, we know almost nothing about your world," Antares concluded.

"Then," Kailan said, "there must be a great deal that *you* would like to know."

Antares inclined her head in acknowledgment.

Kailan touched her shawl, as though in thought. "I feel somehow . . . that I can trust your . . . intentions. It is a most odd sensation." She blinked slowly. "I cannot promise to answer all your questions. But perhaps some. Please ask."

Antares drew a slow breath, and tried to project calm onto Li-Jared, who was making little gulping sounds beside her, trying to restrain himself from interrupting. "Do all of you," she asked with great deliberation, "live beneath the sea? And are you a leader of your people?"

Kailan made the dry-leaf sound again, wordlessly. One of the other Neri females said something, and she answered in words

Antares could not follow. "*We,*" she said, "live beneath the sea—though there are others who do not. As for me, I am called the *obliq.* The keeper. I am not a leader, precisely, no. But I assist our leader with the knowledge and wisdom of generations past." The Neri seemed to chuckle to herself, but it was not precisely a sound of mirth. "Sometimes they remember to ask me, and sometimes they do not."

That, Antares thought, her mind flickering back to her home-world, is something I can understand well.

"The work of the obliq," Kailan went on, "is to remember and to remind." She touched the stones at the side of her head. "I have much new to try to understand, including the function of these—" *qualay* "—stones." Her gaze shifted to Li-Jared, then back to Kailan. "But I believe that the young guard who decided to bring you here chose wisely. Because I must try to understand *you.*"

"We will do what we can to help you," Antares said. "May I ask what has become of our friends? They were separated from us, and we have heard nothing of them."

Kailan turned and spoke into the shadows behind her. Another Neri woman emerged, and they exchanged words; then the other Neri disappeared back through the curtains. Kailan turned back. "My assistant, Elbeth, will inquire."

"Thank you."

"I am sure there are other things you wish to know. Perhaps to help us both understand why you are here."

"Oh, yes," said Antares.

Kailan gestured to cushions along the edge of the floor. "Then let us sit and see if these are things I can tell you. Perhaps something of the struggle with the folk of the land—?"

"Yes?" whispered Antares.

"Or perhaps of the great maw at the bottom of the sea that threatens to destroy us all?" Kailan loosened her shawl and settled gracefully onto a cushion. "You know nothing of these matters? Then indeed there is much that I must tell you."

CHAPTER 8

The Summoning of a Quarx

BANDICUT HAD INTENDED to rest, simply rest. But a few weary questions asked of L'Kell had left him buzzing with exhaustion, and filled with both curiosity and dread. L'Kell had spoken briefly—but with great intensity—of strange poisonings of Neri explorers under the sea. Of raids by land-people on caches of machinery, apparently lost or abandoned for many years, but prized by the Neri. Of mysterious rumblings in the ocean abyss, deeper and farther offshore from the undersea city.

Even as L'Kell spoke, Bandicut thought he felt a soft shudder beneath him. He blinked and rubbed his eyes; now he thought he'd seen faint rays of light dancing in the darkness.

"L'Kell, wazzat—" he started to say, but stopped, realizing that he was slurring his words with tiredness.

"I think," Ik murmured, "that you truly need rest, and perhaps L'Kell might leave us for a short time. All this talk—"

Bandicut grunted. "Yah. Could you give us a little time?"

"Very well," said the Neri. But by the time he was gone, Bandicut knew he was still too charged with adrenaline to go right to sleep. Had they really landed in the midst of a world about to erupt in war? Were he and the company supposed to stop it? If so, how? He sent tired thoughts in the direction of the translator-stones. /Why didn't you warn us? Why didn't you tell us what to expect?/

Though the quarx hadn't been addressed directly, he nevertheless answered with bitter laughter,

/// Would you have come, if you had known? ///

/Well, I—/

/// Don't be ridiculous.
It's the last thing you'd have chosen. ///

Bandicut could hardly argue. After the struggle with the boojum back on Shipworld, the last place he wanted to be was a war zone. /How about you, Charlie? Would you have chosen—?/

/// Mokin' A, no.
I didn't want this, don't want it,
don't intend to put up with it. ///

/What do you mean?/ Bandicut was stunned by the sharpness of the quarx's words. This wasn't like Charlie—at least, not any of the Charlies he had known before. He glanced at Ik, sitting motionless in sleep-meditation. /What do you mean, you don't intend to put up with it?/

There was silent laughter in his mind.

/// Didn't L'Kell just say,
if we don't help with the healing,
we'll be considered enemies? ///

Bandicut froze. /Meaning—?/

/// I think you know. ///

Bandicut sat silent, thinking. Rising up through the center of his fear was a rod of anger. /Don't play games. Are you saying, you hope the Neri *kill* us—so you won't have to worry anymore?/

/// They wouldn't necessarily kill us.
They might just kick us out of their territory.
And we could go home. ///

Bandicut didn't even bother to point out that they *had* no

way to go home. He felt something snap inside. /Listen, you self-centered sonofabitch. If you want to check out, go ahead and check out, but don't try to take me with you. Or my friends. You hear me?/

Charlie didn't answer.

He immediately felt guilty. Charlie *had* just helped heal Ik, after all. But that didn't give him the right to set them up as enemies of the Neri—a suicide pact signed by one. /Look—/ he said, trying to find something to take the sting out of his previous words /—I know you helped Ik, and I'm grateful. But that doesn't—/

He paused. The quarx wasn't listening. In fact, his presence wasn't there at all anymore. He'd slammed the door and gone to another room.

Mokin' A, Bandicut thought. What was *with* this Charlie? He seemed full of sullenness, with a core of dark desperation. Was this just the luck of the draw with quarx incarnations? Or was it something that had been present, but maybe just subdued, in the prior Charlies?

Bandicut peered scowling out of the shelter into the night-time sea, and thought again about the Neri and their conflict with the people from the shore. People from land. Not Neri, though he wasn't quite clear on who or what they were. A different species, apparently; but the Neri had never actually made face-to-face contact with them, and knew little about them, not even their name.

This was not a war with armies clashing by night, or even battles raging beneath the sea—though it sounded as if it could come to that. It sounded more like a war of attrition and desperation; a war of failing support systems, and of Neri sickening and dying. And what in God's name could he and Ik hope to do about it?

But as he thought about it, there was something in L'Kell's description of *how* the Neri got sick, especially in certain locations, that nagged at his memory. What was it? Activities undersea. Military activities? Pollution? There were indeed places where poisons or chemical wastes were being discharged into the sea, and L'Kell had said that some Neri swimmers had encountered such pollution and become gravely ill. But that was not what Bandicut had seen today. These swimmers had fallen ill after visiting a location disturbed by the landers—but with no detectable pollution. Something else had to be killing them.

And why couldn't the Neri simply avoid those areas? L'Kell had seemed reluctant to answer, saying only that they had no choice; they needed what was there. Which was—? Bandicut asked. And L'Kell studied him with those huge, haunting eyes before hissing, "Machines, that is what. *Machines.*"

Machines? Bandicut thought. Why would machines be indispensable to the Neri? "Are these machines you need, that you do not have?" He shook his head in puzzlement. "Or that you cannot make yourselves?"

"We take them from the *seafloor,*" L'Kell hissed vehemently. "They are *ours* to take, not the landers'!"

Bandicut rubbed his eyes in weariness. "So you are fighting with these landers over . . . sunken machinery?"

L'Kell had looked perplexed. "We might have been willing to share, if the landers had not started just . . . *taking* them. And if they had not sent their sickness to kill us. But we need the machines, yes. Our—our—" *rhusssss* "—makers are breaking down. We are becoming unable to make new machines, as our old ones break down. Without them, we will—" He stared at Bandicut.

"What?"

"Die," said L'Kell.

———

L'Kell would be coming back soon.

The conversation reverberated in Bandicut's mind as he tried to rest, tried to think it through to an understanding, tried to put it out of his mind altogether. It was too confusing. And overlying it was the more immediate question: could Charlie be persuaded to help try to heal the sick Neri? Because if the answer was no, then these other things were the least of his worries.

He wanted to call Charlie out to talk about it; but he felt a powerful inner resistance, and a sudden wave of overwhelming sleepiness. Jeez. He'd known he was tired, but—

And then he knew why he was feeling such a pull toward sleep—and it wasn't just his own urgent need—but by now it was irresistible. He slumped over on the floor of the bubble, not far from the resting Ik, and before he could even cushion his head on his arms, he was asleep.

He slept restlessly and unhappily, his dream-thoughts streaming along shifting pathways, through treacherous subterranean passages, and over sliding cloudlands; he walked a dark woods and glided through cemeteries of the night, and he streaked up and down skyscrapers of some strange city, rising and falling inside the buildings and outside them. And through it all he was stalked by ghostly figures luminous with a hideous glow . . .

He woke, drenched in sweat. He had felt, or dreamed of, rumbling sounds and lights in the distance. It took a few moments to remember where he was. As he groped for the dream images he had just lost, he felt a shiver up and down his spine. There was something important in those . . .

The visions came back in a rush, the glowing figures, and he knew at once what they meant. *Radioactive glow.*

Were the Neri being killed by radiation poisoning? They had the sophistication to know if the waters were being poisoned by chemicals—they breathed the water after all, but they— *Dear God, they breathed the water, and if it was contaminated with radioactivity . . .*

Bandicut sat up. "Ik," he croaked. "*Ik.*"

The Hraachee'an opened his eyes. "Urrm?"

"*Damn.* Ik, I think I know what's killing them."

His friend blew a deep breath out through his ears, as Bandicut explained. "It would be consistent with what L'Kell said," Ik agreed. "I should have thought of it sooner."

"We both should have. What's important is, can we do anything about it?"

Ik rubbed his bony head. "Can we heal the sick, or can we do something about the radiation? I'm not sure about either."

Bandicut thought, it all depends on Charlie, doesn't it? /Charlie? You there?/ He felt a strange silence, and then Charlie's voice as though through a deep, dense fog.

/// Radiation sickness?
I don't do radiation sickness! ///

And then all feeling of his presence was gone again.

Bandicut closed his eyes, trying unsuccessfully to curb his anger. He knew he should be grateful to Charlie. And he knew Charlie was xenophobic; at least, an earlier Charlie had been. But so what? People needed healing. Would Charlie really rather stand back and let all those Neri die? If so, that was just . . . cowardice.

His thoughts flickered in and out of focus. The urge to slip back into sleep was almost . . . *was* . . . overwhelming . . . Charlie messing with his sleep center . . .

Ik might have been saying something, but he drifted away without hearing.

He dreamed of a struggle, of figures rising and toppling in the night, of hand-to-hand combat in muddy trenches. He was holding onto someone by the shirtfront, falling and then getting up again, shaking his adversary violently; but the fabric was tearing, and the person, whoever it was, was pulling away, escaping.

He walked in a cemetery again, rows of markers stretching out into a night sky of infinity, stretching to the stars. There were spirits awake in the cemetery, but every time he turned to speak to them, they vanished with a whisper of wind. He was alone, completely alone, with only the voices of the stars for company.

And then the stars began to vanish . . .

When he woke, it was to a terrible grogginess, and emptiness. Everything felt different inside. He experienced a stab of fear.

/Charlie?/ There was no answer, no sense of the quarx's presence. /*Charlie?*/ No, he thought. Don't tell me. Charlie couldn't — wouldn't have —

And then he heard a voice. A *feminine* voice, puzzled.

> /// *Is Charlie my name?*
> *Or the name you use for all of me?*
> *All of us?*
> *This all seems odd —* ///

/Uh?/

> /// *— your response to a name.*
> *Would it seem*
> *more natural if you called me . . .*
> *Charlene?* ///

Bandicut felt faint. He took a sharp breath, worried that he might fall over. He knew Ik was looking at him with concern, but he couldn't speak. Oh Jesus. /Did you say . . . *Charlene?*/

> /// *You can use Charlie if you like.* ///

He exhaled hard. /Well, no, I . . . whatever you say. Charlene, if you like. I'm . . . John Bandicut. And we . . . I guess, have a lot to talk about . . ./

> /// *Still so much I don't understand.* ///

So much *you* don't understand? He took a deep breath and opened his thoughts for Charlene, for Charlie-Five, to explore. A new Charlie . . . his head spun thinking about it. What had happened to the old Charlie? Had he just vanished? Died in his sleep? Why hadn't there been . . . some *warning*, or something. It wasn't as if . . . as if he had died in a sudden attack or something, the sonofabitch had just gone off and . . . slit his wrists or whatever a quarx did . . .

> /// *I have the sense,* ///

said Charlene, as if raising her head from a stack of books and tapes,

*/// that your old Charlie wasn't
very happy. ///*

/No. No, he wasn't./ Not happy. Definitely not happy. /I don't know why./

*/// And that he might have
taken his own life? ///*

Bandicut blinked, struggling, actually fighting back tears, because that was his thought and he hated the idea. Was it possible? Could the quarx have committed suicide? /I don't know,/ he whispered. /You would probably know better than I. Could he have . . . done that?/

The new quarx, Charlene, seemed uncertain.

/// I'm . . . surrounded by reverberations . . . ///

Like bits and pieces of memory in a great whirlwind, a cyclone spinning . . .

And yet she seemed far clearer and more knowledgeable than any new quarx he had ever met.

*/// Hard to tell which are his, really,
and which are yours, but— ///*

/This is strange. *Very* strange. You're not like . . . any new quarx I've ever had. How do you know so much?/

/// Well, I'm not sure— ///

/It's as if you've been listening in, and learning. Or as if—I don't know—as if you have a little bit of everyone else already in your head. Did Charlie-Four know you were coming right behind him? I'll bet the sonofabitch *did* commit suicide!/

/// Does that make you angry? ///

/Yeah, it makes me angry. Because he couldn't *lower* himself to help the Neri—/

/// Perhaps it was not that simple— ///

/What do you mean? What do you know that I don't? It's not as if you were here—/

*/// You're right, of course, but just now ...
Could I ask you some things, to try to understand? ///*

Bandicut sighed. /What do you want to know?/ Everything, obviously. She needed to know everything. He was stunned by the degree of sophistication she'd had from the moment of awakening—like no other Charlie before her. But she could hardly know the details of the situation they were trapped in right now. And she *needed* to know, because L'Kell would be coming soon for his answer.

*/// Some of it I can see right here on top.
But the rest—if you could just fill me in— ///*

Bandicut's head was spinning. But he had to adjust; he had no choice. He had to get used to Charlie-Four being gone, *dead*, and a new Charlie here, and a female one ... and there was just no time. They had to move on, however difficult it might be. /Okay,/ he whispered. /Here goes .../

By the time the bottom of the bubble shimmered and L'Kell appeared, Bandicut felt as if he were on a runaway carousel, images circling him in an endless stream of thought, Charlene raining questions onto him, his dizzy, half-conscious mind answering and his answers prompting new questions. He blinked and stirred, and forced himself to rise, on shaky legs, to greet the Neri. "L'Kell," he said huskily.

The Neri peered at him, then at Ik. His demeanor seemed less friendly, more reserved, more businesslike. Was he prepared to turn their relationship into the status of enemies, if Bandicut didn't promise to try to help the Neri?

Ik spoke first. "We have been resting, and have just awakened. We have not yet had a chance to talk."

L'Kell looked at Bandicut. "I believe," he said, "that you had the most to think about. I have been sent to ask your decision. Will you help?"

/Charlie—Charlene—I know you haven't had much time to absorb this, but—/

/// Yes.
Tell him yes. ///

He blinked, startled by the certainty of tone. How could she be sure she was capable of what was being asked?

"John Bandicut?" asked the Neri.

He let his breath out slowly. "We will try. We will do all that we can. My . . . friend, the quarx . . . has had a change of heart." He touched the side of his head.

"Then," said L'Kell, "let us go." He picked up the gong and struck it four times. He waited expectantly, gazing over Bandicut's shoulder. Bandicut turned and saw two Neri swimming downward toward them, holding something between them. It was the access tube.

CHAPTER 9

Life Signs

BANDICUT WATCHED AS the end of the tube stuck to the bubble like the suction cup of an octopus. A small amount of water trapped in the suction cup drained away, and the junction circle turned shadowy grey. L'Kell gestured. "Are you ready?"

Bandicut nodded. "Let's go."

The Neri leaned headfirst through the connector, and climbed easily up into the tube. From within the bubble, Bandicut watched L'Kell's shadow move up the incline. He glanced at Ik. "Follow me?"

"Hrrm."

Bandicut poked his head cautiously through the membrane, then attempted to follow L'Kell up the tube. He didn't get very far before he started to slip. /Damn, I left my good sneakers at home!/

/// Excuse me? ///

/Never mind./ He yelled up. "L'Kell, I can't get up the slope!"

"Wait."

Half a minute passed. Then a line came snaking down the tube. He grabbed it and began hauling himself hand over hand up the steadily increasing incline. He was gasping by the time he reached the top. /To think I used to climb up the kids' slides all the time./

/// What's different now? ///

/I'm not a damn kid anymore./

As he reached the top, two Neri arms caught him under the shoulders and hauled him out. He wiggled his jaw at the slight pressure drop. L'Kell peered down the tube for Ik. Ik shouted to them to pull in their line. The Neri did so; Ik's rope was attached to its end. Ik's rope began contracting, and Ik appeared, holding on and sliding up almost effortlessly. The Neri looked with interest at the Hraachee'an's rope, but did not interfere as he tucked it back in his belt.

"This way." As they followed L'Kell through the passageway, Bandicut gazed out at the Neri city, aware of a perceptible improvement in his attitude toward it. Being freed from prison had an amazingly salutary effect on him.

They passed through the chamber where they had met Askelanda; it was deserted now. They went beyond it to another connector, and then on to an entirely separate habitat. This one was divided up with curtains and partitions, and had an almost human feel to it. The closeness, and the flimsiness of the partitions, reminded Bandicut of Triton Station. He felt a pang of homesickness, and at the same time wondered why he didn't miss his homeworld more; maybe he was just too busy. Still, he half expected his friend Krackey to emerge from the shadows and ask him what was wrong. *You been acting kinda strange there, Bandie. Sure you aren't having one of those silence-fugues again?*

He shivered at the thought, and hurried after L'Kell.

They entered a curtained chamber. The air was warmer, staler, almost stifling. Several other Neri were present, including Askelanda, but it was the one lying on the pallet that drew his attention. It was one of the sick Neri he had watched arriving, and the Neri appeared to have grown weaker since. "This is Lako," said one of those attending the patient. Bandicut turned, and realized that he had seen this Neri before, too. "My name is Corono. I am a healer." Corono indicated Lako. "He will die soon if nothing can be done to help him."

"I understand," Bandicut said.

"And we will see if your offer of friendship is genuine," Askelanda remarked, before withdrawing into the background.

Bandicut let out a long breath. Ik touched his arm in reassurance. "John—I had not expected that you could do what you did for me."

"Me neither." Bandicut stepped closer to Lako. "I will do what I can," he said, to no one in particular. L'Kell stood close by, and Bandicut asked, "Is he a friend of yours?"

"Yes," murmured L'Kell.

Bandicut swallowed hard. "I must tell you, it will be very difficult. I do not know—" He caught himself and shook away the thought.

/// I have hope, ///

said Charlene, in a voice that was surprisingly calming.

/Do you have any notion of what to do?/

/// Some images ... memories.
Can you touch Lako? ///

Bandicut reached out slowly. He touched the Neri's arm—and almost jerked his hand back. Lako's skin was hot.

/// Is that ... fever? ///

Charlene's voice was quiet, concentrated.

/In humans, we'd call it fever. I don't know if it's the same thing here or not./

/// But if it's radiation poisoning—? ///

/Charlie, I don't know much about radiation poisoning in humans, much less Neri. We'll have to learn as we go./ His hand was resting firmly now on the warm skin of the Neri. Lako was trembling. His eyelids were fluttering, a disturbing sight on such large eyes. The eyes themselves seemed cloudy.

/// Shall I reach out now ...
cross over? ///

He was aware of L'Kell standing close. /Yes, let's try. But don't lose your anchor in me./

/// Stepping across . . . ///

It was startlingly different from linking with Ik. The first sensation was of piercing cold. If Lako was burning with fever on the outside, he felt paralyzed and frozen in the strange realm of his nervous system. And yet . . . it was not that there was no activity. But it felt like humming wires, a metallic singing of frantic nerve impulses. This being was struggling not to die. But he was dying.

/// Deeper.
Look for pathways we can
interpret and use. ///

/You're going to understand more here than I will, I think. Interfacing with nervous systems is your department./ He found the quiet whisper of the female Charlie's voice reassuring. Maybe they could really do this. But they had not yet come to grips with the Neri's real physical damage, or even his pain. The test would be trying to guide Lako's own body into healing.

/// Here— ///

His sight darkened and his ears filled with sound; it was like stepping into a darkened room where an orchestra was tuning up, each instrument subdued, but the combination of reeds and horns and strings and synths sounding like a quake threatening to happen. He felt hot and cold at once: streams of ice water running through glowing lava. Clouds of steam. He listened for voices. Could he make contact with Lako's mind? Should he try?

Charlene was either a very fast study, or she had enough memories from her predecessors to perceive the general patterns of a functioning nervous system. She extended her presence until they were touching, ever so gently, the streams of nervous energy. Ice water. They were throbbing with pain, and with conflicting signals. The network was burning with fever, trying to cool itself;

trying helplessly to heal, withdrawing from pain, hopelessly in turmoil. It was edging slowly toward a silent, dark abyss in the distance. Surrender? Death?

Calm the systems, he thought, and realized that it was Charlene's thought, too. They were moving in lockstep now; he could sense the quarx riffling through his memories even as they moved cautiously through the terrible landscape of the wounded Neri. They were walking among flame and wreckage. Blistering, inside and out.

A question was flickering through his awareness; was there radioactive material still in Lako's body? Not too much, he guessed. Not too much.

He was feeling dizzy and hot himself. Got to keep cool. Where is the center of the distress? Where is the center of healing? You found the centers in me, he thought, the centers that directed the healing; and you, the Charlies before you, sped everything up, like a master chemist orchestrating the movement of chemicals, firing the motors of reconstruction. But we don't know yet how this Neri is *made.*

There was something new moving behind him, a presence approaching, from the outside. It was an alien presence; a Neri presence. L'Kell, bringing his translators close, trying to see what was going on. *What can we do, L'Kell? Can you tell what needs to be done?*

The contact was too tenuous to allow words to pass, but he felt L'Kell's recognition of their mutual presence. L'Kell was just as confused about what was happening in Lako's body as he and Charlie; he would not be of much help with physiological knowledge. But there might be one way L'Kell could help. *If you can calm him, calm Lako, help him relax and let us do our work. Can you calm him?*

It was doubtful L'Kell could understand what he was asking. And would he have the power to do it even if he understood?

A moment later, Bandicut felt a buzzing of energy, like feedback in an audio circuit. The Neri was trying to help. At first it was just disconcerting; then it began to rise, and to distort his ability to connect, and to *hurt*. He was losing his bearings. *Stop it!* he cried. *Too much, too much!* The wail lasted for a heartbeat longer, and then began to ebb, taking L'Kell's presence with it. But it didn't fade altogether. Bandicut heard a sound almost too low to hear, like the invisible muttering of a brook.

Okay, he's doing it. Calming Lako. Work quickly now.

The quarx was already moving; she had found a way to slip through the interstices of the dying Neri's nervous system and get a fix on the control centers. Bandicut felt himself being pulled like elastic thread along the intertwined pathways; then he felt the sudden pulse of neurons firing around him. The quarx was touching and testing, trying to make contact—not to orchestrate the healing herself, but to coax the healing centers to work more effectively, to take over all of the body's available resources, to subordinate all else to the healing of the devastated tissues.

/Charlie, is it working? Charlene?/

The quarx was too busy to answer, but there was a quickening of movement, a rallying of spirits. She was touching *something* that seemed to be responding. But was it enough?

L'Kell's presence grew a little stronger again, a little brighter, as if he felt it, too.

Don't expect miracles, he thought.

They *were* making headway. But it was going to be a tough battle.

Waves of sound and sensation came, went.

At one point he thought he heard words. Not from the quarx, not from L'Kell. It was dizzyingly hard to tell.

Help . . . must . . . keep . . .

Burning.

Shivering.

Must keep . . .

Waves of nausea rushed through him like an incoming tide. They had touched a vital pathway. He steeled himself against the nausea and kept going.

The inner voice was gone. He thought it had been Lako's, but he wasn't sure. Now he heard other words, filtered through whispering shadows of thought . . .

Feel his strength being turned . . . his eyes brightening, showing life. (L'Kell? Corono?)

Bandicut struggled to keep his own strength flowing, to lend what he could to the quarx.

On the outside, he knew L'Kell's hope was growing.

When the breakpoint came, it was like being picked up on a powerful wave and turned inside out, spinning. Something in Lako's body or mind had suddenly retaken control. He felt himself being squeezed . . . forced . . .

Where?

Over a waterfall. Dropping, falling. After about three of his own heartbeats, he began to feel faint around the edges, began to panic. Was Lako dying? Were these the death convulsions? If he was caught in the middle would he be able to pull himself free? Or would he be dragged down the funnel of consciousness into oblivion?

Yes . . . no . . . what's happening . . . ?

/Charlie . . . Charlie . . ./ His cry and the other sounded faint, like dying moans on the wind. He could no longer feel the quarx's presence, though he was sure she was there. She had to be.

He hit the bottom of the waterfall, and a great hand caught him and squeezed him, squeezed around his lungs. He was losing his breath. He was out of the waterfall, but there was a powerful wind here, howling and spiraling, and it was trying to blow him down a tunnel, a long dark tunnel. He didn't like this, didn't want to go . . .

/// Hang on! ///

The quarx's voice was the most heart-lifting sound he could have heard. Though spinning out of control, he was no longer alone.

/// Trying to find the way— ///

/Where?/

/// Out.
Trying to throw us out. ///

/But—/

/// We've set it in motion.
Hold on—see if it works—! ///

The wind swept away the quarx's words. He felt a *WHOOOOOOSHHH* like a balloon letting go . . . he was picked up like Dorothy in the cyclone, being lofted to Oz. But Charlie still had some control; everything was being damped down, not in the whirlwind, but in his own senses. Everything was starting to go dark, his consciousness being drained away . . .

/Charlie, what are you—?/

And then he was flung into the blackness of the void.

———

Awareness shifted in and out. A light flickering. He worked at clawing his way back . . . conscious thought, physical sensation. Sharp pain in his lower back as he straightened from a slump. His eyes flashed open. He was staring straight into the gaze of Ik.

"—" he said, then realized that nothing had come out. He'd meant to say, *Did it work? Is he still alive?*

Ik clearly understood his intent. He canted his head, directing Bandicut's gaze. L'Kell was bent over Lako, conferring with someone who was touching and examining Lako . . . with Corono, the healer. L'Kell raised his head to peer in amazement at Bandicut.

"He is fighting. Gaining strength," L'Kell whispered.

Bandicut nodded, swallowing. He wanted to speak to L'Kell; he struggled to form words. He was aware of Askelanda hovering nearby.

/// Don't try. Not yet, ///

the quarx advised.

*/// We've just been thrown out by Lako.
It was a tough exit. ///*

/I wondered who was doing that . . . couldn't tell if he was dying . . ./

/// Not dying, no. Not when we left— ///

L'Kell was trying to explain what he had seen. "—eyes began to sharpen—trying to speak—"

Bandicut tried to listen.

"—movement of gills—lungs—"

Bandicut focused on the trembling form of Lako. The Neri's muscles were tensing and releasing in small, spasmodic movements. Bandicut gazed at the tortured face. The eyes were flicking, blinking; soft moaning sounds were coming from Lako's throat.

Corono was saying, *brekk-k* "—fever very hot now, but the presence in the eyes—"

Bandicut shook his head and tried to draw a full breath. "L'Kell," he said huskily. "Is he going to make it?"

Askelanda was closer now, listening intently.

L'Kell looked at the healer.

Corono said, "We'll have to wait . . . see." He spoke with a sigh that sounded like the wheeze of a bellows. "But I think, perhaps . . . we must watch the fever, but he seems to be stronger now. Whatever you did, human Bandicut—" he paused "—I am hopeful."

Bandicut nodded, and stared at Lako, at the obviously once-strong face struggling to survive. "Good," he whispered. "That's good." He turned away, rubbing his eyes, then his temples. He took several deep breaths. After a moment, he realized that everyone was watching him. "Is there something else?"

The Neri spoke quickly to one another.

/// Oh no— ///

He sighed soundlessly. /How can we say no, if there's someone else—?/

/// But— ///

"Can you?" asked L'Kell. "There is another. He is in worse condition."

Worse condition? Bandicut closed his eyes, dismayed. "We will try," he said hoarsely.

/// This might be very hard on you;
you've been through a lot. ///

The quarx fell silent as L'Kell beckoned Bandicut into the next curtained room. Another cot. Another dying Neri. Bandicut stood silent a moment, gazing down at the blistered face. "What is his name?" he whispered.

"Thorek," said Corono, stepping to the other side of the cot, touching the patient's forehead. Thorek's eyes were three-quarters closed, and a hazy yellow. His breath was extremely shallow, his nostrils and gill openings barely moving.

"Thorek," Bandicut murmured. He crouched close to the cot, trying not to draw back from the smell of illness, of decay. He was gratefully aware of Ik's presence close behind him.

/// Let's go, then. ///

He touched Thorek's arm. It was cold and rubbery to the touch. He closed his eyes, and let the quarx take him over the boundary . . .

———

He felt at once a sense of quiet, of cold. Not the cold of ice; the cold of space. The cold of dark, stony passages.

Charlene moved silently through the inner landscape of this being, and found that it was not quite as dark or deserted as it had first appeared. There remained tiny veins of warmth streaking the cold, remnants of life trickling through a harsh land. Threads of nervous connection left when the main presence of awareness had fled, seeking escape. He couldn't help thinking of Charlie-Four, fleeing into darkness. Dying.

Don't think of that. Not now.

The quarx probed through the threads and began to track backward, searching for whatever life might still be found . . .

Amidst the ruins of mind and body, Charlie began to pick up scintillations of something. A consciousness? A soul? She called out softly. And felt it withdrawing.

Withdrawing?

Charlie, should we—

The quarx was already in pursuit. Up the threads, following the spark . . . toward something far in the distance, a center of presence. It was like a spidery path to a floating city, high on the horizon, dim and remote. Was this like an image in the net, something he could use to focus his movement? Or was it a hallucination, a false, crazy hope?

What about the body, Charlie? It's failing fast. We might not have time—

Can't heal until we find a connection to the center. He can only heal himself.

I know, but—scary, this is scary. Is that what's up ahead?

Let's hope so.

Again, it happened quickly. But differently.

There was a brightening on the horizon, and for an instant he felt a link, a ray of hope, a touch of Thorek's presence and soul . . . in terrible pain. But the pain was shimmering out of focus, changing.

I do not know you . . . you are not the spirit of the sea . . . do not need you . . .

Not in words, but in wordless thought. Then the connection faded, and the spot of brightness flared and went out. He blinked, stunned by a sense that the light had not gone dark, exactly, but rather had been drawn out of this existence through some portal he could not see. It had seemed eager rather than sorry to go.

And then darkness and a bone-piercing cold closed around him. He withdrew in silence, not speaking even to the quarx.

———

He gazed wearily at L'Kell, knowing he did not have to speak. L'Kell had sensed Thorek's passing. Behind L'Kell, Ik moved out of the way, making room for Askelanda. Bandicut turned, thinking, will he blame us—blame me—for Thorek's death?

Askelanda stood beside L'Kell, gazing at Thorek's body. He was muttering words, but Bandicut could not make them out. Words of anger? Mourning? Tribute? The elder Neri raised his eyes to look at Bandicut. "His spirit has returned to the sea."

"I could do nothing," Bandicut said. "He was too far gone." And, he thought silently, the manner of departure was very different from what I expected. Almost as if he welcomed death.

"He will be missed. But not all passings are unhappy ones," Askelanda said, almost as if he'd read Bandicut's mind. His tone was not exactly rejoicing, but he seemed accepting of the event.

Bandicut's thoughts flickered to Charlie-Four, and he pulled them back with an effort. "Then you believe that there's life—"

"He swims now in new currents, new paths through the deep. Many have gone before him, and many will follow." Askelanda spoke briefly to Corono, then turned back to Bandicut. "Will you come into the other room with me?"

Bandicut blinked, wondering if he was now intruding on the privacy of the dead. He glanced at Ik. The Hraachee'an was drumming his chest with his fingertips in puzzlement.

"Come," said Askelanda sharply, and strode back into the other room.

Bandicut sighed. After this draining effort with Thorek, had Lako died, too? He followed Askelanda through the parted curtain, and found the Neri leader standing beside Lako's cot. No one was speaking. *Damn,* Bandicut thought. He moved to Askelanda's side.

Lako's eyes were open, seemingly clear and focused, black pools staring at the ceiling. The Neri was breathing, his nostril and gill slits opening and closing. Bandicut's heart skipped. As he leaned forward, Lako's eyes shifted in small movements until they met Bandicut's. His mouth moved.

Bandicut shook his head, indicating he couldn't hear.

"He is asking, 'Are you the one?' Are you the one who saved his life?" Askelanda's voice was filled with intensity, and yet seemed expressionless.

Saved his life? Bandicut thought. Had it really worked, then?

"What shall I tell him?" There now seemed to be a twinkle of humor in Askelanda's eyes.

Bandicut blinked in astonishment. "You can say," he replied huskily, "that I had a lot of help. From the stones." He rubbed his wrists, then pointed to his temple. "From someone who lives inside me." And he turned and nodded to L'Kell, who had joined them. "And from L'Kell."

L'Kell's fingers moved in a graceful flutter. "I did nothing. I merely watched, and hoped."

Bandicut shook his head. "You helped, all right. I felt it, from within him."

Lako's eyes shifted, like luminous orbs in a face of scarred black rubber. His mouth was moving again, and this time he made an audible, hissing rasp. And Bandicut heard the words, "Thank you."

He stood motionless, eyes welling.

/// Say you're welcome. ///

"You're welcome," he whispered.

"I think," said Corono, standing on the other side of Lako, "that we should let him rest."

/// Do you think we could just . . . check? ///

At first he didn't know what the quarx meant. Then he nodded slowly. "Do you mind if I touch his arm again, for a moment?"

Corono gestured permission.

Lako was still very warm to the touch. But as Bandicut felt his senses flowing down into the Neri, he felt that the feverish, chaotic heat had changed into something different.

/// He's hot, but it's the heat of
accelerated healing. ///

/Good./ He started to remove his hand.

/// Wait. ///

He hesitated, but couldn't tell what the quarx was doing.

/// Yes. Take care, and be well.
Okay, John. ///

He lifted his hand. /Did you actually speak to Lako?/

/// Not in words.
But in thought. Feeling.
Emotion. ///

/And . . . how is he?/

/// He is in a haze of pain.
But he is aware, and knows that he is recovering.
He will not soon forget you, John. ///

/Us, you mean./

/// Us, ///

the quarx agreed.

"John!" Ik interrupted.

He turned with a start, and realized that Askelanda had been talking to him, and he hadn't heard a word.

"Do we want to go someplace comfortable, to rest? And talk?"

"Yes, of course." He sighed and touched Lako's arm again in farewell, then followed the others out of the room.

From a domed room at the top of a multilevel dwelling, Bandicut and Ik looked out into the sea. They watched three separate schools of fish sweeping one way and another through the city; they saw a large creature that looked like a jellyfish in the shape of a great curved, hanging curtain. Several Neri swimmers were moving around it, trying to herd it away from the settlement. A poisonous animal, dangerous to young Neri, L'Kell explained. It was interesting, but Bandicut was too tired to keep watching. He was still coping with two deaths and one rescue, and deep exhaustion that was more emotional than physical.

Askelanda—after thanking Bandicut with grave, soft-spoken words—sent word that more comfortable quarters should be prepared for the visitors in this larger habitat. "In the meantime," he said, "please make yourselves at home here. Are you hungry? Is there anything else we can do for you? If you have questions, perhaps . . ."

They had many questions. Too many to focus on. Askelanda spoke for a few minutes about those who had died, whose spirits had returned to the sea. They would be remembered in a service later; perhaps the visitors would like to observe.

Ik acknowledged graciously, then said, "Askelanda, we would like to know what has become of *our* companions. May I ask, will they be permitted to rejoin us?"

Askelanda conferred with one of his aides. "They are in conference with the *obliq*," he said after a moment. "They will be invited to join us when they are finished."

"The *obliq*?" Bandicut asked.

"The keeper . . . of our knowledge." Askelanda paused, as an expression of—what?—tension?—crossed his dusty face. He readjusted his stole, with a soft clinking of the bound shells. For a moment, he seemed even older than before. "I expect," he continued in a gravelly tone, "that the obliq is providing your companions with a great deal of useful information."

He suddenly gestured to his assistants and barked something, in response to which several large cushions were carried in. "Please—try to be comfortable. There is food coming shortly. In the meantime, I wish to tell you—"

Askelanda was interrupted by a sudden vibration in the floor. For a moment, he appeared unconcerned, but the vibration grew quickly in intensity—until the whole habitat was shaking. Bandicut exchanged worried looks with Ik. Earthquake? Attack?

The Neri muttered among themselves, and then one of them barked out a warning, pointing outside. Several of the smaller habitats were visibly moving in the disturbance, straining at their anchors. Clouds of silt were being agitated up from the sloping seafloor. And a greenish yellow light was radiating in great fan-shaped swaths through the undersea city.

And it was coming not from overhead, or from any of the structures, but from the darkness of the depths below.

INTERLUDE

Julie Stone

IT WAS SOME time after the contact, after that lecherous Doctor Switzer was through examining her, and the exoarch leaders had debriefed her, that Julie Stone finally got a chance to lie down on her bunk and work it through in her head. Not that she understood it all, by any means; but at least she could go over the events in detail, and the words, and try to put them into some sort of perspective. She had made contact with an alien presence, or rather it had made contact with her. And though the physical details of the contact were a blur to her now, she knew that the translator had conveyed to her some terribly disturbing thoughts—only some of which she had shared in turn with her colleagues. There were other things she didn't dare speak of, not until she had thought them through.

Something out there which is trying to destroy your world . . .

She was virtually certain she had heard those words, though she could not now visualize the moment of receiving them. The thought was ominously reminiscent of what John Bandicut had related to her in his letter, explaining why he was doing those crazy things—stealing a spaceship from Triton Orbital and flying off on a suicide mission across the solar system. But John hadn't said anything about something *trying* to destroy the Earth; he'd just talked about a rogue comet. And maybe, just maybe, he had managed to save the Earth from it.

Maybe?

That was just it; no one knew for sure. The official position here at the MINEXFO camp was that Bandicut had gone crazy, probably as a result of that old neurolink injury, and killed himself. A few people—Georgia Patwell, Julie, maybe John's friend Krackey and a few others—believed what John said. There was no question that the ship had vanished from the immediate neighborhood in a way that *nobody* could explain. And how could John have faked that radio transmission from halfway across the solar system? And the propulsion flame—he'd said put a telescope on it. Someone had—not officially, of course, the officials were all too busy explaining why it wasn't possible—but someone up in Triton Orbital had gotten pictures, very strange pictures. And none of it made any sense unless you took some pretty peculiar technology into account. Like alien technology.

Earth-based observers had spotted the comet, too, just coming out from behind the sun relative to the home planet. It *could* have been on a collision course with Earth—but they didn't have enough data to establish its orbit with much precision, and anyway, no one at that point could have predicted the effects from solar heating and subsequent vapor eruptions on the comet and its trajectory. No one saw the stolen spacecraft emerge from the glare of the sun, if it was there at all. But several telescopes caught the flash, the explosion, way in near Mercury's orbit. And no comet ever came out, though a cloud of fine dust and debris was observed.

Maybe saved the Earth?

Julie blinked and stared at the ceiling over her bunk. *No maybe, not anymore. It told me,* she thought. *What John said was true, every word of it. He took the ship and collided with the comet.* She ought to be happy, knowing that he hadn't died for nothing. That he was a hero. And she would have been, except . . . now the translator wanted her to do something, too. Something crazy, like what John had done?

Mission yet to fulfill . . . require your assistance . . .

And the clear sense that it wanted her to keep it to herself.

She rolled over and grabbed her pillow, and clutched it to her. And, as she thought about John, her tears began to flow once more.

CHAPTER 10

Breakaway!

THE NERI BEGAN shouting to each other. Their voices were a cacophony of rasps, too fast and confusing for Bandicut's stones to follow.

The quaking was growing in violence. In a matter of moments, this had gone from a curiosity to an emergency. Bandicut and Ik stayed out of the way, while Askelanda barked instructions to Neri who ran in and out of the room. Bandicut had visions of the dome around them shattering, but he told himself that if that happened, it wouldn't matter if he was close to the dome; he'd be just as dead either way. He stood at the edge of the dome, trying to see what was going on outside. The dome gave good horizontal and top visibility, but to see down at all, he really had to crane his neck. The light from below had brightened, almost to the point of illuminating the undersea city. It reminded him of a brightly lit stadium, seen far off through a dense fog.

"L'Kell!" Bandicut called to the young Neri leader, who had run in and out several times, and was now awaiting Askelanda's attention. "What is it? Are we under attack by the landers? Is it an earthquake?"

It seemed to cost L'Kell a great effort to shift his eyes and thoughts to Bandicut. "The landers? No. It is the—" *kraafff* "—the Monster, the Devourer—in the heart of the abyss—"

L'Kell's answer was interrupted by a sudden violent swaying of the habitat. Bandicut and Ik both staggered, Bandicut thumping into the dome. His heart nearly stopped as he imagined crashing through the dome, and pushed himself back from the clear material. What had just happened? He turned his head and saw a school of mottled silver fish streaming by the dome, moving downward at an angle. Something was odd about it, and it took him a moment to realize what: they were swimming *upward*, into the current, and still were being carried down into deeper water.

What the hell kind of bottom current would carry something downward with that much speed and power?

"It is what I spoke of before," L'Kell continued. "The Maw of the Abyss. We have never gone deep enough to see it. But we know it well, and hoped it would not awaken."

"Then, hrahh—" But Ik's question was interrupted by a sudden, bone-jarring CRUMP! that seemed to rock the entire structure.

"*Haiii, kallah, Askelanda!*" cried L'Kell, darting to the edge of the room to peer into the sea. His words were too quick for the stones to catch. But the reason for his outcry became apparent a moment later.

KREEEE-E-E-E-E-CHH—!

Bandicut fell back from a wrenching shriek so distorted by the water that he could not have guessed its source if he hadn't been staring right at it. Just upslope from them, a habitat twisted, tilted sickeningly, and tore free from the cluster that was holding it. The habitat spun, trailing bubbles, as it came loose; then it rose with seemingly impossible grace out of the larger structure. It ascended rapidly, vanishing into the mist of the sea above.

"John Bandicut!"

Ik's cry made him tear his gaze away. Most of the Neri had dashed from the room. Only L'Kell was left, and he was shouting down a passageway to someone. He turned to Ik and Bandicut. "I have to go. You can stay here. You should be safe."

"Hrahh—like hell!" Ik growled. "We will go, if we can help."

"Right. But where are we going?" Bandicut asked.

"To the subs," L'Kell said, waving for them to follow. "We must see what we can do."

"Lead on," Bandicut said.

They ran.

Antares had listened with alarm as the obliq Kailan described the mysterious peril at the bottom of the sea, in the abyssal trench that lay not far off from the site of the Neri city. The Neri did not know what the thing was, except that it had appeared in the midst of a great cataclysm generations ago. But *whatever* it was, it caused—at unpredictable intervals—both earthquakes and inexplicably powerful downcurrents of water. And not just seawater, of course, but anything loose in the water, such as Neri swimmers who had the bad luck to be caught in the surges. Through the years, a good number of Neri lives had been lost that way. The worst eruptions were always accompanied by a puzzling glow that somehow radiated upward from the deepest abyss.

"Why do you stay here, then, with your city so close to it?" Li-Jared had asked, with more logic than tact.

"Because our factories are down there—"

"In the abyss?" Li-Jared said, his electric-blue eyes wide with amazement.

"Not in the abyss itself, but on the ledge near the drop-off," Kailan said calmly, facing them where they were seated on the floor of her chambers. Her facial expression was dominated by her enormous eyes, which made her appear intensely curious. "Without the factories, we will die, say our leaders. Perhaps they are correct." She was silent a moment. "In recent times, the Maw has not been too active. It has been years since the last very bad eruption."

No sooner had Kailan spoken those words than the floor suddenly began to shake. Antares and Kailan looked around in alarm. Li-Jared sprang to his feet and began pacing nervously. *"What's going on? What is it?"* Antares caught him by the arm and calmed him. Following Kailan, they hurried back to one of the domed rooms from which they could see for themselves what was happening.

Just as they got to the windows, a piercing sound of tearing metal began to throb through the floor. It grew to a shriek, drowning out the background rumble. What they saw was dozens of habitats, mostly downslope from them, swaying on their moorings. But one, just a few bubbles over, and a little deeper, was twisting alarmingly on its mooring. For a moment it looked as if it were being pulled downward; then, with an awful ripping sound, the mooring let go and with a cascade of bubbles, the habitat floated up and away, and vanished.

Antares looked at Kailan in horror. "This is a bad one?" The obliq was staring silently, radiating alarm.

This was one of the bad ones.

Kailan turned and asked questions of one of the other Neri in a rapid-fire stutter. She listened impatiently to the frantic reply, then stood a moment, frozen in thought.

"Were there people in that bubble?" Antares asked.

Kailan glanced at her. "Yes. If they can get out before it breaches surface, they might survive. But the habitat—could—"

"What?"

Kailan's thoughts were obviously far ahead of Antares' question. She whirled and ran with surprising agility back to her chambers. "Elbeth! Instruments on—full overhead scan!"

Antares glanced at Li-Jared for only a moment before racing after her.

They swept into Kailan's second room. The lefthand wall was lined with consoles; three of them were glowing. They were slightly concave and shaped like fat crescents with blunt horns pointed down. Antares stared, caught by surprise. Even in the submarines, she had seen no indication of such electronic technology. All three instruments showed variations on a ghostly image that might have been the ocean outside, with some kind of light intensification. Several washed-out spots looked like habitats above them, just at the edge of view near the righthand horn of the center console.

Li-Jared jabbed a finger. "What's that?"

Antares looked harder, then saw it—a group of dark spots, moving into the brighter gradient, then fading. Kailan worked at the console, trying to improve the image. "Teams in pursuit. But I don't think they can catch it in time." Her fingers moved like a musician's along the bar-shaped controls. "Askelanda won't like this, but I wonder if we can do something from here."

She touched a round depression, and all three screens blinked and changed. The flanking screens switched to abstract images that were probably graphic representations. The center screen changed to something that still looked literal, but more like a long-range radar or sonar image, with icons that seemed to indicate moving bodies.

"What's that?" Antares murmured, nervous about interrupting.

"Same view, overhead, scanner composite," Kailan said. She seemed to be trying to center a circle on the screen over a large symbol, beside which text characters were changing rapidly.

"Is that the habitat?"

"Yes."

"It almost looks," said Li-Jared, "as if you are targeting the thing. Is this a—?" He caught himself, as though afraid to ask the question. But Antares felt the timbre of his fear and heard herself thinking the question: *Is this a weapon?*

Kailan called to Elbeth, "Raise Askelanda! And don't take no for an answer."

By the time they reached the hangar, all the other subs were gone. Ik and Bandicut scrambled down the conning tower hatch and got out of L'Kell's way as he sealed the vessel and took the controls. They submerged with surprising speed and accelerated away from the hangar, through the glowing city. Bandicut peered out the nose window and clutched for something to hold onto as L'Kell banked around a habitat cluster and then raised the nose and began ascending quickly. "Where are we going?" Bandicut asked. It was disconcerting to watch the yellowish-green aura of the settlement recede below; the city had come to represent more security than he had realized. "Are we going after the breakaway habitat?"

"Yes, if we—" L'Kell interrupted himself at the sound of a Neri voice warbling scratchily from the console. He replied in a low, quick voice—then, with a single warning cry, took the sub into a sweeping turn and angled it back downward into a dive. "We've been given a new assignment," he said. Bandicut's stomach lurched at the suddenness of the change, and he braced himself from the nose window. The motors changed pitch, then finally hummed to a higher speed as they accelerated downward.

The sub swayed drunkenly, and Bandicut realized suddenly that L'Kell had just steered them into the powerful downwelling current that they had observed from the habitat. They were riding it downward. But to where? His breath caught as they passed the undersea city, now off to their left, and continued in a steep descent. The flickering glow from the abyss was in front of them now, and below. It looked like lightning embedded deep in the heart of a thunderstorm. Was that where they were headed? To confront the Devourer?

"L'Kell?" he murmured.

They were approaching the seafloor now, and began to follow the slope, like a terrain-hugging aircraft. It was mostly rock and silt, moving past in a featureless blur.

"They've got people going after the breakaway," L'Kell explained finally. "We have a different job—to follow the current and see if anything's been dragged down." He was interrupted by a squawk from the console. He exchanged further words with a distant Neri comm operator, then said to his companions, "A docking cradle broke loose, and was last seen being carried downward, toward the factory. We must check for damage, and see what we can do."

Bandicut glanced over at Ik, whose eyes were sparkling with an inner fire. Excitement? Or alarm? "We're not going to—go all the way down to the—what did you call it?" he asked in a husky voice.

"The Demon of Darkness, the—" *kraafff* "—Maw of the Abyss," murmured L'Kell, his gaze fixed out the window. "I hope not. There is a lot between us and it."

Bandicut began to breathe a little more easily.

"Still—" L'Kell's eyes shifted toward Bandicut for a split second "—there are never any guarantees. Are there?"

Bandicut blinked, and suddenly wished he hadn't asked.

Kailan was working intently. She had the targeting circle over the symbol representing the breakaway habitat, and was now studying a display that Antares took to be tracking data. "The habitat will breach surface in three minutes," Kailan said. "There's a good chance it will hit the collector array first."

Without knowing exactly what Kailan was referring to, Antares felt a cold sense of distance. Kailan and Elbeth were working with urgent speed, and Antares was deliberately keeping her own emotions isolated, so as not to interfere, even while trying to follow what was happening.

"I have Askelanda," said Elbeth suddenly.

"Obliq," said a dry voice, from the console. "We're very busy right now. We've lost a habitat."

Kailan touched the console. "I'm tracking the habitat. It will pass through the solar array in two minutes, with probable impact. It will breach in two and a half minutes."

The answering voice seemed startled. "How do you know that?"

"I am using the beam-targeting scanners you consider nonfunctional. There is no choice—I must take action. Please order your subs clear."

Askelanda's voice was sharp and angry. "I can't order them clear! They're trying to catch it! It's the only thing we can do."

"They cannot reach it. But I can stop it. *You must get them clear.*"

"Obliq—I don't see how you think—"

"I am going to hole the habitat and sink it. Are the people out yet?"

"We don't know—there's no contact! What do you mean, *sink* it?"

"We've got to keep it from breaching. If it hits the surface, they'll die for sure. If I can put a hole in it, we might be able to bring it back down before it hits. Think of the array, Askelanda! We can't take the chance! *Get those subs out from between me and the habitat!*"

"But surely you don't mean to use that ancient weapon—"

"Ten seconds," Kailan said evenly.

"But you can't—all right—we're calling them."

"Seven."

"Give us time!"

"I can't. It'll be too late. Five." Kailan's fingers were flicking over the console. She peered up at the screen with her enormous eyes, narrowly webbed finger poised on one key. "Two—"

"They're telling us—"

"Can't wait. Starting pulse-beam now." She pressed the key.

The screen on the left blinked back to a visible view overhead. A thin beam of light shot up green, vanishing into the mist. Three bright pulses flashed up the light thread, as though riding the beam, too fast to follow. Antares glanced at Kailan. She was staring at the center screen, where three twinkling icons were closing in on the large symbol and circle. She pointed to another symbol that was clearly a chase sub, and gestured frantically as though to sweep it out of the way. It wasn't moving fast enough.

The first twinkle grazed the sub and blossomed. Kailan tensed. The second cleared the sub and intersected the habitat symbol. So did the third.

The symbol billowed expanding red rings.

CHAPTER 11

Rescue

THE SUB'S HULL creaked disconcertingly as they descended into a darkness broken only by the occasional glimmer of lightning below. Bandicut was reminded of a time, years ago, when he had made a toursub dive onto the site of the sunken *Titanic*, four thousand meters down in the North Atlantic, on Earth. It had been a haunting experience, watching the carefully lit wreck emerge from the darkness of the ocean grave, thinking of the hundreds who had gone with the ship to their personal graves. The wreck had lain undisturbed for decades, and even now, though it was a historic park, there was a sense of quietude about it, a somber sense of tragedy that would never go away. He had thumbed off the commentary in his earphones and just watched the floodlit ship loom before them in the perpetual night, a haunting presence of silence and solitude.

Floating detritus streamed backward past them now in the sub's headlight, which was the only thing that told Bandicut that they were descending even faster than the current. He could still feel the current, as some occasional turbulence caught them and swayed them close to the limits of L'Kell's control. From time to time he heard a whispering rush of air and felt his ears popping, as the sub's internal pressure adjusted in stages to the growing pressure outside—not keeping the two equal, but reducing the differential. It made him think of the habitat that was rocketing toward the surface, if it hadn't already reached it, and he shuddered at the thought of the explosive decompression that must be occurring. When he asked L'Kell, the Neri answered, "With luck, anyone inside got out. They could survive a pressure change much of the way up—but they'll certainly die if the hull breaches and ruptures."

Bandicut was silent after that. He wondered, where in all of this were Antares and Li-Jared?

/// Your other friends?
You miss them. ///

/I'm worried sick about them. What if they're in the breakaway habitat?/

/// They might die. Is that it? ///

/Of course that's it. They're not like you, Charlie. Charlene, I mean. They don't spring back to life the way you do./ At least not as far as he knew.

/// You can call me Charlie if you want.
This matter of dying is
an important business to you,
isn't it? ///

/What a question! Jesus, Charlie—yes! It *hurts* to have your friends die./

/// Yes, I suppose it— ///

/And I must tell you, it doesn't help to have you and your fellows dying all the time, usually just when I need you the most./

He could almost sense Charlene pursing her lips in thought.

/// Just like Charlie-Four, before me? ///

/Well—yeah. Don't get me wrong—I'm happier with you here. I suppose you could say that that death was a good thing./

/// Really? Why?
Would you say that if I died? ///

/No!/

/// Don't get upset.
I'm just trying to understand. ///

Bandicut let out a slow breath, suddenly aware of his inward tension—stunned, in fact, by the rage and grief and bewilderment that were welling up inside him. /Listen. Charlie-Four was a mean-spirited, bad-tempered sonofabitch./ But even as he said it, he felt his inner voice catch.

/// So you aren't sorry that he died. ///

/I didn't say that!/ He struggled to find the words. /I am sorry! It hurt, it always hurts. But you know as well as I do that he wouldn't have done—well, what *you* did, to save Lako, for instance./

/// You're sure about that. ///

/Yeah I'm sure. He flat-out refused. Things got tough, and he checked out. I never knew quarx could commit suicide./

/// If that's what he did. ///

/Well, that's what it seemed like./

/// And if he did . . . was that a bad thing to do? ///

Bandicut peered moodily out into the streaming turbid flow, and wondered how deep they were and how much deeper they were going. L'Kell was piloting with silent concentration. /Yeah, it was, I think. An act of cowardice. Except . . . I am glad for its result. I'm glad you're here now./

The quarx hesitated, and he sensed that she was debating whether or not to voice disagreement.

/// Thank you, ///

she said finally. And then she fell silent, and Bandicut found himself wondering if he had somehow missed something in the discussion.

The water became gradually clearer even as the bottom slope appeared to become siltier. It also became steeper, for a while. Then some irregular topography loomed into the headlight beam: the slope almost leveled off, then rose in sharp little peaks, which L'Kell had to steer over or around. Then it dropped again, leveled, and peaked; and that pattern was repeated several times, in a series of stepped ledges punctuated with low ridges and hills. For a time, the flickering light from below disappeared or was blocked from view. Something about this topography rang a bell in his memory, but he couldn't quite place it . . . until plumes of dark, smoky material suddenly loomed in the headlight beam, billowing up out of chimneylike formations on the seafloor. The plumes bent sideways as they were caught by the current, and then streamed downslope in coiling, turbulent ribbons that flowed over the ridges toward the abyssal depths. Bandicut drew a sharp breath.

/// You know these things? ///

/On Earth they're called smokers. Volcanic vents on the seafloor. If these are the same, they'll have boiling hot water pouring out with the smoke—/

"We must steer around these hot vents," L'Kell said, banking the sub into decelerating turns. "We are almost there."

/There?/ Bandicut started to ask, then had a thought. /Ah, I think I understand./

/// What? ///

/I'll tell you in a moment. If I'm right./

/// You could share the thought,
whether you're right or wrong. ///

Grunting, he strained to peer into the distance. He was rewarded seconds later by the sight of silt-covered domes and derricks and other machinery emerging from the darkness.

/That's it! There it is! Their factory is located on the vent ridge! Unbelievable./

/// Why would they do that? ///

/Heat and raw materials, I suppose. Of course! Those smokers are billowing up plumes of chemicals and superheated water. With the right equipment, they could probably use that—/

"Our factory," L'Kell said suddenly, "uses these plumes for mineral extraction and heat. When it is working correctly, it can—"

"Hrahh, what is that?" Ik cried, interrupting the Neri. He pointed to a conglomeration of greyish machinery rising from the ledge ahead—and lodged against it, just visible in the headlight, what looked like a metal framework holding a ghostly bubble. As they drew closer, two small shapes became visible, moving around inside the bubble.

"Mokin' fokin' lay me in hell," Bandicut whispered. "Is it really?"

/// What? ///

/Not what. Who. It's Napoleon and Copernicus. That's our bubble. Our star-spanner bubble./ Bandicut felt the tightening of fear in his stomach. "L'Kell—"

"Yes, I know," said L'Kell, in a tone that implied he was very busy at the moment. He steered close to the structure holding the star-spanner bubble, then swung the sub around with motors singing at high pitch, countering the movement of the current. L'Kell was trying to hover close to the star-spanner bubble, and the current was trying to sweep them away into the darkness. He finally had to give up and move away. It appeared that the factory was perched on the edge of a sharp drop-off. Bandicut caught sight of a glimmer of lightning in the abyssal gloom, straight down beyond the edge.

"I hope the current will ease soon," L'Kell said. "At that point we will return to do what we can about your bubble. In the meantime, we must inspect the area for anything else that might be caught—and for damage to the factory." He didn't elaborate, but Bandicut remembered his earlier remarks. The Neri's machine-makers were breaking down. And without them, the Neri faced disaster.

"Will you bring teams down to repair the factory?" Ik asked.

The Neri completed a maneuver before answering. He was guiding the sub over the neighboring landscape, angling this way and that to inspect what looked like an abandoned alien settlement on the bleak surface of a moon. Finally he said, "We would—if we knew how."

Bandicut opened his mouth to say something, then closed it. What could he say? What could either of them say?

"Obliq, turn off your weapon! You've hit one of our subs," rasped a male Neri voice, not Askelanda's. "We need to get help to them."

Kailan's finger was poised for more shots. She held off, watching the display. The sound of three concussions thumped through the walls, delayed by distance. "We've hit the breakaway," she breathed, "but did we put a big enough hole in it?" Her finger traced the likely path of the habitat up to a series of long, horizontal lines on the screen. "Still rising. It takes time to flood."

"Obliq, please acknowledge!"

"Message received," Kailan snapped. "Standing by. But keep the line of fire clear!" Kailan hesitated, watching the display. "It's not slowing fast enough. Okay—your sub is clear. Firing again!"

Three flashes went up the thread of light.

They hit the habitat symbol.

The symbol was still rising, approaching the horizontal lines that represented the solar array, not far below the surface. But the habitat was slowing. It nearly touched one of the array symbols, as it came to a stop. It hung there for a few moments, then began to sink.

Three thumps, delayed.

"Obliq!" Askelanda's voice again, sharp.

"Turning off power to the weapon," Kailan said. "The habitat is coming back down. It may have struck one solar collector, but I believe not. Can you get a grapple on it now? If there's anyone still aboard, they'll need help."

The answer was a mixture of angry acknowledgment and shouts and orders in the background.

Kailan stepped back from the console and said to Elbeth, "We must meet with Askelanda. Please ask for a sub, as soon as they can send one." She turned to Antares and Li-Jared. "There will be trouble over this, I am afraid. Askelanda and I do not see eye to eye on all of these matters. And now it will only be worse."

"Why?" Antares asked. "Because of the habitat?"

"Because the Maw of the Abyss has awakened," Kailan answered. Gesturing to Elbeth, she asked her assistant to lead the guests back to the submarine hangar. "I'll meet you there," she said, and quickly slipped away through a doorway on the far side of the room.

The current finally slackened, and tapered off into a leisurely horizontal flow. L'Kell was clearly relieved when he no longer had to fight to keep them from being dragged deeper into the abyss. The eerie glow had flickered out. Once it was gone, Bandicut felt an even greater sense of depth, as they moved about in darkness broken only by their own headlight. He wondered just how deep they really were now—and decided that he would rather not know. On Earth, as he recalled, volcanic vents were thousands of meters deep.

L'Kell turned the sub. "We'll go back to your bubble in a moment, but I must check something first." They glided above some machinery that seemed half buried in silt—the result, apparently, of the powerful downward flow just now. He made a rasping sound that Bandicut interpreted as displeasure.

"Is something wrong?"

The Neri pointed to a spot not far in front of them, where four short masts stuck up into the current. Just beyond them a smoldering vent billowed a thick cloud of smoke. It took Bandicut a moment to realize that the masts were broken; something had been attached to them, quite recently. "That was the last exterior loading assistant, for moving equipment out of the factory and into subs. It has broken away." L'Kell stared at the spot in obvious dismay.

"Can't you replace it?" Bandicut asked. "Surely there must be a way."

"The factory itself used to make repairs like that," L'Kell said softly. "But it does not do so anymore. And I—we—do not know what to do about it. We do not have the knowledge, and even we cannot work easily at this depth."

Bandicut stared at him, then at Ik, who was silently contemplating the problem. And he suddenly thought, /You don't suppose . . . you know, I wonder if it could be—/

/// I see your thoughts, but do not understand.
"Nano-shit"? ///

/It's only a guess, but it stands to reason. I'll have to ask L'Kell. But if he doesn't have the knowledge—/

/// Submicroscopic machinery?
Self-replicating assemblers?
Self-repairing construction units? ///

The quarx's voice became subdued, as she tried to interpret his memories, which included a complex amalgam of feelings. Nano-assemblers were an important part of the infrastructure of the human civilization he had come from; but it was misprogrammed nanomeds—microscopic cellular repair units injected into his body—that had destroyed his career by crippling his ability to neurolink. It was the nanomeds that had left him vulnerable to attacks of silence-fugue.

/// Whoa.
This is something I need to know more about,
yes? ///

/I suppose so. Help yourself to the records. Ask me if you have questions./ He didn't want to think about it right now. He especially didn't want to think about it while he was a couple of miles underwater and as vulnerable to claustrophobia as he was ever likely to be in his life. He shivered in the dark, trying not to look beyond the little pool of light projected by the sub's headlight. The things that could come out of the dark . . .

The thought faded, probably with help. He thought a quiet thanks, and said to L'Kell, "Can you tell me anything about how your factory works? I have a reason for asking."

L'Kell was occupied for a moment with the controls. "I don't know how it works, really. It takes the raw materials, and the heat. And in—" *klaa* "—tanks filled with liquids, the machines that we need just . . . appear. Or they did." He brought the sub around to a new heading. "Perhaps it is—" *kraff* "—magic, and the magic is gone. Or perhaps the—" *kraafff* "—Maw has done something, has decided that it should not be allowed to continue."

"Or perhaps," Bandicut mused, "the nano-constructors have quit working because they have broken down. Or because their programming has gone wrong. I wonder—" And he suddenly realized that he was speaking aloud, and wished that he'd kept silent until he knew more.

But L'Kell had heard him. "You wonder what? Do you have the power to heal machines, as well as people?"

Bandicut shivered, and shook his head. Ik was staring at him in puzzlement. Charlie was waiting for him to voice his thoughts, too.

The sub's headlight crawled over a rising mechanical structure, and within the pool of light the broken docking frame and the star-spanner bubble suddenly appeared. The sub slowed as it approached the bubble. In its shelter, clearly visible, were the robots Napoleon and Copernicus.

"*I* can't heal machines," Bandicut said finally. "But maybe *they* can."

Li-Jared and Antares stood fidgeting on the dock of the sub hangar, waiting for Kailan to join them. The water surface, inches from their feet, was jiggling with vibrations from the current outside, and perhaps fading aftershocks from the quake. Li-Jared hated looking down into the water, so he tried to distract himself by talking to Antares. "Has it stopped yet?" he murmured, turning sideways to inspect the walls.

"It's not going to stop until we leave this planet," Antares mused, and he was startled to realize that there was a hint of humor in her voice. He felt Antares brush the under-layers of his mind, and knew that she was trying to help him. But she seemed pretty edgy herself.

"I meant the quake," he said.

"I know." The Thespi's hand touched his arm for a moment. He closed his eyes, regaining his center, grateful for her calming presence. "Actually," she said, "I think it is abating. But there's a lot of movement of silt out there. A strong current. I hope we don't go out in that."

Li-Jared bonged softly to himself. "I'm sure they know what they're doing. But why do they need *us* to decide what to do about this—" he took a hissing breath "—Maw of Darkness?"

"I suspect it is no coincidence that we are here to assist with this problem," Antares said. But if she had other thoughts on that, she did not voice them.

It seemed as if they had been waiting forever. But by the time Kailan arrived, Li-Jared was feeling better. Still, he was surprised to see the obliq carrying something about the size of a briefcase-satchel, and two of her assistants carrying similar cases. "May I ask," he said, "what we're about to do?"

"We are going to see if we can convince the *ahktah* that we would be better served worrying about what lies below us than worrying about what lies above us," Kailan said. "I do not know if we will succeed. But you two . . ."

Li-Jared waited. "We two what?"

Kailan's black, huge-eyed face was unreadable. "You two come from the stars beyond. So, I believe, does this demon, this

Maw of the Abyss. Therefore, if anyone can help us to understand and control it, you can. Would you not say so?"

Li-Jared felt Antares' surprise and dismay before he even turned to meet her eyes.

Using the sub's external manipulators, L'Kell worked for some time rigging attachment lines onto the docking frame. He had already called for assistance, and by the time he had his lines on the frame, another submarine had joined them. This one attached lines on the other side of the docking frame. Inside the starspanner bubble, at least until the silt swirl obscured it from sight, the robots could be seen watching the proceedings with apparent interest. There had been no communication with them, and it seemed unlikely that they would have been able to see Bandicut's face through the glare. He wondered what they thought was happening.

Both subs applied gentle power. The lines tightened, and the subs began lifting from opposite sides of the bubble. Huge clouds of fresh silt swirled up from the bottom, largely obscuring the view. The motors groaned, and so did the lines and the hull, as they lifted the docking frame and bubble. Bandicut glanced around nervously.

Something clanged, and a jar reverberated through the hull. One of the lines had caught somehow, and was causing the sub to yaw to the right. L'Kell called to the other Neri pilot and touched a control to subdue the movement. Everything settled back to the bottom. "Something's hanging up when we lift."

"Would it help," Bandicut asked, "if we could talk to the robots? Convey instructions to them?"

The Neri's round eye peered at him for a moment.

"Is there any way to amplify our voices out there?"

"You mean *really* talk to them? Oh. Sure." L'Kell touched a switch on the console. "Go ahead."

"CAN I JUST TALK?"

Bandicut started at the sound of his voice ringing outside the hull. He blinked as he heard a distant, scratchy voice in reply. "Hello? Is that you, John?"

His heart raced. *"NAPOLEON! COPERNICUS! CAN YOU HEAR ME? IT'S BANDICUT!"* His cry seemed to reverberate along the ocean bottom. L'Kell adjusted the control to reduce the volume.

"We hear you, Cap'n. Can you advise us what is happening?" It sounded like Napoleon.

"We're trying to rescue you! But you're snagged on something." Bandicut glanced at L'Kell. "How can they help?"

L'Kell peered out into the silt-obscured sea. "Ask if they can see anything, like the docking frame and that structure they're lodged against. Maybe *they* can tell us where they're caught."

"Nappy? Coppy?" he called. "Can your scanners penetrate the water at all? Our vision is obscured. We can't tell where you're hung up."

"Aye, Cap'n. It's this overhang above us, and half a meter aft of center. Can you see it?"

Bandicut peered, but the water was too turbid. L'Kell spoke on his comm to the Neri in the other sub, then said, "Can they say which way we need to move?"

Bandicut relayed the question, and the robots replied that they needed to *drop* slightly, then move forward until they were clear of the obstruction.

L'Kell made a rasping sound. "Difficult, difficult." He spoke to the other sub. They started their motors again, and the lines tightened. He applied sideways thrust as he lowered the sub until it was so close to the bottom that it was scraping up silt.

"Napoleon?"

"Forward thrust, please. *Wait! Wait!*"

The sub suddenly slewed, and there was a thump as the docking frame jarred into a new obstruction. L'Kell muttered as he cut the motors. The sub veered, then slammed into a boulder buried in the silt. L'Kell fought to regain control of the sub, while Bandicut struggled to catch his breath.

"The lines are catching—too low," Napoleon reported. "Hold on. We're going to try to get the star-spanner bubble to help us with buoyancy control." Napoleon fell silent, then, while Bandicut and Ik looked at each other in puzzlement, and L'Kell worked to keep the sub steady.

"Okay," said the robot finally. As they peered out in amazement, the bubble slowly sank about one-half meter. "You can take us out now. Straight and level."

Bandicut blinked and relayed the instruction. With great care, L'Kell and the other pilot guided their subs forward, with the load slung between them. They moved in near-blindness at first; then the remaining current carried away enough of the suspended silt to reveal most of the docking frame and star-spanner bubble.

"You're lifting us again," called the robot.

They eased back and allowed some slack in the lines.

"That's good. Forward again."

A minute later, they were clear of the obstruction. "Well done!" Bandicut cried. He was answered by a series of clicking, rasping whoops from the robots.

The two pilots increased power and carried the frame-and-bubble, suspended between them, to a point of safety, well away from the edge of the abyss. Then they set it down to rearrange their lines for proper, long-distance towing. As L'Kell brought them close to the bubble, Bandicut waved joyfully to the robots, who flashed their lights in reply. The two pilots spent some time changing the rigging, and at last began the laborious climb back toward the city—the bubble and its frame floating well above the bottom, slung between the subs.

It was going to be a long trip back—but a better trip, Bandicut thought, than the journey down.

CHAPTER 12

Aftermath

"IF WE HAD allowed the habitat to breach," Kailan snapped, "not only would it have killed *everyone* on board, instead of just three, it would have destroyed part of the solar array, too."

Antares ducked out of the way to avoid being hit by webbed hands as the two angry Neri strode around one another, gesturing. She and Li-Jared moved farther to one side.

"And that, Obliq, is how you justify firing upon one of my submarines?" Askelanda stretched his hands wide. "How can you dismiss the deaths of three people so casually?"

"I am *not* dismissing their deaths," Kailan said with rising indignation. "They were my friends and I'm as sorry to send them on their spirit-journeys as you."

Askelanda made a gesture of apparent supplication, from his breast toward her, as though to acknowledge her grief. But what Antares felt coming from him was disbelief. "So, then," he said, "please explain why you—"

"Nor did I fire upon your submarine!" Kailan interrupted. "*Our* submarine. I gave warning, I begged you to move the sub. But you did not get it clear in time. There were lives at stake— and not just in the habitat and the sub."

Askelanda turned, arms crossed. *Explain.*

Kailan strode a few paces, then glanced at Antares and Li-Jared, perhaps to make sure they were listening. "Askelanda, imagine a habitat bubble bursting into the air—probably exploding from decompression. How much clearer a signal could you send to the landers: *Here we are, if you want to find us!*"

Askelanda stopped his pacing and peered at her. For the first time, he seemed to take her point seriously. "Perhaps, Obliq. *If* landers had been on the water, watching. But really—what were the chances of that?"

Kailan gazed at him with palpable annoyance. "Ahktah, if we know they have been working at the new salvage site, is it not possible that they might be found elsewhere on the sea, as well? Isn't it possible that they might have scanning equipment for searching above the sea, as we have it for searching within— which could enable them to detect an explosion?" She paused for his reaction. "No? You didn't believe in my instruments, either, Ahktah."

Askelanda turned away with a low, grumbling sound.

Antares listened in fascination to the verbal sparring. There was clearly more at stake here than whether or not Kailan did the right thing in destroying the broken habitat. Askelanda the ahktah—the male leader—was struggling, not just with the obliq's actions, but with the power that she wielded in her use of a technology he did not understand. How, Antares wondered, could that be? Were Askelanda and the male Neri so preoccupied with their explorations and their sea-farming and their search for salvageable equipment that they could not comprehend the value of the obliq's knowledge? It seemed a peculiar kind of blindness. But not one that she couldn't have witnessed on her own world, in one form or another.

Li-Jared spoke up, with a bonging apology. "Excuse me—very sorry—but just so I can understand, don't the landers already know where to find you?"

Both Neri leaders paused to gaze at the Karellian. "If they knew where to find us, they would have been here by now," said Askelanda. "It may be the only thing that has kept us from open warfare—instead of these skirmishes by night, where we barely even see each other."

Kailan drew her shawl close around her, the golden threads glittering. "I doubt," she said, "that they think much about us, or *care* where we live."

"They care enough to poison the sea," Askelanda said softly.

"Or," said Kailan, "they *don't* care enough, and so they poison the sea."

Li-Jared was clearly confused. "Then your conflict—"

"Is not an open battle, no," said Kailan. "In my opinion, they don't regard us as much worth troubling about. Nevertheless—" and she turned to Askelanda to complete her point "—if we continue to probe a salvage site which clearly interests them, and which my technicians have not found a way to make use of anyway—"

"I was not aware you had given up," Askelanda said.

"We have *not* given up. But why risk this—when we have a larger enemy to worry about, and a factory that no longer functions?"

"If the factory functioned, we wouldn't *have* to risk it," Askelanda said, with exasperation.

Li-Jared interrupted again. "By larger enemy, you mean—"

"Of course," said Kailan. "The Creature of Darkness. The Maw of the Abyss. Perhaps *you* can tell us how to stop it. But if not, and without the factory—" She turned her gaze to Askelanda. "Why remain here, facing disaster?"

"Why move, and risk losing everything that way, Obliq? The Maw has been sleeping for many years."

"Sleeping fitfully, Askelanda. Very fitfully. And now it has awakened."

Askelanda started to reply, but instead turned to stare out into the sea, where scores of Neri swimmers were hard at work repairing damage from the quake, and where the last of the returning rescue subs were gliding into the city toward their docks.

"If you don't mind," L'Kell said, as he assisted the others out of the sub and onto the dock, "I would like to take your plan directly to Askelanda."

"Of course," said Bandicut. "But first—"

"After you check on your robots," L'Kell said, with a husky hiss that Bandicut was beginning to recognize as laughter.

They waited at the edge of the hangar while a crew of Neri maneuvered the star-spanner bubble into a makeshift docking collar. A floating platform was tied into place, and at last Bandicut was able to step over to the bubble and crouch alongside it, peering down through its curved top. The two robots blinked at him, their sensor-arrays turning this way and that.

"Would you like to use this?" Ik said, handing him his rope.

"Thanks." Bandicut held the coiled rope close to the bubble. A glow blossomed from around his hand through the closest portion of the bubble membrane. He reached through without difficulty, shook the coil out and dangled one end of the rope toward the robots. The other end he passed back to Ik, who ran it over an overhead brace on the docking collar, then dropped it onto the floating platform, where it secured itself.

After a moment, there was a tug, and the rope began contracting, lifting the first robot. Copernicus emerged from the bubble, dangling from the rope like an oversized puppy, and Bandicut hauled awkwardly to pull him over onto the floating dock. "Coppy! Am I glad to see you! Are you all right?"

The robot ticked and whirred, his wheels rotating slightly before he touched down. "Cap'n, we are now. We did not think we would survive, once we were carried away in that downdraft."

"Well, you can thank L'Kell here for getting us to you—"

"Thank you," said the robot.

"—later, I mean. First, can you help me get Napoleon out?"

"Of course." Copernicus's sensor-array spun. "Ik! How good to see you unharmed. May I ask where Antares and Li-Jared are?"

"Hrrrm, well, we don't actually know—"

"Guys, let's get Napoleon out first," Bandicut interrupted.

"Of course." Copernicus turned and extended a metal arm to help pull on the rope.

"Hold on. Let me drop it to him." Bandicut fed the rope back into the bubble, and soon Napoleon emerged. As they hauled

Napoleon onto the dock, Copernicus backed his rear wheels dangerously close to the edge. "Whoa, Coppy—watch it! You can't swim!"

The monkeylike Napoleon hooked a metal hand onto Copernicus and leaned back, holding him. "I have you," he said, staggering a little.

Ik hrrm'd. "Let's try not to lose both of you. Are you robots waterproof?"

"I think I once was," Copernicus answered. "But my seals and bushings have suffered the effects of wear."

"Let's get away from the open water," Bandicut urged. He was trying to think how they could possibly put the robots back down at that crushing depth and have them do any useful work.

"I've just been told," L'Kell said, helping them onto the encircling walkway, "that a farewell—" *kresshh* "—service is about to begin for those who recently died."

"Thorek?" Bandicut asked, suddenly sober.

"And those killed in the quake. One by rockslide, and three in the habitat that broke away."

"Rakh—it breached, then?" asked Ik.

"No." L'Kell explained how it had been brought down. "A controversial action. But five others were able to swim out as the habitat fell back down."

Another Neri called to L'Kell from across the hangar, and he answered, "In a moment." To the others: "I must go join the parting swim. You may watch from inside, if you wish."

With the help of two of the other Neri, Bandicut and Ik saw to it that the robots were safely parked in a room just a short ramp up from this level; then they hurried up a companionway to one of the domed rooms next door.

The farewell swim began in the open-water space between two large clusters of habitat bubbles, a sort of plaza in front of the artificial reef they had passed on their trip into the city the first time. Ik and Bandicut peered out the dome window at fifty or so

Neri swimmers gathered around the seven fallen—two more than L'Kell had evidently been aware of. The dead were floating on narrow litters, their bodies garlanded with long coils of sea-fronds. Each litter was kept steady by four Neri, and as they began to swim, all the others began a procession, surrounding the dead on all sides. At the head of the procession was a Neri dressed with long trailers of sea-frond, similar to the dead.

The procession moved through the plaza, passing in front of the dome where Bandicut and Ik stood watching. They had been joined by Hargel, the young Neri who had briefly served as their jailor. "They will accompany the fallen out of the city and into the great Sweeping Current, where they will rejoin the circle of the sea," Hargel said.

"Will they simply float on forever, then?" Ik asked.

Hargel looked at him with apparent puzzlement, as if he had not understood the question. "Look there," he said, pointing up into the darkness ahead of the procession.

Movement was visible in the water, but faint, like ghostly impressions, fleeting in the water. "*Pikarta*," he said. "Spirit carriers."

Bandicut squinted into the darkness. The quarx momentarily increased his light sensitivity. The room glared painfully around him, but out in the darkness, he caught a glimpse of large white streamlined shapes. "Eaters," he murmured, as the brightness faded again.

/// Sharks? ///

/Something like that—/

Hargel turned his large black eyes for a glance at Bandicut. "Yes." He looked back out, watching the procession pass below them. "They have been drawn to us by an offering."

"An offering?"

"Towed by a sub."

Bandicut shuddered. "And they won't attack . . . prematurely?"

Hargel made a rippling gesture with his hand. "They usually strike only when there is rapid or violent movement in the water. Or smells of an offering. But the smells are being carried on the current ahead of the procession." Hargel watched the movement of the accompanying swimmers. Many of them were now moving in a kind of ballet around the dead, turning and spiraling and falling through the water.

/// They are grieving . . . ///

/Saying farewell,/ Bandicut agreed, and suddenly his heart became full of grief for Charlie-Four, whatever the reasons for his departure, and Charlie-Three not all that long before him, and all the Charlies he had lost to time and death. And he thought of Julie Stone, and of Earth, and it was all he could do to remain standing, one hand on the dome window.

/// It is good to grieve, I think. ///

/I suppose./ He wasn't sure that it felt all that good, but there was a comfort in sharing his grief with the sea-people, who sent their fallen out to rejoin the circle of the sea. And, he realized after a moment . . . in sharing with this quarx, with Charlene.

/// I do share it, ///

she whispered, and he knew that she meant not just *his* grief, but her own, for all of the quarx who had gone before, perhaps even for the quarx race itself.

"Is that," said Ik, "the healer leading the procession?"

"Yes, that's Corono," said Hargel. "He is our *holtoph*, our spirit leader. Those who cannot be healed, he leads on the spirit-journey."

The healer and the procession were soon past Bandicut and his companions, making their way through the habitat clusters and out of the city. "Just beyond the edge of the darkness, where our channeled current rejoins the Sweeping Current, they will set the travelers free."

They watched in silence, and soon after the last of the procession had disappeared into the undersea mist, the first of those returning reappeared. Bandicut thought he saw a faster movement in the distance, and nudged Charlie into giving him a few moments of heightened sensitivity. The world around him turned bright; he saw a few quick movements of white, before his vision blurred. /Was that—?/

/// Pikarta striking? I'm not certain . . . ///

Bandicut thought it was. He looked up and gazed across the plaza at the panorama of habitats. "John Bandicut," he heard Ik say, and he turned to look to his right, toward the next habitat in the cluster that they were a part of. He noticed that others were peering out of domes at the procession, as well. Two of them waved, and it took him several heartbeats to realize that they were Antares and Li-Jared.

Li-Jared sprang forward, bonging, to meet them, embracing Ik and springing away, then embracing Bandicut. His eyes were alive with fire—two narrow, vertical, almond-shapes of gold, bisected with electric-blue bands. Antares' eyes had their own shimmer of pale gold around black pupils. She was behind Li-Jared, but she ran forward, stones sparkling at her throat with pleasure and welcome. Bandicut threw his arms around her and squeezed her in a long embrace, and only after he'd stepped back, holding her long-fingered hand for a moment, did he quite realize what he'd done. "*Damn*, am I glad to see you!" he murmured huskily.

Antares seemed startled, but not displeased by the hug. She radiated a burst of warmth, her mouth crinkling—then, a second later, visibly drew back into her more familiar reserve. "I am very happy to see you, too. Both of you." She turned and squeezed Ik's arm in greeting. "And the robots? Have you heard from them?"

"They're safe. It was a near thing," Bandicut said. His mind, at that moment, was full of the sensation of Antares pressed against him, and her faintly piney scent. He blinked and shook his mind clear.

*/// I'll have to ask you
more about these sensations.
Especially— ///*

/Not—now—/

Bandicut explained what had happened—and nearly happened—to the robots. "And you two?"

He and Ik listened as their friends described their meeting with Kailan. "Who *is* this obliq?" Bandicut asked. "Is she here with you?"

"Kailan swam with the procession," answered Antares. "I expect we'll be able to rejoin her soon."

"Along with L'Kell," said Ik.

"You mean," said Bandicut, "that we can actually relax for a few minutes?" He let out a long, slow sigh. "I don't think I can believe it."

He heard footsteps behind him just then, and L'Kell's voice. "Have you found each other? Good! I hope you were comfortable watching the procession. Are you ready for a conference?"

Bandicut opened his mouth and closed it. Approaching behind L'Kell was a taller Neri of slighter build, greenish skin, and very different dress—instead of the harness, a shawl that glittered with gold-colored thread. This Neri—a female?—had two daughter-stones glimmering on the sides of her head. He bowed slightly. "Are you Kailan?"

"Indeed, and I have heard of your actions on our behalf," said the Neri. "I am pleased to meet you, John Bandicut and Ik. Is it true that your robots might have the ability to repair our factories?"

Bandicut blinked in surprise. Word traveled fast. "Perhaps," he said.

"Then let us go where we can speak of such matters," said Kailan.

———

What that meant, as it turned out, was adjourning to a large meeting room where no fewer than a dozen Neri could pace endlessly around each other as they talked. It seemed to be the Neri method of holding a conference. Bandicut found it dizzying. It was like trying to talk to a school of fish, weaving back and forth, around and around. The Neri seemed to have significant areas of conflict among themselves, but his proposal had them intrigued. He was starting to wish that he'd kept quiet about it until he was sure.

"I do not understand this *nanotech*," Kailan said, waving her hands as she paced. "What is it you mean?"

Bandicut spread his hands, trying to think how to make it clear. "That's the term we used back on my homeworld, Earth. It means machines smaller than you can see with your eye, almost smaller than you can imagine. It was an important part of our technology—for making things, repairing things, even . . . healing people." He couldn't help wincing a little over that last.

At the word *healing*, Askelanda wheeled around, his expression filled with a new intensity. Did he understand the difference between what Bandicut had done in his healing and what was being described now? Or did he regard Bandicut as a kind of alien wizard, who had performed certain services as requested, but now was holding out a little?

Bandicut tried to explain. "Not like what I did with Lako. That healing—" and as he groped for words he touched his temple, wishing he could touch Charlie and show them "—was different. That was . . . mind to mind. I didn't actually heal; I only helped Lako heal himself. Nanotech is different. It's machines."

Askelanda relaxed a little, and continued pacing, while listening.

"What I'm talking about now," Bandicut continued, "is manufacturing processes, which I *think* may be similar to what you use in your factory. I'm *guessing*, please understand—but it sounds right, because of what L'Kell described, about your factory using minerals from the hot vents, and tanks of liquid that objects are made in. I'm betting that your factory uses tiny machines that reproduce themselves rapidly, then work together to turn raw materials into much larger machines." He weaved his head, trying to follow Askelanda and Kailan.

Askelanda said nothing. But Kailan paused and peered at him with interest.

"And on my world, those tiny machines are—or were—controlled by programming, much as my robots are." He decided not to mention that he wasn't really sure how much his robots were controlled anymore by their original programming. And as for whatever had taken its place—could he even call that programming? It was more like a life process. "It's difficult to explain, really."

Kailan said, "We understand . . . programming, I think. Some of us do, anyway—a little. *Ochile*, we call it." She paced toward Askelanda, and veered away. "We use it in our repairs and modifications. Our—" *kraaa* "—changers—repair devices—require us to specify the changes we want them to make."

"Then you *do* have some knowledge of how these things work," Bandicut said, startled.

"Very little," she admitted. "The knowledge that produced the changers is lost to us, or at least inaccessible, and we are limited to using the devices as best we can."

Bandicut took a moment to absorb Kailan's words. "Then your—changers—"

"Can sometimes heal malfunctions, and sometimes alter machinery from one purpose to another. But their capabilities are limited, and they cannot construct from raw materials," Kailan said.

"Then," said Ik, "is that what you do with salvaged machinery?"

"That's right. It's our only way to maintain our surroundings in the absence of new equipment," said Kailan. "And the more equipment is lost, or falls into a state of final disrepair, the more our chances of long-term survival decline."

"And—" Bandicut swiveled back and forth between Kailan and Askelanda "—who among you actually maintains such knowledge and skill?"

Askelanda spoke in a rumble. "It is Obliq Kailan and her assistants who maintain the stores of arcane knowledge, and perform most of the technical alterations—while those who serve directly under my authority—"

/// —*meaning the males?* ///

/I think so./

"—are busy provisioning, and searching out new sources of supplies, and when necessary, occupied with self-defense." Askelanda stretched out his arms. "And with extending our reach and knowledge of our present world."

"We *all*," said Kailan, "work at trying to understand what is happening in the world around us. Especially in the abyss."

Askelanda waved his hands, pacing back and forth. "The obliq feels that I am too focused on keeping the present salvage area open, given the setbacks and losses—despite the growing need for new machinery to maintain our city."

"That is correct," said Kailan. "It is the Maw of the Darkness that most threatens us." She wheeled back toward Askelanda, arms wide.

Li-Jared scrambled out of the way, bonging softly. He'd had enough of the pacing. From Antares came a soft sense of: *Patience. Have patience.*

"We will not settle that disagreement here," said Askelanda. "But since we have no other hope of repairing our factories, we *must* consider our visitors' plan to assist us. But we must also protect our salvage areas, which may be our only remaining source of equipment."

"Quite so," said Kailan. When the senior Neri showed surprise, she said, "Let us hear our guests out."

"Very well," said Askelanda, turning to Bandicut. "Would you continue?"

Bandicut glanced at his friends. Antares was swaying slightly back and forth, as if to join in the pacing without actually moving from her spot. Bandicut wanted to scream at them all to stand still, but instead, he drew a breath and said, "My plan was to connect Napoleon and Copernicus to the factory control system—and see if they can determine what has gone wrong."

"Is this possible?" asked Kailan, peering at him. "They are not even of our world."

Bandicut shrugged. "That is true. But they have had some experience in joining with machines of alien origin." Though as he said it, he thought: Even on Shipworld, they didn't do anything like this.

"But surely they cannot rebuild broken factories," said Askelanda. "Can they even function at that depth?"

"I'm hoping that *you* can find a way to protect them from the depth," Bandicut admitted. "But no, they would not repair the factory themselves—any more than I repaired Lako when I joined with him. If I understand correctly, your factories are supposed to be able to repair themselves."

"That was true, until the repair machines broke down," Askelanda said.

"Then is it not possible that they might be restarted with a programming change?"

Askelanda paused, staring.

"If the repair units are self-replicators, and if there are *any* repair units still intact, the factory might have a chance of repairing itself. It might be that the programming itself has failed, or needs adjustment."

"Are you certain of this?"

"Not at all. I'm saying it's *possible.*"

Askelanda and Kailan exchanged sharp looks and quiet words, then Kailan said, "You give us hope. What we face now is certain death—or undoubted losses, if we attempt to move our people. But even your success with the factory might not be enough."

"You mean, the Maw?"

Kailan made a low, murmuring sound. "Whatever happens with the factory, it will still be there. And I'm not certain that we can survive that threat if we stay."

"Hrrm," said Ik. "Are you saying that it might be necessary to move . . . your entire city? Could you do that?"

The tension between Kailan and Askelanda became palpable. "Very difficult, and very dangerous," Askelanda said at last. "And without the factory—"

"Your whole way of life is threatened," murmured Ik.

*/// Unless they learn to manufacture
what they need themselves. ///*

/No way they could do that in the short term. Not with so much of their life support based on things like those membranes which *we* don't even understand. That's gotta be nanotech./

"Nevertheless," said Kailan, "Neri have moved in the past, and we might have to move in the future. Unless—" and she peered at each of the company in turn "—you who come from the stars can find a way to stop the Maw from destroying us."

/Mokin' foke,/ Bandicut muttered silently. /*That's* why we're here, isn't it?/

There was a long silence. Finally Askelanda said, "Let us worry about one thing at a time. John Bandicut, what do you need to enable your robots to attempt this thing?"

Bandicut drew his thoughts back to the present. "They need to be protected from water and pressure—and somehow connected to the control center. Do you have a way to do that?"

"If you need it to be done, we will find a way to do it."

"Thank you."

"You saved Lako. Perhaps you can do this, as well. Whatever you need, ask L'Kell." And with that, Askelanda strode from the room.

But Kailan's expression seemed exceedingly worried as she watched the ahktah leave.

CHAPTER 13

Factory Expedition

THEY SPENT THE night in surprisingly comfortable quarters, several levels above the "conference" room. The Neri provided them with cured fish and various kinds of fruit, including juice squeezed from seaweed berries. For sleep, they were given coarsely textured blankets woven from cottonlike fibers. Bandicut, Ik, and Li-Jared slept in one room, Antares in an adjoining room.

One by one, they awoke—and sat, nibbling at their food in silence. Was there an almost imperceptible lifting of the darkness outside the habitat? Bandicut thought so, as he rubbed his eyes and wondered what time of the day it really was. According to his wristwatch, they had slept for six or seven hours. But he had no idea what the length of a day was on this planet, or how the Neri kept track of time in the endless dark.

By the time Hargel came to attend to their needs and to escort Bandicut back to the sub hangar, Antares still hadn't awakened. So Bandicut said good-bye to Ik and Li-Jared and followed Hargel to supervise the outfitting of the robots for contact with the deep-sea factory. He found Neri techs—females, Kailan's people—hard at work on the outside of one of the subs, altering a set of cables that fed out through the pressure hull, connecting the interior of the cabin to the outside. He got his first look at one of the "changers" that Kailan had referred to, a fat cylindrical object about the size of a breadbox, worn as a frontpack by one of the technicians.

The flat end of the cylinder was pointed outward, and seemed to be made of an extremely malleable substance, like soft putty. One end of the sub's cable was engulfed in the putty right now. A second tech worked at a small console connected to the changer, apparently tending the ochile, or programming.

"What are you doing?" Bandicut asked.

The Neri holding the changer glanced at him but didn't answer. The putty end of the changer began to squirm, and a moment later it spat out the cable, which had a long, bulbous probe on its end—apparently new. "We had to lengthen the cable and put a changeable connector on its end," the tech said. "Now we'll attach it to one of the extending arms."

As the techs began working with one of the sub's telescoping manipulator arms, Bandicut began to see what the purpose was. The probe, attached by cable to the robots inside the sub, would complete the link to the factory outside. "What about the hookup to the robots?" he asked.

"They're preparing that on the inside," the tech answered, without taking her eyes from her work.

Bandicut peered through the sub's nose window, and saw Napoleon and two Neri techs crowded together in the cabin. He made his way around to the hatch and lowered himself into the sub. He had to crouch near the back of the cabin to watch them work. "It is good that you are here," said one of the techs. "Your robot did not appear to want us to attach the changer to it. But we must alter one of its electrical fittings."

"Eh? Alter it how? What about that, Nappy?"

The robot clicked. "I sensed they wanted to change part of my equipment, Captain. I was reluctant to approve, not knowing what other tasks you would have in mind."

"Well, I have no idea what other jobs we will have. How drastic is this change?" Bandicut looked from Napoleon to the techs and back.

"We must form a connector on its output point. We can restore it when we are finished with this job," the tech said. "But we will have trouble making a physical connection without doing this."

Bandicut sighed and crossed his fingers. "Okay."

The changer went onto Napoleon's side, where an I/O socket rested flush against his skin. When the tech pulled the changer away, it left behind a small, pod-shaped connector. The other tech stretched a cable from the sub's console and somehow snapped it into the pod. Then she touched several controls on the console. "Are you detecting a connection?" she asked, swinging her newtlike head around.

Bandicut relayed the question.

Napoleon clicked, several times. "A connection, yes. But I cannot verify compatibility. It may be difficult to establish a working interface with their circuitry."

"Are you opening your internal bus to the console?"

"Negativissimo, Captain."

"Eh?"

"I do not wish to risk my circuitry without evidence that I can actually manage the connection."

Bandicut rubbed his chin. "Well, Nappy, I'm not sure we have much choice, if we want to help them with their factory."

"I do want to help them. But John Bandicut—" Napoleon turned his robot eyes toward the human.

"Yes?"

"I would appreciate it if you did not call me 'Nappy.' My name is Napoleon."

Bandicut stared at the robot. "I beg your pardon?"

The robot rose a few inches on its metal legs, then settled back. "I just feel that it is somewhat undignified to be called 'Nappy.' I would prefer to be called Napoleon. Captain."

"Captain?"

"John Bandicut, I mean." The robot clicked thoughtfully. "Old habits are hard to break, aren't they?"

"Yes," Bandicut said softly. "Yes, they are. Very well, Napoleon, I will do my best to remember."

"I can ask no more. Now, then. I believe that I can set up a code filter to protect me from dangerous software commands. It's an adaptation of the condom protocol that the shadow-people gave me on Shipworld. But I'm concerned about the actual voltages and so forth."

"But I thought—"

"Possibly if I crosslink with Copernicus, we can combine our hardware to provide the necessary diagnostic elements."

Bandicut shook his head. "I thought you had all sorts of electrical diagnostic tools. Don't you remember when you used to hop onto my rover, back on Triton, and tell me what was wrong?" He remembered it clearly, himself. It had been an annoyance, actually, when the first Charlie was attempting to account for Bandicut's seemingly bizarre actions by faking an electrical malfunction.

"My memories of Triton are a little hazy, to be honest. But yes, John, I did have that stuff. I guess the shadow-people must have thought it was outmoded, or unnecessary. They seem to have removed or converted it. That may have been a mistake on their part." Napoleon fiddled with the connecting cable with a manipulator, tugging at it as though testing its strength, while the Neri techs looked on with alarm. "It's the first time I've ever found myself questioning the shadow-people's judgment. It's most unsettling."

Bandicut grunted, shifting position in the little cockpit. "I guess if you're going to become sentient, you have to learn to expect this sort of thing—questioning other people's judgment from time to time. You'll get used to it."

There was movement at the back of the cabin, and L'Kell appeared. "Are you ready for us to bring Copernicus down?"

"I guess so. Are you ready, Napp—"

"Sir?"

"—oleon?" he said, catching himself. "Do you want to try linking Copernicus into the circuit?"

"Whenever you're ready, Cap—John Bandicut."

"Okay." Bandicut squirmed toward the hatch. "Let me get out of here and make room. Call me if you need help translating or something."

He watched from topside while several of the Neri lowered Copernicus into the sub. They had not yet worked out where he would be riding himself, but he was having trouble imagining how he could fit inside that sub, crammed together with two robots and L'Kell or another Neri pilot, for the duration of the repair mission. If claustrophobia didn't get him, muscle spasms would.

/// Is it essential that you be with the robots? ///

Charlie asked. She had been following the events with interest, learning all about his odd friendship with the robots.

/Well, I think it would be pretty hard to pull this off without me there. For one thing, the robots don't speak Neri./

*/// The stones and I might be able
to do something about that. ///*

/Oh? Well—that's an interesting thought. Still, I'm the only one around here who seems to know anything about nanotechnology. Not that I know so much./

/// Do you know more than the robots? ///

/Good question./

/// Why don't we check? ///

/Okay. But I can't teach them much, if they don't already know it./ He paced along the dock at the edge of the hangar, angling his gaze down into the green illuminated deeps. He was proposing to dive down there again in one of those tin cans. The thought made all the muscles in the back of his neck tighten in a spasmodic ripple. /Charlie, is there some reason you're trying to get me not to go? Do you have some insight I ought to know about?/

*/// I think I'm just feeling nervous.
Concerned for your safety.
And—I'm embarrassed to admit—mine. ///*

/You weren't scared during the last dive, were you?/

/// Not during.
But I had nightmares last night,
while you were asleep. ///

Bandicut was dumbfounded. Charlie—having nightmares? But then, he supposed, why not? It shouldn't be any harder to believe than anything else about the quarx's inhabiting his brain and his emotions and . . . being female. /Well,/ he said.

/// I'm not trying to get out of it.
If we have to go, we have to go. ///

"John Bandicut," he heard, before he could answer. He blinked back into contact with the world outside his skin, and was surprised to see Antares approaching along the dock. She stood beside him, gazing at the silver-grey submersible that would be taking his robots, and perhaps him as well, back down to the edge of the abyss.

"Hi," he said. "How'd you sleep?"

"Well enough, I suppose," she answered, in a tone that he thought suggested a polite lie. "I came to see how you were doing in your preparations. Will you be leaving soon?"

"I'm not sure," he admitted. "We're still working on hooking up the robots without blowing either their circuits or the sub's. If we can patch them into a working connection, then I hope they'll find a way to talk to the factory's control system. They're damn clever robots, you know."

"Indeed they are," Antares said, with a clicking that sounded like a chuckle, but wasn't. "If anything went wrong, I would miss them." She turned to peer at Bandicut, and her almost Asian-looking eyes, gold circles around black pupils, caught his. "And I would miss you, too, human of Earth." Her nostrils trembled as she breathed. There was an enchanting combination of delicacy and strength in her features.

"Thank you," he murmured. "I don't think we're leaving right away, though. We'll need to learn all the Neri can tell us about the factory."

"Of course," said Antares. She hesitated, then continued, "You know . . . even though we haven't known each other long, I have come to like and respect you, John Bandicut."

He flushed. "Call me John."

"John. You *and* your norgs. I hope . . . wish you to return safely. All of you."

Bandicut nodded, and tried to get a fix on his own reaction. Every once in a while, the fact that she was both female and strikingly . . . *beautiful* wasn't perhaps the right word, but intensely *interesting* . . . caught hold of his brain down on some deep, primitive level. His breathing was somewhat erratic just now, and he self-consciously tried to even it out. "Thank you," he whispered.

Antares looked pensively out over the water. "You know—in truth, I didn't rest too well last night." She turned her head to gaze at him.

/// *What's that mean—that look?*
Is she interested in you?
As a . . . lover? ///

/I—dunno, I—/

"I felt lonely," Antares said, "being separated from you and the others." Bandicut was startled. Antares had slept in a separate room partly out of consideration to the Neri, among whom males and females appeared to lead somewhat segregated lives. But he'd also had the impression that it was Antares' wish. On her homeworld, she'd remarked, third-females were never permitted to lodge with males. *I did so once, and it almost cost me my life,* she'd said.

"I guess everything feels different, here on an alien world," he said awkwardly.

"Yes," she said. "Very different."

"Ik and Li-Jared will be here. They can help look after you." He knew at once that it was the wrong thing to say. As if Antares couldn't take care of herself. "And—" he added hastily "—I hope you'll look after them, too. They're good, trustworthy companions."

And in an attempt to sound a little less somber, added, "Even if Li-Jared *is* a bit excitable."

"Yes," Antares said, and this time he was sure there was amusement in her voice.

"Do you know yet what you'll be doing while we're gone?"

"I'll be working with Kailan, to see what I can do to help them learn more about this Maw of the Abyss," Antares said, radiating a sparkle of excitement. He blinked. He had noticed in the last day that he was picking up her emotions more overtly than before. Was he just getting to know her better?

> /// *The difference is in her, I think.*
> *She's letting her empathic abilities*
> *flow both ways.* ///

/Ah./

"The obliq," she continued, "has a variety of instruments, some of which she does not know the use of. Askelanda has never believed them to be useful, but she thinks they are—if we can just learn their functions. In any case, we'll be probing the seafloor, to see what we can learn."

"And do you—" Bandicut hesitated, not wanting to say, *Do you know enough science to be helpful?* His own experience with the Triton surveys probably qualified him more than anyone here to understand seafloor geology. And that wasn't saying much.

Antares' eyes twinkled. "I will tell you and the others everything that I learn. Don't forget, Li-Jared was something of a scientist on his own world."

Li-Jared, a scientist? Bandicut realized, with a start, that his time with his friends had been so filled with relentless urgency and confusion that he had never learned what Ik and Li-Jared had done for a living on their own worlds—or even if "earning a living" was a concept that would have made sense to them.

"Some sort of mathematical theorist," Antares continued. "I don't understand it myself. But I'm depending on my knowing-stones' helping, in any case. They seem to understand much that I don't."

Bandicut peered at the stones glowing in her throat. He realized suddenly that he was taking care not to stare at her chest, and he chuckled inwardly. As if he had any idea whether staring at her stones was any more acceptable to a Thespi third-female than staring at her four breasts!

*/// You do not stare at the breasts
of the women on your own world? ///*

/Not if I know what's good for me./

/// ??? ///

/Let's just say I—try not to get caught at it./

*/// But your memories . . .
there was someone named Julie,
and she seemed to . . . ///*

/That was different./ His pulse fluttered. /There's a time and a place, and right now isn't the time—/

"Is everything all right, John?" asked Antares.

"Uh?" He'd lapsed into his moron-stare again, focusing inward. "Yes. Sorry. Talking to Charlie." He waved a hand at his head. "I've got a new Charlie, by the way. A female, this time. Charlene. Very interesting."

"Indeed!"

*/// John, do you suppose she would be willing
to join stones briefly?
It might help me
get to know her a little. ///*

Bandicut hesitated. /I don't know. I guess I could ask./

/// Please. ///

He cleared his throat. "Um—Antares? Charlie and I were wondering if you would like to . . . pool . . . that is, share knowledge. Join stones, I mean." At that moment, he had to flatten himself against the wall to let some Neri workers pass by on the dock, and it occurred to him that he could not have picked a more awkward time or place to ask such a question. "To understand each other better," he tried to explain.

Antares' eyes narrowed, brightened. She made a sound that was both a click and a chuckle. She seemed troubled, amused, and receptive all at the same time. Finally she said, "Not just now, I think. But perhaps, at another time. I would like to know, not just you, but also your friend . . . Charlie . . . better. Would that be possible?"

Bandicut nodded. He was saved from an awkward silence by L'Kell's reappearance beside them on the dock.

"I think the robots would like you to come speak with them," L'Kell said. "I can't tell for sure."

"Right. Okay." Bandicut touched Antares' arm. "Thanks for coming by. I'll see you before—"

"Actually, I will be leaving soon to go join Kailan," Antares said. "Her habitat is—I don't know exactly, but somewhere upslope from here. I have to take a sub to get there. I don't know when I'll be back, so I'll say good-bye now." Her mouth crinkled, then she stretched out her arms.

Bandicut gently embraced her. He smelled something like a blend of seaweed and balsam in her hair. "Bye. Let us know what you find out."

"I will," she said with a hint of throatiness. "Take care down there and stay away from the Maw. Okay?"

He smiled. "You can be sure of that," he said, and with a final squeeze of her hand, turned to walk out onto the deck of the little sub.

Inside the cramped cabin of the sub, Napoleon and Copernicus were now linked to each other, while Napoleon remained connected by cable to the console. Bandicut noticed flickering activity on the console. He squeezed in next to them and sat crosslegged beside the Neri tech. "How's it going here?"

Napoleon answered. "We now have a working connection, Captain. We're exploring how the control system on the submarine works. We thought if we understood that, we would have a better chance of understanding the factory when we got there."

"Plus," said Copernicus, "we thought it might be helpful to know how to pilot the sub, in case of emergency."

"Makes sense," said Bandicut. "What else?"

"Well," said Napoleon, "we were wondering if you would be willing—" The robot hesitated.

"Willing—?"

"To let us link with you—with Charlie, really."

Bandicut rubbed his eyebrows in silence, thinking, didn't I just have this conversation? I liked my first idea better.

/// It's okay with me, ///

said the quarx.

He sighed and answered, "Sure. No problem. Anything in particular you were after?"

"Well," said Napoleon. "We just thought it might be helpful to know something of the Neri language. In case we need to deal with them alone . . ."

Peering out the viewport, Antares felt a pang, as the Neri pilot steered the small sub away from Askelanda's habitat. Already she missed the company—all of them, but especially John Bandicut. John. She hadn't expected to feel this way, but she did; and she wondered at it. If she were still on Thespi Prime, it would be a very dangerous feeling. Not that it was *wrong*; but if it developed further, and led to personal intimacy . . . that way lay temptation, and possibly death, for a third-female. Her role in life was to facilitate, not to embrace, or to experience for her own.

She had succumbed to temptation once, and would have died for it had it not been for the intervention of the Shipworld Masters and the stones. *Ensendor.* Just the memory of that name caused old fury to rise up in her. And some of the old desire, as well— even after the betrayal. The memory of Ensendor's testimony against her—on trial for her intimacy with *him*—was as clear as if it had happened yesterday. The immediacy of the memory was astounding. His words, damning her in the eyes of the council, while he walked away praised for his candor and honesty. His eyes, touching hers in a glancing flicker, with a hint of regret but no compassion, no grief, no shared responsibility. Even with all that clear in her mind, she still could feel the flush of the old desire.

And what did all of that have to do with these disquieting feelings about John Bandicut, who was not even of her own world? Perhaps nothing. Perhaps everything.

Antares narrowed her gaze through the portal of the little submarine. Glowing habitats moved slowly by, like ghosts in weightless space. A small school of silvery fish flashed through the sub's headlight, then a bulbous creature moving on pulsing jets of water. The bottom slope was flowered with a variety of pastel-colored lifeforms, feathery things, waving and drifting in the slow-moving currents. This gave way to a bed of long kelp, cultivated under artificial light. Ahead, finally, she saw the shape of the obliq's habitat, where Kailan would be waiting.

The sight of Kailan's bubble only reminded her that far below, far out of view, lurked the Maw of the Abyss, the monster she was being asked to help identify and tame. How she would do this, she did not know. Would it be like the way Bandicut had taken on the boojum, with almost no real information—with nothing to go on but courage, hope, faith?

She sighed. At least in this, she had something she could search for. Truth. Objective, physical truth.

If she could even recognize such a thing anymore.

———————

As the small flotilla of subs dropped away from the undersea city, descending toward the factory, Bandicut felt sudden pangs of doubt. Was he just offering the Neri false hope of repairing the facility? He wished he could have another private talk about it with the robots, but they were in the second sub.

/// What's the matter, John? ///

What was the matter was that he feared that this whole mission was just pride and wishful thinking on his part.

/// You don't seem overly proud to me. ///

/No? Then why did I make it sound as if I knew all about nano-factories? If that's even what these things are! Hell, I don't even know anything about *human*, much less Neri, nanoshit./

*/// Maybe not,
but you understand the general concept.
The translator-stones are pretty resourceful.
And from what you've told me,
the robots are, too. ///*

/Yeah. But none of us really knows what the kr'deekin' hell we're doing here./

*/// Have faith, John.
I'll check back with you later. ///*

Before he could answer, Charlene was gone—off in the stacks of his brain's library, whistling softly, seeing what else she could learn about John Bandicut and the Charlies that came before. She was a good student, this Charlie.

He couldn't help wishing that Ik and Li-Jared were here, even though they'd all agreed that it was the right decision. There wasn't much either of them could offer in the way of expertise, and they were probably more likely to be useful to the Neri city, making themselves available to Antares and Kailan, or anyone else who might need help. Plus, Li-Jared would probably have had a nervous breakdown if forced to travel in any direction except toward the surface. Didn't matter, though; he still missed them.

L'Kell, beside him in the cockpit, seemed to sense his pensive mood. "We'll make a survey of the area first," he said. "There are several possible sites where I think we might find connections to the central controller. But we'll just have to see when we get there."

Bandicut nodded, as the last visible signs of the Neri city vanished astern. Only the foreboding darkness of the endlessly falling seafloor lay before them now, sprinkled sporadically with bottom-feeding animals, some finned but most on spidery legs. And somewhere far below, the Maw of the Abyss. They were going to work terrifyingly close to the drop-off, and the plan was simply to pretend it didn't exist. What else could they do? Half the terror came from not knowing what the devil the thing was. But he reminded himself that whatever unknown threat the Devourer posed, the threat of a nonfunctioning factory was a matter of clear physical need. The Neri had no way to replace damaged or aging subs and habitats, the solar arrays that fed them power were reportedly degrading, and their deep-sea farms could last only as long as the artificial light lasted.

"Tell me something," he said, trying to shake his mind loose from this train of thought. He glanced sideways at his friend.

"Ah-huh," said L'Kell, peering from one side port to the other, checking formation with the other subs.

"If we do get the factory going again, how will you bring the manufactured goods up to your city? How did you do it before?"

L'Kell murmured softly in thought. "We have two cargo subs left, which we use in our salvage operations. One of them is at the new site, the one where Lako and the others were poisoned. The other is not in working order."

"That doesn't sound good. Is it something Kailan's people can fix?"

"Well," said L'Kell, "that seems to depend on whether the salvagers can find some equipment that can be modified by the changers to fit their needs."

"Hm."

"It is said that there is a large cargo carrier trapped in one of the factory's loading docks—and that if we could get *it* free, then we would not only have the sub and all the machinery in its hold, but we could free the whole mechanism. I don't really believe that last part, but we've never been able to prove the question one way or the other. Nobody's been able to find the dock."

Bandicut grunted. It was amazing to him that the Neri had survived as long as they had, with the factory mostly out of commission for a generation of Neri. No large shipments had been received in L'Kell's lifetime, though products had been received from one of the smaller docks in more recent memory. But that last dock had stopped working when L'Kell was still a trainee sub pilot, and now its entrance was buried. The Neri really were living on borrowed time, as far as the factory was concerned. It was almost as if they had been waiting for someone to come along and help them fix it. "And all this time, you've had no idea how to repair it—or even how it works?"

L'Kell, before answering, made several adjustments to the sub's attitude and speed. "The factory was not built by us," he said, "but by our—" *hrrullll*

Bandicut's stones twinged with uncertainty. "Your ancestors?" he guessed.

L'Kell seemed at a loss.

"Those who came before you . . . gave birth to your parents?"

"I understand the word. The problem is—well, according to the obliq, our ancestors were not exactly *us*. Not Neri. They were something different—from which they made us—"

"Huh?"

"They took themselves, and made us . . . and we were different. *Changed.*" L'Kell steered carefully over a ridge in the bottom slope. "I do not believe that they lived in the sea."

Bandicut's mouth opened; it took a moment for words to come out. "Engineered?" he murmured. "You were engineered? Are the *landers* . . . your ancestors? Or creators?"

L'Kell hissed. "Those creatures—killers—are no ancestors of ours!"

"Then what—?"

"Our ancestors," L'Kell said, with a snap on each word, "are *dead.*"

And before Bandicut could think of a reply, the Neri was touching controls on his panel and sending them sharply downward, over a plunging drop-off into darkest night.

CHAPTER 14

Contact

THE GREYISH-WHITE forms of the factory area emerged from the gloom like ghosts in a graveyard, or old bones sticking out of the earth after a quake. Bandicut swallowed back a feeling of dread and tried to peer out with rational calm as the submersibles swept slowly over the area. He touched a comm control and spoke to the robots, in sub two. "Napoleon and Copernicus, start keeping a watch for anything that looks like a port where you could jack in. L'Kell says he's really not sure where they are, so if you have any ideas, let us know."

"Roger," said Napoleon. He was silent a moment, then, "Captain?"

"Yeah?"

"This stuff looks really, really old. As if no one's been here for a long time."

"Yeah. But remember, it's partly because that quake covered everything in silt. I don't have to tell you about that, I guess."

"Yes. But Captain?"

"John."

"John? If it's been a really long time since the Neri actively controlled the facility . . . how do we know that it will want to recognize their, well—"

"What?" Bandicut said. "Their authority?" He glanced at L'Kell, who rolled his eye slightly as if waiting to hear what would come next.

"Exactly," Napoleon said.

When L'Kell didn't volunteer an answer, Bandicut said, "Well, I don't think you can assume that every control system is going to develop consciousness, the way you and Coppy have."

"Oh," said Napoleon.

There was no talk for a few moments. Then Copernicus announced, "Cap'n, I am reading substrate structures that could imply the presence of transmission wires and oplink cables. I believe there is a juncture of some sort approximately twenty meters ahead of us."

"Okay, Coppy. L'Kell?"

The Neri responded by speaking to the other Neri pilots, and nosing his sub lower and closer to the silt-covered bottom. "Unable to confirm that reading," he said after a few minutes.

"We are now coming directly over the juncture," Copernicus said.

"Are you sure?" Outside Bandicut's sub, there was a straight ridge that appeared to slope down toward one of the smoking volcanic vents. There was nothing to suggest an entry port.

"I'm certain of the presence of the structures, Captain. But I cannot state their purpose, nor tell if there is any kind of outer access."

"I believe," said L'Kell, "that we are looking for units large enough for one of the subs to dock with, or at least make connection. However, the entire structure may have transmission lines running through it. Just knowing that lines are present isn't enough."

Bandicut spoke to the robots. "What we need is probably a larger structure—something we can nose right up to, or even go inside. Probably you've found some kind of secondary node. It might help to trace those lines, to see where they lead."

The subs continued gliding, their headlights probing the night. The sea was clearer than it had been on their previous visit. Most of the silt had either settled out or been carried away by the currents. The current was gentle now, and according to L'Kell, normal for this place—following the lines of the natural ridges, parallel to the orientation of the abyssal valley, rather than down into it. The Maw was quiet for now.

The search continued.

The first sighting came from sub three, scouting downslope of them. L'Kell steered toward the location. All they could see was the glow of the other sub's lights, just beyond a minor drop off. But the glow was bright; the other pilot seemed to be directing a search-beam toward them, against the underside of the drop-off. With a soft whir of motors, they crossed the ridge and maneuvered to come alongside the other sub. "Ah," said L'Kell, shining his own light up under the ridge. It was hollowed on the underside—and looked artificial, not natural. The headlight shone, through a blizzard of silt stirred up by the sub's jets, into a dark cavity that seemed just large enough for the nose of a submersible or two.

Bandicut had a sudden memory of being a child standing under a sports stadium, beneath a seating section that sloped upward overhead. It was a dizzying, claustrophobic image, and for a moment, he felt himself beginning to slip away into a daydream. A rumble of bubbling air—or maybe rock movement—brought back a sharp awareness of the ocean over his head, and the pressure squeezing in against the hull of the sub. "Is this it?" he murmured.

"Possibly," said L'Kell. "We must explore carefully." Indeed, though the area under the ledge was less heavily silted than that above, there was still enough sedimentation to obscure the details of the structure—including anything that might have indicated the presence of a docking port.

L'Kell touched the controls, and the sub shuddered as a jet of water shot forward from the thrusters, kicking up a tremendous, blinding cloud of silt. Bandicut swallowed, holding back a sudden rush of fear.

*/// Do you want me to help
quiet that reaction? ///*

/Not yet. I've got this instinct for a good reason./ He took a deep breath, and waited for it to stop, for the silt to clear.

L'Kell moved the sub with exquisite care. Bandicut glimpsed the other sub to their right, looming out of the murk. He tensed, saying nothing. Working together, the two pilots were sweeping the area of accumulated silt. Gradually the murk dissipated, carried away by the slow-moving current. L'Kell called for sub two, with the robots, to move in.

Bandicut heard the whine of the robots' sub before he saw their lights. Nabeck, the Neri piloting the sub, asked L'Kell what he wanted them to do.

"Can you scan anything in there?" L'Kell asked. The headlight beams beneath the overhang now illuminated contours that suggested the possible presence of mechanisms—indentations and protrusions that might have been control surfaces. Or entrance archways. Or who knew what.

"Scanning," said Copernicus.

And then: "We think we've got something. Can we move in closer?" That was Napoleon.

"Carefully," said L'Kell.

"Always," answered Napoleon.

Nabeck did as the robots asked.

Nabeck's sub had been motionless for a while. It looked like a large, foraging bottom-feeder against its own lights. It was impossible to tell what was going on, until the call came from Napoleon: "We believe we are detecting—correction, we have penetrated an air cavity with the probe. Inserting further. I believe I've found a point of electrical contact. Testing . . ."

Bandicut's heart pounded. Were Napoleon's circuits being fried, or had they found what they had come for?

"Definitely a signal input/output."

"And—" Bandicut swallowed "—is anyone home?"

"Indeed . . ." said Napoleon, in a preoccupied tone. "There is activity. Attempting to make out the language."

Bandicut glanced at L'Kell. The Neri was staring intently out the front port, as if by staring hard enough he might penetrate the haze. Bandicut had a feeling that it was all L'Kell could do to keep from parking the sub and swimming out there to see for himself—except that he might not survive the experience.

"Yah," said Napoleon.

"Yah, what?"

"There's someone here. A control system. But it's . . . I don't know exactly how to explain it, Cap'n." The robot's voice was tinny and cold through the comm.

"Try, Nappy."

"It seems very confused. As though . . . it's been working with some kind of malfunction, or handicap, for so long . . . that it doesn't remember exactly what it's supposed to be doing. Or how it's supposed to run the facility. I don't think it knows exactly what's wrong."

"Napoleon, hold on a minute. Is this thing a person—or a mechanism? Or a program that needs reconfiguring?"

"Captain—"

"I'm trying to understand. Copernicus, are you hooked in, too?"

"Roger. Captain, I think there's more wrong here than just a failure of the self-repair mode. I have a sense of deprivation, of starvation. I do not know what it is deprived of, however."

Napoleon spoke, with a voice that seemed more attenuated, as though he were speaking from a greater distance. "Could it be . . . lonely, do you think?"

"Napoleon? Is that your answer?"

"I believe it is something else," said Copernicus. "But we cannot tell for sure without surveying the processing layout, the memory, the stored histories . . ."

Bandicut drew a breath. "Can you do that?"

"We are having to redraw some of the pathways, Cap'n," said Copernicus. "Since the failure of the self-repair functions, many of the pathways have atrophied and failed, and alternate pathways must be called up—within the physical limitations, of course."

"Okay."

L'Kell finally broke in. "What are they doing?"

Bandicut shook his head. "I'm not sure if they're repairing it or reinventing it, but it sounds as if they're deep inside the control system, so I think we'd better let them work."

L'Kell muttered softly to himself, but did not argue.

It was not long after Bandicut had departed when Ik became aware of a commotion outside their guest room. He had just finished describing Bandicut's healing of Lako to an anxious Li-Jared, trying to reassure the Karellian that their present situation was perhaps not so hopeless as it seemed. There were things that they could accomplish here.

"What's all that—" *bwang* "—racket outside?" Li-Jared cried, as they both turned at the sound of Neri running past the curtained entrance to their room.

Ik rubbed his chestbone and tugged the curtain aside to look out. Now the Neri were shouting on a lower level of the habitat. "I guess we'd better go see."

His Karellian friend uttered a twang of annoyance, but hurried after him. They followed the short passageway to a platform that overlooked an open room below. A dozen or so Neri were engaged in rapid conversation; some were running in, and others were running out. "Can you make out what they're saying?" Ik asked Li-Jared.

The Karellian was springing up and down lightly on his feet, leaning forward over the bar that constituted a railing. "If you can't, how do you expect me to?"

Two of the Neri looked up at the sound of their voices. Ik called, "Is something wrong?"

A Neri named Jontil, who had assisted them in their room, called up agitatedly, "A problem with the landers. A raid on a site. I doubt that it's anything you can help with."

"Hrah," Ik said, "perhaps we could help with our *experience*—" And then he hesitated. Their experience?

Jontil replied, "If you want to come down and join us in council with Askelanda—"

"Urr, coming," said Ik. Only after he had turned to climb down the ladder did he realize the fear that was showing in Li-Jared's electric-blue eyes. "I spoke without thinking. Li-Jared, do you think we shouldn't go?"

"No choice now," Li-Jared gulped. "It's just that—"

"Is it the landers you're worried about?"

"Not the landers. Don't care about the landers," mumbled the Karellian. "It's the whole thing of . . ." He angled his eyes, and then Ik understood. It was the ocean over his head, the thought that they might have to venture out into the turbid depths. If only the normalization had taken away Li-Jared's fear of the water!

"Hrrm. Let's go, then," Ik said softly, and dropped to the floor below.

Jontil escorted them into the adjacent habitat, where a group of Neri were gathered around a troubled-looking Askelanda. The elder Neri noted the presence of the visitors without comment, and paced as he spoke. Ik and Li-Jared stepped off to the side to keep out of the way.

"Our people at the salvage site are being openly attacked by landers."

"Attacked? How?" cried one of the newcomers.

"They're wearing breathing gear similar to our neos'—and by all reports are overrunning the site. They've got vehicles of some kind, and explosive weapons. Our people are mostly in hiding within the site right now. Many are wounded." Askelanda paused in his movement. "We've sent nine swimmers, but they might well be on their way to disaster. We have at most one or two vessels available to send more help. Will any here swim to the aid of their fellows?"

In answer, the movement of Neri around him changed, and there was a folding-in of ranks, and a rising murmur, as virtually all of the Neri present declared their willingness.

"You must be cautious," Askelanda said, "of the poison that killed Thorek and the others and almost killed Lako. That may be what has harmed many at the site already." He wheeled and addressed Ik. "If I may ask our visitors—"

"Yes, Askelanda," Ik replied.

"Do you have knowledge of these poisons, knowledge that could help our people to avoid them?"

Ik hesitated. "I have some little knowledge. Unfortunately, the poison is invisible—to me, as much as to you. Do you have any instruments that can detect radiation?" He sensed, even as he said it, that his voice-stones were having difficulty translating *radiation* into something that the Neri could understand. They simply had no words for the concept. "Without the proper equipment, I don't know if I can help you avoid it." He closed his eyes for a moment; the pacing Neri were making him dizzy.

Askelanda paused in front of him. "I know of no such instruments." He seemed almost to sigh. "Perhaps the obliq might know of such things."

Ik looked at Li-Jared. "Could you work with Kailan on that question?"

The Karellian looked simultaneously dubious and relieved. "I could try," he murmured.

"And you?" the Neri leader asked Ik.

"I—hrrm, could go with your brave people to help those in trouble. If you have a vessel that can carry me."

Askelanda bowed and turned in a sweeping turn. "Shall we grant space in our vessel to our courageous guest? To Ik?"

The response was a rumble of approval.

Ik wasn't sure whether to be glad or sorry.

"Take care, my friend."

"You also, Li-Jared. Give my regards to Antares and Kailan." Ik sighed through his ears and stepped out onto the deck of the little sub. He turned back. "And keep your eyes closed on your ride back to Kailan's!"

Bwong. "Don't think you're the only one to go fearlessly into the deep, Hraachee'an! I'll spot more fish than you do." With a wave that hid his nervousness, Li-Jared strode away.

Ik dropped down into the sub. He was greeted by his pilot, a Neri named S'Cali, and took up the passenger position on the left. They were joined by a second Neri, Delent'l.

Soon they were gliding through the depths lit green and yellow by the sub's lights. From time to time, in the edge of the illumination, he glimpsed a formation of Neri swimmers flanking the sub in its course. Remarkably, it seemed that they were capable of moving as fast under their own power as by submarine. They were truly well engineered for the sea. And that was what they were, he had gathered from S'Cali—creatures engineered for the sea by a now-vanished race of air-breathers.

The habitats of the city dwindled behind, and he settled in for a cruising time, accompanied by the hissing and creaking sounds of ascent—not straight up, but on a long course following the bottom slope toward shallower water. The sub was depressurizing as they climbed through the depths, and he made his own sinus adjustments and prayed silently that the stones and the normalization could protect him from the decompression as they had from the effects of depth.

In time, he was startled to see one important change outside: natural illumination, not from the headlights but surrounding the sub. It was sunlight from overhead, diffused through the depths. *Thank the moon and stars*, he thought. Whatever the risks of this trip, at least he was going to see sunlight. Real sunlight— not that they would be going all the way to the surface. Their destination was a wrecked ship, sunk in comparatively shallow water—shallow enough that the air-breathing landers could reach it.

"We are drawing close," S'Cali said, interrupting his thoughts. "Do you have a special way of preparing for battle?"

Ik rubbed his chest in silence.

"Now would be a good time," said Delent'l, crouching near the rear of the sub and the lockout chamber. "I'll check your breathing gear for you."

Breathing gear. It had been fitted so hurriedly back at the habitat—adapted from breathing aids used by juvenile Neri with immature gills—that he had thought little about it. So much for taking the long view, he thought.

"I have never thought of myself as a warrior," Ik said finally, not knowing what to say except the truth. "If I have any strengths to offer you, it will be in sharing my knowledge. If I see something in your salvage site that I think may be a source of your sickness, I will tell you at once."

The Neri pilot made a muted sound of acknowledgment; the other said nothing at all. Never, Ik thought, had he made such an ineffectual-sounding offer of help. But he could think of nothing to add.

S'Cali flicked off the headlight.

A twilight gloom closed in around them. The illumination from the surface was substantial, but there was little or no color. The bottom landscape was becoming visible in shades of grey.

Silhouetted like a charcoal sculpture against the misty blue-green ceiling ahead was the jagged, broken shape of an enormous sunken vessel. The salvage site. He could not tell what kind of a ship it was, perhaps a very large submarine. As they drew closer he glimpsed, swarming around the wreck like insects, a number of small, black objects.

They did not seem to move like Neri.

He had scarcely even begun to wonder if the landers had detected the approaching sub, when it became obvious that they had. They were already turning and gathering to meet the Neri.

CHAPTER 15

Repair and Rescue

THE ROBOTS WERE trying to report to Bandicut when a conflicting transmission came through from another source. L'Kell rasped something in reply, drowning out the robots' efforts altogether.

Bandicut waited until he thought the channel was clear, then called, "Say again, Nappy! You have a link with what sub-section?"

The robot's voice was a partially garbled hiss. "Operational records, Cap . . . block in which malfunctions . . . think we know why . . ." At that point, Napoleon's voice became inaudible again.

"We have something new coming in—sorry," said L'Kell, and called for everyone to be silent.

This time, the incoming message was clearer, though still scratchy. ". . . under attack. Salvage party trapped inside, many sick with poisoning . . . swimmers have gone to their aid . . . one sub, one of the visitors . . . may not be enough."

"*Do they need our help?*" L'Kell called back, with a sharp glance at Bandicut. Most of the available subs were either here on *this* expedition or tied up on jobs such as repairing damage to the Neri city.

L'Kell's glance lingered, and Bandicut suddenly realized what the Neri was thinking. He wasn't asking whether more *subs* were needed; he was asking whether the stricken Neri workers needed

John Bandicut to come heal them. /Oh, no. I think we're about to be pulled out of here . . ./

/// Whatever we need to do, ///

Char said calmly.

Perhaps Char didn't understand how hard that would be for him. After committing so much energy and will power to this mission, he wanted to see it through to the end.

/// You don't want to leave Napoleon and Copernicus. ///

A statement, not a question.

/No./ He took a breath and said to L'Kell, "I'll help, wherever you need me."

The Neri grunted in satisfaction and muttered something back into the comm. Then he gestured outside. "They haven't asked for us yet. So let's find out what your friends were trying to say."

Bandicut called, "Can you try giving me that update again, Nappy?"

After a certain amount of static, Copernicus reported, "Cap'n, the good news is that most of the internal circuitry appears to be in working order. However, the programming is not. Napoleon is trying to diagnose a faulty code module that appears to be recycling through the main processor."

"That's fast work."

"Well, Captain, the central program apparently attempted to compensate for an operational self-repair problem—a mechanical breakdown, perhaps caused by seismic impact, combined with an unexpected materials shortage. The compensation failed, and errors became compounded. Once self-repair failed, there was no way to recover without outside intervention. But there *was* no such intervention."

"And now?"

"We have hopes for a restart."

Bandicut thought of the healing of the Neri and decided that nothing was impossible. "Will you need help from us?"

"Unknown at this time."

"Any idea how long it might take?"

"Unknown, Cap'n."

Bandicut asked L'Kell, "Did you follow that?"

"Some." The Neri adjusted an outside light, which was shining along the flank of the robots' sub. All they could see was the blunt form of the sub with its nose stuck under the overhang, its forward probes buried in a juncture membrane. The robots, presumably, were motionless inside the sub; everything they were doing was invisible, electronic signals sent into the heart of the factory. "You probably should ask," said L'Kell, "if they could carry on without you, if they have to."

Bandicut stared into the green and yellow and grey world carved out by the headlight. "Better find out if Nabeck and the robots can understand each other, first."

"Yah," said the Neri.

The next communication from the city indicated that matters were worsening at the salvage site, but stopped short of asking them to pull up and go. L'Kell looked troubled, though. The darkness around them was shivering with occasional faint flashes of light from the direction of the abyssal valley, like heat lightning before a storm. It made Bandicut nervous.

He keyed the comm. "Copernicus—"

"Yes, Cap'n." The robot's voice sounded distracted. Napoleon remained occupied in the subsystems, with Copernicus trying to understand what was happening. Bandicut imagined Copernicus standing by with a tool chest, reaching for the appropriate wrenches as Napoleon asked for them.

"I need you to make a judgment. L'Kell and I may be needed elsewhere. But this repair is every bit as important as what we might be doing. Do you think you can carry on without me?"

"Cap'n—it is difficult to know."

"Do you mean because of you and Nabeck?"

"Well, we *can* communicate with Nabeck—" Meaning, with effort, they could make themselves understood. "So that's—"

Copernicus was interrupted by a piercing tone in the comm.

"*Coppy?* What was that?"

There were some confused electronic noises. Finally Copernicus said, "That was the factory control, trying to broadcast a message."

"Trying to broadcast? Then it really is awakening?"

"Hold a moment. Napoleon thinks it was just a subsystem reflex. Possibly in response to our activities—but we haven't been able to decipher it yet."

"Oh." Bandicut let out a slow breath. "Does that change your assessment?"

"Negative," said Copernicus. "Captain, we suspect that the factory may indeed have initiative, but not necessarily consciousness. We'll just have to wait and see."

Bandicut blinked in surprise. "If it *does* turn out to be conscious, do you think you can handle the situation?"

Copernicus did not speak for a moment. Then he said, "Remember the shadow-people." The noncorporeal, fractal-dimensional beings who were in charge of systems maintenance back on Shipworld: Copernicus had spent considerable time in communication with them, and had done just fine without Bandicut's help.

"Ah. Yes. Of course." Bandicut looked at L'Kell. "I think . . . if we have to go, the robots can manage by themselves."

"Are you certain?" said L'Kell.

Bandicut shivered. Hell, no, he wasn't certain.

/// If you're not, then shouldn't you— ///

"Yeah," Bandicut said to L'Kell.

/// Never mind. ///

"In that case," said L'Kell, "I think our friends above could use some help right now."

Bandicut looked out into the mist overlooking the alien abyss and felt one mission slipping from his hands as another was thrust into them. He turned back to the comm. "Coppy, you and Napoleon are in charge. We'll be back when we can."

He swallowed hard, glanced at L'Kell, and jerked his thumb upward.

L'Kell squeezed the controller. The engines hummed, and the sub backed away from the overhang, then lifted from the abyssal ledge and drove upward into the perpetual night.

———————

The Neri swimmers dropped out of formation with Ik's sub and dispersed for cover along the sloping seafloor. They would continue making their way toward the looming, sunken ship. They were far swifter than the lander swimmers coming to meet them, and better able to conceal themselves. The landers were close enough now that Ik could see that they were bipedal, and encumbered by bulky diving equipment.

A cloud of bubbles approached out of the haze, and from it emerged several landers riding a mechanized, powered sled. "Rakh," Ik muttered, watching the vehicle sweep in an arc ahead and a little to their left. Three landers dropped away from the sled, swimming, air bubbles streaming up from their heads. He couldn't see them too clearly, but they all seemed to be holding something in their hands. Weapons. They were fanning out, looking for the Neri swimmers—but for now, keeping clear of the sub. Maybe they thought the sub had bigger weapons.

S'Cali steered in a skirting detour to approach the salvage site from the right. Above the shadowy form of the sunken ship, Ik saw several white flashes of movement. Not the landers. More like a school of fish. He pointed. "Are those—?"

"Pikarta," S'Cali said.

"The deathfish?"

"Yes. They could be dangerous to both sides. If there's fighting, and the scent of blood gets into the water—"

Ik gave a grunt. He had lost sight of the Neri swimmers now, as well as most of the landers. "Do we need to help your people out here?"

"They can take care of themselves," S'Cali answered. "My

biggest concern is the wounded inside the wreck. Maybe you'd better go back and put on your gear."

Ik clicked his mouth shut at the thought of swimming out there—among the landers and the pikarta—with diving equipment designed for juvenile Neri. "To be honest, S'Cali, if I am to be of use to you, the longer I stay inside this vessel the better. Outside, I may quickly become a liability."

S'Cali assessed him with large, dark eyes. "Perhaps so. But be ready. If they attack us with bursters—"

"Understood," Ik said. "But since we're concerned with the injured, let's see if we can stay clear of the fighting long enough for me to help you discover the cause of the sickness—yes? Radiation cannot be seen—but perhaps this ship was powered by some kind of reactor. We should be alert for a large, heavy structure or compartment somewhere inside—probably with thick metal shielding around it, maybe cracked or breached."

"There could be many places fitting that description," Delent'l called from the back of the cabin. "Our people have been opening compartments all through the wreck, combing for useful equipment. Any one of those could have been what you said."

"But not just a compartment," Ik interrupted. "It might be *in* a compartment, but it would be large, and inside the shielding would be tightly packed machinery—coils, wires, quantum crystal arrays—"

"I do not understand those last words," S'Cali said, turning his eyes from the viewport for an instant. "What exactly do you mean?"

Ik struggled to find a way to make it clear. "I can't say *exactly*, but there must be some kind of—" he flexed his fingers in frustration "—*reactor*—" he knew no other word "—that's leaking radiation into the water. And—*by the stars, why didn't I think of this before?* There might be a blue glow around it, or inside it." Secondary radiation, in the form of visible light.

"We'll ask," said S'Cali. He was steering the sub directly toward the wreck again. It was a shadowy shambles in front of them now, with what looked like large, dark openings in the hull.

"It would be very dangerous to approach. Your people *must* stay away from it, if they find such a thing." Ik could have kicked himself for not thinking of it before. Secondary light emission might or might not be present, but if it was, it would be one sure tip-off of radioactivity.

"We'll try to get inside, up ahead here," S'Cali said. "At some point, though, we'll have to leave the sub and swim."

"Okay, but the longer we can stay in the sub, the better," Ik said. "If there's radiation contaminating the water, the sub's hull will give us protection."

S'Cali grunted. They were very close to the wreck now. Ik still couldn't tell what *kind* of vessel the thing was, sunk and broken on the bottom. It was roughly cylindrical, and enclosed all around; it could as easily have been a spaceship as a submarine. Ik rubbed his chest. A spaceship? Now, that could raise interesting possibilities. "Where did this ship come from?" he asked suddenly.

"We don't know," said S'Cali. "It is very old. And very different from our ancestors' other ships." He pointed. "Look there." A pair of Neri swimmers had emerged from the wreck and were darting along the bottom to meet the sub. They stopped halfway and gestured urgently toward the ship.

"What's happening over there?" Ik asked suddenly, peering at the shadowy breach in the wreck's hull. He realized the answer even as he asked. A group of Neri were engaged in hand-to-hand combat with lander divers. That was what the two swimmers were gesturing about. "Can we help them?" he asked. "Do you have weapons on this sub?"

"I thought you were no fighter."

"Rakh. When I must, I can be of service."

"I am glad," said S'Cali. "No, we do not. But that does not mean we're helpless." He squeezed the controller, and the sub accelerated. He flicked the headlight back on, as they bore down on the fight. Three Neri and five or six landers rotated in the water, pausing momentarily in their battle. In the instant the landers were frozen, the Neri swimmers darted out of the way. This was Ik's first good look at the landers. They were encased in suits and face coverings, but appeared to be somewhat smaller than the Neri. They wore artificial fins and air-breathing gear. Of their faces, he could see nothing through the reflective glass.

Was S'Cali intending to ram them? If so, the hull of the wreck was going to make a damned hard stop. At that moment, S'Cali pulled the control back, reversing thrust. The sub braked hard, and the landers in front of it tumbled wildly, caught in the powerful jetwash. The sub slowed to a halt, and hung directly in front of the hull breach.

Ik leaned close to the window, peering out in an effort to spot the landers. Had they been knocked away to a safe distance? Or better yet, had they fled?

S'Cali spoke into the comm. "Neri outside the hull, please report." His voice reverberated, amplified by speakers on the outside.

An answering voice, thin and distorted: "Many injured and sick on the inside . . . unable to get away."

"We're here to stay with you," said S'Cali. "More swimmers are coming."

Before there could be an answer, a new cry came: "Landers returning!" There was a thump on the outside of the hull, and Ik glimpsed webbed Neri feet flying past the port as Neri swimmers maneuvered to greet a new attack.

S'Cali swiveled the control, and the sub rotated in place, facing outward from the wreck. A group of landers was coming in, swimming furiously; two of them raised weapons and fired darts. One glanced off the sub with a ding. S'Cali caught them in the headlight and roared out toward them. As they began to turn and disperse, he yawed the sub violently left and right, threatening to sweep anything and everything out of his path.

Ik was unprepared as S'Cali reversed thrust again, repelling the attackers with the jetwash. He was thrown forward, catching himself with one hand against the viewport. He clacked his mouth, wondering how much impact the pane could withstand.

S'Cali backed the sub toward the wreck, with Delent'l calling out directions from the stern, where he was peering out a small porthole. Out in front, though, Ik caught sight of a lander sled approaching amid a cloud of bubbles. Ik saw something erupt from the sled and streak toward them. "S'Cali!" he cried.

The Neri shouted a warning on the outside comm. "Burster coming! Take cover!"

A moment later came a flash, followed by a concussion and a clap to Ik's ears. The sub jarred, and Ik's ears were left ringing. The hull seemed to hold well enough, but as Ik shook off the effects, he wondered how the Neri outside were faring. "S'Cali, are they hurt out there?" He glanced sideways, and realized that S'Cali himself was stunned. "S'Cali—can you hear me?" He took hold of the Neri's arm.

S'Cali peered at him in apparent puzzlement, then came back to the present. His large eyes blinked, and he turned and snapped out a call on the outside comm. "Neri swimmers, what is your condition?"

The replies came in scratchily, like distant shouts. A couple of Neri had been injured, and were being helped back inside the wreck by others. But Ik realized, peering out the viewport, that several lander divers had been injured by the explosion, too. Most of them were withdrawing from the area; but one was floating not far from the sub, looking dazed.

Two Neri swimmers converged on the lander and grabbed him. "Can you have your people hold that one?" Ik urged, pointing. "Perhaps we can talk to him, find out what they want!"

S'Cali looked doubtful for a moment—but barked an order. The two Neri responded by wrestling the lander out of sight behind the sub, into the shelter of the wreck.

"What now?" Ik asked.

S'Cali had no time to answer. A shadow passed over them, moving quickly, then another. S'Cali's eyes rotated upward. "Pikarta!" he called. "Take cover! Pikarta over the site!"

Ik tensed, craning his neck to peer up. Three creatures nearly as large as the sub had sailed over, and were now circling to return. They were shaped like enormous, elongated raindrops with mouth openings on the front. In the mouth openings, Ik could see teeth. But something was odd about the teeth, some trick of the light. As the pikarta sped back toward the sub, Ik finally saw what it was: their teeth were rotating in their mouths like huge, spinning rasps.

"Is everyone inside?" S'Cali cried, maneuvering the sub to try to provide cover to the swimmers.

The first deathfish slammed into the top of the sub with a sickening impact and grinding screech—teeth spinning on metal. Its hindquarters and tail convulsed in front of the viewport; then the fish careened away. S'Cali fought to keep the sub upright. Ik could only hold on desperately, squinting out the window. The second and third pikarta veered away from the sub, seeking easier prey.

The landers were fleeing, but the pikarta were much faster. Ik watched in horror as one turned and caught a free-swimming lander. From where Ik lay, the lander was just a small, shadowy shape. Even so, he could see its body turn instantly to a cloud of blood and shreds. "Moon and stars," Ik breathed aloud, thinking with a shudder that it could just as easily have been him, or any of these Neri. He felt no better about it being a lander, for whom he held no hatred.

"They may be coming back," S'Cali said. "We've got to get inside." He touched the comm. *"Is everyone in?"* He was already turning the sub toward the hull breach.

"What about the Neri who came with us?" Ik asked, thinking of the swimmers on the far side of the wreck, whom they had left trying to evade lander divers.

As though in answer, he felt a sudden concussion, but muted. "Was that—"

"Landers on the other side, probably. We can't do much for our people over there now," S'Cali said. "But they know how to hide, and fight if they have to. I'd guess the pikarta are a bigger threat to the landers right now than to our people. Those bursters may have been aimed at the pikarta." He completed the turn and was directed into the hull opening by a Neri, almost invisible in the shadows of the wreck.

"Are you sure we can fit?" Ik asked nervously, eyeing the jagged edges of the opening.

Another concussion hit much closer, the shock wave nearly carrying them into the side of the wreck.

"No choice," said S'Cali. "Our wounded are inside. We can't help them from here."

True, Ik thought. It was either drive the sub in, or get out and swim. He peered close to the viewport, and tried to gauge the clearance. S'Cali was steering them expertly into the breach. The wreck loomed around them, as they moved into the near-darkness of the interior.

Then Delent'l shouted a warning from the back—and bursters started going off directly behind them. **Thud! Thud! Thud!**

S'Cali cried a warning—and the sub pitched nose-down, surged forward, and slammed into a heavy bulkhead. Ik was thrown headfirst into the viewport. The lights sputtered and died, and he heard water gushing into the compartment.

CHAPTER 16

Rings of Fire

ANTARES WAS STILL trying to learn what everything did in Kailan's chamber. It all looked so incongruous down here in the Neri realm. The instruments that the obliq had used during the breakaway habitat crisis were just a small fraction of the total. The room, a curtain-lined den filled with consoles, seemed to be a combination library, laboratory, and long-range sensor control—or, as her stones rendered it, a *knowledge-center*. Kailan's instruments provided a range of environmental scans. Some Kailan seemed to understand fairly well; others not at all. Who had built all these instruments? Antares wondered, and how was it that the Neri had forgotten so much about them?

Kailan and her assistant were activating the consoles one by one. "My people," Kailan said, referring to the female Neri under her authority, "have the duty of maintaining the knowledge of the Neri people. But it is difficult, in the face of failing equipment and understanding."

"Then your instruments—"

"Were provided from the beginning, to help us keep a watch on changing conditions in our world—and to maintain our scientific and historical knowledge. But many years ago, our knowledge began to disappear, partly from equipment failure, and partly from problems in organizing and retrieving it."

Antares sensed suppressed emotions tickling outward. "Who,"

she said carefully, "provided the equipment?"

"Those who built the city, I presume," Kailan murmured, adjusting a console. "One of the deep factories probably manufactured the equipment, though I can't even say that for sure. I'd guess that there is a lot of historical information still in the system somewhere, if we knew how to get at it."

Antares sensed regret, but no defensiveness, over the admission. "Then this began long before your time?"

"Oh yes. I have tried, like the obliqs before me, to recover and maintain all that I could." Kailan tapped a small unit that seemed not to be responding. "Elbeth," she said to her assistant, "there seems to be no power here. Do we have a recharged battery for this one?" As Elbeth went to check, Kailan continued, "But there is so much I don't know about the instruments and their purposes—including how they work. They are very sturdy—which is fortunate, because the changers do not have the necessary programming to repair all of them."

Kailan adjusted her shawl and peered over the top of a nearby instrument, which she had called a seismic imager, and fiddled with a connection. She looked back at Antares. "I seem to be telling you how many things there are here that are beyond my understanding. Well, I would appreciate any knowledge that you, who come from other places, or—" she closed her large eyes for a moment "—that the stones of knowing, might bring. I am already beginning to understand a few things, I think."

Antares looked around the chamber. Something had been bothering her. "Kailan, were these consoles actually made for you? For the Neri? Some of them seem—well—"

Kailan straightened up. "Awkward? Unsuitable?"

"Yes. As though they were designed for someone else's hands." Antares pushed her hair back, her empathic faculties afire, but quietly, like banked coals. She sensed that there was a stew of knowledge and emotion simmering beneath the surface of Kailan's mind.

"You are right," Kailan said. "These instruments were not designed for us, but for—" she seemed to have trouble saying it "—those who created us."

Antares stepped closer, touched by a sense of the Neri's sadness and loss. Kailan's eyes shifted and focused on the instruments, as Antares felt a strange tickle in her stones. There was an inner tension in the obliq around this question. "Those who created you?" Antares asked. Was this a religious question?

"I'm sorry, I thought you knew. I mean those who designed— *changed* us, to live in the sea." Kailan seemed to sense Antares' astonishment. "There are some among us now who do not wish to believe this, for whom it seems more like tale than history. They find it hard to believe, and do not *want* to believe it. But it is true. Whoever we were before, we were altered for this world in which we live."

"And your creators?"

"They lived on land. Before they died. Before the Maw came and destroyed them."

Antares was struggling to put this together. "Then they're not related to—the landers? The ones you are fighting now?"

The obliq made a soft hissing sound. Laughter? "Not to the landers, no." She turned back to her instruments. "Where the landers come from, we do not know. But they are not of this world. There are stories that they landed in a great fireball. That they were brought to this sea by the—" *huuum* "—One Who Brings All Things Together. That they spurned the gift and fled to the land. I cannot say. But they do not come from this world, of that we are sure."

Not of this world? Antares thought. Like us? No wonder we were greeted with suspicion.

"And of course, my friend-from-another-world, there is the Maw of the Abyss, which, I believe, also did not come from this world." Kailan looked up for a moment. "These matters, I am certain, are all connected. But whether they are by design, or by chance, I do not yet know." Her barely-webbed fingers hesitated, then moved quickly over the instrument controls.

Antares suddenly realized she had stopped breathing, so closely was she listening. She drew a deliberate breath.

"But now," said Kailan, "we must focus our thoughts on this thing at the bottom of the sea. We must try to learn what it is *now*, regardless of its origins. You and your stones must help me understand it. I believe our future rests on this—on a battle that sometimes seems as much as anything a war of the spirit." Kailan urged Antares to join her at the console. "Here, let me show you what we can study."

Antares crouched next to her, thinking, Well, friend-from-another-world, let's hope you can help . . .

The images reminded her of the multicolored feathers of a whoailabird back home—stirring and fluttering just before flight, when the bird would loft itself into the air like a pillar of crimson and gold flame. The preparatory flutters were less flamboyant than the actual launch, but were captivating and bewildering in their complex movements, shifting and fanning.

The images of the seafloor shifted and changed like that, as the obliq changed the processing from one mode to another, searching for meaningful patterns, but mostly just confusing her Thespi guest. Kailan would point to a shape and say, "Does this suggest anything to you?" and Antares would think a moment, then murmur in the negative, and Kailan would change to something else. It was clear that, while their knowing-stones provided them with a common language, her own lack of training in this area could not help but make matters difficult. She was looking at depictions of valleys and geologic fault lines, and graphs of seemingly chaotic forces. She could guess at the meaning of some of them, but to think that she could offer any insight was ridiculous.

Kailan was undeterred. "What I'm showing you now is background. From some intact records, we have historical seismic information—that is, about sound waves traveling through rock. We're still getting some new data, from a network of sensors put down long before I was born. Plus, we have current sonar readings—sound through water—but if we ever had historical records of that, they've been lost. Now, let me show you some visible light images of—"

"Kailan, how much of this do you actually understand?" Antares interrupted. "It all seems . . . highly specialized."

"It is," said Kailan, moving to the next console. "But if *I* don't try to understand it, there's no one else who will. Most of my people are busy in technical maintenance, or in the nurseries caring for the young. And the males, under Askelanda, seem to have lost their curiosity about it—and anyway, they're too busy in salvage and farming for food." She looked up at Antares. "So it's up to me and Elbeth, plus Maerta, whom you haven't met yet, who's apprenticing when she has time."

"It sounds pretty difficult."

"It is. But we're doing what we have to do." Kailan pointed to another display. "There—that's what it looks like when the rift opens. When the Maw begins to devour."

Antares watched. It was a holographic light image of the abyssal valley, as viewed from the ledge near the factory. The image was amplified and enhanced in some fashion, so that it looked as though they could peer downward through the depths for a mile or more. This was not sunlight, but monsterlight. A flicker of brightness appeared in the center of the image, and grew. She found it frightening, without quite knowing why. It seemed to be coming toward her, swelling out of the console. Suddenly it *opened*, like a billowing ring of fire. Amplified through the deepwater haze, it looked like a ghostly presence that was not just frightening, but *threatening*—as if it were attacking. She pressed her long fingers to her throat, and thought, /Please tell me—does this mean anything at all to you?/

There was no answer, but she sensed that the knowing-stones were focusing just as intently as she. Probably the image *did* mean something to them, but they were not yet sure what.

"Here's where the real trouble starts," Kailan said, pointing to the dark area in the center of the ring. Antares peered. What was it? She had assumed rock, but apparently it wasn't.

Kailan pointed to a neighboring screen. This one was in false colors, not a visible light image; some kind of sonar, a current-mapping thing. A flow was beginning toward the ring, and into the center. "Water currents?" Antares asked.

"Yes."

"*Into* the ring?"

"Exactly." The obliq touched a control, and the mapping image flicked to a topographical display, which Antares had seen before. It was changing, as she watched. Where she had just observed the current flowing, there was now an opening in the seafloor that had not been there before, like a tremendous funnel at the bottom of the ocean. It looked as if seawater was *draining out of the ocean basin.*

"That's impossible," Antares whispered. "Isn't it? Where's the water going?"

Kailan changed the display again, to one showing a global view of the planet. "Watch."

Antares stared at the console. The glowing red funnel appeared to represent the Maw. Apparently the flow of water was going down into the planet, and then . . . disappearing.

"That's how it starts. But then—" Kailan touched a control to change the display. "This is actually slowing down the image, so you can see it better." Something was changing inside the planet—as if a worm were tunneling through the middle of the globe, looping and curving through an intricate tangle of pathways. When the tunneling was done, the flow was being channeled in impossible loops through the planet's interior. And then out . . .

"Back into the ocean?" Antares stared in wonder.

"Back into the sea, but not anywhere near here. Somewhere on the other side of the world."

"You're observing this? Measuring it somehow?"

The obliq brushed her finger across the globe. "Those who built our realm were very thorough. There are measuring units scattered all over the planet—far more widely than we ourselves are scattered. We only live here—" she pointed to the region near the funnel "—and in smaller settlements here and here—" she pointed to a few places north and south, not far out from the shoreline of the neighboring continent "—and a couple of outposts in the arctic zones." She touched two spots much farther north. "There were at one time splinter settlements elsewhere around the globe, but we've lost contact and we no longer have subs that can travel that far." She displayed a sprinkling of dots on the screen. "But here are the sensor locations. Most are still linked to the imagers here. As they fail, though—" she pointed to a few that were orange rather than blue "—we no longer have any way of replacing them."

Antares flared her nostrils. "What about these other settlements—the ones that are closer? Are you in contact with them?"

Kailan's answer was interrupted by the return of Elbeth, carrying a round, lozenge-shaped object the size of a dining plate. Apparently it was a battery; Elbeth lifted the top of the nonfunctioning console and removed a similar object before inserting the new one. Kailan tried the console, and nodded when it came on. "We are . . . to a degree." She looked back up at Antares. "In the past, we were cooperatively interdependent. The other settlements looked to us after their smaller factories began failing, perhaps a hundred and fifty years ago. We were not only the largest city, but the only one that could guarantee new equipment. Still, they performed much salvage of lost technology from our ancestors, and often had richer fishing grounds. The trading was mutually beneficial."

"But—" said Antares.

"But not everyone saw it as equally beneficial. Then when *our* factory failed, we had less to trade. Contact dwindled. As times have grown more difficult, so have our efforts to stay united with the other Neri," Kailan said. "We still have communications, through the midwater sound transmission layer—"

"*Uuhll?*"

"A middle layer of water that is confined by warmer, lighter water above, and colder, denser water below," Kailan explained. "In good conditions, sound can travel around the world through that layer, bouncing endlessly between the two boundaries. It's erratic, but we do send messages. And until recently we still sent the occasional sub, or even groups of swimmers, to call on the other settlements."

Antares watched the movement in the mapping screen, and recalled the powerful downward currents she had witnessed during the recent eruption. "Do you think there's some *purpose* to the creation of these currents?"

Kailan was silent a while. "That's what I'd like to know," she said finally. "Certainly *I* have no idea of the purposes of the Maw—if it has purpose, or intelligence, at all." She looked up at Antares, and now the Thespi sensed a real undercurrent of longing, hope, need. "Do you have knowledge—?"

Antares sighed wistfully before the question was finished. "Perhaps one of my friends will. Perhaps Li-Jared, or—"

"Did I—" *bwong* "—hear my name?" said the Karellian, striding into the room behind a young Neri guide.

"Li-Jared!" Antares cried. "Have you come alone? Where's Ik?"

"My Hraachee'an friend was called away," Li-Jared said, and Antares felt a darkness in his words, and in his gaze. "There has been a raid of some kind. I'm afraid that it might be a bad business. But I trust him to take care of himself." He bowed to the young Neri. "Thank you, Maerta." Then to Antares and Kailan, "Can I help? What is all this?" He waved at the row of consoles.

"Do you have training in sciences?" Kailan asked cautiously.

"I *might*. You needn't sound so surprised," Li-Jared said.

Antares had to suppress a hiss of laughter. "I think, Li-Jared, that few Neri males are trained in such matters. But I am sure Kailan would appreciate all the help you can offer."

"Then," said Li-Jared, with a great display of confidence, "let us get down to it, shall we?"

Antares sensed confusing emotions, and could not quite tell if Li-Jared's confidence was genuine or acted. But she had no time to ponder the question, as Kailan continued her explanation as though there had been no interruption at all. "We believe," she said, "that this thing is what killed our ancestors."

"You mean your—"

"Designers. Our forebears. All record of contact with them—or such record as we have—ends at the same time as the Maw's appearance. There are reports of terrible cataclysms, above and below the sea. But we under the sea apparently fared better. Why, we do not know."

"And this was—?"

"About three hundred years ago."

Antares felt an electrifying tingle. Something appeared on this world three hundred years ago, perhaps destroying an entire civilization on land, and now endangering another civilization in the sea? Was *this* why she and her companions had been sent to this world? If so, what could they possibly hope to do about it? But surely they wouldn't have been hurled across the galaxy to this place, if there was nothing they could do . . .

A strong likelihood you are correct. We suspect an approaching convergence.

/Convergence of what?/

Uncertain.

So. They would still be fumbling their way. But she felt a renewed sense of hope, that perhaps they were not merely adrift here, without something useful to do. Some purpose. And, perhaps, the tools with which to do it.

Kailan suddenly became agitated and moved to the next console. *"There,"* she said, pointing to the screen, where irregular red and yellow shapes, clustered incomprehensibly, were sprouting from a slowly scrolling scan of—what was that again? Seismic activity? "That may be a sign of another flareup, coming soon."

Antares hissed breath through her teeth. "How bad? How soon?"

"I cannot say. We have not established the meaning of these patterns. But they have something to do with gravity-density. And such patterns have at times preceded major events."

Antares pressed her fingers to her stones in the vain hope that they might have some answer. /Please—if you can make sense of this—share it with me./

From her stones she sensed intense interest, with undertones of urgency. But there was no answer at all.

CHAPTER 17

Drowning in the Dark

IN THE DARKNESS, it was hard to be sure of anything. But Ik could still hear water streaming into the sub. S'Cali and Delent'l were chattering to each other, too quickly for his stones to follow, and were taking things out of storage areas behind him. Ik, still a bit shaken from the crash himself, was having trouble getting his own thoughts in focus.

He drew a long, measured breath and called out, "Urrr, what is our condition? Are we flooding—" His breath caught as his leg, straightening toward the rear of the sub, sank into icy water.

The two Neri fell silent, and for an instant he heard only the gurgle and sucking of water. Then S'Cali answered, "Yes, Ik—sorry. We are flooding. But we have some time yet. The drain membranes will keep us from filling up too fast." There was more rustling, and then a glow appeared from the rear of the cabin. S'Cali had unsheathed some kind of trouble light; it shone like a chemoluminescent globe, in a seaweed bladder.

Ik turned himself around, with difficulty. He rubbed his eyes, and the saltwater made them sting. "What do you mean, about the drain membranes?" he asked. The two Neri were holding pieces of the diving gear they had stowed for his benefit. He shuddered at the thought of venturing out as a free diver in this water, not even close to the undersea city.

"The one-way membranes," S'Cali explained, "are letting water out. But not as fast as it's coming in."

"Ah. But we're going to have to abandon ship. Is that what you're saying?"

"Yes. Now, let's see if we can get this hood on you." The thing S'Cali held out looked like a large, open-ended bladder with hoses attached. It was made of a cloudy material that reminded him of seaweed.

Ik rubbed his fingers against his chest, trying to think optimistically. They were in a disabled, flooding sub, yes, with diving gear made for alien children. But there were a lot of other Neri around to assist. Except most of them were sick or wounded. He had come to rescue *them*. Surely other subs were being sent from the city, though. Or would be, if a message had been sent.

S'Cali handed him the helmet, and he examined it in the dim light. Remade from equipment designed for Neri young, the hood had been reshaped for his much larger head. The glue-seams looked . . . fragile. Apparently the nanoshit changers were not reprogrammable to make this change; it had been done by hand. Attached to the hood by the hoses was a strange-looking apparatus which seemed to contain feathers, enclosed in a semirigid housing made of a flimsy, transparent material. This was probably the oxygen extractor and gas-exchange mechanism. There were no tanks, just a small, flexible air bladder. He could not imagine how it would work efficiently enough to provide for his needs, but he had to assume that it would. He hoped his physiologic needs were reasonably close to that of the Neri young.

"Did you, urrrr, happen to get a signal out to the city, telling them what happened?" he asked, hefting the helmet.

"Unfortunately not," S'Cali said, gesturing to him to put it on. "We were already inside the salvage ship. But eventually they're bound to check on us."

Ik sighed through his ears and put the helmet on. The Neri craftsmen had done their best to fit it, in the short time available to them; nevertheless, it fit snugly on the crown of his head, and loosely around the neck. He couldn't see anything except shadows through the hood. "Can we still talk?" he asked, his voice echoing around his ears.

"We can hear you," answered Delent'l, who was busy attaching the other components to the hood. His voice sounded muffled, but understandable. "Once we're in the water, it'll be a little more difficult. The techs didn't have time to finish the comm unit." The Neri touched the side of the helmet. "So if you need to say something when we're out there, speak clearly."

Ik grunted. "What do we do, once we're outside?"

S'Cali gestured toward the nose of the sub. Peering through the foggy hood material, Ik imagined that he saw a couple of swimmers in the gloom. "We'll regroup with the others," S'Cali said. "And you can show us how to avoid this radiation sickness."

"Ah," said Ik, wondering how he could even remotely hope to do that, swimming blind, in freezing, pikarta-infested waters.

"We'll meet with the wounded," said S'Cali. "I understand that you star people have the power to heal? I think there are plenty of injured waiting for you."

Ik could only stare in dismay.

———————

Seawater was swirling around his legs now, but S'Cali and Delent'l seemed in no hurry to get out. They were sorting equipment, so Ik took off his hood and used the time to ask about the layout of the wreck. He had two main concerns: finding his way around, and trying to guess where a leaking reactor might be.

The Neri, it seemed, did not map the layout the way he would have done it, in terms of ups and downs and relative spatial locations. Instead, they spoke of moving "with the slow current, until the walls open," and stopping where "turbulence brings you to a still spot, and the water is staler and saltier," and then swimming "just above the bottom-hugging, faster current . . ." This was no help at all to Ik in trying to build a mental picture of the layout. But then something clicked in his mind. Delent'l had just said, ". . . into the corridor where the current runs warmer . . ."

"What was that you just said?" Ik asked, as the Neri continued his description.

Delent'l seemed puzzled. "Which?"

"Something about warm water? Warmer than the rest?"

"Oh, yes. There is something in the ship that warms the water in one area. It flows into a corridor, and this is where the sick are staying, until you can heal them."

Ik felt a rush of dizziness. The sick were staying in the corridor with the warm water? Terrible. Terrible! "Do you know where the warmth is coming from?" he asked hoarsely.

"There is a grate-covered opening," Delent'l told him. "The water flows out through there. We have not been able to get inside to see what it is."

"Good!" Ik cried in a whisper. "If you got inside, you would probably die. You must move those people at once!" If it is not already too late, he thought helplessly.

Delent'l and S'Cali looked at one another in surprise. "Move them?" S'Cali asked. "But the warmth comforts them."

"Please!" Ik drew a breath. "You *must*. It is almost certainly the warm water that is making them ill!" As the two tried to comprehend that, Ik craned his neck to peer out the viewport. Several Neri swimmers were hovering outside the sub. "Can you call outside and send word?"

"Yes—I think so," S'Cali said. "But are you sure? You have not yet seen—"

"I know I have not seen it," Ik said quickly. "But I am *nearly* sure—and if I am right, then every minute they stay will make them sicker. Please!"

S'Cali had to fiddle some with the switches, until he got power back to the comm; then he relayed the message. But he looked back in puzzlement at Ik.

"If water is leaking out of a reactor, then it would very likely be warm," Ik explained. "It is probably contaminated with radiation." Then he clacked his mouth shut and hoped that he could stay alive long enough to be of some help.

We can assist in maintaining your physical integrity.

/That's good,/ he said to the stones. /Can you help me heal radiation sickness?/

Uncertain.

/You saw me being healed./

Yes.

Ik waited.

They answered finally: *We will do what we can.*

The water in the cabin was up to Ik's waist when the Neri made final adjustments to his air supply and strapped on a weighted vest to compensate for the buoyancy of the helmet. The visor, now wet, had become transparent. S'Cali's voice sounded thin and distant through the helmet. "We'll go out one at a time. If you have trouble swimming, we'll tow you. All right?"

"All right."

In the gloom, he watched Delent'l wade past him, the Neri's webbed feet brushing past his legs. Delent'l touched something, and Ik felt a slight change in the water movement. Then Delent'l sat in the water, and with barely a ripple, sank out of sight through the floor of the cabin.

S'Cali tapped his shoulder. "Go ahead!"

Ik checked one last time for his rope, wrapped around his waist, then felt for the membrane-opening with his feet. He gasped at the cold as he bent to find a handhold, then dropped with a lurch down through the flooded pressurelock chamber below. There was a frightening rush and gurgle of cold water all around him, but he forced himself to keep going, until his feet met open water and finally his shoulders and head cleared the bottom of the sub. He felt Delent'l's hand guiding him, then pulling him off to one side.

He suddenly realized he still had his moccasins strapped on, which was probably stupid. But there was nothing he could do about it now. Delent'l looked like a sea monster in front of him, waving—probably asking if he was all right. Ik waved back. The air seemed perfectly breathable, if a bit seaweedy-tasting, and he wasn't nearly as cold as he'd expected to be. But he was too buoyant; he was floating upward, hitting the underside of the damaged sub.

Delent'l saw it, too. Had they not weighted him enough? After a moment, Ik looked at his hands and realized what was happening: his voice-stones had provided a forcefield barrier around his skin, sealing in a thin layer of air for insulation. That's what was making him too buoyant.

He exhaled experimentally, and found that with his breath almost completely out, he was just about neutrally buoyant. /Can you let out just a little of that air?/ he asked the stones.

A flurry of very fine bubbles surrounded him. He began to sink. He drew a sharp breath. He was floating now. Good.

S'Cali came alongside, and the two Neri took hold of the ends of Ik's rope and began to swim. Ik tried to swim, but couldn't hope to match the Neri's speed; he soon gave up and held the rope to steady himself and allowed them to tow him. They glided across the empty cargo hold where they had crashed, a space dimly illuminated by sunlight coming in through the breach in the hull. Several other Neri joined them as they turned to survey the sub.

The small vessel was jammed into the lower corner of the hold, wedged among some oddly shaped struts that appeared to be part of the sunken ship's original structure. There was little outward damage to the sub, but no doubt plenty of trouble inside, given the flooding. Ik hoped that the Neri had the knowledge and resources to fix it.

He felt himself being pulled around in the water. S'Cali and Delent'l were towing him away, and at a surprising speed. He was breathing hard, and glad he wasn't trying to keep up under his own power. They passed through a sizable bulkhead opening into a darker space. A number of dim glowlights were visible ahead, looking like deep sea fish—handlights carried by swimmers, no doubt. After a few moments, his eyes had adjusted enough to the gloom to see that they had entered a wide corridor, which would take them deep into the wrecked ship.

His breathing was coming just a little harder now. Probably the difficulty of holding his body in a streamlined position while the Neri pulled him.

He tried to settle his mind for visualizing and remembering the layout of the ship. The more he learned, the better. And he needed to be alert to any cues, any hints at all as to the nature of the radiation leakage.

Except he was having trouble focusing. It was his breathing. He hauled in a deep breath and felt it burning in his chest. It wasn't the physical exertion; it was the air. Something was wrong with his air.

Respiratory problem . . . immediate action required.

Moon and stars! What could he do? Try to get back to the sub? He struggled to call out to S'Cali and Delent'l, but he could not draw enough breath to shout. He fought a surge of panic; then he clacked his mouth and yanked hard on the rope.

S'Cali turned first. Ik waved urgently, and in the process caused himself to tumble so that he couldn't see either of the Neri. He tried to recover, but his hands caught on the lines and it took him precious moments to get untangled and turned back around. By that time, S'Cali and Delent'l had reached his side.

"Can't . . . breathe," he gasped, grabbing his hood with both hands. The water seemed to be closing in around his head.

He could hear S'Cali and Delent'l speaking, but their words didn't quite penetrate his hood. He must have communicated his need, though, because they launched into motion, turning him around and heading back toward the sub.

Good! he thought. Good! We can make it . . .

Two Neri swimmers came streaking through the bulkhead toward them. They were gesturing frantically—and crying out— and this time he heard the words.

"Into the ship! Landers coming! You can't go back!"

And as Ik strained for breath, S'Cali and Delent'l hauled him in a tight turn and sped inward into the ship, away from the only source of air he knew.

CHAPTER 18

Shipwreck Rescues

L'KELL PILOTED THE sub with silent concentration, as Bandicut angled his gaze backward from the side of the nose viewport, trying to see if that ghostly light from the abyss was still visible behind them. It unnerved him to have something like that at his back. And he hated leaving the robots in danger.

/// You really think of them as friends, don't you?
As living, thinking beings. ///

/Well, yeah. I mean, don't you think of the translator that way?/ Bandicut wasn't sure when he had stopped thinking of the robots as *almost* sentient, and started regarding them as members of the human community.

/// My thoughts of the stones
and what memories I have of the translator are . . .
I don't know what you would call it.
Not masters, nor servants exactly,
but not friends, either.
Do you regard Ik and Li-Jared and Antares
as human? ///

/I guess so./ Bandicut shrugged inwardly. It wasn't that he'd lost sight of their species differences. But somewhere along the line he had come to think of humanness, or maybe *personhood*, as being determined by more than a particular DNA coding. /You too,/ he added.

The quarx didn't say anything, but he felt a flicker of acceptance, belonging.

All this talk, though, got Bandicut's thoughts going. /Tell me something,/ he said a little later. /What about Charlie-Four? Do you think he ended his own life so he could get out of the way and make room for you? Because he knew he wasn't the right quarx for the job, or the time?/

/// It's possible, I suppose.
What makes you ask? ///

/I dunno. It's been bothering me—the way he seemed to just give up like that./

/// You're thinking maybe it was
self-sacrifice? ///

/That's what I'm asking you. I mean, it doesn't square with the Charlie-Four I knew. And yet—/

/// Well, I do have residual memories
that make me suspect, anyway,
that he was not wholly forthcoming with you
about his feelings. ///

/Meaning what?/

/// Meaning I think he tried
to be more of a sonofabitch
than he really was. ///

Bandicut rolled that around in his mind. /But why?/
Charlene hesitated.

/// I don't know. ///

/Well, if you don't know . . ./ Bandicut sighed and looked back out the window.

As they ascended along the slope of the seafloor, they were

encountering a greater number and variety of animals, from slow-moving fish to large jellies to spider-legged things half a meter wide that sprang in long, slow-motion leaps through the head-light-smudged darkness. He kept wondering if they would ever see daylight in the water, and then reminded himself that they were still far too deep . . . and then, to his surprise, he blinked and saw what looked like the palest haze of moonlight filtering through the water. "L'Kell, is that sunlight I see?"

The Neri flicked off the one remaining headlight, to let Bandicut see the difference; there *was* a faint, colorless glow in the water. Then L'Kell pointed off to the port side. There, some distance off and below them, was a cluster of yellow-green lights.

"The city? We passed it?"

"At a distance. I think you were asleep."

"I was?" He had not been aware of dozing off at all.

"We still have some distance to go to the salvage area. The relief force hasn't been heard from since they reported sighting a large number of landers."

Bandicut's stomach knotted, as he thought of Ik. /Mokin' fokin' A./ He had come to depend so much on Ik, he could not imagine what life would be like if anything happened to the Hraachee'an.

/// *It's still perfectly possible that*
they're okay, isn't it? ///

/Yeah, sure,/ he said. /We don't know a thing, so I should quit worrying until I know more. Right?/

/// *I'd say so. Will you?* ///

/Not a chance,/ Bandicut said, and rubbed his eyes as he peered ahead into the mists.

Ik couldn't last much longer. Towed by the Neri, he was floating down an endless corridor. His chest was searing now, his breath going in and out in frantic little movements.

Remain as still as possible. We are modifying the forcefield.

He tried to obey, but it was not easy to keep his body still, and straight, and streamlined while being pulled by a rope through the water! He prayed that the Neri knew where they were going; if he could just hold on . . .

We are attempting to speed the exchange of gases through the forcefield, out of the water. We are also attempting to dampen your metabolic rate. You may feel faint . . .

Faint. The darkness actually seemed to be lightening around him, as everything went grey and grainy, out of focus. He no longer felt the burning; he felt only the numbness.

And then even that slipped away, as he entered a kind of shadow world of awareness . . .

Movement of light and dark . . . without bodily sensation . . .

When he blinked back to a fuller consciousness, there was still motion. Something was ahead, something blurry. Shimmery. Like a mirror, but only a flicker of light on it. What would be shimmery?

Air?

Some part of his mind wanted to launch into a furious swim. He moved his hands ineffectually, but his body could no longer respond. He could only hang limply behind the Neri, mind in a fog, as water flowed past his body.

And then the shimmer was in his face, and around him, and he broke through a boundary layer into *air*, blessed air. He could feel his head and shoulders out of the water, but the helmet was still suffocating him. He gasped, trying weakly to reach—then felt other hands on the helmet, releasing straps and ties, and finally lifting it from his head.

Ik's windpipe rasped as air flamed into his chest—wonderful, life-giving, air. It felt like fire, but he didn't care. At least a dozen long, ragged breaths went in and out before he even noticed how stale and metallic it tasted. It must have been trapped here for a long time. He slowly became aware of what was holding him up out of the water—four or five Neri kicking in the water, supporting his weight. He could only wheeze in gratitude.

Readjusting metabolic parameters.

His strength returned slowly. More and more Neri appeared around him. Additional globe-lights came up out of the water, and he could finally see the faces of S'Cali and Delent'l on either side of him. They were in a sizable chamber, apparently an empty hold, with an airspace allowing four or five meters of headroom between the water line and the ceiling. Over his head he could see a number of struts and fittings on the walls and ceiling. The sounds of breathing, and lapping water, echoed around him. His mouth was full of the tastes of salt, metal, and old seaweed.

"Can you breathe all right now?" called S'Cali, his voice filling the chamber.

"Hrrr—yes," Ik answered—then choked, gurgling, on a mouthful of water. "I'm—okay—" he gasped.

S'Cali asked Ik if he thought he could climb up onto a ledge that ran along one side of the chamber. Ik looked where S'Cali was pointing. The ledge was tilted a bit toward the water, but it was fairly broad, and Ik thought he might be able to hang on, if he could get up there.

The Neri, in concert, moved him sideways through the water. Once he had an arm up on the ledge, he felt a little better. More lights had been brought into the chamber, and he could see other Neri moving beneath the surface of the water. "Can you—urrr, push me up?"

The answer was a powerful push under his feet, vaulting him up onto the ledge. He turned awkwardly, with his gear still draped around him, and sat facing the water. The ledge was metal, and it was cold and slippery. He could feel the stones increasing the insulating forcefield layer beneath him, but he started to slide at once on the cushion of air. /Turn it off!/

His cry was unnecessary. The stones killed the field instantly. Better to be cold than back in the water. He shivered—then thought of his rope, still cinched around his waist, with the two ends trailing in the water. He pulled the ends up and stretched them out behind him, on the ledge. /Try it again, just for a second./

He felt a tingle, and began to slip. But the rope held fast, keeping him in place. He drew a long breath. "Thank you," he said hoarsely, to the Neri gathered around him, heads out of the water.

Delent'l climbed up beside him and began removing his breathing gear. "We must try to repair this."

"Thank you for coming," said one of the other Neri.

Ik gazed at the speaker for a moment, absorbing the meaning of his words. "I hope I am not more burden than help." He gestured awkwardly. "I don't know what I can do for you here."

There was some muttering, before one of the Neri said, "We have many who are sick. If we bring them here, will you heal them?"

Ik felt a sudden rush of something like claustrophobia, only worse. *Heal them.* "I . . . will try. John Bandicut—it was my friend John Bandicut who healed. And his companion, the quarx." Ik struggled to find words of apology. "I have never, hrrm, attempted this . . . healing."

"But your—" *rasp.* The Neri pointed to his head.

Ik touched his temples. His stones. Doubts crowded into his mind, and in anguish he pushed them away. "Yes. I will try. It is all I can do."

"We will bring the first of the wounded," answered the Neri, and then he and several of the others sank out of sight.

Ik glanced at S'Cali and Delent'l. "What about the landers? Will they try to reach us here? Are they still fighting?"

S'Cali answered, "They've taken the hold where we left the sub. But we think they will come no further. The passages are narrow, and we can defend them. For now, however, we're trapped here."

Ik rolled his tongue in thought, wondering what the landers would do with S'Cali's abandoned sub. But that reminded him of something else. "What about the lander your people captured? Are you holding it somewhere inside?"

"It's in another chamber," said one of the other Neri.

"With air?"

Discussion among the Neri, too quick to follow. "No. It is wearing breathing devices."

Ik blinked his eyes in alarm. "There might be a limit to how long its devices can keep it alive underwater. Can you bring it here? Or at least to an air chamber?"

S'Cali seemed surprised. "We had not decided what to do. You think it is important to keep it alive?"

"Rakhh—*yes!*" Ik exclaimed. "Have you never made contact—or tried to communicate with the landers?"

More Neri discussion, this time with sharp, spiky edges to it. Finally S'Cali said, "We have never spoken with them. We do not know how."

Ik pressed his fingertips to his temples. Never spoken . . . Moon and stars! This was just like the situation he had tried—and failed—to correct on the world of the Kuy. How could he hope to do any better here? *But you didn't have Li-Jared and Bandicut and Antares with you then,* he reminded himself wearily.

/Do you think,/ he murmured to his stones, /we might be able to help them speak to the landers?/ In reply he felt a faint tickle.

Several Neri light-globes were moving closer in the water just below. They broke the surface. Two Neri were supporting a third; several more gathered to help boost the injured one up beside Ik. Ik turned himself carefully to face the Neri. "This is—?"

"Rencandro," murmured someone.

Ik touched the Neri's arm. It felt burning, freezing; he couldn't tell which. "Was Rencandro swimming in the warm current?" Ik asked in a throaty voice, knowing the answer already. /Can we do anything for him?/

We will try. Call for Bandicut if you can.

/I would if I could,/ Ik sighed. He had never before heard the stones sound hesitant, wistful, afraid. It made him shiver. /Shall we?/ he murmured. With a great effort, he sank into a meditative trance, his hand on Rencandro's arm. Around him, the echoes of lapping water and Neri voices faded to a whisper . . .

Bandicut jerked his head up at the sound of L'Kell's voice. He must have dozed off again. It seemed impossible; but then, he couldn't remember the last time he'd had a good, sound sleep. "We are nearly there," the Neri said quietly. He was eating some berries and dried fish, and he offered some to Bandicut. The berries had a sharp, tart flavor; the fish was meaty and bland, with just a hint of salt.

As he finished eating, L'Kell began guiding the sub closer to the bottom, practically skimming the rock formations—probably to remain hidden as long as possible.

"What's the plan?" Bandicut asked. He thought, with a pang, that instead of sleeping, he should have been helping L'Kell prepare.

"We should be relatively secure, as long as we are in the sub, and don't come too close to any of their—" *rasp* "—bursters. Explosives."

Bandicut nodded. Bursters. He hadn't given much thought to the tactics of battle. Military tactics were not his specialty.

"We must find a way to contact our people. They may be sealed up inside the wreck, if the landers are still outside."

"Okay," Bandicut said. "How do we do that?"

"I'm not certain. Actually, all of them may *not* be inside. Some of them might be waiting outside. Or they might all be in battle—" He paused suddenly and peered intently out the window.

Bandicut squinted. "What is it?"

L'Kell pointed. There was enough sunlight in the water now to identify landscape features through the blue twilight. "There's the wreck. Now, I need you to keep a sharp watch. Tell me if you see *anything* moving."

Bandicut hunched close to the window. The wreck was a long bulge rising from the bottom which he had at first taken for a ridge of stone. He felt a surge of adrenaline. He began scanning methodically.

"There!" he said, pointing to the left of the wreck, which had already grown larger and clearer. Several small, dark figures were moving just above the bottom.

L'Kell murmured. He was piloting very close to the silt and rock now. Bandicut squinted upward for a moment; he thought he'd seen a momentary surface flicker. He guessed they were a hundred or so meters down. The air pressure in the sub had been bleeding off gradually. He thought about bends, and prayed that his normalization would hold.

/// If you have any problems,
I'll try to smooth things out,
increase your vascular pressure,
and so on. ///

/How much can you do?/ he thought with a dry throat.

/// Quite a lot, I hope.
The bends factors are complex;
it's pressure change, but not just pressure change.
It's mechanical, and chemical, and
affected by nucleating bodies in the blood.
We can try to minimize a lot of that.
If it works for your dolphins and whales,
it ought to work for you, too. ///

Bandicut took a deep breath. /Right. Good. I'm glad./

/// Hey, you're my only friend.
I don't want to lose you. ///

Bandicut blinked. /Thanks,/ he whispered.

L'Kell was circling to the right of the wreck. "Those were landers you saw. We'll steer clear for now. If our people are outside, they'll hear us."

No sooner had he spoken than a small group of Neri rose from the seafloor ahead of them and closed in alongside the sub. L'Kell slowed to bare maneuvering speed and turned on the outside comm. "What is your situation?"

The answer was too low, rapid, and distorted for Bandicut to catch, but L'Kell seemed to understand it well enough. "If the landers' numbers aren't too great, we might be able to force our way in," he said to the swimmers. "Stay close for now. I'll try to bring us all in together." He began gradually increasing speed. "It's going to be difficult," he said to Bandicut.

"The others are trapped inside? Ik, too?"

"They think so. They couldn't see what happened on the far side. But they heard bursters, and have since heard sounds from within the wreck." L'Kell made a hissing sound that Bandicut interpreted as anger, and frustration.

Bandicut peered ahead to the looming shape of the wrecked ship. Was it an ocean ship or a spaceship? The perspective was difficult, and the thing was half buried in silt; but it didn't look quite right for a submarine, and it was too streamlined for an orbital-parking ship, but not streamlined enough for an atmospheric lander. Perhaps configured for aerobraking—?

/// Does it matter what kind of ship it is? ///

/Yeah, actually, it might. If it's a spaceship, it could have very different characteristics inside—reactor powerplant, for one thing—from a seagoing ship. And depending on where it came from, and who was in it . . . well, we might need to consider the implications of its being here in the first place./

/// Meaning— ///

/Meaning, who owns it? And are its owners around? If they're going to be fighting over this, it would help to know some facts. And if the Neri have never communicated with the landers . . . there's really no way of knowing, is there?/

/// Unless we do something about it. ///

Bandicut sighed darkly. /Yeah. Unless we do something about it./

L'Kell brought them around to the far side of the ship. At least a dozen figures were hovering near the wreck. At the sub's appearance, they gathered in formation and moved to confront the Neri. L'Kell applied power, and with Neri swimmers keeping pace on either side, he began driving in fast, slewing S-curves toward the landers. It appeared they were entering into battle. And as far as Bandicut could tell, they had no weapons whatsoever.

CHAPTER 19

Healing in the Hold

THE RUSHING WATERS, the heat, the cold, the cries of pain and hope and despair, the desire to be healed, or to be put over the edge into the quiet of death . . .

Ik had never experienced anything like it.

He had felt empathic connections before, and the linkage of stones with Bandicut—and the near-telepathic fury of the ice caverns on Shipworld—but this was different; this was a full link into the *body*, not just the mind of another. And not just one, but one after another, starting with Rencandro. His stones must have learned more from Bandicut's than he had realized, because they had risen to the challenge. It was not quite the full, miraculous healing that Bandicut and his quarx had managed with Lako; but Ik had pushed Rencandro and another in the direction of recovery, given them a breath of hope—without actually orchestrating the entire healing, which he knew was beyond his abilities. Touching the third Neri, he'd had to retreat in the face of an overwhelming desire to die. That Neri breathed his last, shortly after Ik broke contact.

He was now working with his fourth, and achieving some success. But it was time to withdraw, before he lost too much of his own strength. The warning signs were there—the faintness, the loss of concentration. And the stones agreed. He shivered as he slowly drew away from the Neri. He sat a moment with his hand on the Neri's arm, gazing at the dark, silent face.

Rest now.

The stones were right, of course. But it was hard to let go. /There are so many more. So many to help./ Ik peered at the growing collection of disabled Neri, brought into the chamber by their fellows. /How can I rest?/

Who can you heal, if you fail, yourself?

/Hrahh,/ he murmured. To the nearest Neri, he said, "I must pause awhile. I must rest." And he was surprised by how tiring it was even to speak those words.

The Neri buzzed among themselves, and he sank almost involuntarily into a fleeting meditative trance, starting in and out of it even as the Neri voices echoed their raspy echoes around him. The air in the chamber was starting to become depleted, and there were now so many Neri out of the water, on the ledge beside him, that they were using up the air much faster than he would have alone. Ik searched tiredly until he found S'Cali, who was right beside him, gazing down at the Neri he had just attempted to heal.

"He seems a little stronger," S'Cali said. "Will he live?"

"I don't know," Ik whispered. "But the air is growing bad in here. Can these people recover as well in the water as in the air? I am finding it—" he paused, drawing air "—increasingly hard to breathe."

"I will see if there are some extractors available to freshen the air. If necessary, we can move you. And we can certainly move some of the ill," S'Cali said. He pulled something out of the water, which had been hanging from a line. It was the air supply pack that had malfunctioned and almost killed Ik. "This has been repaired. You must have struck something leaving the sub. The intake vanes were bent, blocking the flow of water through the air extractor. They have been straightened."

Ik muttered his thanks.

"If you need to sleep, you might be more comfortable in the water," S'Cali offered.

Ik hissed a restrained laugh. "No thank you," he said. "But I am glad to know that I can put this on, if I need to."

"Shall we leave you alone, then?" asked S'Cali.

"Alone? Please, no!" Ik barked. He hissed, and this time his laughter was a release. "Perhaps one or two of you could stay, with some lights."

"It is done," said S'Cali.

As L'Kell drove his sub into the path of the oncoming landers, Bandicut caught sight of more of them, riding powered sleds of some kind—one sweeping in from each side, trailing what looked like jet contrails, strangely beautiful in the twilight blue water. The contrails rose like a curling aurora borealis behind the sleds. He assumed that the sleds were armed. After he pointed them out to L'Kell, the Neri grunted, smoothed out his final S-curve, and bore down with full throttle upon the formation of lander swimmers.

Before the sleds could get close enough to harm them, the Neri swimmers were in the midst of the landers. A melee ensued, not so much a battle as a mutual scattering, with the lander swimmers futilely attacking and then trying to get out of the way of the faster and more maneuverable Neri. Bandicut saw some flashes of spears and knives, but couldn't tell if anyone was actually being hit. At last the sleds, moving a good clip faster than L'Kell's sub, churned in close.

"If those things are armed with bursters—" L'Kell muttered. He veered again toward the thickest concentration of lander swimmers. The sleds roared past without firing. One contrail, then another, boiled past the sub's nose. "They don't want to hurt their own people!" L'Kell cried jubilantly. Indeed, the lander swimmers were too close now for explosives to be used safely. L'Kell turned once more, keeping the sub moving through the midst of the landers. There were two loud clangs on the hull as spears hit the sub.

Bandicut craned his neck to follow the landers' movements as the sub passed them by. "They're fleeing! They're heading up, toward the surface."

L'Kell made a rasping sound. "We've scared them away! All it took was a show of force!"

Bandicut grunted. The landers were indeed ascending, moving as quickly as they could away from the Neri. A few Neri swimmers gave chase briefly, but dove away when lander sleds returned to guard the retreat. As the landers disappeared into the misty water overhead, Bandicut noted that they seemed to be moving at a cautious rate. "*Maybe* we scared them," he murmured to L'Kell.

"You think they're not fleeing?"

"They're fleeing, but I'm not sure it's just because they're frightened."

L'Kell cut the sub's speed to let the Neri regather around him. "What do you mean?"

"They're from the surface," Bandicut said. "They might be running low on air. And I doubt that they have your ability to withstand pressure changes." L'Kell turned his eyes in puzzlement. "Remember I told you it might kill me if I went straight to the surface from your city?" L'Kell had been surprised at the time. The seapeople seemed practically immune to the bends. But if a human tried to make the kind of depth changes that the Neri made routinely— without being "normalized" on Shipworld, anyway, and without stones—he would die in agony as nitrogen bubbles fizzed out of solution in his body. It seemed likely that the landers were vulnerable to the same problem, since it arose from basic gas physics and only a highly adapted physiology could circumvent it.

L'Kell was steering the sub toward a large, dark gash in the side of the wreck. The ship now loomed before them, and for the first time, Bandicut could see an encrustation of sea growth on its surface. He squinted, trying to get a better look—and his heart nearly stopped when three landers suddenly flashed out of the wreck, chased by Neri swimmers. Two of the landers made their escape upward, but the third took a spear through its abdomen— and sank, writhing, toward the bottom. Bandicut shuddered, as the dying lander and the pursuing Neri dropped out of his view. He hadn't even gotten a good look at the lander, but he didn't have to, to feel the horror.

"This sickness?" L'Kell said, without mentioning what they had just seen. "It might keep them from returning?"

Bandicut grunted. "It would mean they can't stay down for more than a short time, without getting sick or dying on the way back up. They're probably partway up right now, hanging at an intermediate depth—"

"Waiting to come back down?" L'Kell barked. "We should go after them!"

"No!" Bandicut said, shaking his head. He didn't want a blood-bath on his conscience. "I mean they're decompressing slowly, on their way up. If I'm right, they *can't* come back down—not right away, and probably not today. Although others might come, I suppose."

L'Kell muttered darkly to himself. "Then we'll station guards, while we investigate inside the wreck. But I hope you are right about this, John Bandicut."

/I hope I am, too,/ Bandicut thought.

Steering the sub into the breached-open hull, L'Kell pointed to another Neri sub, almost lost in the shadows—jammed against an inner wall of the hold. "It's S'Cali's. And look." L'Kell pointed to the nose of the sub.

Bandicut couldn't see much, no real sign of damage. But no light shone within its interior, and there was no movement in-side, and—wait a minute. Was it *flooded?* Yes, there was an air pocket near the top of its viewport. Bandicut grunted, trying not to jump to conclusions. "The landers attacked it?" he said, not voicing his real fear, which was that Ik was inside, drowned. And if not, then where was he?

L'Kell spoke on the comm to several Neri swimmers who had emerged from the shadows, then reported, "Your friend is alive, inside the shipwreck."

Bandicut's breath went out in a rush. "Is he all right?"

"I do not know his condition," L'Kell said. "But you are needed inside. We must get you in there."

"How?" Bandicut frowned. "Will the sub fit?"

"We'll have to swim. And we should hurry, before any pikarta turn up." Parking the sub beside the other, L'Kell crawled back to the aft compartment. He brought out a set of gear that resembled something from an old Jules Verne holo, with an odd-looking hood and a backpack that looked as if it had been handmade from old junk. Bandicut shuddered; he'd been hurriedly fitted for the gear before setting out, but he'd prayed that an emergency requiring it would never arise. "It is quite safe for our young," L'Kell said, as though reading his thoughts. "There is no reason why it shouldn't serve you just as well."

Bandicut could think of plenty of reasons. "Is Ik wearing one of these?"

"I don't know how else he could have gotten out of the sub."

Bandicut held up the hood. /Charlie, old boy—/

/// —old girl— ///

/I hope you're ready to do some emergency resuscitation./

*/// Do we know there are Neri in need
of resuscitation? ///*

/I wasn't thinking of the Neri./

/// Oh. ///

With L'Kell's help, Bandicut began to put the thing on.

It was unnerving, swimming with a hood over his head that might have been made of leather and transparent seaweed, and a flow of air that was cold and salty and filled with a dozen unidentifiable smells. Bandicut tried to keep up with L'Kell, but without swim fins it was difficult. L'Kell offered to tow him by his straps, but Bandicut waved him off and began boosting himself along the corridor by grabbing wall protrusions and bulkheads.

He had kept his clothes on, counting on a ghostly forcefield created by his stones to keep him dry. Buoyancy control had proved a bit of a problem, until L'Kell had attached some small weights to his vest.

They had left the chamber where the sub was parked, and were making their way down a long, dark corridor into the heart of the ship. There were few sea-growths on the inner walls; apparently the local varieties required light to thrive. Chemoluminescent lamps carried by the Neri provided the only illumination. Bandicut thought he felt a current moving through the corridor. He also thought he saw ghosts and sea monsters drawing back out of sight every time he turned his head. /What the hell are we doing here?/ he thought with a shiver.

/// Is that a rhetorical question? ///

He didn't bother answering.

They swam some distance, making half a dozen turns in the ship's corridors, until they arrived in a largish space where a number of Neri were gathered in the water. It was a surreal-looking gathering, a slow dance of dark, big-eyed creatures of the night, caught in the ghostly glow of the Neri lanterns. One other thing caught Bandicut's attention—a rippling shimmer off to one side. No—it was overhead. An air space! L'Kell led him upward, and they broke the surface. Bandicut sculled the water with both hands as he peered around out of the awkward Neri hood. The visor started to fog up, but before it did, he glimpsed a semi-level surface above the water, with several figures on it.

/// Was Ik there? Did you see him? ///

/No./ Bandicut felt a gentle push. He was being nudged toward the ledge. He tried to propel himself, and realized that it had been a long time since he had tried to swim with scuba gear on the surface, especially with no fins and a fogged visor. It was harder than it looked.

Someone gave him another push from behind, and L'Kell had his straps now and was towing him the remaining distance to the ledge. Then he had his hands up on it, and felt a rocketing boost under his feet. Before he knew what was happening, he'd made an effortless vault onto the ledge. Gasping, he turned and sat with his legs dangling in the water.

/// Do you suppose this air is breathable? ///

Charlene asked.

Before he had time to wonder, several sets of hands began disconnecting his gear and lifting the hood from his head. His first breath was an involuntary gasp; then he caught himself and tried to sample it more critically. It was metallic, and smelled like low tide, but seemed perfectly breathable.

L'Kell perched beside him as he looked around in the lantern glow. There was no sign of Ik, but a half dozen or so Neri were sitting or lying on the ledge. It was a good-sized chamber, maybe a hold—or more likely, a working room; he could see obscure-looking machines mounted on the walls above his head. Instruments? Tools? Is that what the Neri were salvaging? He wondered if the ship had come to rest upright, or on its side; maybe they were sitting on a wall or partition. If it was a spaceship, he wondered what the bridge looked like. Or if it had a bridge.

/// John? I think you'd better
take a look at these Neri. ///

He turned and looked more closely at the Neri behind him. They didn't look good. "The sick and wounded," L'Kell said. "Can you do anything for them?"

Bandicut suddenly felt as if he had just landed in a transmogrified war holo, in one of those scenes in a field triage unit, where the wounded are everywhere and the doctors and nurses are desperately trying not to show their despair. "I don't know," he admitted. "Do you know where Ik is?"

L'Kell was talking to another Neri. Suddenly he pointed. "Down there, I think."

Bandicut squinted into the water. Lights were moving, and shadowy figures. Moments later, the water broke, and someone surfaced wearing a helmet much like his, and was practically catapulted out of the water by his escorts. Bandicut reached out a hand to steady him.

"Jesus, Ik, am I glad to see you!" he said hoarsely.

Ik couldn't speak until he was freed of his gear. "Hrahh!" he cried in return, his voice strained. "John Bandicut! You came! But I thought you were down in the abyss." The Hraachee'an's eyes sparkled with an inner fire of joy.

"I was," Bandicut whispered, squeezing his friend's arm. He was so happy to see Ik he nearly wept. "But I heard you needed a doctor here."

He meant it with a trace of humor, but Ik looked around and said soberly, "It is true, my friend. I have done what I can—"

"You mean you can heal, too?"

"My stones have learned some things from yours. I hope I have helped some of the patients back in the other chamber. Only time will tell." Ik rubbed his temples with what seemed great weariness. "They brought me out because the air was going bad and they didn't have the equipment they needed to set up air purifiers." Ik turned and scrutinized the air space surrounding them. "We can last a while here, I suppose. And then we will have to put our equipment on again. I don't know how many spaces like this there are in this wreck."

"Do you know what the wreck is? Is it a spacecraft?"

"That is my guess. But I do not know for certain. And I do not think that the Neri know. Perhaps, for now, it doesn't matter."

"Maybe," Bandicut said. "Maybe not." He rubbed the back of his neck, frowning.

Ik turned to peer at the Neri lying on the ledge. "We should not delay. Many of these people are very ill."

Bandicut took a deep breath. /Are you ready?/

/// Ready as I can be. ///

"Then let's begin," he said. He slid over and touched the arm of the nearest patient on his side. /It's going to be a long night./

It was an even longer night than he had imagined—perhaps not by the clock, but in the toll it exacted from his mind and body. When he finally looked up and met Ik's gaze, then L'Kell's, he could barely register their expressions. He had labored long and hard, imagining himself a physician working deep into the night in a city hospital . . . and as a Neri healer, striving with inadequate tools to bring together spirit and flesh . . . as one of the shadow-people of Shipworld, probing intricate and mysterious systems . . . as a mage from ancient fairy tales, tirelessly spinning enchantments of healing and power. In the end, though, it was just himself and Charlie, working with the stones. And not far away, Ik working in his own silence.

Glancing to one corner, he noticed someone sitting between two Neri—a little smaller than the Neri, its face obscured by a mask and an array of tubes and hoses. Bandicut rubbed his eyes, wondering if he was dreaming, in the surrealistic near-darkness. He glanced at his friends and glanced back. The being was still there. Who was it? Or what? A lander?

The quarx seemed to be trying to find an opening in his blurry consciousness to speak.

/// John— ///

/Yeah,/ he sighed, forgetting the strange sight as quickly as he had noticed it. /You did . . . good work./ He felt a flicker of pain as he said that. They had lost three patients that he knew of. He thought they had healed more than they had lost—five, maybe, or seven. Truthfully, he had lost count.

/// I think . . . you know . . .
you had better get to some fresh air. ///

/Fresh air?/ he thought muddily.

/// John, I'm . . . John . . .
I'm trying to compensate,
but the air has gotten really depleted . . . ///

He rubbed his eyes again. He was dimly aware, now that he

214 | Jeffrey A. Carver

thought about it, that he was breathing shallowly and rapidly. Waves of lightheadedness were passing through him. He was suffocating. So was Ik, probably. Damn. He turned his head to squint at L'Kell, and had trouble getting words out.

"Rrrrm . . . hrahh . . ." Ik looked unsteady, as well.

He managed to fumble for the helmet of his breathing gear. It slid away from him and splashed into the water. Sank.

Dear God.

/// John, I don't know if— ///

There was another splash, and the helmet flew back up onto the ledge, propelled by a Neri hand. Someone else grabbed it before he could move. *Wait . . . I need that . . .*

There was some jostling around him, and then the hood came down over his head like an oversized hat, and someone was strapping the breathing gear onto his back. He gasped; the air in the hood was no better; in fact, it was worse. He started to grope blindly.

Something pushed him from behind. He flailed. The water crashed around him, deafening him, enveloping him. Drowning him. *Please . . . no . . . I need . . .* The water was cold, momentarily overwhelming his insulating forcefield—and jolting him alert for a second.

He choked, air rasping into his lungs. On about the fourth breath, it started to seem different. Better. He gulped . . . sweet, oxygen-rich air. Panting out the carbon dioxide, he was still dizzy; he was tumbling through the water. Then someone was holding him.

/// Are you . . . okay . . . John? ///

/Yes,/ he whispered. And gradually his vision and his thoughts cleared. And slowly he comprehended what the Neri had done. The breathing gear had only a small reservoir of air; it drew fresh oxygen from the water, and flushed out the carbon dioxide. The only way they could revive him was to get him back into the water, fast.

Someone was floating in front of him, peering worriedly. Finally he made out who it was—L'Kell. And beside him, also slowly recovering, was Ik.

/// That was close, John.
We couldn't have gone much longer. ///

She was right. But why hadn't his body's own warning systems alerted him to the danger, before the critical point? The stones, at least.

/// I think we were all
too focused on the healing. ///

/We all?/

/// The stones included.
They lost track. ///

/I'll be damned,/ Bandicut whispered. He shook inside his helmet and gave a little laugh. /The stones make mistakes. I can't tell you how much that cheers me./

/// ??? ///

/You'll either understand it, Charlie, or you won't./ Peering at his friends, Bandicut slowly raised his right hand and held up a circled thumb and forefinger, first to L'Kell, then to Ik. The standard diver's signal: OK / OK?

His two friends looked at him in apparent puzzlement as he wondered: might the stones have passed on this bit of linguistic obscurity in their exchanges?

Ik finally raised his right hand, attempting to reproduce the gesture. He had trouble deciding which of his two thumbs to close with which finger, and finally presented Bandicut with a double-O, and a single unopposed finger sticking up. Bandicut nodded and looked at L'Kell. The Neri was trying, too, but the webbing got in the way, and his forefinger didn't seem jointed quite right for the gesture. Nevertheless, the intent was clear. Bandicut nodded.

"Are you recovered?" he heard in a scratchy voice from L'Kell. He had forgotten about the comm in the helmet.

"I'm okay. But we can't breathe this air any longer."

"We know," L'Kell said. "Let's swim. There will be more air in the corridor, where there's a moving current." They kicked downward, making their way slowly through the flooded gloom.

Their swim was interrupted by a rasping outcry and sounds of a commotion. Bandicut paused, turning in confusion; he couldn't tell where it was happening, but several Neri streaked past them, on their way out of the compartment. "What is it?" he asked.

L'Kell shot ahead briefly, then returned, looking agitated. "The lander prisoner!" he cried. "It escaped while we were distracted over the air! It's fled out into the ship."

Ik and Bandicut exchanged glances. Ik's voice rasped incomprehensibly; his comm didn't seem to be working. Bandicut wondered what Ik knew about the prisoner. That must have been the creature in the face mask. L'Kell was trying to get them to move faster—as if they would be of any use in trying to capture an escaped lander. They did their best, but in the end they simply limped along behind L'Kell.

They reentered the long corridor and followed it around several bends. The lander was long gone, but according to Neri who were swarming about, it apparently had fled further into the ship, rather than trying to get out past the Neri guards. Perhaps it knew it had no chance that way. Perhaps it was suffering from air problems itself and was delirious.

Bandicut felt a twinge of sympathy for the being. Even if it got away, where would it go? It was unlikely that its people would be waiting directly outside to rescue it—and could it even survive the decompression after so long at this depth? Quite possibly it was acting in blind desperation, with little or no real hope.

The layout of the ship remained unfathomable to Bandicut; he had seen nothing, really, except winding and turning corridors. But one thing he had noticed was that there were curves bending in all three dimensions in the corridors, which suggested that it was designed for either zero gravity or variable gravity.

If that was the case, what was a spaceship—starship?—doing on the bottom of the ocean? What had brought it here, and was there any relationship between it and the Neri, or the landers?

> /// *The stones are pretty much with you*
> *on this one.* ///

/Meaning what? They know what it's all about, but don't want to tell me?/

Char seemed puzzled by his tone.

> /// *I don't think they know the answers.*
> *But they suspect some of the same connections*
> *that you do.* ///

/And what connections do I suspect?/

> /// *The ship. And the landers.*
> *Probably not the Neri.* ///

Bandicut frowned, peering down the tomblike corridor. A pair of Neri were down at the far end, exploring with their lamps. L'Kell and the others nearby were looking forward and back now, uncertain which way to go. Bandicut had a sudden thought. If he were the lander, an air-breather in a foreign environment, trying to get away from pursuing fishmen, where would he go?

> /// *I don't know.*
> *Is there an answer to that?* ///

Bandicut turned to L'Kell. "I'm betting he won't try to get out right away. He's been down too long for easy decompression. If it were me, I'd try to find an air chamber I could hide in until my own people came back. That's if he's in his right mind."

L'Kell looked puzzled. "Why wouldn't he be?"

"He might be injured, his air might be bad, who knows?" Bandicut gestured. "*I* was pretty frantic when *I* started to run out of air. And if that's the case, we have to find him fast or he may die." He thought desperately. "Are there other air chambers? Places where he might hide?"

"It's a large ship," L'Kell said. "We've only explored a fraction of it."

Bandicut chafed. "But isn't there—"

A Neri sped into view from over his shoulder. "The lander has been spotted upcurrent, moving deeper and higher! Two swimmers have gone after him."

"Toward the room of madness?" cried a Neri named S'Cali, with alarm in his voice.

"Room of madness? What is that? Is that the reactor? A place where you think there's radiation?" Bandicut turned around, his own fear growing.

"I don't think so," said L'Kell. "At least, there's no warmth in the current there, and no glow. We don't know what it is. But—"

"What?" asked Bandicut.

"Two of our people ventured there when we first started exploring—and it drove them—" *rasp* "—mad. Not like the radiation sickness. It was their minds. They died—crying and babbling." L'Kell looked around among his companions. "Why would the lander go there?"

"Maybe he doesn't know," said Bandicut. "Maybe he has no idea, or he's gone crazy. But if he's trying to hide, and that's a place your people are staying away from—"

"We'd have to swim in after him," S'Cali said, and there was fear in his voice.

Bandicut drew a breath. "Can you take me that way?"

As they approached the expanding end of the corridor, where the room of madness was said to be, the Neri grew increasingly apprehensive. Bandicut met Ik's gaze flickering through the hood, and could practically read his thoughts: John Bandicut, do nothing foolish.

/// That is good advice.
Why are we doing this? ///

/I'm not sure. A hunch. He might have gone somewhere else, and maybe they'll find him. But if he's gone to this room, Char, we've got to go after him. That lander might be crucial. The first chance for contact, for communication. We *can't* let him go. And we *might* save his life./

The quarx hesitated a moment.

/// *Okay.*
I just wanted to be sure you had a reason. ///

/I'll need you and the stones to help me./ Bandicut took several deep breaths. /They're sure they can stop radiation with that forcefield?/

/// *For a time.*
It might put a drain on their reserves.
And they might not be able to stop everything. ///

/Okay. And the rest?/

/// *Well, we don't know what to expect,*
do we? ///

/No. But if this is a starship—well, I have some memories of "spatial transformation" on the way from my home star out to Shipworld. It was really, *really* weird—but the stones helped pull me through it. But the *Neri*, now—it would be even more alien to them—and without stones, it might well kill them./

/// *You're making a pretty big guess here.* ///

/I know. You ready if we have to go in?/
The quarx said nothing. She was ready.

CHAPTER 20

The Madness Room

TWO NERI WERE waiting near the entrance to the room, and they both looked nervous as hell. They reported that they had lost sight of the lander, but thought it had come this way.

"You don't know if it's in there?" asked L'Kell.

"We think it is. We saw *something* move in there. But we didn't want to go in," murmured one of the swimmers. "We didn't know what might happen—"

"Very well," said L'Kell, with a glance at Bandicut, who thought, /This is it, Char./ With L'Kell, Ik, and S'Cali, Bandicut moved cautiously past the swimmer and peered into the chamber opening.

The room was oval and about the size of a small gymnasium, and completely flooded. It was hard to see clearly, with only the Neri lanterns for light—and one other, tiny light source visible on the far side of the room. The lander, with a stolen Neri lantern? If so, it wasn't moving. Bandicut and his friends hovered just outside the entrance, taking a careful look. In the center of the egg-shaped room, a dark mass hung suspended like a petrified yolk; there was nothing but water where the white would have been. Bandicut could not tell, in the dim light, what supported the yolk. But there were definitely invisible forces active in the room. Even at the entrance, he could feel an indescribable tingle somewhere at the edges of his senses. He couldn't put a name to it, or even say which sense was affected, but it made him jittery in a physical way, like the effects of too much caffeine.

He took a slow breath to steady himself, and surveyed the perimeter of the room—the inner surface of the eggshell. It was not smooth, he realized, but festooned with spiky, spiral-shaped structures that looked almost like antennas. Was the whole thing some kind of space-time transformer? It was possible he was completely wrong; but it seemed to him that there was more visual distortion than could be accounted for by the water alone.

/// I feel resonances— ///

/Of—?/

*/// Ancient memories . . . transformations . . .
long voyages, before I knew you. ///*

Bandicut held his breath. */So you think—?/*

/// Your guess may be right. ///

With a grunt, Bandicut turned in the water to face the others. "I'll go in. I think the quarx and I can handle it."

L'Kell's huge eyes peered at him. "That would be very dangerous. I question whether—"

"I know, but I think it's worth the risk. L'Kell, if that's the lander over there, I might be able to bring it out, save it." He turned to Ik. "Can we use your rope as a lifeline?"

Ik's voice was weak and distorted without a comm. "Hrahh." He began stretching out the rope, attaching it to Bandicut.

When the rope was secure around his waist, Bandicut called to L'Kell. "I can't swim very fast, so I need all of you to give me a good, solid push, straight toward that light. Okay?"

"John Bandicut, I don't know—"

"Let's just do it, okay?"

"Very well," said L'Kell, waving to S'Cali and another Neri to help. "Be careful, my friend."

Bandicut nodded, double-checked the rope, then caught Ik's eye and raised a circled thumb and forefinger. The Hraachee'an returned the gesture, and Bandicut turned to face the open chamber. He stretched his body so that he was floating horizontally, arms straight ahead. His heart pounded. "Ready!"

The Neri, with a long thrust, propelled him forward. "Let go!" he cried, then realized that they already had. He held himself rigid, stretching his momentum as he sailed through the water, across the open space, to the left of center. The tingling grew stronger around his head and shoulders and waist. As he felt his momentum failing, he gave a breaststroke kick and raised his head to check his position.

At least, that was what he'd intended. But instead of confirming his long, smooth glide, he found himself tumbling. /Wait— that's not right—/ Where he'd expected to see the central mass, he glimpsed a spinning array of spines, rapidly drawing closer. With a muffled cry, he tried to tuck, to change direction.

/// *Don't make any sudden movements!* ///

the quarx cried, applying just enough inhibition to slow his actions.

/What are you doing? We're going to hit—/

/// *I don't think so!*
It's an illusion!
Try turning your head—slowly. ///

He swallowed hard, turning. A spinning dizziness came over him, the world flipping . . . flipping again. Something was disrupting his equilibrium. He caught a sharp breath, reaching for his flight skills in spatial disorientation: When feelings contradict reality, ignore the seat-of-the-pants, suppress the instinct, follow the instruments. But there were no instruments here—just vision, and Ik's rope to pull him back. Ik's rope! He felt it slithering loose from his waist, and grabbed for it—too late. Gone! The spines and spirals were growing before his eyes. It was like silence-fugue, bad—but it wasn't silence-fugue, it was real.

/Charlie, help me!/ he whispered.

/// Working—the stones— ///

The answer was breathless, but the quarx was true to her word, and an instant later, he saw a spidery grid superimposed over his vision. /What's that—?/

/// The stones are
tracking your course changes.
I'll interpret— ///

He tried to answer, but his breath went out and he couldn't do anything except let go and allow the knowledge of the stones to flow through the quarx into his muscles.

He rotated slightly and stroked once, hard, with his arms. The deadly outer shell of the room ballooned and distorted, and opened up like a billowing curtain. In the center of the opening was the central mass, the egg yolk quivering like gelatin in zero gravity. A wave of dizziness passed through him. And along with it a feeling of another kind, a feeling that something or someone was nearby.

The lander?

The feeling was indistinct, reminding him of the neurolink. But there was a sense of disconnectedness, as if a gulf of space, or wavelength, or phase separated the someone-else from him, like a silent wall. He probed the surroundings with his thoughts, as he might have probed a neuro, trying to find the source of the feeling.

He felt a stirring in response, but couldn't identify it as animate or inanimate. He was losing his visual connection to this place, as if the dark mass had softened and surrounded him; he felt as if he were probing, falling through a wall of smoke, or something wispier yet firmer, light as smoke but solid, like an aerogel. He felt a boundary layer between where he was and where the something-else was. There was nothing humanlike about it; but it was aware of him, reacting to him, making ripples through some level of space-time to which he was sensitive.

/// I feel a sense of something long . . .
very long. ///

/Long, like in local terms?/

> /// *Long, like . . . cosmic.*
> *Like a thread, or a tunnel,*
> *stretching to infinity.* ///

Bandicut shivered, suddenly wishing that he had not come here, had not made this connection. He felt utterly impotent, and ignorant, in the face of these forces. What did he think he was going to do, remake them? He thought he knew what this was now, thought it was a kind of reactor—or no, not really a reactor, it was a—

> /// *Stardrive,* ///

the quarx murmured.

/Yes,/ he answered. And maybe it was disabled, or broken, maybe it no longer had the power to move a spacecraft—but it was not dead, not yet. He vividly remembered "threading space" with Charlie-Two aboard *Neptune Explorer*, and though it had seemed mind-bogglingly strange at the time, he suspected that this thing was more exotic, perhaps more like the "spatial transformation" that had propelled him from the solar system to the cold darkness of intergalactic space.

> /// *Possibly. Possibly true.*
> *But . . .* ///

The quarx was uncertain, and he knew she was trying to piece together his old memories with her old memories, trying to weave in whatever understanding the stones were able to give her.

> /// *The tunnel I feel here is more like . . .*
> *the star-spanner, I think.*
> *Not driving you, exactly, but firing you*
> *through the light-years.* ///

Char's words gave him a sudden, cold fear. /This thing is a star-spanner?/ Was it about to hurl him across interstellar space, ripping him from his friends and his last vestiges of—?

/// No, I don't think so.
It doesn't seem on the verge of that.
But if it is a star-spanner,
the stones think it's not from Shipworld. ///

/Then—/

/// And here's the other thing:
you're not actually in its presence—not yet.
It's not here with you. ///

Not in its presence? Bandicut thought. Then whose presence was he in? He felt himself rotating slowly in the water, and had a vision of the room's core, the central mass, curved around him like a doughnut. There was some serious bending of space-time happening here, and he didn't know whether to be fascinated or terrified.

/// John, I find this very confusing—
and yes, terrifying.
I don't want to stay here any longer than we have to. ///

Bandicut peered around anxiously, remembering with a jolt that he had come in here looking for the escaped lander. But his eyes were wavering, and he wasn't sure he would recognize the lander even if he saw it.

/// John, whatever we're directly in the presence of
is connected to something far more powerful,
and dangerous. ///

Bandicut drew a breath of dank air—and suddenly knew what the quarx was referring to. /The Maw of the Abyss? Are you telling me that this *spaceship* is connected to whatever's down there in the bottom of the ocean?/ He reeled at the thought.

Char didn't answer, didn't have to.

/I will be b'joogered,/ he whispered. And his thoughts began spiraling off in a way that might have led to silence-fugue or worse, but somehow stayed controlled. Maybe it was Char's influence, but whatever the reason, his thoughts were spinning in an uncanny convergence of rationality and intuition. He was coming to an understanding, and not by the usual route; it felt like speeding in an airplane around racing pylons, and scooping up words and data and clarity in a whirl that left no time for breath or articulation of thought.

He came to, with a shivering intake of breath—and a realization that he was rotating physically. He was peering down the barrel of a long, faintly glowing tube, and moving slowly toward it. That was what Char feared. He was not *in* the Maw, but he was close to it in some terrifying fashion; this thing surrounding him was intimately connected to the Maw, and had been since its arrival on this world.

/That's it,/ he whispered.

/// What's it? ///

The quarx had been trying to keep him together all this time, and she was dazed.

/That's what happened to the ship—I think./

/// You mean . . . ?
Wait—the stones are getting
some kind of data download. ///

/Data download?/ He waited, not speaking. As Char gathered the data, he let his mind fill with the resulting images, and slowly realized . . . *were they downloading from some interstellar blackbox recorder the events that had brought this craft down?* The images formed quickly and bewilderingly, but he caught the central event:

The stardrive, its tendrils extended into whatever tortured reality defined its operating regime, was caught in intersecting space-time fields projected by something deep in a distant planet. It should not be possible, but it was; it was trapped in a tightening web, unable to free itself. From orbit, unable even to turn itself off, it was being drawn into a deadly, spiraling descent . . .

The landing was cushioned by the same forces that caused it. The spaceship, half in and half out of normal space-time, did not so much crash as *materialize* at the bottom of the atmosphere, meters above the ocean surface. The impact, though hard enough to shatter critical stardrive components, was not so hard as to kill most of the passengers. It remained on the surface awhile, sinking slowly enough to allow for evacuation of living inhabitants and some hardware and supplies; and then it sank beneath the waves, leaving a scattered armada of rafts and makeshift boats to struggle toward shore.

The stardrive remained locked in the deathgrip of the strange thing that had doomed it. It moved a little, by fits and starts, closer to the thing. And its people, those it had carried across the stars in search of a new home, vanished over the waters and made themselves known only by whispering, half audible transmissions. Soon they did not even seem like the same people. They seemed even less so when they returned later, much later, to begin stripping the wreck, without so much as an attempt to speak to the soul of the stardrive.

There seemed a note of . . . regret? . . . or more like sadness . . . in the images. Was that a reflection of the beings who created the machine, or was it merely Bandicut and Char's interpretation?

Bandicut thought he heard something—a voice. Char?

/// Not me. ///

Then it spoke again. Not in words. The stones seemed unable to translate, or even put an overlay of meaning upon it. But he felt the stones' increasing *desire* to understand it. It was a thrumming kind of sound, like a string bass simulating a human voice. At first he'd thought he had heard it in his mind; now it seemed to be vibrating through the water, surrounding him, making his skin tingle.

And then it faded away.

/Did you hear that? Do you know what it was?/

/// I tried. But I couldn't—
wait, I feel something closer.
Do you feel it? ///

Bandicut strained, let his awareness drift back from its focus on the stardrive. There *was* something out there, something much smaller and weaker. Not a part of the stardrive connection. But it felt alive: confused, frightened.

/// Can you see it . . . with your eyes? ///

He blinked. He had become so engrossed in the inner contact that he had nearly lost his sense of the physical. The light was uneven, wavering, warped by the distortions of the stardrive core. He slowly turned. One instant, the stardrive seemed an archway surrounding him; the next, it was a strangely glimmering pinpoint in front of him.

And then he saw it, floating just beyond the pinpoint: a dark shape, bent and curled. It took him a moment to realize what it was, helpless in the fields of distortion. /Char—/

*/// Yes, that's it.
It's the lander, the one we came for. ///*

Bandicut nodded slowly; he'd had trouble remembering how this sojourn had begun—in an effort to capture, or rescue, the lander. /What now? I don't know if I can get over to it./ He moved his arms and legs, not so much to propel himself as to establish whether he *could* propel himself. He quickly found that his movement in the water was almost uncontrollable; there were invisible, and turbulent, currents here that he could not compete with.

/// Arms out—hold them still. ///

/Uh?/ He did as Charlie requested, but without understanding.

*/// If we can't control the currents,
maybe we can ride them. ///*

After a few moments of using his arms as vanes, he saw that it was indeed having an effect. He felt the current turning him and carrying him downward, but away from the lander. /Ride them where?/ he asked worriedly.

/// Toward the lander, I think. ///

/But this isn't—/

> */// The currents do not move in straight lines.*
> *The stones have been trying to track them.*
> *If we can sweep around ... ///*

He was, in fact, drifting below the core now, in a slow arc that perhaps would take him toward the lander, after all. At the same time, the shape of the room had begun changing around him, in a slow, elastic twisting. He steadied his nerves, and waited for the stones' grid to reappear in his vision; and it did, but just for a moment, and then the grid distorted and dissolved.

> */// They're losing track ...*
> *they're not sure anymore. ///*

He grunted, and blinked in a slow, methodical rhythm, taking in the surroundings each time his eyes opened, but taking care not to keep them open long enough for the blurring to make him any dizzier. He must have drifted into a more active zone of the space-time-altering fields. Now how the hell was he going to get out of it?

> */// Try to descend, ///*

murmured Charlene's voice, as though from a very great distance.

Descend? How could he possibly even know which way was down?

> */// Exhale ... streamline ... ///*

Of course; he had forgotten his basic diving skills. He expelled all the air from his lungs, pressed his arms to his sides. He felt himself beginning to sink.

A rainbow flashed around him once, twice.

And then he heard the voice of the stardrive, a chime singing to him.

/Please, stones—what are they saying?/

He was descending out of the field, he thought . . . or perhaps not. Something was propelling him forward, a current. He drew in a shallow breath and expelled it, trying to keep his negative buoyancy. Was the stardrive core over his head now? He could see only a haze of sparkling things that, for a startling moment, reminded him of the colony creatures called the Maksu. He called out silently, *Can you hear me? Can you stop this madness?*

The current carried him forward, and then he began rising in an arc that no amount of breath control would affect. And he heard a voice that was a little like the husky voice of Ik, and a little like the impossible metallic groan of the Maksu, and a little like a dozen other kinds of voices, saying, *"This one needs you. Can you help him to freedom?"*

And in that instant of uncertainty, he suddenly saw the curled, crippled shape of the lander directly before him. He reached out and caught the lander in his hands, and an instant later felt the current coiling about him, pulling him into a slow half-somersault. He struggled for a moment to slip out of the current, but it was hopeless. Ik, pull me in! he thought—then remembered that Ik's rope was gone. He drew a slow, even breath, and allowed himself simply to tumble with the disorienting movement of the current.

Lights seemed to sparkle and flash around him again, and then they went out; and he was lost in the darkness, the alien helpless in his arms.

CHAPTER 21

Deep-sea Express

IK STEELED HIMSELF to remain calm, even after watching his friend glide out into a dark emptiness which almost immediately came alive with bizarre glimmerings and twists of light. Bandicut had appeared to tumble, then fall feet-first into a ghostly whirlpool. Soon after he'd vanished from view, Ik felt his rope go slack. When he gave it an experimental tug, the other end sailed out of the darkness back to him, and the rope contracted into a coil in his hand. He could only curse in silence.

The strange lighting effects did not go away, but kept mutating, like a living thing. The Neri floating with Ik looked extremely agitated, and were no doubt terrified. One of them fled. Even S'Cali and L'Kell looked as if they wanted to. L'Kell was gazing somberly into the room, probably convinced that their friend was gone. For Ik, though, the continued play of light signified hope for Bandicut's survival. John Bandicut was a difficult person to kill. If something in there was still reacting to his presence, then perhaps Bandicut was still alive.

Ik kept silent, reminding himself to take the long view. And that meant not just faith in Bandicut, but a willingness to accept it if Bandicut were really gone. It was a good and useful exercise. And it was a damnably hard viewpoint to keep up.

It seemed he had been waiting a lifetime. He waited a few more lifetimes—and then he saw movement. He lost his composure

232 | Jeffrey A. Carver

and shouted madly at the Neri to move, move, *move!*

The madness room flickered and went dark, and John Bandicut came tumbling out of the darkness like a bouncing ball, head over heels. Ik was too clumsy in the water to assist, but the Neri flashed into position like fish, catching Bandicut with ease—Bandicut, and the lander he held in his arms.

The lander!

Ik made rapid arm strokes, moving slowly toward them. "John Bandicut!" His voice wasn't getting through. But now he could see Bandicut's eyes fluttering inside his helmet. Obviously he was disoriented, and possibly he was hurt. As Ik reached out to catch the human's arm, he got a look at the lander, limp in its diving gear. Was it alive? Ik couldn't see its eyes. He touched it, felt for movement or warmth, but couldn't feel a thing.

The Neri were crowding around them, L'Kell saying, "Let's get out of here. Let's get to the transport, before something else happens." L'Kell's voice was thin and metallic, but vibrating with urgency. He waved to the other Neri, and Ik felt two of them grab his straps, and they all began moving. He kept a tight grip on Bandicut and the lander, and counted the moments until they could get back to open air.

Bandicut was conscious but woozy as the Neri towed them down one corridor after another, toward . . . no, it didn't look as if they were returning to the chamber they had come from. He hadn't heard the plans. Maybe they were going to another air chamber. He wanted very badly to get this helmet off and stop trying to be a fish. He wanted to get his breath and rest. He could hear the Neri talking among themselves, but he didn't bother straining to hear what they were saying. They would tell him soon enough.

He kept a viselike grip on the lander's gear straps, dimly aware that he and it and Ik were all being towed together like a harpooned whale. He caught momentary glimpses through the creature's faceplate, as the lantern light came and went with the swimmers' movements. He could just tell that the lander's eyes were open, though it looked more dead than alive. Probably it was deep in some equivalent of shock. Was it suffering from air starvation? Or from the effects of the stardrive room? He wondered if there was anything he could do to help it.

/// I'm, uh, feeling a little better.
Maybe I could take a look— ///

/If you do,/ Bandicut muttered, /be damned careful./ One of these days, the quarx was going to reach out to make contact with someone, and they would regret it.

". . . okay? . . . let us take him? . . . try to relax . . ."

Who was that? He finally realized that it was L'Kell, talking to him. "Um—what did you say?" he grunted, probably not loudly enough to be heard.

"John Bandicut, are you all right?" L'Kell's voice was clearer and more urgent now.

"I think so . . ."

"Can you let go of the lander?"

"I—"

/// Don't. This is difficult. ///

His breath caught, and he realized that Charlie was already trying to make contact across the suit, water, and skin boundary. "Uh, no—" he said hoarsely to L'Kell "—let me carry him. He's hurt, I think. Needs help."

The Neri looked at him in puzzlement, but allowed him to maintain his grip on the lander. "We're going to try to get you all out of here," L'Kell said, and they glided down the gloomy, curving corridors like spirits in the night, or bats in a haunted house.

/// Hold on.
The stones are picking up
some radiation. ///

He was startled. /Radiation? What kind of radiation?/

234 | Jeffrey A. Carver

Bandicut blinked, and shouted to the Neri, "Stop, please! Radiation!" The Neri halted, alarmed, as he turned slowly, trying to look around. "Where are we? What is this passageway?" Was that a blue glow he saw ahead? Cerenkov radiation?

L'Kell moved closer. "We are making our way to another part of the wreck. There is a large—" *kkriiikk* "—cargo submarine, which we will use to transport the wounded and the captive. We believe this may be a good time to get out. It will soon be daylight outside. But there are not many landers around right now."

Bandicut was surprised. "You have a cargo sub here?"

"It is docked inside, on the other side of the ship. It is used to transport machinery, but it has been unable to get away. Until now, we hope."

Used to transport machinery? Bandicut suddenly recalled an image he had glimpsed during his contact with the stardrive: a view of the ship's passengers leaving the wreck after the crash and going ashore—and later, much later, returning to begin removing pieces of the ship. But there were different kinds of beings who came, and who took away pieces. Landers. Neri.

He suddenly realized that L'Kell had spoken again.

"John Bandicut—the radiation?"

The radiation! /Charlie?/

*/// It seems to be primarily in the gamma wavelength.
Probably emanating from a fixed source,
not radionuclides being carried in the water. ///*

Bandicut tried to think that through. If radioactive materials weren't physically being dispersed through the water, then they must have strayed close to the reactor itself. "L'Kell, we need to back up. Are we near anything like a cracked bulkhead—or any other indication of the reactor that I warned you about?"

L'Kell waved the others into retreat. "Something that we think *might* be the reactor is nearby, yes—but we've stayed upcurrent of it. We thought as long as we were upcurrent, and the water was cold . . ."

"Yeah, that's what I thought, too. But maybe there's a shield missing from the reactor area."

/// The radiation is falling off, ///

Char said, as they retreated around a bend in the corridor.

"We're safe here," Bandicut said to L'Kell. "But we have to find another way around."

They began backtracking, searching for a new route. This was clearly a part of the ship that the Neri did not know well. The corridors seemed to Bandicut to curve around like coils of rope unwinding. He wasn't sure if it was the layout of the ship, or a change in his perceptions resulting from the encounter with the stardrive.

/// A little of both, maybe.
This is very intriguing, John. ///

/Glad you're enjoying it. Have you made any progress—any contact?/ The lander was starting to stir in his grip.

/// Of a sort, though not verbal.
I believe he is aware of my presence,
without comprehending it. ///

/That's probably a good way to leave it for now,/ Bandicut thought. The last thing he needed at the moment was an internal alien encounter.

It took him a while to work it out, but the passages were apparently laid out in helical patterns that corkscrewed through the ship like worms tunneling through an apple. Possibly drunken worms. There were frequent openings and intersections, many of them set at odd and awkward angles. Several times, they passed through wider chambers in which strange-looking machines hugged the walls. Science labs? Control rooms? Cafeterias? It all looked, in the glow of the lanterns, like the remains of civilization from some mythical Atlantis, completely transformed from its original function.

"Do you know where this ship came from?" Bandicut asked L'Kell. He wanted to bite his tongue the instant the words were out. *Not now,* he thought.

L'Kell seemed puzzled by the question. "You know we don't. The sea is full of sunken vessels. This one is different, but—"

"As though built by someone else?"

L'Kell swam closer, then away, almost as if pacing in a Neri conference. "Yes," he said. "It's different, not just in machines, but in shape. We have often wondered what offshoot of our ancestors built it."

"I think," Bandicut said, "it is far more different than you know."

L'Kell, without answering, seemed thoughtful as he swam on.

———————

Eventually the passageway opened into a very wide and high space, relatively well lit by a large number of Neri lanterns. Occupying the floor of the space were several small, alien-looking vessels—spacecraft?—plus a submarine of considerable size. They swam closer. As they approached the sub, the space lit up with a burst of dazzling light—*sunlight,* Bandicut realized, squinting. The far wall of the great room was being opened, tilted outward, by Neri swimmers. Hangar doors! It must be morning outside, and even the pale sunlight that reached this depth was dazzling after the interminable gloom of the ship's interior.

L'Kell led them to the sub, where long doors were propped open, revealing flooded cargo compartments. Bandicut noted plenty of salvaged machinery littering the floor of the hangar, while the sub's cargo bay was filled with the outstretched forms of disabled Neri—including, he thought, some of the individuals he and Ik had attempted to heal. "Medical express to the city, on track one," he murmured.

"This is the only working sub left here, except the one you and I came in," L'Kell said. "We're going to leave the small one for those staying behind." Bandicut said nothing, but wondered why they were leaving Neri swimmers here. To maintain their claim on the ship? Or to guard and repair the damaged sub? "We can lock you through into the dry compartment," L'Kell said.

Bandicut felt a sudden jerk, as the lander started twitching in his grip. He caught a glimpse of the being's eyes, and thought he saw consciousness—and fear. Perhaps he couldn't accurately identify fear in the gaze of a lander, but he was sure of one thing: the being was in distress. "Can you lock the lander through, too?"

L'Kell hesitated. "We should secure him in back, I think."

"He won't survive there," Bandicut said sharply. "He should ride with us." The lander was struggling weakly as they spoke.

L'Kell opened his webbed hands. "I don't see how we can—"

"You can secure him up front, for God's sake! I doubt his diving gear can tolerate the depth of your city. For all we know, he could be running out of air right now!"

"But—"

"His diving gear might not pull air out of the water the way yours does! Trust me! We can guard him inside!"

"Very well," said L'Kell, looking genuinely puzzled. "He will be inside." Bandicut heard mutterings of complaint from some of the other Neri; but having decided, L'Kell held firm.

They floated into the forward cargo compartment, and Bandicut and Ik maneuvered into position beneath the airlock. They held the lander between them, and Ik gave his rope a couple of turns around the being. When the airlock membrane shimmered grey, L'Kell gestured, and they hoisted the lander up into the airlock, where Neri hands from above took hold and pulled him inside.

Bandicut went next. It was an awkward business, getting through the airlock with the breathing gear. By the time he was in the sub, he was panting from the exertion. The lander was slumped against a bulkhead. Bandicut squinted through his foggy visor, trying to see whether it was still breathing; it looked motionless. *Damn*, he thought. *It's dying.* "Get it out of its helmet!" he shouted, through his own hood. The attending Neri jumped at the shout, and began removing *his* helmet. "No, no!" he protested. But it was hopeless; he let them finish, and as soon as the thing came off his head, he shouted, "Get *his* helmet off!" and pointed urgently at the lander.

The Neri looked puzzled—and reluctant. Bandicut struggled to clamber over on his hands and knees, still wearing the awkward gear on his own back, to where he could get at the lander's helmet and mask. He fought to pull it off, but it wouldn't budge. Where was the clasp? He clawed at the thing, but was too exhausted to think straight, and with sweat and salt water in his eyes, he couldn't see very well, either.

The Neri finally moved in to help. They hissed and squawked at each other, but quickly removed the helmet. When the lander's head was exposed, they murmured excitedly. Obviously they were all seeing a lander for the first time.

Bandicut's first thought was that it looked a little like a short-nosed fox. It had the triangularity of face, and the tufted ears, and the short brown fur. Or perhaps it was not fur, after all, but a coarsely textured skin. Its two eyes were closed to thin slits, and Bandicut feared that they really had been too late.

/// May I? ///

/Uh? Of course./ Bandicut reached out a shaky hand and touched the lander on the side of the head, just a light brush of the fingertips. Its skin felt rough, and cool to the touch. Bandicut drew back slightly at the sensation.

/// It's alive, John.
Returning to consciousness. ///

Bandicut muttered in silent gratitude, and wished he could speak to the lander.

/// I'm trying to do just that. ///

The creature's eyes fluttered momentarily, then closed again. There was a noise behind Bandicut. Ik staggered from the airlock, followed a moment later by L'Kell. The Neri hastened to take Ik's helmet off, and the Hraachee'an leaned close to Bandicut. "You were in time!" he rasped.

The lander's eyes were open, staring at Bandicut. Its eyes had round pupils like a human's, surrounded by concentric rings of iris, and no white at all. The iris rings were colored in shades of brown, yellow, and orange, giving it an intense-looking gaze. It stared at Bandicut for a long time, then finally flicked its eyes around the compartment, taking in the Neri, and pausing for a moment on Ik. Then its gaze returned to Bandicut. Was it aware that Bandicut had saved it, or that he was the source of the quarx's inner touch? It had seen Neri before, no doubt, but what did it make of a human face, or the bony, sculpted features of a Hraachee'an?

Bandicut placed a finger to his lips, then his ear. "Can you hear me?" The lander's pointed ears perked slightly. "My name—" he pressed a hand to his chest "—is John. *John.*"

Clearly the lander *heard* him, because its ears twitched and moved like small antennas. But it made no sound in reply. Did it have a voice? Bandicut wondered. Perhaps it was in too much shock to speak.

"We do not mean to harm you," he said, resting his hands in his lap, with palms open. He glanced up at the Neri crowded around in the cramped passenger compartment, and hoped that they would honor his statement of reassurance, even if they personally desired retribution for their ill and wounded.

/// *He does not understand you.* ///

/I didn't expect he would. But I want him to know that we're at least trying to communicate with him. I thought, if nothing else, he might sense the tone. It was a long shot./

/// *I have inquired of the stones,*
whether they would like to offer
daughters to the lander. ///

/And?/

/// It's not an option.
They need a much longer period of regeneration
before they can divide again. ///

/Too bad,/ Bandicut thought, cocking his head to study the lander.

"We should be underway shortly," L'Kell said. He urged the other Neri forward to the cockpit. "The last of the wounded are aboard, and we're draining the holds. Do you want to get your gear off?"

Bandicut had almost forgotten the encumbering Neri diving suit. With L'Kell's help, he shrugged out of it; then they helped Ik out of his. Finally, with care, they removed what they could of the lander's gear. The being made no effort to resist. "Gonna be a crowded trip back," Bandicut murmured. The compartment already stank from the closeted bodies of four different species from various worlds. But he was grateful they were all still alive to be making the trip at all.

"How are the wounded?" Ik inquired.

"Some better, some worse," L'Kell answered. He stowed the gear and called forward to see if they were ready to move. He was answered by a lurch, as the Neri pilot applied thrust.

Bandicut could just see out a small side window. He glimpsed the walls of the wreck's hangar, then felt the brightening as they passed out into the sunlight. After the tomblike darkness of the wreck's interior, even this attenuated sunlight was like having a curtain of gloom stripped away.

"*Guuh.*"

He blinked, turning his head. The lander had just spoken. It was craning its neck to try to see outside. Bandicut sat back to give it a clearer view of the window. Probably that burst of sun-light was like a breath of fresh air to it; probably it was hoping against hope that they would, somehow, be heading surfaceward.

Bandicut closed his eyes for a moment and sighed, feeling for the captive. It was only a few seconds later that he felt the sub angle downward, beginning its descent. If there were any lander divers in pursuit, they would soon be left behind.

The lander probably thought he was deep in the ocean now. You don't even *know* what deep is, Bandicut thought pityingly. Get your last view of sunlight while you can. It could be the last view you'll have for a long, long time.

INTERLUDE

Julie Stone

"THERE'S SO MUCH I've been wanting to say, Dakota—to explain—as much to myself as to you. I only have enough time allowance for one full-holo transmission, but I want you to hear this, face to face—even if it's just one-way. And I want to get it right." Julie paused to adjust the holocam angle. "I know you have a lot of questions, and so do I. I'm still looking for answers. But I'll try to tell you what I can about your uncle, and what he did here."

Julie looked up at the shelf over her cubicle desk, where a grainy image of John Bandicut looked out at her. It was an image that Dakota Bandicut had emailed her—clipped from a family photo of a few years ago. He looked visibly younger than the man she remembered, his features a little softer, his brown hair free of those first strands of grey. She would have liked to see what the other Bandicuts had looked like.

"Thank you for the photo of John. It's hard to believe I didn't have *any* pictures of him—except one tiny image off a group photo that our friend Georgia took once. He had his eyes closed in that one. Sometime I'd love to see the rest of the picture that you took this image from; I don't know a thing about what John's family looks like. Please send me a picture of yourself?"

She drew a breath.

"This is so hard, Dakota. Before I say anything else, let me just say again—even though I've said it by email—that I am convinced that your uncle John saved the Earth from a terrible disaster, no matter what anyone else thinks. You know the evidence that's been made public. Well, I've gained some new information to support it." She swallowed. "Though I'm not sure how much of it I can share at this point."

She paused the camera to think. She paced for a few moments around her sleep compartment, then resumed. "I've had an experience that shook me, and also *might* lead to some of the answers we've been looking for. You know about the alien translator— know what John said about it, anyway, which was all any of us knew. Well, I know more now. I've spoken to it." She cleared her throat. "I've actually . . . met it and communicated with it. And it made one thing clear—and that was that John was telling the truth."

Was it okay to say that? The existence of the translator was public knowledge, but details were classified. Not that this was exactly a technical detail. But still, she had to assume that her transmissions were monitored, and she didn't want anyone coming down on twelve-year-old Dakota because of something she said. But she did want John's only surviving relative to *know*.

She backed the recorder up a couple of sentences and paused after the words, ". . . all any of us knew." She started again. "We're starting to learn more now. We've had some communication with the device, and it definitely confirms John's story . . ."

That wasn't much different from what she'd said the first time. She shrugged and let it go. But probably she shouldn't say much more about it—not until matters were clearer with the research boards. This business was far from over.

Yesterday's hearing had helped crystallize some things in her mind . . .

———

"Ms. Stone, do you have any idea why the artifact resists all of our efforts to communicate with it? Or for that matter, why it took five weeks from the time of first sensor contact for it to finally reveal itself physically to us, and—more intimately—to you?"

244 | Jeffrey A. Carver

Julie Stone studied the government representative for a moment before answering. This wasn't like a group meeting of the exoarch department; this was a preliminary hearing for the oversight bodies, and she didn't entirely trust those who were running it. She knew they were in a power struggle among themselves, vying for control of the translator, and anything she might say could be subject to misuse—or at least, narrow interpretation. "No," she said finally.

The three members of the hearing board glanced at one another. Government rep, MINEXFO (Mining Expeditionary Force), and science board. No one from exoarchaeology was on the hearing board; they were supposed to be represented by the science member—a man who had arrived on Triton just a week ago. The government rep, Macklin, spoke again. "You seemed to have to think about that, just now. Do you need time to reflect?"

"No," Julie said, without hesitation this time. In a way, she trusted the government man more than the others; he made no bones about his goal, which was to secure government control over the translator as soon as possible. But there were issues of ownership and interplanetary law that complicated the matter. Thank God. "I don't know why it resists your efforts," she said mildly.

"But it did communicate with you," Macklin pointed out.

"Yes, but it's not as if it told me everything I wanted to know."

"Well, then—no offense meant—did it indicate why it chose *you* for its contact? Was it just arbitrary, because you were the first on the site?"

Julie hesitated. "It didn't say, exactly. But I *suspect* it might have chosen me out of deference to John Bandicut. Because we were friends. And because it and Bandicut . . . worked together." Her words produced a silence, and she cleared her throat to fill it. The name John Bandicut was not one that met with wholehearted approval around here. Nevertheless . . . "I have a feeling—and it is only a feeling—that John *recommended* me to the translator."

The panelists continued to gaze at her. "I see," said Macklin after a moment. "Did it give any indication about its reason for maintaining secrecy, for staying in hiding?"

Julie shook her head. "My guess is that it was observing, and waiting for confirmation—which I know it got somehow—that the comet had been destroyed by *Neptune Explorer.* Perhaps it wanted to defer contact until then."

That look again from the panelists. Macklin scratched his head. "Yes, well . . . you know, it might take some time yet before the science teams are able to establish whether or not there was a cometary impact—"

She stifled a sigh of exasperation.

"—since the evidence, as I understand it, is not wholly compelling, either way."

"I find the evidence *quite* compelling," said Julie.

"But you have, as you've indicated, a personal bias."

"I don't have a bias that would make the translator *tell* me that he destroyed the comet, do I?"

Macklin shrugged his shoulders. "In any case, you say that the translator told you that it wanted your assistance with some future activity. Is that correct?"

"Yes. And I can't really tell you more than that, because it didn't *say* more." Which, she suddenly realized, was not quite the truth. She closed her eyes for a moment. *Something out there which is trying to destroy your world.* Had she really heard that, or was it just a lingering impression, or a dream? She felt a powerful reluctance to share it; too much ambiguity and uncertainty. Or was that just a rationalization? No, she thought—she wanted confirmation before she said something that inflammatory.

"You understand, Ms. Stone, that the object is not your personal property, nor under your personal protection." That was John Hornsby, representing the Interplanetary Science Board.

"Of course I understand," she said, bristling.

"Yes, well," said Takashi, of MINEXFO. "Since we have not yet established *who* will have permanent custody of the artifact, I suggest that we not get sidetracked on that issue." He did not actually look at Hornsby as he said that, but the tension between the two was evident.

Julie drummed her fingers on the table for a moment, trying not to seem stiff or defensive. "I have a suggestion, if you're interested."

"Of course," said Macklin, while Hornsby frowned.

"Two suggestions. One is you let me go back to the translator and try again. The other is—well, that you let the translator take the lead in communicating. It's been here for a million years already, and maybe it has its own ideas about who it wants to talk to and why."

"We keep coming back to that, don't we?" Macklin said. "It talked to you—and everyone wants to know why."

Julie flushed, wondering why she had to feel defensive about that. "I want to know, too. And if you'd let me try, maybe we'd get some answers."

Hornsby looked faintly ruffled. "That might, in time, be possible. But we have a full schedule of physical studies planned, which is not something we can lightly interrupt. Also—with respect—" an insincere smile flickered on his face "—we cannot afford to have the object treating any one person as sole designated representative. If you can understand that."

Julie said nothing, but thought, you might not have any choice in the matter.

"My own feeling," said Macklin, "is that we ought to just take the damn thing to Earth and quit screwing around with it here. Hell of a lot more resources for studying it, back home."

Julie felt a sudden flicker of panic. If the translator were shipped to Earth, and she were left here on Triton . . .

"That might not be feasible right away," said Hornsby. "There are issues of safety, of course. And we need to make detailed in situ studies. Plus—" he glanced at Julie "—I rather expect that the exoarchaeology branch would like some time to examine the site. Is that correct, Ms. Stone—if you can speak for your department?"

She nodded, her panic subsiding.

Takashi voiced his agreement, though no doubt for different reasons. Triton MINEXFO's claim could lose much of its power once the artifact left Triton.

Macklin shrugged. "I guess, then, that that's all the questions we have for you right now, Ms. Stone. Thank you for your time. You may be excused . . ."

Julie shook off the memory. She still felt guilty for what she hadn't said. And the questions weren't going to get any easier. A lot of people wanted access to the translator, for a variety of reasons. But the translator, she knew, would allow access to whom it wanted, when it wanted. She feared what could happen if an attempt were made to move it by force.

She restarted the holocam recording. "There's so much we don't know about the translator, Dakota—so much I look forward to learning—we all look forward to learning. This will be an exciting time. We may never get all of the answers. But we do know the one answer that counts—that John did his work well, his work of protecting the rest of us—you, me, everyone."

She hesitated, not daring to add the final thought: *And I'm afraid that work is not yet over.*

CHAPTER 22

Deadly Change

IT WASN'T LONG before Bandicut noticed that the lander was starting to look ill. His eyes were moving erratically and his breathing sounded labored.

/I wonder what—oh, mokin' A. Why didn't I think of it earlier?/ He reached out and touched the lander on the shoulder.

/// What do you—oh, I think I see.
The air mixture is becoming toxic for him
with the increasing pressure. ///

/He doesn't have the benefit of our "normalization." We're going to kill him by taking him that deep./ Since they'd begun their descent from the shipwreck, the internal pressure in the sub had been increasing to match the outside pressure. Bandicut had been so preoccupied keeping his ears and sinuses equalized that he'd forgotten the less obvious but far more critical issue: the need to adjust the balance of oxygen and other gases in the air as they went to greater depth.

"L'Kell!" he called. When the Neri came back from the cockpit, he explained the problem. "Can you delay pressurizing this compartment any more and still get us to the city okay?"

L'Kell's great black eyes studied the lander for a moment. "I suppose so. But we can't keep him indefinitely at a different pressure. I'll see what I can do for now, though."

Bandicut nodded, and kept his hand on the lander's arm. He felt the quarx trying to make contact. If she could even just calm him a little, that would be helpful.

A few minutes later, L'Kell returned from speaking to the pilot. "We can maintain this pressure without risk to the sub. But we'll have to use airlocks to enter the habitats. The pressure difference will be significant."

"Is there some way to give him a different gas mixture—if we could figure out what it should be? Or better yet—set up a chamber in the habitat where he could be kept at a lower pressure?" It was not just the immediate problem they had to consider; the deeper they took the lander, the harder it would be to return him to the surface later. Bandicut didn't know what the Neri's intentions were for the lander. He doubted they'd thought much about it. But returning the lander to his own people was very much Bandicut and Ik's hope.

The journey back down seemed much longer than the trip up. Maybe he'd just forgotten. With the pressure stabilized in the cabin, he managed to doze off for short stretches, sitting huddled on the floor of the cabin with Ik, the lander, and two Neri.

By the time they docked at the undersea city, the lander was breathing a little more easily—mostly from the calming influence of the quarx, Bandicut suspected. But he did not look well. His hands, brown and pebbly, with fingers shaped almost like pincers, were shaking. Bandicut glanced worriedly at Ik—who didn't look any too great himself, with dim eyes and a dull stare. In Ik's case, he hoped it was just exhaustion. The Hraachee'an had gone a long time without much rest, and that in addition to repeated rounds of healing—and oxygen starvation.

They were all in need of recuperation. But the lander . . . he wished he could do something more for the lander.

*/// If only we were able to transfer
a daughter-stone.
A stone could physically intervene. ///*

/If only,/ Bandicut murmured. /If only . . ./

Li-Jared was restless at the instruments—more than restless. He couldn't sit still. They had been trying to pin down these readings to predict the next eruption of the Maw, and the longer they worked at it, the murkier it became. He paced around Kailan's lab in agitation. His pacing didn't seem to bother the obliq or her assistant Elbeth. Probably he was getting on Antares' nerves, but he couldn't help it. He was sure she understood what he was feeling; she'd been emanating her own waves of frustration for a while now.

"So what *do* we know?" he muttered with a twang. And at the same time he voiced a plaintive inward query, /Can't you help with this at *all?*/ But from the stones there was no answer; they seemed highly preoccupied. They hadn't been much help lately.

"We know, star friend," said Kailan, answering his question, "that our Maw's reach extends up from the abyss, and down through the depths of the world—and now, you suggest, it reaches perhaps even beyond! That is more than I knew before—so do not be discouraged. And you have helped me understand three different instruments that were confounding me."

Li-Jared stopped pacing and shivered. He was cold, and hungry, and the feeling of being eternally damp was driving him crazy. But he admired this Kailan and liked working with her. She was smart and determined, and for all the gaps in her scientific knowledge, he was stunned by how much she did grasp. And it was remarkable how closely some of the Neri instruments resembled equipment familiar to him from Home, and from Shipworld. Form followed function, he supposed. He had tried to explain the basic concepts of spatial distortion to Kailan—that the abyss thing didn't just shake the planet's crust open to draw water through, but rather, opened the very fabric of space-time to create the channel. But knowledge and language barriers had made it difficult. He hadn't found an adequate way to explain how the Maw might be distorting space-time in a far more dramatic fashion than just channeling water.

He strongly suspected that the Maw had drawn the star-spanner bubble in from the stars like an iron flake to a magnet. No doubt the star-spanner had *intended* to put them here, but the Maw had provided the perfect homing beacon. And that was why they had landed so amazingly close to the Neri city.

"Li-Jared, do you have any idea how far the thing's reach might extend?" Kailan asked, drawing him back to the present.

Bwang. "No, Kailan—the instruments do not give that much information." He shook his fingertips in frustration, thinking, /I'll bet someone back on Shipworld knows, or has a pretty good idea, though—because they sent us here. Don't you have *anything* you can tell me?/

The obliq studied his expression carefully, with those enormous eyes in a black rubber face. "I think I perceive some of what you are feeling," she murmured.

Li-Jared cocked his head slightly, and felt his eye-slits tingle with electric fire, as myriad frustrations and hopes spun through his thoughts. Before he could answer, though, the silence was broken by Elbeth, who turned from a nearby comm unit. "A cargo sub has just returned from the salvage site with many sick and injured on board. Also Ik, John Bandicut, and a *lander captive*, in physical distress."

"Lander captive!" Li-Jared said excitedly. "Are they—"

"*Who* is in physical distress?" Antares cried. "Are Bandie and Ik all right?"

"I do not know. I do not know," said Elbeth. "I will try to find out. But they've reported a strange encounter with a—*machine*—on the salvage wreck, possibly involving a connection with the Maw! They request that we come quickly."

"Yes? Yes?" Li-Jared said excitedly, his weariness and frustration evaporating. "What sort of encounter? They must be all right if they want to tell us about it quickly! What did they say? When did it occur?"

Elbeth made a helpless gesture. "I do not know. But the time? Well, it had to have been hours ago."

"Ho?" Li-Jared raced to the console where he had been working, and urged Kailan to join him. "Can you bring back those readings from when we saw the fluctuation and the spike? Good, good. Now, can you superimpose a map with the location of the salvage site?"

Kailan worked quickly at the console.

"There it is!" Li-Jared jabbed excitedly at the display. "The field bends, and that's where the fluctuation starts! Whatever they found, it *is* connected to the Maw!"

"Is that good or bad?" asked Antares. "Shouldn't we be getting over there right away?"

"Yes, absolutely! I don't know if it's good or bad. But I do know we need to see Ik and Bandie. A sub! Kailan, can you get us a sub?"

"Of course," said Kailan, pointing. Elbeth was already making the call. "We must all go, at once."

The lander was having difficulty again. Bandicut reached out and touched his arm one more time. Whatever benefit he and the quarx were providing, it seemed to last only as long as they maintained physical contact. There were too many physiological forces trying to squeeze the life out of the lander for them to be able to just nudge his healing systems in the right directions. And Bandicut couldn't keep this up indefinitely. /You know,/ he murmured to the quarx, /if it isn't possible to split off new daughter-stones, it occurs to me, what if . . ./ He hesitated. /Now, let me think about this for a second./

The quarx waited a few moments, then said,

/// I didn't want to suggest it. ///

/What do you mean? Why not? Never mind, I know why. Still . . ./ He drew a deep breath, and said, /What if I were to let him use *my* stones for a while?/ Even as he said it, the thought made him shiver, thinking of all the ways that he depended upon his stones. He would feel helpless without them. But would he be, really? /Can *I* survive without them? What do the stones say?/

/// They . . . don't rule the idea out.
But they seem reluctant to commit to it. ///

/Well, if *they're* reluctant—/ He could feel himself drawing away from the idea in relief. Then his eyes focused again on the lander, who would die if something wasn't done.

/// There are risks.
Your normalization offers some protection,
against pressure and so on.
But there is another danger, not so much to you
as to the lander. ///

/Huh? What's that?/

/// Well, if their new host
doesn't wish to give them up later,
they might not be able to return
without severe trauma. ///

/Trauma to the lander—?/

/// Yes. ///

/—or to the stones?/

/// Both.
A bond must be formed, and while they will not
forget their bond to you,
you will have to give up a certain authority. ///

Authority? he thought. Then he remembered the time on Shipworld when he had commanded the stones to leave him, just to see if they would obey. But if they would do that, would they not return to him here?

/// I believe they will return,
even if there is a conflict of will.
But if the lander resists
and the bond is severed unwillingly,
it could— ///

/Kill him?/ Bandicut felt the quarx's affirmation, and his own fear and doubt as he looked back at the lander. The creature was trembling; its eyes looked unfocused. Had he saved this creature's life, only to watch him die—either right here and now, or later, if the stones had to leave by force? No, he thought—that's not good enough. There has to be a way. /Could we transfer just one? Which stone does this sort of work?/

/// Mainly the black one.
But they can't really work separately. ///

Bandicut swore silently. /If I give them both up, I won't be able to communicate with the Neri. What the hell good will I be to anyone then?/

/// I don't know.
I'll help as much as I can.
For what that's worth. ///

Bandicut swallowed and thought, Charlie's help is worth quite a lot. /Just tell them . . . I really, *really* want them to come back, okay?/ He turned to the Hraachee'an. "Ik," he murmured, "there's something I want to do. You're probably going to think I'm crazy . . ."

Crazy indeed, Ik thought, watching his friend. His own stones had refused to split for the lander, saying that it was not yet their time—and thus leaving it to Bandicut to take the chance. Ik felt a throbbing guilt, even though it was beyond his control. But here, in Bandicut, was a being who knew how to take the long view. Willing to risk his life, his future—his voice-stones—to save a being whom the Neri regarded as an enemy. Someone ought to compose a song about it someday, Ik thought. It was an act of compassion. But it was more than that, he knew. It was a calculated gamble. Maybe not calculated consciously; but it was calculated somewhere in that human's soul—to do whatever it took to bring these two races together. Or at least get them to stop killing each other.

Ik approved of the goal. But he was terrified of the risk to his friend.

He dared not speak a word of warning. Bandicut knew the risks. Now he needed only courage.

The human raised his wrists to the lander's head. L'Kell and two other Neri were watching silently. Bandicut's attention had turned inward. Ik had watched him do this once before, on a train in Shipworld; but then, it had been a rash experiment, a demonstration, in a place of relative safety. Ik could only guess how much the human might be depending on the stones for his survival here in the crushing depths.

There were two small twinkles, one on each of Bandicut's wrists. Then answering flashes on the sides of the lander's neck. Bandicut slumped suddenly, wrists dark. "John?" Ik called. The human was still conscious, eyes open, but obviously drained of energy. The lander started, its breath rasping in its windpipe like a saw. It jerked its gaze around wildly, its eyes seeming to spin. It clawed at the sides of its neck, where the stones had imbedded themselves.

"John!" Ik said more loudly, and was startled to hear his voice sound distinctly unHraachee'an. His own voice-stones were transforming his speech into the human's language.

Bandicut blinked with difficulty, looking up at Ik, then at the lander as if for the first time. He raised a trembling hand. He seemed to realize that the lander might hurt himself trying to claw the stones out. Ik started to move to restrain the lander, then thought, better if Bandicut intervened. "Stop him," Ik urged.

Bandicut grunted, and leaned forward, reaching for the lander's hands. There was a flash of movement, and Bandicut's hands were caught in the lander's pincer grip. He howled in pain. The lander jerked reflexively and let go. Bandicut swore, bent over his bleeding right hand, and barked something that Ik's voice-stones struggled to interpret. The lander jerked his head—as if he had heard, and perhaps even understood, Bandicut's words. Or maybe the intent, if not the words. He brought his hands to his chest, away from Bandicut, away from his own neck. And he stared in astonishment. There was no ambiguity now. Ik could read the astonishment in the lander's eyes.

"Can you hear me?" Ik asked.

"*Whhhhum!*" said the lander, furrowing his facial skin. He was still breathing with difficulty, and obviously fighting an urge to scratch at the stones. But as Ik watched, he saw the intensity of the expression slowly subside, and the lander's breathing grow just a bit easier. The stones were probably preoccupied with trying to ease the lander's physical distress. Ik decided to hold off a few minutes on trying to communicate.

Bandicut was looking worse—disconcerted by the loss of translation, no doubt, but probably more than that. Loss of the protective forcefields, for one thing. Normalized or not, who knew how much work the stones had to do to keep him healthy, if not actually alive. Bandicut was starting to shiver, and he looked a little frightened. "Are you all right, Bandie?" Ik asked softly. Human words again.

Bandicut looked puzzled, then nodded painfully.

"*Whhhummll,*" muttered the lander, looking from Ik to Bandicut and back. Ik felt his voice-stones twinging and tickling in his temples. "*Uummlll.* I . . . better . . . why . . . ?" said the lander.

"Hrahh, it will become clear," Ik said. "You must be patient." But there's hope. There's hope, there's hope . . .

For Bandicut, hope was gone. He'd thought he was prepared to lose his stones, but he was wrong. He was cold, he was frightened, he felt as if he'd been struck deaf and dumb, and the half mile of ocean over his head suddenly weighed on his spirit like nothing he had ever known. He felt a massive loss of strength and will. He was still aware of what was going on, though, and understood what was happening to the stones. He was glad to see the lander look more alive.

But only a little glad. His hand where the lander had pinched it was aflame. Ik's voice, even transformed by the Hraachee'an's stones for his benefit, sounded foreign, garbled, alien. Alien, he thought. How long had it been since he had thought of his friend Ik as alien?

He tried to reassure Ik that he was okay, but in truth he felt half dead, removed from this realm of being, as though he had just gone through one of the shadow-people's fractal shifts.

/// This feels very strange . . . ///

/You're here? Thank God you're here./

*/// Oh yes. But it's not the same.
It's just not . . . ///*

Bandicut closed his eyes. /Don't you start. There's no room for both of us to be moaning, complaining, whin—/

*/// Don't say it—not whining.
It's perfectly normal confusion. ///*

/Yah./

At that moment, the lander leaned toward him, ears cocked and pointed, eyes brighter than he had yet seen them. The lander said something incomprehensible.

"Yes?" Bandicut grunted. At least this was progress.

Ik spoke in a rumbling voice. At first he was impossible to understand; then his words changed to that alien-sounding English. "It is working, John. The lander . . . understands me. It says . . . are the stones for it . . . to keep?"

Bandicut blinked in confusion. Was that what he had just answered yes to? "Tell it no—it's just for the time being. Just for now." And what am I going to say if it doesn't want to give the stones back?

*/// You can't worry about that.
That's the stones' problem. ///*

/Can't worry?/

/// Shouldn't worry. ///

"John," said Ik. "John!"

He raised his eyes.

"Li-Jared and Antares! They're on their way!"

"That's . . . wonderful," he whispered. And he meant it, somewhere down in the depths of his soul. But something else was
happening down there, too . . . something stirring in the darker,
hidden places . . . and now rising up, and beginning to gibber in
strange voices . . .

Locking through to the sub's lower cabin pressure seemed to take
forever. Antares and Li-Jared crouched together, decompressing,
with no room to move or stretch. At last the hatch opened, and
they climbed down into the cabin.

Antares sensed at once that something was wrong—or at least
different. Ik raised a hand in salute, and caution. An alien—the
lander—sat on the other side of the cramped compartment. Between
them, Bandicut sat reeling. Not visibly, but internally. It took her
a moment to realize what was different; she felt it before she saw
it. *The stones.* They were no longer glimmering in his wrists. She
could feel his distress, the absence of the connection—and his
physical discomfort, as well.

She suddenly realized just how much the knowing-stones had
been doing to maintain his, her, all of their well-being and comfort
down here under the sea.

"John Bandicut," she said, crouching close to him. "Are you
all right?" She hesitantly reached out to touch his arm with her
fingertips. "John?"

Her words must have been reaching his ears as foreign sounds.
She felt a sudden sharp pang of regret for not having joined her
stones to his when he'd made the offer. The stones were able to
translate well, in concert with other stones, but alone, they lacked
sufficient knowledge of the human's native tongue to reproduce
the sounds.

Bandicut blinked at her, and cocked his head. His eyes didn't
look right. Something was definitely wrong.

Antares felt a twinge of her own fear and blocked it away from
Bandicut. She looked up, turning. "What's happened, Ik?"

"He gave his stones to the lander," Ik replied. "The adjustment is proving very hard for him."

"This is more than just a hard adjustment." Waves of confusion and fear were welling up from the human. "He is having a very bad reaction of some kind." She placed her hand flat against his upper arm, her three long fingers pointed up toward his shoulder. "Bandie, can you hear me?" she said softly. "John?"

His eyes flickered. He groaned.

"He has," Ik said, "spoken on occasion of something called—" *rasp* "—'silence-fugue,' a difficulty of the mind that afflicts him from time to time. I wonder if this could be it."

Antares hummed in answer. The translation of the word was uncertain. But it was clear that whatever was happening now was threatening to overwhelm her human friend. Perhaps there was something she could do. "Bandie," she murmured, "perhaps you cannot understand my words right now. But I hope I can help you to calm yourself, to regain mastery over your inner self. I will do what I can."

She half-closed her eyes, and began reaching out with that unseen extension of her being, touching and soothing the human's raw emotions that were turning more and more to fear.

CHAPTER 23

Stones of Fire

BANDICUT'S MIND WAS afire with silence-fugue. The hallucinations were all inner visions now—not aliens attacking from the outside, but creatures and vapors crawling through the pathways of his mind. There was no place to go, no place to hide. He was shivering, burning with fear. Charlie was supposed to be here to help him, but someone had unplugged her. No, not Charlie. Char. Where was she? He heard a distant echo, and wondered if that was Char. He wanted her back, needed her.

/// I'm here, John, but I . . . ///

A distant voice. /Please come back,/ he whispered. /Wherever you are./ He wished he could see her in the flesh. Protect her from these voices, these beings. What sort of a woman would she be if she were human?

/// John, I can't seem to find— ///

No no no, this was all wrong. All wrong.

/// It's as though— ///

The creatures were drawing closer; he was keeping lower, hoping to stay invisible to them. /Trying,/ he whispered. /I'm trying to keep us safe. But can't you—?/

/// Spinning, John. I'm spinning.
I'm lost. I'm afraid. ///

/Don't be afraid,/ he whispered, with a flicker of lucidity. /It's the fugue, there has to be some way . . . some way . . ./

In the midst of the turmoil, he felt a sudden tingle, like a trickle of electricity moving up his arm. Then it became more diffuse, a warm flow, like a comforting bath coming over him. He couldn't quite figure it out; but in the face of it, the creatures of mist and vapor turned abruptly and fled. His eyes blinked open, closed; open, closed. He suddenly noticed Antares—when had she arrived?—and she seemed to be trying to say something to him. But he couldn't understand.

/// No stones . . . ///

/No stones? That's right . . ./

And then he realized that this feeling of warmth had something to do with Antares. But how could that be? /Can you hear me?/ he whispered. /Antares?/ He shuddered, desperate for contact. He felt so lonely. So isolated. Except for that strange warmth. Was it Antares, reaching out to him? /Char? Char, is that Antares, trying to make contact?/

/// Antares?
Yes . . . she is touching us now . . . ///

The quarx helped him to refocus his eyes. To see Antares, crouched in front of him. She was gazing intently at him, her hand on his left arm. That was where the tingle came from, the empathic contact. His faculties returned a little more, until he was able to open his mouth and use his vocal cords. "I, uhh . . . you came . . ." And those hoarse words seemed to pull him most of the rest of the way out of the fugue.

But Antares' reply was garbled. Was he still in fugue, after all? Perhaps so. *No.* It wasn't fugue garbling her words, it was the loss of the stones. But he felt her presence distinctly now, touching him inwardly with the empathic balm of her connection. That was why she was here, why she was kneeling in front of him, calming him, trying to help him through the isolation and the silence-fugue.

He raised a trembling hand, and she took it in hers, and she touched the darkened spot on his wrist where the daughter-stone had been.

/// Yes, ///

whispered the quarx at last, in response to Antares' presence, and he sensed great relief in the single word.

Watching his friends clustered around the lander, around Bandicut, Li-Jared felt at a loss as to what to do, how to help. Antares was helping; he could not even get close. Bandicut had apparently given up his stones, and was suffering through some terrible trauma. Li-Jared shivered, his thoughts distracted by memory. Memories of his homeworld: its night sky ablaze, the nearby plasma clouds lit by neighboring, energetically sputtering stars, beautiful and deadly. And the meteorite blast near his home: the ionic halo passing quickly, but leaving the stones of knowledge burned into his breast. The disorientation, trying to understand the stones—the bewildering linguistics, the stones' intentions, purpose, origins. The language barrier had passed quickly. The rest he was still trying to understand—the meaning of the stones' appearance, and their transformation of his life.

And now . . . here was John Bandicut struggling to talk, to *exist*, without his stones. *Why had he given them up?*

The whole business made Li-Jared very nervous.

Ik leaned close and whispered, "John Bandicut is in a very difficult condition. We must help him all we can. I do not know if he can survive without his stones."

"And the lander?" Li-Jared asked, looking at the alien. "Is it working?"

Ik squinted. "I think so. He was near death, until John lent his stones."

"But—if they both need stones—"

"Hrrm. Exactly." Ik gazed at Li-Jared. "John's stones cannot split off new daughters, at least not yet." Ik muttered softly to himself. "I asked my own if they would."

"And?" Li-Jared asked uneasily. He thought he sensed what was coming.

Ik answered in a grave tone. "They were unwilling. Apparently they think they're needed somewhere else—or for some*one* else." Ik was no longer looking at Li-Jared now.

But Li-Jared knew exactly what his friend was thinking. Who else among them had not yet contributed daughter-stones to the cause? He could feel the stones twinging in his breastbone.

The very thought made his twin hearts race, and in none too great a synch with each other. Was that what was expected of him? It made sense, certainly; it was logical. So why did the thought scare him? It was true he had never quite made his own peace with the stones and their role in his life; certainly he had never come to see himself as their master. And yet they were crucial to his life now. If he doubted it, all he had to do was look at John Bandicut. *Suppose he asked his stones to split, and they left his body instead?* That was it, he knew; that was the fear. He shuddered at the thought of all this alien ocean around him, without the stones to protect him. His two hearts banged seriously out of rhythm for a few moments before settling down again.

He glanced again at Ik, and knew that Ik knew what he was thinking. He felt ashamed. He wanted to cast aside his fears and offer his stones up to this lander, so that Bandicut could have his back. But he could not make himself do it.

The lander moved suddenly, and said something that he strained to understand. *Groff* "What do you—" *homm* "—want with—me—here?"

Li-Jared glanced around to see who would respond. L'Kell was the one who should, but he was forward in the cockpit, talking to someone on the comm. Ik finally answered the lander's question. "We hope . . . that is, the Neri and those of us helping them . . . hope that we can speak with you. With your people."

The lander's arms closed in front of its body. "Who—" *hroff* "—are the Neri?"

Ik pointed to the nearest, one of the crew crouched in the entrance to the pilot's compartment. "He is one of the Neri. The sea-people." He cupped his hands. *"L'Kell, I think you're needed."* Ik brought his hands back to himself, pointing inward. "I am Ik, a visitor to this world." He gestured around. "This is John Bandicut, who lent you his stones. Antares. Li-Jared."

Li-Jared gave a small gesture of greeting with his hands.

The lander clearly was struggling to follow. "I am—" For a moment, further words seemed to fail him. Then he drew a breath and said, "Harding."

"Harding," Ik repeated. "That is how we may address you? Good. Harding." He pointed around the room, repeating each name. "But . . . you must meet L'Kell, of the Neri. L'Kell?"

The Neri leader had turned from the comm, and was now leaning out of the cockpit. "Is the captive talking?" He carefully stepped into the crowded compartment to stand facing the lander, who was still sitting on the floor, very much at a disadvantage. *Not good,* Li-Jared thought.

Ik gestured, introducing L'Kell. "The lander's name is Harding."

"Harding," L'Kell repeated. "Do you know, you are the first of your kind to enter our city? I am glad you can understand us. There is a lot we must talk about."

Harding leaned forward slightly where he sat on the floor. "You called me . . . *captive.* What do you intend to do with me?" He seemed to show his teeth just a little more. Li-Jared felt Antares trying to maintain a soothing presence, but her efforts were having limited effect.

L'Kell drew back slightly, as if trying to recall his words. "Perhaps I should have said, *guest,*" he murmured. But his voice seemed to have a bite to it as he continued, "You must stay here for now. Until we can prepare a place for you."

"Here," the lander repeated, with a slight hand movement. It was clear he might as well have said, *jail.*

Li-Jared squinted at Bandicut, wondering how much of this the human was able to follow. John didn't look so good. "Bandie? Are you all right?"

Bandicut's eyes flickered, probably responding more to the sound of the Karellian's voice, and the eye contact, than anything else. Li-Jared felt a pang. It was like watching an invisible force strike his friend deaf and dumb. Was this what it would be like for the rest of his life?

What you contemplate might be possible. But not without risk.

Li-Jared started. /What might be possible?/ he thought, closing his eyes.

To make contact. To divide. To share in the place of your friend's stones.

His hearts beat quickly. /And the risk?/

If the host is reluctant, or too fragile . . . it could do serious harm to the host. And to the other stones. And to us, if the feedback is too severe.

His hearts went out of synch again for a moment. /And if I don't, Bandie will stay like this. Or worse. Right? Do you have any other suggestions? Could you split and go to Bandie instead?/

He needs his own stones back, the stones that know him. But we are prepared for this risk, if you wish to try.

Li-Jared felt paralyzed, listening to the voices in the compartment around him, unable to open his eyes.

If you wish to try.

It was a little like the way a bird must feel sitting on a high wire in a thunderstorm waiting for a lightning strike, Bandicut thought. It was not just the emotional trauma of losing the connection—like losing his neuro all over again—though he certainly had been flashing on that, over and over, in the eternity since he had given up the stones. It was also physical. He was shivering. And not just from cold: it was also the effects of high pressure, much higher than anything his body had been meant to withstand. Was he getting too much oxygen or too little? Probably too much, but he couldn't really tell. He felt himself flickering between euphoria and despondence. If something didn't happen soon, he would lose his mind and his body both.

The fugue was gone, at least. But he was left with a hazy understanding of what was happening. Conversation with the lander. Harding. Antares gripping his hand, three slender fingers squeezing with surprising strength. Rising and falling empathic connection, waves of sensation. A rush of concern, fear, affection. A more controlled wave of reassurance, of calming. She was scared, scared for *him*. But she was also trained to submerge her own emotions, to listen and respond and reflect, according to the needs of the one in her sphere.

/// She is . . . you know,
she cares about you, John.
She does.
It would almost feel like love, I think,
if she weren't . . . ///

/It's not the time, Char, let's not think about that. If she weren't what?/

/// She's conflicted. I can feel it.
But she's trying very hard
to pull you out of this, John,
she's trying hard. ///

He started to think of an answer, and couldn't, because he was suddenly aware that his breathing wasn't working quite right. Shallow, panting; that's not right. But he couldn't stop. Was something wrong with the air—?

Beside him, the lander Harding had stopped talking to Ik or L'Kell or whoever it was, and turned his head to look at Bandicut. Did he see Bandicut's distress? Or had perhaps the stones noticed, realized the danger . . .

There was another movement now, Li-Jared. Moving forward to crouch beside Antares. Peering at Harding. Peering at Bandicut.

Ik's attention had been divided between concern for John Bandicut and the need to foster communication between the lander and the Neri. Since Antares' and Li-Jared's arrival, he had been focused more on the latter. As they spoke, L'Kell seemed to absorb the fact that Harding might be not just a war captive, but a potential negotiator. But what was L'Kell really thinking—and what would Askelanda think? There were a lot of sick Neri, and angry Neri, who he supposed would be just as happy to see a lander captive fed to the pikarta.

"L'Kell," Ik said, "if you and Harding could allow the stones to help you understand one another . . ."

The Neri glanced at him, but it was the lander who spoke. "Are you the leader of these people?" he asked L'Kell.

L'Kell made an unfamiliar gesture with his hands. "I am *a* leader. Perhaps later, you will speak to the one who leads all of my people."

The lander gave a little shiver. "If I survive your bringing me to the bottom of the ocean."

L'Kell answered with a rasp. "My greater concern is for my people who are sick and dying, killed by *your* people."

Harding's head jerked a little. "That is not—"

His words were interrupted by another Neri's arrival through the airlock. It was Hargel, who had attended them previously. "L'Kell," Hargel said urgently, "we need Ik and Bandicut at once!"

L'Kell gave him a sharp look.

"The sick are worsening. Corono is trying, but some will certainly die soon, without the aliens' help."

Ik sensed the tension in the Neri leader's face as he turned. "Are you able to assist?" he asked Ik.

"I will do what I can. But John Bandicut, hrrm—" Ik peered at his friend. "John—are you able to—?" He stopped, stunned by the pain he saw, and the difficulty Bandicut was having breathing. "I'm afraid," he said to L'Kell, "that John Bandicut *is* one of the injured now. I do not know if he will live, without his stones."

Ik turned back to Bandicut, and was startled to see Li-Jared reaching out to touch first Bandicut, then the lander.

It had all come in a rush to Li-Jared. The pain and confusion on the human's face, the concern radiating in waves from the Thespi, and now the need of the Neri. Not those in positions of power, but the Neri dying in the hold, or in the habitat.

Li-Jared found himself crouching in front of Bandicut, listening to his labored breathing. "Bandie," he murmured. "Can you—" He paused, realizing that his words would not be understood. He turned to the lander, who was watching with an indecipherable expression. But Harding had the human's stones, and should be able to understand the words, at least. "Will you," Li-Jared said, twanging with nervousness, "allow me to save the life of the one who saved yours?"

CHAPTER 24

Turbulent Clarity

BANDICUT'S THOUGHTS SLIPPED and drifted, then cleared just in time for him to notice the points of light flickering through the air. From Li-Jared to the lander. From the lander to him. Like liquid jewels spattering from one to another.

His wrists burned. He watched stupidly as two marble-sized orbs of light shrank down to pinpoints and embedded themselves in his wrists, diamond-white on the right and black fire on the left. He suddenly felt faint, as though from the pain. Dizzy. He struggled to hold on. It was not the pain; it was the stones reconnecting . . .

/// It's working— ///

"John, are you—"
"John Bandicut?"
He could scarcely distinguish Antares' voice from Ik's. And then with a long, slow shiver, he felt the fog lift and blow away.

/// They've made the transition, ///

the quarx whispered.
"I'm . . . okay," he said, with a little gasp—and if his voice didn't work too well, the words did. Ik hrrm'd in satisfaction, and Antares squeezed his hand, sending waves of relief; and Li-Jared, his electric-blue eyes blinking like a lighthouse, was bonging in

relief and amazement, "John Bandicut, John Bandicut, can you hear me can you hear me can you understand?"

And he laughed and nodded to Li-Jared, whispering thanks, and squeezed Antares' hand tightly before finally letting go.

The physical strength came back more slowly. His wheezing subsided, as the stones poured their effort into rebalancing his body chemistry and getting his breathing back to normal. After a few minutes, he could feel new strength start to flow back into his limbs. He sat up straighter, held his head up, watching the others.

Their attention had shifted back to the lander, once they were satisfied that Bandicut was safe. Harding was obviously having some trouble getting used to yet another abrupt change. He kept shaking his head, like a dog with something in its ear. But he did not seem angry. Bandicut understood, perhaps from his own stones, that Harding had agreed to the change, had willingly let the stones return to their original host, to make room for new daughters from Li-Jared. And now he was struggling to incorporate the new in place of the old.

"I—" *hroff* "—don't—I think I can—" He shook his head with a jerk.

Bwong. "Can you understand what I'm saying? Are the words clear?" Li-Jared was shifting his weight back and forth, left to right, peering nervously at the lander.

"Yes—" *hrrrr* "—yes, I begin to understand. Li-Jared. Yes, I—yes. I am beginning to." Harding blinked his eyes, the concentric rings of his irises seeming to spin. He rubbed the side of his head with his pincer-fingered hand. "I was very—" *hmmm* "—dizzy. But I think we can speak now. Yes."

"Harding," Bandicut whispered.

The lander turned his head, fixing his bull's-eye gaze on Bandicut. For several heartbeats, they simply stared at each other, with locked gazes. Then, at the same moment, they both whispered, "Thank you."

"John Bandicut," said L'Kell, interrupting. "I don't know if you were able to understand a few minutes ago. But there are swimmers inside who need you, desperately. They are dying, John. Do you think you could . . ." His voice trailed off, perhaps because he had suddenly realized the intensity of the exchange he had interrupted. "I am very sorry to ask."

Bandicut wanted very badly to talk to Harding. But he swallowed and closed his eyes. /Can we do it? Can we do some more healing?/

The quarx seemed to share his unutterable weariness as she replied,

/// *If we have to, then we can, I guess.* ///

Bandicut glanced at Ik and nodded. "All right," he said, through a throat that felt like sandpaper. "Let's go."

Compressed air bled rapidly into the airlock, taking them to ambient pressure. When he stepped out into the sub hangar, Bandicut felt such a powerful feeling of *homecoming* that it stunned him to realize that he had been gone for less than two days, as he reckoned time. Led by Hargel, he and Ik walked through the habitat to the place where the sick had been brought—not the healing center, which was far too small, but the open meeting area where they had first met Askelanda. They paused at the entrance, horrified by the sight of Neri laid out on cots, on cushions, on the floor before them. Inside the shipwreck, it had been dark—and they had never seen all of the radiation victims gathered together. There, it had been a desperate first-aid station; here they faced a full hospital floor, just as desperate.

"My God," Bandicut whispered.

"Moon and stars," Ik murmured in the same breath.

Hargel strode forward, calling out, "Corono! The aliens are here! Where shall they start?"

The healer was on the far side of the room. But at Hargel's call, many of the Neri lying on cots turned their heads to look.

Some peered at them with large, cloudy eyes. Others ignored them completely. Even before Corono came to join them, the answer to the question was almost obvious: start just about anywhere. Many of the Neri they had not yet helped at all; many of those whom they *had* helped were failing again. Corono quickly identified the most urgent cases. Without a further word, they began.

The passage of time was something almost outside of Bandicut's awareness, as they worked. It might have been another day, or another century, when they were joined by L'Kell and Kailan, who interrupted them to ask for instruction in using their own stones for healing. Bandicut stared at them in weary disbelief, too tired to be really surprised, but wondering why no one had thought of it before. It wouldn't be easy, he told them, without a quarx, and without the experience of neurolinking to help them get started. But the need was great, and the Neri were willing; and they pressed their stones close, L'Kell to Bandicut's, and Kailan to Ik's. And soon the two Neri were working alongside their alien friends, coaxing their people back toward life.

Bandicut was scarcely conscious by the time he was escorted to his sleeping room and given some food and drink. He was soon joined by Ik, but they were too tired to talk much. Ik sank into a deep meditation, and Bandicut lay down with a thick blanket wrapped around him. His mind was crowded with the events of the day. Without Char's help, he might have tossed and turned for hours. But the quarx touched him in the right places, and he slipped off quickly into a leaden sleep.

He awoke, hours later, reverberating from intense dreams in which the stones took on the forms of dancing brooms, scattering great clouds of dust in the air, then vanishing into a murky darkness, only to reappear swinging overflowing buckets of water, water in which he began to drown.

/// That came from somewhere
deep down in the memory stores. ///

/Yeah./ He rubbed his temples, and then his wrists. There were two almost imperceptible bumps where the stones resided. He heard voices in the next room. That was probably what woke him up. Ik was nowhere to be seen. /I wonder how long I slept./

/// A long time.
You were tired, guy. ///

/Yah. So how'd you pass the night?/

/// With catnaps.
I don't need sleep the same way you do.
I worked on my studies of the history
of John Bandicut. ///

/Oh. I hope you enjoyed it./

/// I did. What's next? ///

Bandicut stretched slowly. /I dunno. More healing, maybe./

/// What I thought.
I wonder what they're talking about
in the other room. ///

/Let's go see./ Bandicut stood, wobbling.

He went next door and was greeted by Hargel, who was pacing with three other Neri. "Corono says most of the swimmers you worked with will probably recover," Hargel said. "L'Kell and Kailan were able to keep going while you and Ik slept."

"That's good. I notice you said most, not all."

Hargel's voice became gravelly. "We lost one coming back on the sub, and two more last night. There will be mourning about that. But it could have been a lot worse. Askelanda wants to see you as soon as you're ready."

"Fine. Where's Ik?"

274 | Jeffrey A. Carver

"He's with Corono and the sick. Want to stop there first?" Hargel beckoned to him to follow.

They found Ik walking back and forth among the Neri patients like a priest murmuring inaudible prayers and sprinkling holy water over everyone in sight. Instead of Hail Marys, Ik was hrrrm'ing and hrah'ing under his breath. He wasn't really saying anything, Bandicut thought, just voicing sounds of reassurance. When he saw Bandicut, he gave a wide-fingered wave, but did not cease his patrol. Bandicut began his own walk among the Neri, touching arms, gripping hands, murmuring encouragement.

"They weren't doing this well when we left last night, were they?" asked Ik, drawing near.

Bandicut shook his head. "L'Kell and Kailan must have been very busy."

"Hrahh." Ik peered around in satisfaction.

"Where are they? Sleeping? And have you seen Antares or Li-Jared?"

"L'Kell and Kailan are sleeping. Li-Jared stayed with the lander, I understand. And Antares . . . is with Askelanda. Shall we join her?"

They followed Hargel through the Neri maze to the same domed room where they had once stood and watched the habitat break free, shaken from its moorings by the Maw. They found Antares and the Neri leader seated on cushions on the floor, in the midst of a discussion about when the next eruption might occur. Hargel brought more cushions, and they formed a circle of four, while Hargel waited by the door. Antares peered at Bandicut with questioning eyes, and he whispered, "I'm fine." Antares touched his hand in relief, before turning back to Askelanda.

"We owe you a debt," Askelanda said, leaning forward. "I thank you for the lives of my people."

"You're welcome," Ik murmured, and Bandicut said, "I think L'Kell and Kailan deserve as much thanks as we do."

"So I understand," said Askelanda. "But they could not have done it without your help, and your *stones*." He hesitated, and for a moment Bandicut thought that the elder Neri was going to ask for his own set of stones. Askelanda rubbed the side of his dusty-grey head, as though in contemplation. Then he said, "But we now have other problems to solve. If you would care to offer your thoughts . . ."

Bandicut inclined his head. Perhaps the Neri was too polite to ask for stones—or too afraid of what they might do to him. Just as well, since he had none to offer. "If we can help, we will, of course. May I ask, have you spoken yet with the lander—with Harding?"

"The captive is resting quietly, I am told," Askelanda replied, not quite answering the question. His large-eyed gaze seemed very somber. "I understand he has been making demands. We will speak with him, perhaps, when L'Kell and some of the others are with us."

Bandicut nodded silently.

Askelanda gestured to Antares. "Your friend was just describing their efforts to study the thing that awaits us . . . below. I confess I am uncertain what to make of their work. Perhaps your friend could explain."

"We think," Antares said, "that the Devourer—the Maw—might be on the verge of a major eruption. Li-Jared and Kailan have studied certain patterns of activity that have preceded quakes in the past, and they think the signs point to another one approaching. But we don't know how soon."

"Rakh," Ik muttered in dismay. "Do you have any idea what the Maw *is* yet?"

Antares made a soft clicking sound. "No. But Li-Jared believes that it functions by opening channels in space-time, much as a . . ." She hesitated.

"Stardrive would?" Bandicut asked.

"Exactly," said Antares. "How did you know? Have you spoken with Li-Jared?"

Bandicut shook his head. "No, but in the sunken ship—"

"You reported an encounter—and Li-Jared found activity around the Maw, at the same time." Antares was beginning to stir with excitement. "Please tell us what happened?"

"Of course. But finish what you were saying," Bandicut urged her.

Antares pushed her fingers back through her hair. "I cannot explain much more, because I frankly do not understand it—but we know that the Maw's functions are *somehow* connected to the sunken ship. Is it in fact—?"

"A spaceship?" Bandicut said. "Yes. I met its . . . stardrive . . . in person. I was lucky to get out alive, with Harding." He had the attention of everyone now, especially Askelanda, who fixed him with an intense gaze. "I don't know exactly how they are connected, but I am certain that *it was the Maw that caused the starship to crash.*" He hesitated a moment, then decided he might as well tell it all. "And I believe it was through that crash that the people you call the landers came to this world."

He could hear the Neri's breathing sharpen. In surprise, or dismay? Askelanda gazed at him with an expression he could not quite decipher. "We have had certain legends . . ." the Neri began, speaking with difficulty. He paused in thought, then seemed to decide something. "They are not from our world, then?"

Bandicut took a deep breath. "They are now," he said. And he realized with a start that his knowledge of the landers was far deeper now than it had been just hours ago. His stones had been busy learning, while they were in Harding's care.

"What do you mean?" Askelanda asked sharply.

Bandicut turned his hands up. "The landers—the *Astari*, they call themselves—are not native to this world, no. But they have been here for several generations now. And they have no other place to call home."

"Home?" Askelanda cried, raising his hands. "They call it *home*, but they poison it, and poison our people?"

"I think," Bandicut said softly, "that they have been unaware of the poisoning. I believe their actions have been more thoughtless than malicious. But yes, the spaceship is theirs. Or their ancestors'."

The Neri leader's eyes focused on him for a few heartbeats, as if trying to decide if this was the same John Bandicut who had healed his people. Finally he said, "So the ship is connected to our great Devourer. What are we to make of that? Do they control it? Will they let it keep erupting until it destroys us?"

"They don't control it," Bandicut answered. "How could they, if it was the Maw that caused them to crash on this world in the first place? They too have been at the mercy of the Maw and its quakes."

"How can that be, if they are safe on the land?"

Antares answered, "Were your—ancestors—not safe on the land? And yet Kailan says that the Maw destroyed them."

Askelanda's head jerked a little.

"Your ancestors?" asked Ik. "They are all gone now?"

Askelanda let out a raspy breath and closed his eyes for a moment, muttering some syllables that the translator-stones did not catch. When he spoke again, it was in a more distant-seeming voice. "There was a great convulsion, many generations ago— not long after the Neri came to the sea. There were quakes and tsunamis. Volcanic blasts. Storms above the sea. Our people only barely survived. But our ancestors died."

"All of them?" Ik asked, his voice strained with the emotions of one who knew what it was like for a planetful of people to die.

"As far as we know. Expeditions ashore never found survivors." Askelanda hesitated, before adding simply, "They are gone."

"Destroyed by the arrival of the Maw," said Antares. In response to questioning looks from the others, she said, "That is what Kailan believes caused the cataclysm—the arrival of the Maw, from space. It is still causing destruction—but probably nothing compared to the moment of its arrival."

Bandicut suddenly realized something that had been staring him in the face. "The arrival of the Maw happened soon after the Neri went to live in the sea, didn't it? Was there a feeling—do the Neri fear that the Maw came *because* the Neri dared to move away from the land, into the sea?"

Askelanda's expression froze. "That," he said stiffly, "is a historical and spiritual matter. It is something you would have to ask the obliq. Or Corono."

Spiritual matter? Bandicut wondered. Antares glanced at him with an expression of affirmation, and he knew that he had touched on a point of difficult feelings among the Neri. He raised his hands pleadingly. "But is there any evidence of such a connection?" It seemed unlikely. His guess was that the Maw fell when it fell, and had nothing at all to do with the Neri coming to live in the sea.

Askelanda gazed at him somberly, and started to answer.

But he was interrupted by a call from Hargel, at the door. "Askelanda, the robots have returned from the factory!"

———————

The robots entered, apparently having been hand-carried up through the passageways by the Neri. Napoleon walked to the edge of the discussion circle, Copernicus rolling along behind; Napoleon crouched in a rest position, his scanner-eyes swiveling to take in the entire group. "Captain, we've come back to report. We might have stayed longer, but our sub needed recharging and resupply."

"We're glad to see you," Bandicut said. "What progress have you made?"

Napoleon clicked softly. "We have established contact with the factory control system, and now have a basic understanding of the operating mechanisms. We think we know what went wrong."

Askelanda leaned forward, thoughts of the Maw apparently forgotten.

"And what went wrong?" prompted Bandicut.

"It's complicated."

"Okay, it's complicated. What was it?"

The robot clicked again. "The breakdown apparently occurred in several distinct stages. The first stage was caused by a severe seismic disturbance, which damaged a number of internal control pathways, as well as manufacturing elements in the factory."

"Seismic disturbance? You mean, caused by the Maw?" Bandicut demanded.

"Probably, Captain. The factory head believes so, but has no direct record of the source of the seismic activity."

"Factory head?"

"The primary control system. It ordinarily would have been capable of self-repair, but the damage was too extensive. There may have been fragmentation of certain instructional subsets. In addition, a number of raw materials needed for completion of repairs were unavailable."

"Materials? You mean chemical materials, like minerals, and so on?"

"Affirmative. Minerals that are not present in the output of the volcanic vents, which constitute the primary source of raw materials as well as heat energy. Electrical energy is derived redundantly from radioisotopic generators, as well as from geothermal heat." Napoleon paused as though for breath and seemed to look to Copernicus for confirmation. Copernicus drumtapped.

Bandicut glanced at Askelanda to see if he was following. It was impossible to tell. "So it was missing raw materials."

"Yes, and that was a contributing cause of failure. But the factory might have survived, with a reduced level of productivity, if it had not been for the programming failure—which itself was likely a cascade effect caused by damaged components that were not properly repaired at the outset."

Bandicut sensed that the explanation was beginning to get away from some of those listening. "What's the bottom line, Nappy? Were you able to do anything about it?"

"I believe we have made a start, Captain. I was able to examine the basic programming, and determined that the major failure was something that could be worked around through programming changes, prior to attempting physical repair to the damaged components."

"Urrr!" said Ik, interrupting. "Are you saying that you will be able to physically repair the machines?"

Napoleon angled a sensor toward the Hraachee'an. "We personally? No. However, we hope to be able to assist the factory head in repairing itself—guiding, rather than doing the work for it."

"Hrah!" said Ik. "Just like our healing of the Neri!"

Bandicut grinned, despite himself.

Askelanda interrupted to ask for clarification. The robots had been speaking in a mixture of Neri and English, which Bandicut's translators had been rendering seamlessly to him as English. Bandicut quickly summarized what the robots had been saying. "Do I have that right?" he asked Napoleon.

"Yes," said Napoleon, "except for one more point. The factory still requires raw materials which it does not have, and which apparently it was never expected to find in the volcanic vent stream. The vents are rich with many chemicals, but the factory was designed with the expectation that it would be regularly supplied by the Neri, or by its designers, with supplemental raw materials, as needed."

Bandicut turned to Askelanda. "Is it possible that the subs that once collected manufactured products also carried down loads of raw materials to the factories?"

"It is possible," murmured Askelanda. "I do not know."

"In any case, that supply was interrupted," Napoleon continued. "Possibly by the same cataclysm. It may have so disrupted normal activities that the need to provide supplies was, in the end, simply forgotten. And the factory kept going for a while, using up its reserves."

"What materials do they need to get up and running again?"

The robot answered, "The greatest need appears to be for germanium, molybdenum, gallium, ytterbium, arsenic, and copper."

Bandicut and Ik exchanged uncertain glances. Askelanda simply appeared bewildered. Trying to explain, Bandicut only produced even more bewilderment. The translator-stones were remarkable devices, but even they were hard pressed to translate names of obscure chemical elements to the Neri who lacked the vocabulary of chemistry. He leaned toward Ik and asked, "Were you able to follow it okay?"

"Hrrm, I believe so. If I am not mistaken, those materials would be most likely to be found in . . . intelligent machines," Ik murmured.

"Such as the machines," Bandicut said, "that the Neri were trying to salvage from the sunken ship?"

Ik inclined his head and stroked his sculpted, blue-white temple with a long, bony finger. "Possibly. Quite possibly."

Bwong. "In that case," said Li-Jared, springing into the room with a quicker step than Bandicut had seen in a long time, "perhaps it is time we all had a talk with Harding." Behind him came the lander, walking with slow, determined steps.

CHAPTER 25

Convergence

BANDICUT WAS STUNNED, as they all rose. "You locked him through to this pressure? And he's still alive?"

Harding gazed back at him for a moment, his head moving in a rhythmical, dipping fashion. Bandicut knew the explanation, of course; it was the daughter-stones from Li-Jared. They were giving him enough internal physiological support to survive the pressure increase.

/// I'd guess that the stones are
having to work damned hard at it.
He's the only one of us who isn't normalized. ///

Harding spoke for himself, in labored but understandable words. He gestured to both Bandicut and Li-Jared with his pincer hands as he said, "Thank you for making it possible. But—" and he spoke now to the larger group "—I am not certain how long I can survive this environment. It is—" *ffrrrrrr* "—difficult. I also do not know if I will survive a return to the surface. So please, let us use the time that I do have."

Askelanda walked in a slow circle around the lander, as though inspecting him. It occurred to Bandicut that the scene was something out of a nightmare: a black, rubber-skinned mer creature with enormous eyes, gill slits, and a mantle of seaweed, circling ominously around a pebbly-skinned, fox-faced being from the world of air, who was breathing with difficulty and standing stooped with pain. The Neri leader halted in front of the lander. "You were part of the team that attacked our people on the sunken ship?"

Harding raised his head slightly. "I am of the—" *ffrrrrr* "—folk of earth and wood—" *ffrrrr* "—travelers—" *ffrrrr* "—Astari." He peered around. "We were attacked by a group of—amphibians— your people—when we tried to protect our property."

Askelanda's breath came in a rasp. "Your property? It was an abandoned wreck. Empty."

"Empty at that moment, perhaps. But we have been salvaging it. It is ours. It belonged to our ancestors."

Askelanda turned angrily, then swung his gaze back around. "And the land you live on belonged to *our* ancestors!"

Harding looked startled.

"Not only have you stolen our ancestors' land, but you have been poisoning our seas and killing our people!"

Harding seemed surprised by the accusation. The pupils of his eyes contracted to dots as he contemplated Askelanda's words. "I do not know anything about this poisoning of which you speak," he said finally. "But I do know—since you accuse us of theft of your land, which you do not seem to inhabit—that the land was empty when my people arrived there. Our records are clear on that."

Askelanda's breathing slits flared. He kept his eyes fixed on the lander. "It may be true," he said, "that misfortune had already befallen our ancestors when you arrived. But surely you saw signs of prior habitation."

Harding made a slow whistling sound. "Of course. There are still some abandoned cities, half under the sea and broken by earthquakes, which we have left as we found them." He rubbed his chest with a pincer. "Mostly, anyway. But living inhabitants? No."

Askelanda hissed softly, and paced for a moment. "So you settled the land. But now you attack our people. Why?"

The lander made a coughing sound. "We do not attack. We only defend what is ours. You have never made yourselves known to us. We have only seen our machinery disappearing!"

"As *our* machinery has disappeared from our old cities along the coast—even in the places you have not settled."

The lander studied him for a moment. "This I cannot say. It may be that there are other places being salvaged, which were not the property of our people." He made a rippling movement with his upper body, which Bandicut interpreted as a shrug.

Li-Jared was scowling in concentration through this exchange. Antares inclined her head slightly, and Bandicut felt a tiny inner change, a calming influence. At that moment, Ik spoke. "Might I offer an observation?"

The Neri and the lander turned.

"Hrrm, I have no right to make judgments. I am only a visitor here, and do not know nearly enough about your two peoples. But it sounds to me—" Ik glanced carefully from one to the other "—as if both of you have been salvaging materials from wrecked or abandoned sites belonging to the other's ancestors. Neither of you intended anything wrong. And yet, both of your people feel that you have been stolen from."

Askelanda and Harding stared at him.

"It is difficult when you do not know the other side, isn't it? When you have no way to speak, face to face—either in anger or in friendship." Ik extended a hand toward the Neri leader. "Askelanda, you could not have known that Harding's people came here from the stars—and perhaps never even meant to land on this world. And Harding—" Ik turned to the lander and pointed toward the dome window "—would you have guessed that the Neri had such a civilization down here?"

"No," whispered the lander, and his amazement surfaced like oil bubbling up through water.

"Take a look outside—with your permission, Askelanda? I don't think you were able to see this from the submarine."

Askelanda made a sweeping gesture. "Let him see. If he does not believe that we have a civilization, let him see for himself."

Ik led Harding to the window, from which at least a dozen other habitats could be seen glowing in the darkness. Harding gazed silently into the sea. Turning to Askelanda, he said hoarsely, "I never imagined anything . . . at all like this. And so far down." He seemed to shudder slightly, perhaps with awe, or perhaps fear. "But do you ever . . . go to the surface? You speak as if you have visited the land. But we have not seen you. Or rather, there have been stories—but none have ever been confirmed. We were most surprised by your appearance at the starship."

"We go to the surface . . . on rare occasions," Askelanda answered. "But beyond that, I think, I will not speak right now."

Bandicut wondered what Askelanda was avoiding talking about. Then he remembered that the Neri had solar charging arrays, large fields of solar cells floating near the surface to convert sunlight into electricity. Askelanda was no doubt hoping that the arrays had not been discovered by lander surface ships.

Harding made a husky sound that might have been a grunt. He looked again out the window, before Askelanda said, "You have not yet answered my question. Why do you poison the seas? Are you so determined to keep us from these sunken ships?"

"Poison. You keep speaking of this," Harding said. "But *what poison do you mean?*"

"The poison my people are dying of!" Askelanda snapped, with startling intensity. "You rode here in a submarine filled with my dying swimmers! If it were not for the help of these two—" he waved his hands at Ik and Bandicut "—most of them would already be dead."

"But I did not see anyone dying in the submarine," protested the lander. "Except when the human, John Bandicut—"

"He doesn't mean me," Bandicut explained. "He means Neri who were riding in a lower compartment. They are all ill—and yes, many have died—from something called radiation poisoning."

Harding stared.

"It is hard—" Bandicut struggled for an explanation. "I do not know, really, how much you know—"

And then a rush of information sluiced through his mind, and he suddenly remembered that the stones *did* know something of what Harding knew. And the landers were in one respect much like the Neri: they had inherited some old and fairly sophisticated

technology, but their general knowledge of science was fragmented. Much had been lost, much was disorganized. They—
or at least Harding—had no understanding of reactor technology
or even of basic radiation science. It was a testament to
their determination that they were getting along as well as they
were, using what was left of their ancestors' technology, with
low-tech developments of their own. It was quite plausible that
they might be unwittingly discharging radiation into the water,
or even opening reactor chambers in ignorance of the dangers
they were posing to themselves, to the environment, and to the
Neri.

*/// I suggest you give Harding an explanation
that will enable him to understand, deep down,
how the Neri swimmers are suffering. ///*

Bandicut found himself nodding, as these thoughts poured
through his mind. And he began to try to explain, and hoped that
the stones could somehow make sense of it for the lander. "Radiation is something that you can't see—except for certain kinds,
like sunlight, or the light of these lamps," he said, pointing to
the glowing patches in the walls. "But other kinds, which are invisible, are so deadly that if you simply stand in their presence
for a little while, you die . . ."

The tour of the medical area was Li-Jared's idea. But Ik led the
way, under Corono's watchful gaze, touching the arms of the sick
Neri as he passed them. Bandicut thought he knew how the
Hraachee'an felt. It was as if he *knew* all of these Neri swimmers,
or anyway those whose minds he had touched last night and the
night before. Walking through, he was gratified to feel improvement in most of them.

But not all. Some were too far gone.

Ik paused beside a Neri whose face was blistered and raw. His
eyes were open, but milky, blind. His breath came in a labored rasp,
into lung chambers full of fluid. Ik whispered to him for a few

moments, then spoke briefly to Corono, before turning to Harding. "His name is Ul'Kant. He got too close to the open reactor chamber on the sunken ship, and the radiation is destroying his body. It is beyond our power to heal him, I think."

Corono, touching Ul'Kant for a moment, spoke softly, but with deep feeling. "He will soon be on his spirit journey. It will not be an easy one. He suffers."

Harding stood a little apart from the sick Neri. He seemed to be regarding Ul'Kant with a mixture of horror, fear, and compassion. "He is in great pain," Harding said, and it was more statement than question.

"Yes," said Ik.

"And he will die?"

"Yes," said Ik. "Unless someone with greater healing power than mine can help him." He glanced at Bandicut, but while the two had been speaking, Bandicut had placed his own fingertips on Ul'Kant's arm. The Neri was burning with fever, and felt the same on the inside, within the mind, as he did through the flesh. Even Charlie had trouble not shying away.

/// He is gone ... already gone ... ///

whispered the quarx, with a shiver.

Bandicut shook his head sadly. "I can't do anything for him."

"You—" Harding said to both of them "—healed, using your ... stones?"

"The stones," Ik said, "helped us to help them. We could not have done it without the stones. But the true healing came from within."

"Do you suppose," Harding said hesitantly, "that it's possible that *I* could help any of—" his voice caught, and he pointed to the dying Neri "—or help this one?"

Bandicut glanced at Ik, at Corono—and at Antares, from whom he sensed a sudden wave of ... what? Caution? He peered at her, trying to read her thoughts. He turned finally to Askelanda, wondering if the Neri leader had understood Harding's question. "Our guest has asked—"

"*No!*" Askelanda rasped. He strode forward and waved the lander away from Ul'Kant. He had understood enough, apparently. "Let him die in peace, not at the hands of this—" He gestured at Harding, but words seemed to fail him.

Bandicut felt the tension rising in the room. Corono moved to interpose himself between his patient and the group. Bandicut touched Harding's arm. "It will not be allowed. I'm sorry."

Harding made a low rumbling sound under his breath, and stepped slowly back from the Neri swimmer. "He will die, then," Harding said—and it was clear he was offended, or saddened, or both by Askelanda's refusal.

"He will die as Neri die," Askelanda snapped. "Not at the hands of an alien. He will soon join with the sea." With a sweeping gesture of dismissal, Askelanda stalked from the room.

Bandicut squinted after him.

No one spoke. But Harding's reaction was clear. He stood motionless, his ringed eyes following Askelanda. His face seemed to contort through a startling assortment of expressions—conveying anger, astonishment, dismay, and other, unidentifiable emotions. Suddenly he lurched forward, limping after Askelanda, trying to move quickly in spite of the obvious pain he was suffering himself. Two of the Neri stayed close behind him.

The others began to follow, but Antares raised a hand. "They both want something from the other, and I'm not sure they know what. But they have to find out. I don't think we should interfere much."

"Hrrm, what could Harding want from the Neri, except to be taken home and left alone?" Ik asked. "I think he feels genuine regret about the injury and death. But what can he do about it, except go back and tell his own people?"

Li-Jared suddenly clicked his fingers excitedly. "I think I know. I think I know. He was talking about it in the sub." And without pausing to explain, Li-Jared sprang in pursuit of Harding and Askelanda, with the others close on his heels.

The two were back in the discussion room, arguing. The lander was standing with his foxlike head and snout jutting toward Askelanda in an almost feral-looking expression, while Askelanda's hands were on his hips in a humanlike fashion. The two robots were still there, and looked for all the world as if they were trying to follow the conversation. It was possible that they understood Askelanda, but it seemed unlikely that they could have followed much of what the lander was saying. Nevertheless Bandicut was startled to hear Napoleon saying, in the Neri tongue, "Yes, there are records in the factory's memory of a long history of seismic disturbances. I do not have detailed knowledge of your world's seismology, but it would seem reasonable to expect that this activity affects the Astari as well as the Neri."

Askelanda stopped pacing and stared at the robot with eyes that seemed weary with cares. He scarcely seemed to notice when Kailan and L'Kell entered the room a moment later. "All right. So there are seismic disruptions on land."

"And I should point out," said Li-Jared, "that there may also be severe climate changes associated with disruptions in the ocean currents."

Askelanda clearly did not enjoy having this information brought forward at just this moment. "What does any of this have to do with us?" he asked.

Harding took a step forward, closing two pincer fingers in the air. "It has to do," he said, "with terrible earthquakes and storms originating deep in the ocean. It has to do with my people being hurt and killed. Perhaps you do not control it, perhaps you do not understand it or even know much about it at all. But you are closer to the source than we are. And there are those Astari who wonder if these mysterious, rarely seen amphibians who thieve from sunken vessels might also be responsible for these disasters."

"*Thieve?*" said Askelanda. "Are we back to the accusations again?"

"I think," said Ik, stepping almost casually into the conversation, "that what Harding refers to is the *perceptions* of his people, who do not have the same information that we have."

Askelanda ignored the interruption. "Why—" he snapped, "would anyone think that we control the Maw of the Abyss? The

Demon! We are in greater peril from it than anyone! If it caused your ship to crash, maybe *you* brought it to this world!"

Harding's gaze focused narrowly, his arm muscles swelling. "You do not—"

"I'm sorry to disagree with you, Askelanda," Bandicut broke in, "but *I saw what happened when their ship crashed.* They were as helpless and confused as your own people are when the Maw comes to life."

"How can you know that?"

"I am telling you what I felt in the starship's memories."

Askelanda seemed doubtful. This time it was L'Kell who stepped forward. "I remind you, our friend John Bandicut went into that place at great peril to himself. He risked his life to bring the prisoner—" he inclined his head toward Harding "—our *guest* now, back alive."

Askelanda answered in an inaudible mutter. He seemed to feel that everyone was turning against him.

Bandicut heard a clicking sound. Napoleon was waiting to be recognized. "Captain, if I may say a word? Thank you. I speak now because we learned something else from the factory head which I believe may factor into your discussion."

"That might be helpful," said Antares, her soft voice somehow carrying through the room with greater force than any of the sharp retorts.

"The information," began Napoleon, "was rather technical. But since the Maw of the Abyss figures centrally in your discussion, I believe it may have relevance . . ."

The factory head, it seemed, had been monitoring emanations from the Maw of the Abyss for years. Furthermore, it claimed to possess information about how to make contact with the Maw directly. It had not attempted such contact itself, but in its fragmented datastores were designs for equipment that might enable living beings to make contact. "I am uncertain," said Napoleon, "of the nature of the equipment, or of the accuracy of the claim.

We did not devote too much attention to it, because it did not seem as urgent a matter at the time."

"Not urgent?" asked Askelanda. "How could you not think it was urgent?"

"Remember," said L'Kell, "they were sent to try to repair the factory—not to make contact with the Maw."

"That may be true, but . . ." Askelanda hesitated. "Tell me how the factory could know how to do such a thing!"

L'Kell blinked his great black eyes and spread his webbed fingers in a shrug.

Kailan turned from the window, where she had been gazing out, seemingly not listening to the discussion. "It was built by our creators—who were themselves destroyed by the Maw—but not without a last, desperate struggle. That is what the narrative records suggest."

"If we can believe them," said Askelanda.

"You are right, they are not as historically certain as some of our other data. It can be difficult to distinguish fact from tale in parts of our records." Kailan closed her enormous eyes, as though recalling something she had studied years before. "But certain of the narratives—not clearly identified as histories, just narratives—are surprisingly consistent with the information Napoleon has just brought us. They describe a people—not named, but probably the tellers themselves—who were struggling to make contact with a very great power that was destroying them."

"And?" prompted Askelanda, pacing as he listened.

"According to the narrative, some of them thought they had found a way. But they were too late. Their cities, their culture, were too fragile, too badly damaged. They were destroyed before they could put their ideas to the test. Or perhaps they did put them to the test, but the goal was still beyond them."

"Perhaps," said Bandicut, "they intended for the factory to produce the means of contact, but the factory was already too damaged."

Kailan gestured with her fingers—a shrug. "The narratives do not say."

"You speak of the Maw," said Askelanda, "as if it were a thing that could speak, listen, and think. *Contact* it, you say."

"Yes," said Kailan. "That is how the narratives were written. Do we know that they are wrong?"

Askelanda stared at her, his dark, dusty face lined with uncertainty.

"Perhaps," said Ik, in a dry voice, "it is time someone tried to find out. Hrrm?"

CHAPTER 26

Surface Bound

THE ONLY WAY anyone could think of to test whether the factory was telling the truth was to fix it, then let it try. That meant sending the robots back down to continue their work, as soon as the subs were recharged. It also meant acquiring a supply of the needed raw metals so that the factory could complete its self-repair. The first was no problem. But the second . . .

"You wish—" *flaaaay* "—to take still more property from our ship?" cried Harding.

"Well, it *was* left abandoned at the bottom of the sea," Askelanda said.

"You didn't like it when we took equipment from your abandoned cities . . ."

Bandicut could not bear to listen. There was probably nothing to be gained just now from pointing out that both sides had the same problem, and would benefit more from cooperation than conflict. Instead, he wandered away to look out the window. The underseascape seemed remarkably peaceful; there was little activity visible outside now. As he watched, though, he became aware of animal life moving here and there, always seemingly at the periphery of his vision. When a school of long, flare-tailed, silver fish glided between the habitats, he imagined himself as one of them—free and silent, passing through a strange ghost city of enormous, luminous globes. He imagined himself very far, indeed, from the concerns of those sharing this habitat with him.

The feeling of calm vanished when he saw a glimmer of distant light off to his left, low on the horizon, like lightning deep in thunderclouds: the Maw, stirring. He wondered somberly how many eruptions like the last one the undersea city could survive.

*/// Don't you think they might need
some diplomatic help back there? ///*

Bandicut angled a glance back at the group. A handful of Neri were pacing around the somewhat bewildered Astari, the two robots, and the rest of those from Shipworld. Ik met his glance and, without visibly moving a muscle, managed to convey rueful sympathy. Bandicut shook his head. /We can't settle this for them. They're going to have to work it out for themselves./

As time wore on, in fact, Bandicut noticed that Harding's attitude was subtly changing. The Astari was saying less about his people's ownership of the sunken spaceship, and more about the question of whether anything could be done about the Maw. "I do not know," Harding was saying, "how my people would respond to the possibility of trying such a thing. They know nothing of your people. But if there might be a chance of preventing new eruptions—"

The talk went on for a very long time.

The following morning, while the breakfast meal was being served, Antares realized that something fundamental had changed in Harding's approach toward Askelanda, and vice versa. They were earnestly discussing the virtues of various foods from the sea. The Astari tended more toward the flesh of fish; the Neri toward undersea fruit. The conversation gave Antares hope. It was not that they were wholly friendly toward one another, but the edge had disappeared from their exchanges. They were beginning to speak in positive terms about cooperation. Nothing had yet been agreed to, but Antares now felt hope that the Neri would send Harding back to the surface—as a messenger, at least.

She knew that Harding had been deeply moved by the sight of the dying Neri. She had felt his horror, fear, regret—and the upwelling desire to help. And then, at Askelanda's rebuff, his sudden shift toward anger. The anger had perhaps passed more quickly when he'd gotten his first glimpse of the light of the Maw outside the dome, and felt the faint rumble vibrating through the sea.

For Askelanda, the change had come harder. But one of the Neri had finally pointed out that it could just as easily have been the Neri who had opened the ships's radioactive chambers to the sea. No conflict was needed for the Neri to come back sick and dying.

Now, as she sat nibbling on a cluster of purplish green sea-grapes, she cast her inner senses around the room and thought, perhaps it was time to nudge for a resolution. "Would it be rude of me to offer a suggestion?" she murmured, raising her voice just high enough to be heard. Everyone looked up.

"I would welcome any suggestion," answered Kailan.

"Speak," said Askelanda.

"Very well," said Antares. She felt self-conscious, not only because she was an alien here, a guest making presumptions upon her hosts, but also because it was not the place of a third-female to take a lead in discussions. It might be reasonable, but it was hard. She drew a slow breath. "I would like to suggest that it would be in everyone's interest if Harding returned to the surface as soon as possible. We do not know how much longer his people will stay around."

"At last report from the wreck, they were still there. But they haven't made any further effort to penetrate the ship," Askelanda said. "We still have a small group, with one useful sub and one disabled."

"It is only a matter of time, I think, before fighting begins again," Harding said.

"But you could go and speak to your people," Antares said. "You could give them some understanding of the Neri. Of how they—or we—might be able to help your people."

"I am not certain we can help them," said Askelanda. "Can we promise to quiet the Maw of the Abyss?"

296 | Jeffrey A. Carver

"We can offer hope," said L'Kell. "The best hope we've had that *I* can remember."

"Perhaps," said Kailan, "it would help them even to know that an eruption may be imminent—whether we can stop it or not."

Askelanda made a noncommittal sound.

"That might be true," said Harding. "But even if we were to allow you to remove equipment and metal from our ship, we could not promise that your people wouldn't continue to be poisoned by this . . . radiation."

"Perhaps not," said Ik. "But if you have *knowledge* of the ship, you might work together with them to find less risky ways. Hrrm?"

Askelanda squinted, as though making a decision. Suddenly he rose, getting to his feet with surprising speed. "Then let us do this! The Maw will not wait while we finish our meal. L'Kell—"

"Yes, Askelanda?" The younger leader was already standing.

"Prepare a sub to take our guest back."

"To the shipwreck?"

"To the surface."

L'Kell looked startled. "Very well."

"Harding—I wish you to take leave as our guest. Will you speak to your people of these matters?"

"I will try," said the lander huskily. He staggered a little as he rose, but waved off L'Kell, who stepped quickly to help him.

Antares blinked, surprised but pleased by the speed of the decision. "Wait!" said Bandicut—jarring her with a sharp note of worry. "You can't just take him straight to the surface, you know!"

"Why not? I have approved it!" Askelanda said sharply.

She felt Harding's thoughts darken, as he realized what Bandicut meant. Even L'Kell seemed to understand. But Antares had no more idea than Askelanda.

"I am afraid," Bandicut said, "you would kill him. I doubt that he shares your ability to withstand rapid pressure changes. Harding?"

The lander's pupils were large and dark. He spoke slowly. "That is true. I don't know if I can survive a return to the surface at all. Perhaps the stones can make it possible. But we must go slowly. It might take days. Can your subs do this?"

"We can," said L'Kell. "We'll have to conserve power, though, or transfer from one sub to another, partway there."

"Then," said Askelanda, "the sooner you start, the sooner you will reach the surface, yes?"

———

Bandicut had mixed emotions as he departed on the sub with Antares and the Neri pilot named S'Cali. It made good sense for them to scout ahead—locate the lander surface ship if it was still there, and if it seemed appropriate, make contact to urge it to stay. But he wished he could be with L'Kell and Harding on the slow ascent, learning more about the Astari and his people—a job which, reasonably enough, had been given to L'Kell, with Li-Jared's assistance.

They would accompany S'Cali on a secondary mission, also, to make an inspection of the floating solar arrays. Askelanda was concerned about the condition and security of the arrays—especially with Astari in the area—and there were now fewer subs available for this kind of thing. Ik was remaining in the undersea city to assist Corono with the sick.

"How far up must we go before we see sunlight?" Antares asked, craning her neck at the front viewport of the sub.

"Well, we probably have to get above a depth of a couple of hundred meters. That's quite a ways up. I think the Neri city is somewhere around three hundred meters." Assuming that his stones were interpolating correctly from information the Neri had given him.

Antares hmm'd, and he glanced her way. They were lying side by side in the sub's cockpit, their shoulders and hips pressed together, the hair that streamed from between her shoulders spilling off her back onto his. He could feel her enjoyment of his company, and yet at the same time her . . . not aloofness, exactly, but caution. That's okay, he thought, that's good; caution is good.

S'Cali, on his right, steered out from among the highest clusters of habitats in the Neri city, and into the darkness. S'Cali was murmuring to himself as he piloted the sub. Bandicut puzzled over the sound, then realized that the Neri was humming a tune. It was the first time he had ever heard Neri music. It was husky, and not very melodic to his ears. Nevertheless, he found it soothing. He smiled, rested his chin on his folded arms, and settled in for the ride.

———————

"There it is," S'Cali said, pointing ahead. Bandicut recognized the sunken spaceship, but was surprised how different it looked in another light. He had last seen it in early morning; now the whole setting seemed brighter, bluer, though the sun was still shrouded by the water overhead. It must be close to midday, he thought.

"How close do you intend to go?" Antares asked.

"That depends," said S'Cali, reducing power. "We're not going to try to get past the lander guard, if they're around—but if they're not here, we'll see how our people are getting along."

Soon after that, he cut the power altogether and let the sub drift, ten or twenty meters above the seafloor. He activated some equipment on his console, and said, "Quiet, please."

They listened, studying a sonar display. At first Bandicut heard, and saw, nothing; then he became aware of distant clinking sounds that might have been nothing more than loose pieces of equipment, or the ship's structure creaking in the currents.

A moment later, S'Cali raised a webbed finger. Now Bandicut could make out a faint, buzzing whine. A motor, in the distance. S'Cali pointed to the screen. A tiny point of light was visible above the shadow-tracing of the wreck. "Overhead," S'Cali said, "but on its way down. They must still be keeping a watch, at least." He adjusted a control, and some additional points of light appeared near the silhouette of the wreck. "They're there, all right. It doesn't look as if much is happening, though. Which is good."

"Are you worried that they'll spot us?" Antares asked.

"I don't mind if they know we're here. It might actually help ensure that they stay around. But I don't want them following us."

"Can you broadcast sound?" Bandicut asked.

S'Cali looked at him in puzzlement. "If we need to, of course."

"Could we broadcast an announcement? Tell them that Harding is on his way back up, and they should please wait for him?"

"Can you speak Astari?" Antares asked softly.

He focused inward.

/// Pretty well, I think. ///

"Of course I can," he said.

"As long as they don't come after us," S'Cali said, his hand on the maneuvering control.

"But you can get away from them, right?"

S'Cali conceded the point, and switched on the outside comm. Bandicut leaned close to the mike. He thought a moment, and spoke slowly and clearly. *"Hear this! Hear this! We are the Neri, the sea-people. We have an Astari named Harding in our care. He is coming back up from the deep—slowly, to decompress. We wish to return him. Please wait for us to contact you again."*

He repeated the message, twice—then listened for a reply. No answer came. S'Cali kept a watch on the screen; the lander blip continued descending toward the wreck. "It might have paused while you were talking," he said. "But I can't be sure." S'Cali touched the controls and got the sub back underway again, steering a zigzag course away from the wreck. After a few minutes, there was no sign of pursuit. "Let's go take a look at those solar arrays," he said.

The solar collectors were a good distance from the salvage site, almost directly above the Neri city. Once the seafloor began to fall off rapidly, S'Cali began ascending and then made a steady course at a depth of fifty or so meters. The water was clear and deep blue, and Bandicut realized that they must be getting close to the point where he and his friends had fallen into the sea in the star-spanner bubble.

"It's a lucky thing we didn't hit this array of yours when we landed," he murmured.

"You nearly did," said the Neri. "That was one of the reasons we went out after you in the first place."

Bandicut glanced at Antares, detecting amusement. He was startled to realize that for the first time since they had plummeted into the depths, he could really see the gold flame that haloed the pupils of her eyes. What a difference sunlight made, even sunlight attenuated by over a hundred feet of water! Her eyes were quite striking now, set off by a mouth that was expressive in unhuman ways, and framed by her flowing auburn hair.

"We're picking up a ship overhead," S'Cali said, tapping the sonar. He reduced power again, and watched thoughtfully. Bandicut waited in silence, wondering what this was going to mean. "It's a small one. It seems to be moving away from the direction of the arrays," S'Cali said. "The question is, did it pass over them, and if so, did it detect them."

"What will you do if they *do* find the arrays?" Antares asked.

"I don't know," S'Cali admitted, his eyes following the display. "I don't know what we *can* do about it."

"Except hope that you aren't at war," Antares murmured.

S'Cali didn't answer, but changed his course, and slowly increased power again. He set a new heading to approach the arrays from a wide sweep to the side.

On the screen, they watched as the lander ship slowly moved out of range.

"S'Cali," Antares said, pointing up, "are those the collectors?"

In answer, the Neri raised the sub's nose and began his ascent. There were glimmers of silver visible now—the surface dancing high overhead—and across the expanse, wide patches of darker shadow. "Those are the arrays," he said. "They're floating just below the surface."

"Why so irregular in shape?" Bandicut asked.

"I've been told," said S'Cali, "that it makes them less likely to be noticed from above, by making them look like vast arrays of floating weeds."

/Ah,/ Bandicut thought. /Sargasso. It's just like the Sargasso Sea./

/// ??? ///

/Look for it under "Atlantic Ocean," on Earth. It's a large, calm area where enormous clumps of seaweed float just below the surface. A big habitat for sea critters, I believe./

/// Ah. There. ///

The quarx had located an image from a nature holo seen a long time ago.

/That's it,/ he murmured, pleased that he still had the memory, and pleased that Char was able to find things in the library of his mind.

The closer they got to the surface, the more noticeable was the drop in air pressure. The last ten meters produced the greatest proportional change. Antares had some trouble equalizing her respiratory sinuses, but true to promise, the normalization and translator-stones together kept them from suffering from bends.

It was like looking up through a stained glass window, all in shades of blue and silver, with just the odd hint of yellow-gold. They cruised beneath the translucent solar panels, and S'Cali noted places in need of repair. He steered around the long cables that stretched down into the endless gloom from the arrays, leading to the seafloor and ultimately to the Neri settlements. The cables not only anchored the arrays, but also carried the power.

"Don't you lose a lot of sunlight, having them below the surface like that?" asked Bandicut.

"I suppose we do sacrifice light to the water," said S'Cali. "That's why they're so large. But having them subsurface protects them from wave action—and of course, from being seen."

When the survey was finished, S'Cali steered toward a small habitat bubble flanking one of the larger arrays. "If you've no objection, I believe we'll dock here for the night. It's one of the service habitats," he said. As they ascended, the water continued to brighten around them. It was Caribbean blue, dazzling to the eyes and heartbreakingly beautiful.

Once they were docked and secure, Antares and Bandicut followed S'Cali out through the airlock into the habitat. The Neri's first action, once outside, was to plug a power line into the sub. Where better to recharge? Bandicut thought. Right at the source.

Antares looked around, sniffing the musty air. There was no hangar pool, just a docking port for the sub's airlock. The habitat was mostly transparent, and spartanly furnished. "This is where the maintenance crews stay?" she asked.

"That's right. In earlier times, they used to make observations of the surface from here. And even—" S'Cali hesitated, struggling for the right words. Even in Neri, he was uncertain how to say it. "The holes in the night sky?"

"Astronomy?" Bandicut cried in delight. "They studied the stars in the sky?"

"Yes. That's it." S'Cali stretched the webs between his fingers. "I know little of it, myself."

"But how did they see the stars?" Bandicut asked.

The Neri gestured overhead. "There is a place, a hatch. The top section of the habitat can be adjusted to breach the surface."

Antares' eyes shone golden. "Can you—can we go—?"

The Neri's mouth opened in something like a smile. "Would you like to taste the air of our world? Follow me."

CHAPTER 27

Beneath the Ocean Sky

BANDICUT'S HEART NEARLY stopped as he stepped out under a vast, blue and white streaked sky. He squinted, shading his eyes against the brilliance of the sun. He felt himself grinning like a fool. It seemed like a hundred years since he had been above water; he felt a tremendous sense of release. A second later he realized that the sun was brilliant only by comparison with the world under the sea; it was actually at this moment hidden behind whorled streaks of cloud low on the horizon.

/// This is breathtaking!
I have never seen open space before.
Not through your eyes. ///

Antares stood beside him, gazing across the water. He felt her wonderment before he saw the expression on her face: the widening of her eyes, the irises a thin golden ring around the black pupils. She gasped long, slow breaths as she took in the view. "I had not known," she said at last, "just how closed in I felt. Not until I saw this." She pushed her hair back from her temples, peering around.

He murmured agreement. It was a featureless sea, nearly calm except for slowly undulating, peaceful-looking waves—with nothing in sight except the sea, the sky, and the gently rocking platform that surrounded the exit hatch of the still mostly submerged habitat.

304 | Jeffrey A. Carver

He stepped out to the edge of the platform and peered over the low bumper that protected the edge. They were about a meter above the water's surface. Several Neri ladders were spaced around the edge; if they fell off, they'd be able to get back up. Peering down into the water, he could see the shadowy presence of the solar arrays contrasting with the blue of the clear depths. It didn't look that much like sargasso, he thought, but maybe it wouldn't be conspicuous from the air. Or maybe the landers didn't possess aircraft.

"The arrays move up and down, as needed," said S'Cali, from the hatch. "In high seas, or if the sensors detect something in the area, the array will drop to a deeper level. But it does take time to respond."

Bandicut turned, and had to look twice to spot S'Cali. The Neri's head was just visible below the lip of the hatch. "Are you coming out?" Bandicut asked.

"I . . . don't know if there's any need. Unless you require assistance . . ."

Struck by the tentativeness in S'Cali's voice, Bandicut moved closer. "No, that's all right." Antares put a hand on his arm, and he looked at her and felt a strong sense of, *Don't*. He peered at her questioningly.

*/// I think she means,
leave poor S'Cali alone. ///*

/Why "poor" S'Cali?/

*/// A blind man could see it.
He's afraid of the open space. ///*

Bandicut blinked, suddenly understanding. Of course. S'Cali lived under the sea, spent his whole life there. On an extraordinarily clear day he could see maybe a hundred meters. It must be terrifying to him to be under the openness of the sky. It was not the sea or the waves that frightened him; it was the sky.

"We're fine," Antares said softly toward the hatch. "Why don't you go on with whatever you need to do. We'll come down if we need anything."

"Good," said S'Cali, with obvious relief. He vanished below.

Bandicut looked at Antares. "He must feel the way Li-Jared feels underwater."

Antares hummed assent. "I wish we could bring Li-Jared up to see the surface. It would do him good, I think." She reflected for a moment. "And we must remember to thank S'Cali."

"Eh?"

"For bringing us here. Oh, he has his inspections to do—and yes, we're keeping an eye out for lander ships. But I have a feeling he brought us here as much for our benefit as his." She fell silent, and they stood awhile, soaking up the feel of the open sea. Suddenly she walked over to the hatch and called down, "S'Cali, is there anything in this water that would hurt us if we swam in it?"

Bandicut couldn't hear the answer, but Antares returned a moment later and said, "He says it should be safe. The pikarta don't usually come to the surface. I think I'd like to go for a swim." She peered down into the water. "Would it disturb you if I disrobed?"

He tried not to swallow his tongue. "Uh—no, I guess not."

/// Disturb? ///

/Shut up./

"Will you swim with me?" Antares asked, removing her slipperlike shoes. Before he could answer, she had done something to her pantsuit, and it opened down the front. She turned slightly as she shrugged it off over her shoulders, stepped out of it, folded it neatly, and stood nude in front of him. At last he could see the ways in which she was like, and unlike, a human female. She indeed had four breasts—small and round, with what looked like largish nipples slightly above the center of each. Her body was covered with a fine, silky hair, and something that looked like pubic fur started as a point between her lower two breasts, widened and thickened over her stomach, and thinned again as it narrowed to another point between her legs. Her arms and legs were very humanlike, except that the curves of her muscles were just different enough to be noticeable.

Bandicut said nothing; he was busy trying not to stare. He began to fumble with the closure on his jumpsuit.

"Bandie, I didn't mean—I don't want to make you feel—"

"No, no—it's fine. Yes, of course I'll join you." He opened the front of his jumpsuit.

"It's all right if you look at me. I'm curious about you, too."

"Okay," he murmured as he stepped out of his own clothes. He stood self-consciously before her, thinking, It didn't feel like this when I gave Ik a look at the human form.

/// No, this is certainly very— ///

/Yes, it is./

Antares cocked her head, gazing at him. "You're not so different from a Thespi. So *that* must be your—what an interesting place for it. How do you—never mind, you can tell me later."

Bandicut blushed. "Shall we swim?" he said, turning toward the water.

"Yes, let's."

Antares stood beside him at the edge. "After you," he said—and watched with admiring interest as she stretched and dove gracefully into the clear water. He followed suit—grunting as the water smacked his unprotected groin—and shivered in the coolness, then sighed with pleasure as he surfaced and swam with brisk, strong strokes through the water.

Antares surfaced nearby, her wet hair pulling back from her head. Her lips parted in a Thespi smile, and her stones flickered in her throat, and Bandicut grinned at her. They swam back and forth for a while, then in circles around the platform. Finally, by silent agreement, they returned to the ladder, where they hung in the water for a few minutes, savoring the relaxation. "It'll be getting dark soon," Antares said. She began to climb up the ladder. He floated backward with lazy strokes, watching with interest as she emerged, water running off her back. He waited until she was standing back on the platform, then swam back and climbed out himself.

They stood shivering in the cool air. Without towels, it seemed smart to dry in the air first, then dress. The sun was very low in the sky, half hidden by clouds. But overhead, and to the east, the sky was clearing. Antares' skin glistened with seawater; her nipples seemed larger and more prominent as her breasts contracted with the cold. He could see now that the pubic fur over her stomach covered a depression about where a human's belly button would be.

/// *Interesting.* ///

/To you?/

/// *And to you.* ///

He said nothing. He was starting to feel dry, and apparently so was Antares, because she picked up her clothes and began to put them on. After they were both dressed, they stood together, gazing out over the water.

"Tell me what you're thinking, John," she said after a minute.

"Mm?" And he thought, Not on your life. Not yet. He cleared his throat. "Thinking . . . in what sense?"

She gazed earnestly at him. "In any sense. Bandie, so much has happened so quickly—and we've been thrown this way and that—and I've hardly had a chance to get to know my new friends. People I've come to care about very much, but don't really know. I don't mean just the Neri. I mean you."

He let out his breath softly, nodding.

/// *How exactly does she mean this?* ///

/I don't know. I'm not sure she knows herself. She's trying to sort things out./

/// *Like you.* ///

/Yeah. Like me./

"John?" Antares uttered a low hissing sound: laughter, or maybe a chuckle. "You seemed to go away there, for a minute."

"Ah. Sorry. My idiot face."

"*Uuhhhl?*"

He chuckled ruefully. "It happens when I'm talking to Charlie and I forget to keep up my outer appearance. I wish I didn't do that."

Antares gazed out over the empty sea, then back at him. "John, you asked me once if I wanted to join stones, so that we could know each other better. I think I would like to do that, if you still want to."

He felt something funny in the pit of his stomach, and then a smile taking over his lips. "I think," he said quietly, "that getting to know each other better would be a very good idea."

———

It was cool in the salt sea air, and there was no place very comfortable to sit, but neither of them wanted to leave the open air. Antares went below and found a couple of cushions, and they sat together with their backs to the hatch, facing the water. The chill and the physical discomfort were pushed out of his mind by a sudden spangle of color—sunset over the sea, orange and crimson peeking through the clouds, then a flash of green before it all faded to twilight. Overhead, a handful of stars were already pricking the sky. Bandicut felt his heart race at the sight of stars, and he wondered where in that sky his sun was, the sun of Earth.

Antares' hand touched his. Her lips were parted in a querying smile.

"Whenever you're ready," he murmured.

Antares opened the collar of her suit to expose the two stones glimmering white and deep ruby in her throat. "Bring our stones together? Is that what we do?"

He nodded and raised his hands, and she took them in hers and held them close to her throat. It was awkward, and they shifted around a little, trying to get comfortable. Finally he rested the edges of his hands on her shoulders, and she gently pulled his wrists close to her throat.

He could feel the stones beginning to join already, the aura of her personality welling up to brush against his—and in the back of his mind, but not too far back, the quarx watching the contact with extreme interest. And then the world seemed to recede around them, and he was aware of a current flowing from his stones to hers and back again, and her thoughts stretching out to meet his . . .

John Bandicut, human of Earth and Triton . . .

Antares . . .

Yes. Autumn Aurora (Red Sun) Alexandrovens, Thespi third-female . . .

This is not alien to you, this . . . joining. Is it like what you do on Thespi Prime?

Like, but different. There we joined with emotions only. But you and I . . . we can share thoughts and memories . . .

And even as she spoke in the silence of the stones, he began to feel her thoughts and memories lapping against his . . . and he knew she was already learning from his memories . . . of life on Triton and on Earth, of Julie, of his companion-for-life, the quarx . . .

And in turn he felt the memories of Thespi Prime opening to him. Thespi Prime. A place of very great beauty, a harsh beauty. A place of mountains and rugged forests in the region where she lived; and a harsh people in certain ways, a people of difficult and perilous customs. The images came quickly: her training as a third-female, a station in which she was skilled, joining others together in empathic contact. But it was a life ill-suited to her, a life of confines and restrictions, and tempered desires. He felt in a dizzying rush her time of succumbing to forbidden love, under laws in which she stood responsible but her lover did not; and he felt how close she had come to leaving that world through the gateway of death, imposed by the law. But then the stones came into her life—he could not quite glimpse how it happened, a vision of a beam of light flashing into her prison cell, glittering and swirling, dizzying her . . . and transporting her from this world to another . . . through transitional spaces, along a churning light directed by unseen hands. And if she didn't understand it either, she came in time to know that she had passed through a different kind of gateway, the star-spanner to Shipworld.

It was like a walk through a garden of images, this sharing; more open, more inclusive and intimate than the sharing with Ik had been. And it was not just Antares and John; he felt the quarx joining, as well—and caught glimpses of Charlie's previous lives that Bandicut had never seen before, worlds and peoples lost now in deep time . . .

And all the while, the stones hummed like living things, absorbing and exchanging knowledge and language, and he was dizzily aware that they would never now go back to the isolation that had divided them before. He knew now, they all knew . . . all three of them, so much more . . .

The night sky was full of stars over their heads as the joining slipped away. The first sound Bandicut heard was the lapping of water against the Neri habitat. The second sound was Antares' indrawn breath, and quiet sigh. She still held his wrists to her throat. "You, John Bandicut," she whispered, "are a very interesting . . . man."

Her eyes gleamed in the dark like starlight on gold.

He half-smiled. And since his hands were practically cradling her head anyway, he gently slipped his fingers into her hair and cradled her face in his hands, and he liked the feel of that, and sensed that she did, too. After a moment, he leaned forward and kissed her on the forehead. She sighed again, and he felt her curiosity and liking, and a certain puzzlement about what he was doing, and a certain unusual lack of . . . caution.

Very gently, he raised her chin, and brushed her lips with his, and held the kiss for a moment. He felt a shiver, a thrill; and also uncertainty, a reflex to shake the touch away because it was an alien touch. "Mm?" he murmured, thinking, why do I feel that way? And then he realized that it was not his feeling, it was hers. But her eyes caught and held his as he gazed into her face, and her hands pressed his against her cheeks.

And then he felt a shadow appear, slipping between them, an old barrier of caution and fear. Thespi third-females do not do this, he thought. Especially they do not do this with aliens, non-Thespi. Or perhaps it was not so much the alienness of him as simply the doing . . . of something forbidden.

"John Bandicut," she whispered fiercely, "I am pleased to know you, my friend." And with those words, she brought his hands away from her face, and held them clasped in hers, and then released them. And the moment was over.

He sighed softly, trying to hide his jangled emotions, and the straining physical arousal in his groin, and the unreasoning desire to bury himself in her hair, in her body . . .

/// I am confused.
It is powerful, so powerful . . . ///

"John Bandicut, I feel it, it is a fine feeling, do not try to hide it. I cannot—" *uuhhhl* "—I must—but—" And hissing softly, Antares stopped trying to find words to explain, and finally touched his hands again and lowered her gaze.

He swallowed and murmured, "It's okay, yes. It's all right." And even though it wasn't exactly all right, he wanted it to be so, he wanted to feel those feelings, and he wanted this moment, which had not quite fully materialized, to last forever.

———

They slept below, all three in the one main living compartment, Antares and Bandicut lying close but not quite touching. Bandicut was aware of S'Cali getting up and moving quietly about several times during the night. Apparently he felt too uneasy to sleep, or felt he needed to keep checking on things, perhaps to make sure no landers were about. Some time past the middle of the night—real night, not the perpetual gloom of the deep—Bandicut awoke, aware of a pale light shining down through the ceiling of the habitat, through the surface of the water. He lay awhile, still half asleep, puzzling over the light. When he realized what it was, his eyes popped wide open, and he slipped quietly from his blankets and crept up the ladder to stand on deck.

It was not just one moon, but two, silver-grey, over the sea.

They were smaller than Earth's moon, but heartstoppingly beautiful, crown jewels in the night sky, the higher one about three-
quarters full and the other a delicate crescent not far above the
horizon. He stared at them, entranced, listening to the sea lapping at the habitat. A splash distracted him, then several more:
fish jumping, sparkling like foil in the moonlight. He smiled,
and gazed up at the stars salted across the sky. No patterns
were recognizable to him, no hint of familiar constellations. Not
that he had expected any. The great milky river of the galactic
disk, edge-on, crossed the western part of the sky. It was impossible to be sure, but he thought it looked bigger here than it had
on Earth.

Was he closer to the galactic center? He didn't know, and it
certainly made no practical difference; but the sight, charged by
the reverberations of his joining with Antares, made him practically weep with homesickness. And at the same time, he felt a
vast exhilaration in being here among the stars, first human to
journey from the solar system, galactic wanderer, tossed on the
tides of chaos and swept by the whim of forces he didn't know
and couldn't understand. Friend to wonderful aliens. He wasn't
sure that he would give it up, even if he could. But a heartbeat
later, his thoughts wandered to Julie Stone, and he began to feel
a very different kind of ache . . .

Julie, Julie . . .

His vision blurred, and his thoughts turned into a hopeless
jumble—and when Antares appeared at his side, he nearly jumped.
He felt her instant concern: "John Bandicut, are you all right?"
She crouched close and he murmured back, "Yes yes, fine," and
gestured an invitation to sit.

She joined him, looking at the moon and the stars, and he
began to feel better. She turned a little away from him, but leaned
against his shoulder in a comradely fashion. They were mostly
silent. He found himself aware of what she was feeling—warmth
and loneliness and uncertainty—even while caught up in his own
feelings. Eventually Antares went below again, touching his hand
in farewell, and he remained a little longer, shivering in the sea

air but reluctant to give up his first night under the stars since their arrival on this world.

When he went below again and shivered into his blanket, both Antares and S'Cali were sound asleep.

The morning dawned grey and chilly. He could sense it even below the surface. When he went topside, he found Antares scanning the sky and the sea, which had considerably more chop to it than last night. She greeted him soberly. "S'Cali got a message that there may be an Astari ship headed this direction, so we need to keep a sharp watch. He wants to take us down soon."

Bandicut nodded glumly. He gazed at the fast-moving, low stratus clouds that were turning the world grey, and thought, Please, just one more good look at the sun before we go back under.

S'Cali called from the hatch, "We must depart. L'Kell's sub is almost to the salvage area. They were able to decompress more quickly than they expected. They want us to meet them."

Bandicut turned for one last look. He was rewarded by the sight of the clouds streaming apart and breaking momentarily to reveal one small section of sunlit sky, with a broad sunbeam slanting down over the ocean. He murmured a silent thanks, and followed Antares down the ladder.

S'Cali was busy disconnecting the power lines to the sub and straightening up the habitat. They gave him a hand, and watched as he worked the habitat controls. A sheet of fine bubbles billowed away from the sides of the habitat, and after a minute they began to sink. Looking up, they could see the surface slowly receding, until the overhead hatch was perhaps twenty meters below the surface. Then they boarded the sub.

As they fell away into the depths, the solar arrays seemed to drift upward like a vast, unfurled parachute floating on the wind. Soon they were moving at a steady cruise, with neither bottom nor surface in sight, just continuous blue water. S'Cali steered by some combination of instinct and Neri instrumentation. Bandicut thought of the potential confrontation that awaited, and took comfort in Antares' presence, though not without a tingle of wistfulness.

/// *You will, in time,*
explain these confused feelings to me,
won't you? ///

The quarx spoke with an earnestness that surprised him. Without saying anything more in words, she showed him her own confusion at the intensity of the emotions that she had shared with him, not just as an observer but as one who had personally touched Antares. She too felt a deepening bond with the Thespi woman, but was bewildered, caught up in Bandicut's feelings of sexual attraction.

And in truth, it was not just the attraction to Antares that had stirred Char's emotions, but the reminder of her aloneness in the universe. All of them here were cut off from their own worlds, probably forever, but Char alone believed that her people were probably extinct but for her. Even Ik, rescued from his homeworld's destruction, had reason to think that some of his fellow Hraachee'ans had also been transported—somewhere, somehow—to Shipworld. But the quarx, or at least her predecessors, had been quite convinced of her/his/its existential aloneness. It had been a part of her life for millions of years now. And this new closeness with Bandicut and Antares had put it into bold relief.

/Yah,/ Bandicut said silently. /Look, as far as my own feelings are concerned, I don't know if I *can* explain. I'm not sure *I* understand it. But you have my permission to poke around the subconscious and see what you find./

/// *But . . .*
you want her. Physically.
Don't you? ///

/Well, I—/

/// *Your nerve endings were positively aflame.*
Especially down in your— ///

/Yes, okay, I wanted her. At that moment, for sure. Right now, I—it's more confused./

/// *You're not sure?* ///

/Well, I do and I don't./

/// *???* ///

He sighed. /Look, guys aren't so great at getting all introspective about this stuff./

/// *That sounds like an excuse,*
if you don't mind my saying so. ///

/Huh?/ His face stung. /As a matter of fact, I do mind. Look, people don't like being rejected, okay?/

/// *But she didn't reject you!*
She just . . . she said those feelings were good.
But it wasn't the right— ///

/Yeah, sure. That's one way of looking at it, and it's very rational and so on. But I'm just telling you what I maybe *feel*, which is different from logic./

/// *You're mad.*
You're mad at her, aren't you? ///

Bandicut felt a flush in his face. His eyes were closed. /I'm not *mad*. I'm just—/ He couldn't believe this—couldn't believe what he was feeling. Was the quarx tapping into all of his repressed emotions? /Look, I'm not sure this is such a good line of questioning./

/// *I'm sorry.*
You said it was okay to poke around.
I guess I shouldn't— ///

/No, it's okay. It is. But—well, there are some things that most guys would just as soon leave under wraps./

/// That's really weird.
But if it's a ... guy thing ... ? ///

/Yeah. Don't worry about it. I mean, it's all right for you to look, and ask./

/// Okay. ///

/Okay./ Bandicut drew a deep breath and slowly let it out. He opened his eyes and stared at the blue haze flying toward them as they sped through the water. Gradually, he shifted his gaze over to steal a glance at Antares. She was peering off to the side, scanning the view. She seemed unaware of his inner discussion. Her hair was loose and somewhat tangled over her shoulders. She smelled pinelike, with a hint of musk, which he guessed was what Thespi women smelled like when they hadn't had a fresh morning shower in a while. He didn't want to think what aromas he might be giving off.

Right now, he thought, he didn't honestly want that kind of contact with her, anyway. Make love with an alien? She was attractive, yes, but only in certain ways of looking at her. It wasn't as if . . .

Like hell. He wanted her, all right.

/// Well, I should think so.
You've got an erection again. ///

/Mokin' fokin' . . ./ He shifted position, and quit looking at Antares, his rush of desire dispersed like a cloud of smoke. /Char, that sort of thing just happens sometimes. You can't—I mean, it's not as if—/

/// Yeah, mokin' A right. ///

/Oh, shut up, will you?/ he said, this time with feeling. Startled, Char answered,

/// I'm sorry. Really.
I really hope it happens for you, someday. ///

And then she did shut up. And Bandicut rode in silence, wondering if he was just imagining the soft empathic Thespi voice acknowledging his jangled feelings, and soothing him, saying it was okay . . . and he focused every fiber of his conscious will on listening to the drone of the sub through the water.

CHAPTER 28

Meeting of Minds

LI-JARED, CROUCHED BESIDE Harding at the small side viewport, felt a rush of excitement as he watched the other Neri sub materialize out of the misty distance. It had been a torment, being cooped up in the submarine, feeling cut off from the rest of the world. But the growing natural light outside the sub had helped to soothe his nerves, and now seeing the vessel carrying his friends was enough to make him rejoice.

He'd been thinking about his long talks with Harding during the trip, hearing about the Astari people, how they had carved an existence from the coast of an alien sea, and spread inland but always with a need to remain close to the sea that had claimed their starship. Something in the Astari people had always wanted one day to find a way to return to that starship, to reclaim something of what was theirs. Not so much their equipment, Harding thought, as their sense of heritage. Many of the Astari still felt themselves to be exiles on this planet, stranded by a queer twist of destiny. They believed they would return one day to the stars— either as a people, or individually, in death. It was not too different from the way many Karellians viewed life: as a great endless cycle tied invisibly to the great coils of energy that surrounded and entwined their world.

Li-Jared had a lot in common with this being, besides their stones. He wished they could have spent more time talking. But

Harding still tired easily, and had to share his time talking in the cockpit with L'Kell, who was at least as full of questions as Li-Jared. One thing that was clear, though, was that the Astari were no simpler or more predictable a people than any others Li-Jared had known. Harding guessed that some might welcome his efforts at diplomacy, while others would oppose it. And Harding couldn't even be sure at what level decisions would be made about their proposals; they might be made by the expedition commander, or by the ruling committees ashore.

Harding stirred, rubbing his houndlike nose as he crouched behind L'Kell and his copilot Jontil, and watched the sub carrying Bandicut and Antares come alongside. "One step closer," he hissed, pleased. He had been wheezing some for the last hour or so—and for that matter, so had Li-Jared—but they both generally seemed to have weathered the ascent in good health. The Neri had done their best to provide smooth decompression, but with the constant change in pressure, humidity, and gas mixture, it was not surprising that they felt a little shaky.

L'Kell called back, "We'll be in sight of the salvage site soon. Have you decided how you want to make your approach?"

"I think," said Harding, "that we should just broadcast my voice, and then see what happens. They might not recognize my voice through the water, but surely we'll get their attention."

"Getting their attention," L'Kell said wryly, "was not what I was worried about."

"Then I guess we'll have to trust that they won't want to risk killing me, and will hold off with the heavy bursters." He paused, and in the silence, it seemed to Li-Jared that L'Kell was trying to decide just how serious the lander was being. Finally Harding continued, "They wouldn't expect you to go right up and say hello. If we actually do that, I think they'll take notice—and will want to see what you intend. And then perhaps . . . well, we'll see."

Li-Jared remained silent, though the whole business worried him. This was their show; he was only here to help, if he could, through the affinity of his stones with Harding's. At the moment, that seemed a very tenuous role.

It was not long before they came within sight of the sunken starship. Li-Jared and Harding peered out the left porthole, angling to try to get a good look at the wreck. As the sub swung into a right turn, Li-Jared caught his first clear view. The wrecked vessel was huge and ungainly, and yet at the same time he could see much of its original smooth lines, now broken in places by the crash. Here, in the fog of the undersea world, the starship looked as though it would be perfectly at home in the far vaster sea of space, probing star streams and nebulas.

"Astari in sight," L'Kell said. "Harding, can you come forward?" As Jontil and Harding exchanged places in the cockpit, L'Kell altered course again, cutting off most of Li-Jared's view of the ship—but not before he glimpsed a group of tiny, dark figures floating above the wreck. His two hearts stuttered and momentarily went out of synch. "Say the right words," he whispered softly, speaking to Harding, to himself, to the stones.

"Outside speakers are on," said L'Kell. "Speak into the comm, whenever you're ready."

For a moment, Harding merely cocked his head to peer out the viewport at the shipwreck and his fellows. The sub's headlights were on, announcing their approach. Finally Harding spoke. *"Attention! This is Harding, in one of the vessels now approaching. I am unharmed. I bring important information. The amphibs—the Neri—wish a conference. If you can hear me, flash a light."*

There was a long silence, but no answer. Harding and L'Kell conferred. L'Kell turned up the amplification, and Harding spoke again, with exaggerated slowness, his voice ringing through the hull from the external speakers. *"THIS IS HARDING—"*

He repeated the message twice, before L'Kell said, "Over there—a flashing light. Coming this way."

"Good," said Harding. He spoke into the comm again. *"The Neri have no weapons. They wish to approach, and invite you to escort us."*

A moment later, Li-Jared saw something speed past the side viewport. It was an Astari, riding some kind of propulsion unit that streamed a white cloud of bubbles. It was wearing breathing gear, and in that brief glimpse looked about as alien as anyone Li-Jared had ever seen. He supposed that was what Harding must have looked like in his diving suit.

Harding was making gestures through the forward window, and appeared satisfied with the reception. But Li-Jared couldn't help noticing, as several other landers sped past, that they all seemed to be carrying weapons. He thought of mentioning it to L'Kell, but supposed that the Neri had probably noticed it himself. Soon they were alongside the starship, surrounded by Astari. Li-Jared wondered where the Neri were who had stayed in the wreck. Probably still in hiding. There was a good deal of chatter on the comm, and it sounded as if they were talking about going to the *surface* to meet.

Li-Jared was excited at the prospect of open air, and sun; but at the same time, he knew enough to be terrified—as much for Harding as for himself. They had managed well, so far. But the deadliest decompression came last. In the final ten meters, the pressure would drop by half. If they had problems, that's where it would happen. He didn't want to have come all this way with Harding, only to see him die just before reaching his world again.

He felt a tickle in his chest.

It can be done. But go slow. Warn them.

He blinked, hearts pounding. /Okay,/ he murmured. And he leaned forward to tell them. Because how would it look, he thought with a twinge of irony, to bring back an Astari guest and kill him right before the eyes of his people?

John Bandicut had similar thoughts about Harding's safety. True, he and Antares had gone to the surface without incident. But they and their stones were better prepared. Antares was looking at him, and clearly picking up his sense of unease. "I'm sure they'll be okay," he muttered, leaning to get a better look.

They were ascending now past the top of the sunken starship. He noticed that the Astari accompanying them were gradually dropping away, to be replaced by others coming down from above.

They were ascending faster than the Astari could decompress. He spoke into the comm to L'Kell. "Is Harding doing all right?"

Harding himself answered. "I am well, so far."

S'Cali seemed to read his thoughts. He blinked his wide eyes, and said, "We will ascend very slowly the rest of the way. Plenty of time yet before we reach surface."

Bandicut sat back and tried to relax.

It did indeed seem to take forever.

Bandicut wasn't sure, but he thought he saw some flashes of light coming from below. Imagination? he wondered. A trick of sunlight, playing off deeper layers of water? He glanced at Antares and S'Cali. "I saw it, too," Antares said.

S'Cali looked sharply at both of them.

/We'd better not plan on lingering too long at the surface,/ Bandicut muttered to the quarx.

Char agreed.

/// *That thing down there*
is what we really need to talk to, isn't it? ///

/You have any idea how? Assuming there's something down there *capable* of communicating?/

/// *Not really.*
But you get me in range, and I'll find a way. ///

/Getting in range. That could be the hard part, couldn't it?/ Bandicut stared out the viewport, not really expecting an answer.

———

As they neared the surface, two Astari ships became visible as shadowy shapes overhead. S'Cali and L'Kell steered to one side, to breach the surface at a safe distance. In the final moments, the subs burst through the waves with a sudden rush, and began bobbing as sunlight streamed in through the viewports, which were now half out of the water.

A minute later Bandicut heard a thumping noise overhead. He glimpsed a pair of suited, flippered Astari climbing from a small launch onto the deck of the Neri sub. They were attaching lines.

"What are we supposed to do now?" S'Cali muttered.

"I expect they'll tow us alongside one of their ships," Bandicut said. "Is that okay?" S'Cali didn't answer, but he looked extremely ill at ease. Bandicut wondered which was worse for him—being at the mercy of the Astari, or bobbing around on the surface of the sea. Soon half a dozen of the Astari were in the water, adjusting various lines—which drooped off across the water toward a surface ship, just visible over the waves. There was a jerk, and the sub began slewing from side to side as the lines were winched in, drawing them toward the Astari ship.

It was a bumpy, seasick-making ride through the waves, and by the time they thumped up against the side of the Astari ship, Bandicut couldn't wait to get out of the sub and into the fresh air. S'Cali went first, to open the top hatch. After a moment's hesitation, he climbed out. Bandicut went next, followed by Antares.

The first thing Bandicut saw, shining down through the hatch, was the sun. The second was the silhouette of two Astari heads leaning over the top of the conning tower, peering down at him. He kept climbing, and they backed out of his way and allowed him to step onto the deck. He squinted in the light. On the starboard side of the sub, the hull of the Astari ship rose like a cliff face. L'Kell's sub was moored behind them. A head appeared in the hatch there. It was Harding.

Bandicut waved and started to call out, but his voice was drowned out by half a dozen or more Astari voices shouting to Harding. Bandicut gave up trying, turned to give Antares a hand getting out, then reached for a snaky ladder that was dangling down onto the deck of the sub.

From a look around the deck, Bandicut concluded that the Astari had a fair amount of industrial capability. The ship's hull was steel, the deck wood, and while he couldn't tell precisely how it was powered, he could smell hydrocarbons and steam, and saw a

324 | Jeffrey A. Carver

thin stream of smoke coming from a stack. It was not high tech, but impressive for a people who had crashlanded and been forced to carve out an existence on a new world. Probably they had brought some machinery out of their starship—maybe that's how they'd assembled their diving gear—and Harding had acknowledged that they'd taken some abandoned Neri machinery. But they certainly must have manufactured much of their own equipment. He would have liked a chance to see more of it.

All those who had come in the subs were now on the middeck area, under the watch of half a dozen armed Astari. Harding was surrounded by a group of his fellows, who were questioning him with a combination of solicitous concern and zeal. Li-Jared stood nearby, but was slowly being pushed farther and farther away from his friend. The Astari had shown some curiosity about the Neri and the assortment of otherwordly creatures, but they seemed far more interested in what their own had to say—as if they could trust only his answers, and maybe not even his.

Bandicut watched the Astari in silence, trying to gauge their reaction to Harding. It was like watching a gathering of tall, tailless foxes talking urgently—and yet not like that at all. They were alien, and having so many gathered together somehow made them seem even more alien. Their eyes, with those concentric circles for irises, were hypnotic and frightening. Bandicut could understand fragments of their conversation—though much went by too fast for his stones to pick up.

"—took you how deep?" "—how did you—?" "—those things in your neck—?"

And Harding was answering, or trying to. "Yes, they helped me . . . yes, a prisoner at first . . . but later, it was different—"

And the others murmured, interrupting Harding and each other. "—learn about the amphibs?" "—and who are these others—?"

"—people who helped me—" he struggled to explain "—gave me stones to understand—"

"Understand what—?"

"Everything—they helped me to survive."

"Then who—" "—what—" "—these creatures—?" Pointing at Bandicut, Antares, Li-Jared.

"Not from this world—*listen to me!*" he gasped, trying to silence his fellow Astari long enough to explain. He waved his arms, as if that might make them keep quiet.

But the questions came faster than his answers, and he was falling behind the pace of his fellows. It looked to Bandicut as if Harding was having some trouble getting his breath. Was there no one in charge here? He wondered when the Astari would turn their barrage of questions on him or Li-Jared or Antares—or even the Neri. It would be a relief, if they would let up on Harding. But they seemed to be showing a growing wariness of their returned fellow.

/// They probably think he's been contaminated
by his visit with the amphibs, ///

Char murmured. She had been quiet throughout, but he could feel her concern that the reception of Harding was not at all what they had hoped for.

/// It would have been better
if the stones had stayed hidden. ///

/I think you're right./

Two and three at a time, the landers stepped close to peer at the stones glittering in the sides of Harding's neck. Then they crowded up to peer at the similar stones in L'Kell's head, and Bandicut's wrists, and Antares' throat. When the first landers looked suspiciously at Li-Jared, he shrugged with a flick of his fingers and tapped his chest, then yanked the front of his suit open enough to show that he had them, too. "I think you'd better explain these stones," Li-Jared said to Harding.

"Of course. I'm trying," Harding gasped. "*You must under-stand*," he snapped to his fellows, finally getting a moment of silence, "that these stones are what let us speak with each other. It is how I understand what they say, and how they understand what we are saying." He gestured toward Li-Jared and Bandicut, and some of the Astari pulled back a little, clearly startled by this statement.

One of them pointed to Bandicut. "You—understand—my words?"

When Bandicut spoke, his words reverberated in the Astari tongue: "When you speak slowly, yes. I hope that we can understand each other. And that we can tell you . . . there is no need for this fighting to continue." The Astari's eyes seemed to grow wide, and he took a step backward in surprise, and said something to the others, too quickly for Bandicut to follow. "No need for fighting," Bandicut repeated. "Do you understand my words?"

"Your words?" the lander said, looking back at him. "We hear them, yes. But why should we believe them?"

"Because they're true," Bandicut whispered urgently. "You must speak with the Neri and understand, you can work together."

"We *will* speak to the amphibians—*after* Harding has told us what he has learned." The lander turned from Bandicut in what seemed a deliberate gesture of dismissal.

Bandicut said nothing more, and stood watching as the seemingly random examination of Harding continued. There was a tall, darkly dressed Astari observing from a shaded spot under the ship's superstructure. Who was that? Bandicut wondered. It seemed to him that the lander was standing with a self-assurance that suggested authority, and yet he had made no move to step in. Maybe this was how Astari leadership worked: let the group snarl and snap in apparent aimlessness until a consensus emerged. After watching the Neri in their pacing discussions, that would not be too hard to believe. He glanced around for the Neri. S'Cali and Jontil were keeping as far under an awning sunshade as the Astari would permit, perhaps to stay out of the crowd of landers, perhaps to block the enormous sky from their sight. L'Kell, however, had gradually moved toward the railing at the edge of the deck. Two of the Astari guards were keeping an eye on him, but it was unclear what he was doing. Getting ready to jump back into the sea?

It took Bandicut a few moments to realize the answer. He began to edge that way himself, until he was close enough to the railing to angle a glance over the side. The sunlight flashing off the wave caps made it hard to tell. But he thought he knew what L'Kell had been looking for. Now he saw L'Kell peering at him with those enormous, sober eyes. "Eruption coming?" he murmured softly.

L'Kell nodded, just once, before the Astari crew members herded them back into the gathering.

Li-Jared was worried about Harding. He was looking uncomfortable, and not just from the intense questioning. Finally the Karellian squeezed his way forward through the crowd. "Excuse—" *bwang* "—excuse me. May I speak with him, please? Thank you." The landers gave way with seeming annoyance, but no one actually stopped him from approaching his friend.

Harding was saying, "They have—told me much—and shown me the dangers—" He stopped and gulped air.

"Harding!" Li-Jared demanded, stepping directly in front of his friend. "Are you all right?"

"Uh—?" The Astari looked confused. Too confused.

Li-Jared glanced around for his fellows and saw that he was the only one close enough even to be aware of the problem. "Harding, did we decompress you too fast?"

The Astari's eyes seemed to spin for just a moment. He seemed caught in mid-thought, and unable to restart. The muttering around them fell to silence.

"Are you in pain?" Li-Jared asked. "Are you having trouble breathing—or thinking clearly?" Inwardly, he screamed, /What's happening to him? Is he all right? *Tell me something!*/

A silent voice answered: *Please touch him, if you can.*

Li-Jared reached out a black-fingered hand and touched Harding's chest. Several of the Astari crew muttered, closing in. Li-Jared felt a tingle of contact.

Harding seemed finally to comprehend Li-Jared's question. "I am not . . . sure," he said huskily, blinking his concentric-circle eyes. "I do not feel pain. But I—my thinking does not seem—it feels blurred. *I* feel blurred."

"Blurred," Li-Jared whispered, resisting as one of the landers tried to push him away from his friend. Blurred, as in oxygen deprivation? As in bubbles in the tissues, blocking circulation?

Decompression sickness. The daughter-stones cannot manage alone. He needs help.

Help? Dear mighty stars above. Li-Jared ignored the Astari who were looking at him with suspicion, and wheeled around to shout, "John Bandicut, come quickly!"

He heard an uproar of murmuring—and spun back to see Harding wobbling on his feet, ready to collapse. "Must work—danger—together—" Harding wheezed.

"What danger?" muttered a lander.

"It's the decompression, John Bandicut! The bends!" Li-Jared shouted.

"Must work with them—the Neri—" Harding gasped. And then he fell face forward to the deck.

CHAPTER 29

Decision Points

BANDICUT FOUGHT HIS way through the knot of Astari. He reached
Li-Jared first. The Karellian was swinging his arms to shake off
the landers who were trying to pull him back from Harding. Two
of the Astari crew were crouched near Harding, turning him over
onto his back. Harding hissed; he was conscious, but just barely.
One of his crewmates poked at the stones that were flickering
frantically in his neck.

"Can you help him?" Li-Jared cried, looking up at Bandicut.

"What happened? I thought he was all right!"

"I thought so too! The stones must have been holding him
together!" The landers hissed suspiciously as Li-Jared waved toward the daughter-stones in Harding's neck. "But they couldn't
keep it up. He needs help!"

/// Can you make contact—quickly? ///

Bandicut slipped between a pair of Astari and knelt close to
Harding, who was blinking his eyes in a daze. Bandicut reached
out a hand to touch him, to make the contact that Char needed—
and felt a sudden, sharp, pincer-grip on his left shoulder, drag-
ging him away. "*OW! Damn it, wait!* I'm trying to help him!"
Bandicut struggled to pull free. He was tottering backward now,
about to lose his balance, when another clawlike hand grabbed
his right wrist, and someone jabbed at *his* stones, with a loud

mutter. As he was pulled from the wheezing Harding, he shouted, "If you can speak—Harding—tell them to let me—"

"Yesss—yessss—you mussst—" gasped Harding, struggling to rise. He couldn't, quite, and no one moved to help him.

"What—" called a loud, hollow voice "—have you done to our friend?"

Bandicut turned his head, trying to see who had spoken. It was someone behind him. There—it was the Astari he had noticed earlier, in the dark clothing, moving through the knot of people. Was this in fact the leader?

"We're trying to help him!" Bandicut shouted. "He decompressed too fast!"

"Decompression," hissed another lander, "does not give our people—" *ssss* "—demonic fits—"

Demonic? Bandicut wasn't sure of the translators' rendering, but—

/// *It was close enough.*
They think something is wrong with you,
and with Harding coming back bearing stones.
Demonically wrong. ///

/But that's—/

/// *Crazy, yes. But they don't know that.* ///

Bandicut looked up, trying desperately to think of what he could say to convince them of his intentions. Harding was still struggling to sit up. "I might be able to heal him," Bandicut insisted. "If you'll let me try."

The dark-dressed Astari spoke again as the crowd parted to let him through. "What could you do that his own people cannot?"

Bandicut squinted, trying to meet the Astari's gaze. "Heal him with the help of the stones. We helped him before, when the pressure below was killing him. Will you at least let us try?"

"You helped him by giving him the eyes of a demon?" muttered one of the other Astari.

Bandicut shifted his gaze, trying to find the speaker. "No! Please let me explain, while there's still—" But the voices rose in a clamor to overwhelm him. Bandicut looked at his friends in alarm. He guessed from Antares' face that she was concentrating on the crowd, trying to offer calming emotions, and failing.

Harding was coughing now. Flecks of purplish foam appeared at the corners of his mouth. His eyes looked as if they were going in and out of focus, and he was raspily trying to say something. "L-l-lisssten . . . t-to . . ." He wheezed and sank back.

"He will die if nothing is done!" Bandicut snapped. "Do you want to kill him? Because if—"

He was interrupted by a sudden shuddering in the deck under him. One of the landers lost his balance and fell. Those standing near the railing began to shout. "Explosions in the water!" "A quake!" "They're threatening us with their stones!"

/Damn. Not now!/ Bandicut managed to stumble toward the railing. There were Astari in the way, but he maneuvered past them to see the flashes beneath the surface of the water, like heat lightning in an upside-down sky. Dear God, he thought. Is this it? The big eruption?

The closest Astari confronted him angrily. "Why are you doing this?" "Do you control it?" "Do the amphibians?"

Bandicut hesitated. If the landers became convinced that the sea-people controlled these eruptions, the mission was already lost.

"—stealing parts of our ship to make this happen?"

"No. No! Listen to me! Look at what's happening out there! It comes from the bottom of the ocean, from the abyss! None of us can control that—not you, not the Neri, not any of us!" Bandicut waved his hands at L'Kell. "But his people might have a way to try to stop it!" He swung and pointed to Harding, helpless on the deck. "And he risked his life, to try to tell you to *help the Neri*— for your sake as well as theirs!"

The deck lurched, and the landers began to shout, "Help them?" "Why should we help them?"

A husky voice cried, barely audible through the clamor, "You—must—!" It was Harding, gasping.

Bandicut and Li-Jared, almost as one, broke through the crowd and knelt beside him. His stones were flickering weakly. Bandicut reached out to touch him.

/// That's it. Hold on if you can. ///

He felt Harding's presence. He felt pain. The struggle for breath. Failing of strength. Darkening of hope. Stones helpless to recompress the gas bubbles, Bandicut's stones trying to lend strength . . .

He was wrenched away with a grip that sent a blaze of pain through his shoulder.

/// Damn! ///

"Don't be fools!" he gasped. "Harding—try to hold on!" He wished for a frantic instant that his stones would turn him into a terrifying alien vision, as they had once before—or send out bolts of energy—but he knew that they didn't dare; their mission was to end conflict, not promote it. Even if at the cost of his friend's life.

He became aware of L'Kell calling, "Would it help, John Bandicut, if we took him back down to depth?"

He tried to think. "It might." If they took Harding back down to the Neri city, they might recompress the bubbles; he might recover there.

"No!" shouted a lander. "You took him once already! If he dies here, that's his right—"

"He came back here to help you!" Antares cried out. "Don't you understand? Don't you *want* to understand?"

Hearing Antares' voice crack with emotion, her words falteringly translated into Astari, Bandicut suddenly knew that they had lost. But he was stunned when one of the Astari shouted, "You want to take him back? We'll help you take your demon eyes back!" While two landers held Bandicut in a vice grip, two others picked Harding up like a sack of feed and carried him with a few swift strides to the railing. With a single glance back, they flung him out over the water.

"NO!" Bandicut bellowed. He tore free from the landers holding him and ran to the side of the ship. Leaning out, he saw Harding bobbing unconscious in the waves twenty or thirty feet below.

"Who told you to do that?" shouted the Astari leader.

"Let the amphibians have him back!" someone answered.

The cry was joined by others, and while the landers were shouting at each other, Harding slipped beneath the waves.

Bandicut acted without thinking, only dimly aware of L'Kell doing the same. He climbed up, then jumped from the railing—L'Kell airborne at his side—and crashed into the sea with a tremendous impact, and sank with a rush of bubbles. His shoulder blazed with pain as he kicked back to the surface, then treaded water, looking around for Harding. He gasped, choking as a wave hit him in the face; he caught half a breath and went under again, peering around in the alien salt sea, the water stinging his eyes. He caught sight of L'Kell struggling beneath the waves—the impact from the jump had hurt him, too—but L'Kell had a hand on a shadowy form. He had Harding, and was straining to bring him back up.

Bandicut kicked forward, lungs burning. Together, they broke the surface with Harding. Bandicut gasped for air, fighting to get Harding's head above water. L'Kell pushed up from below, and Bandicut kicked with all his strength. Something hit him in the head, stunning him. It took a couple of breaths to realize what it was—a line, thrown from the ship. He caught it in his right hand, and got his left arm around Harding and pulled him into a cross-chest carry. Then something else hit the water, a log-shaped float, and he managed to get that under his arm. L'Kell broke the surface, looked around, and dove back under to continue supporting them from beneath.

Soon there were Astari in the water, assisting, and the three of them were being pulled back to the ship.

Bandicut coughed, shivering, and bent over the still form of Harding. They were once more surrounded by landers, but this time at a more respectful distance. Bandicut's hand was on the Astari's chest, and Charlene was reaching out, searching . . . but there was no life left in his friend, except some residual energy in the daughter-stones. Even they seemed to have shut down.

/// I'm sorry, John, truly sorry.
He probably died when he hit the water. ///

/He knew he was going to die. I think he knew it, when we made that last contact./ With a sigh of exhaustion, Bandicut rocked back from the body of his friend. Such a short time together, but still a friend. Sharer of stones.

We grieve.

He was startled to hear the voice of the stones, but after that, they were silent. He looked up at L'Kell, who had shaken himself up pretty badly in the jump into the water. And Li-Jared, crouching in bewilderment and grief, Li-Jared whose daughter-stones were Harding's now, and who so obviously could not comprehend what had driven Harding's own people to kill him. "I'm sorry, Li-Jared," Bandicut whispered, touching the Karellian's arm.

Li-Jared looked startled by the touch. His eyes pulsed; the electric-blue, horizontal slit of his pupils widened for a moment, then contracted again. "So—" *bwong* "—mokin' stupid. So mokin' fokin' stupid."

"Yes," Bandicut said. He gazed at Harding's still face and wondered, was there still life in those stones? Some of Harding's life, or at least his knowledge?

/// Maybe. Maybe.
I would say that it's Li-Jared's move. ///

Li-Jared seemed to have the same thought. He reached out a wiry, black-fingered hand and almost touched the lightless stones in the dead Astari's neck. Almost. Whether it was out of concern for what the landers might think, or what their taboos about death might be, Bandicut couldn't tell. But Li-Jared stopped with his fingers poised a few centimeters above the dark stones.

"You . . . risked your lives trying to save this one."

Bandicut turned to face the Astari leader. "Yes," he said simply.

"Why?"

Bandicut straightened painfully, and rose to his feet. "Because he was our friend. And—because he was trying to bring an important message to you."

"What message?"

Bandicut suddenly felt weary to the depths of his bones. If they hadn't gotten the point yet . . . He cast a glance out over the water, and noted that the flashing from the Maw had subsided somewhat. "He was trying to make peace. Between your people and the Neri." Bandicut nodded in the direction of L'Kell, and S'Cali and Jontil, crouching close to L'Kell. "But your people didn't want to hear it, I guess."

"Neri," repeated the Astari. "Amphibs, we call them. We have known about them—a little, anyway. But your kind we have never seen before. Who are you? And your friends?"

"We are not," Bandicut said, "from your world." He drew a breath. "I am John Bandicut, human of a world called Earth." He introduced the others. By the time he was finished, he seemed to have caught the Astari leader's interest.

"And still you risked your life to save this one, Harding."

"I told you why."

"Yes. But you have not told us what you were planning to offer us, or ask of us. And what these *stones* have to do with it." The leader spoke as though it was now irrelevant to him how the other Astari had reacted to the stones. Having watched their passion and anger play itself out, would he now make a rational decision on their behalf?

"I will answer all of your questions if I can. But first, may I ask—how shall I address you? Are you the leader of this . . . ship?"

"You may call me *Morado*. I am the—" *krrrll* "—commander of the salvage operation."

"Morado," Bandicut said. "Well, then." He rubbed his wrist, thinking. "The stones allow those of us who are not of this world to survive in a place that is alien to us. And they allow us to talk to you. They are tools of negotiation."

"Yes? Negotiation?" Morado angled his head slightly. "And if I thought they were demon eyes, and ordered my people to take them out of your body and destroy them?"

Bandicut stared at him for a moment. "I would not recommend that," he said dryly.

Morado said nothing, but gestured to two of the Astari nearby. One of them grabbed Bandicut's left wrist; the other drew a blade nearly as long as Bandicut's forearm. Bandicut grunted, and tried to pull his arm away. The Astari's grip tightened. The knife-point gleamed as it poked at his wrist near the black stone.

/// Brace yourself. ///

A pulse of light shot from the stone, and with a *whump*, a forcefield flared out momentarily, hurling both landers back into the crowd. The concussion made Bandicut's ears ring. A smell of ozone lingered in the air.

Morado watched in stunned silence.

Bandicut stared coldly at the two Astari who had assaulted him, then turned slowly to Morado. "As I was saying," he began. He paused, seeing a movement out of the corner of his eye.

Li-Jared bent to scoop up two marble-sized balls of light, which were suddenly floating above Harding's body. "Here," Li-Jared said. "Perhaps you would like to inspect them." He handed them to Morado.

The Astari leader's eyes seemed to contract with suspicion, but he took the stones from Li-Jared. He held them carefully in what served for a palm of his hand, where they shrank slightly and glowed like illuminated gems. "How do they change like that?" he rasped.

Bandicut and Li-Jared looked at each other. "We don't really know," Bandicut said finally. "We did not make them, and we don't wholly control them. But they don't control us, either." He glanced down at Harding's body, with a pang of sadness. "They tried to save his life, right to the end." Bandicut sighed heavily, and felt a touch on his arm.

It was Antares, who stepped forward to Morado. "May I say something?" Her words were translated more clearly this time, perhaps because she was calmer.

Morado's ringed irises seemed to contract and expand for a moment as he studied her. He looked like a cartoonish nightmare of a fox, gazing at his prey. But Antares remained unfearful. "Were you also a friend of Harding?" Morado said finally.

"I did not know him as these two knew him—through the connection of the stones," Antares replied, "but I spoke with him, and listened to him, and yes, he was my friend. I know how uncertain you are of those stones that you hold. Uncertain whether to trust them or fear them."

Morado's head tipped slightly back, and his lips parted slightly. "And you wish to tell me to trust them?" he asked, raising the stones to eye level.

"No," said Antares, which seemed to startle him a little. "I wish to tell you that they are a very great treasure, and that Li-Jared's gift of them to Harding was a very great gift. And whether or not you *trust* them, you would be wise to respect them."

Morado glanced at Bandicut—perhaps thinking of the demonstration *his* stones had put on—then back at Harding's stones. But before he could answer Antares, there was another flash of light in the sea off the starboard side of the ship—then a rumble, vibrating through the deck. Morado's hands closed over the stones as he shouted, "Crew, to your stations! Secure for high seas! Communications, contact port and warn of possible—" *hssssk* "—crash-waves! Deck monitors, take this crewman's body below." He watched for a moment, then gestured to Antares and Bandicut and Li-Jared to step closer. When L'Kell joined them, he stared at the Neri for a moment, but did not ask him to leave. "What do the stones have to do with this?" he demanded.

Bandicut raised his voice to be heard over the noise of the crew. "Nothing!" He raised his hands helplessly, and finally gestured toward the undersea flashes. "Morado, we know these quakes and disruptions threaten your people on the coast. But they also threaten the Neri, even more. There is a *thing* down there that is causing it. But we hope, and Harding hoped, that a way can be found to stop it. That's why he risked his life hurrying to the surface!" Bandicut pointed to the stones that Morado held. "Those stones, and ours, might be able to help. But the Neri also require the help of your people. They need your cooperation. Materials. Machines."

"Materials. Machines," Morado repeated, his gaze flicking from one to another. "Can *I* use these stones to understand what you speak of?"

"I don't know if that's for us to say." Bandicut glanced at Li-Jared for affirmation.

"We cannot tell the stones whom to serve," Li-Jared said. "They decide that for themselves." His eyes dimmed for a moment, in thought. "I believe that they wish now to return to me."

"To you?" Morado said, in a voice that seemed to suggest disbelief.

"Yes. I am sorry."

Morado stared at the stones for a moment. "I do not think—" he began, and then hesitated and opened his hand to look at the stones again. "I sense that there is—" He thought a moment longer, and finally said, "It is a pity. However, perhaps I will trust Harding in this, and honor his wishes. What is it that you want exactly?" As he spoke, he held the stones out to Li-Jared. When the Karellian touched them, they seemed to brighten, flickering; and then a sudden wave of light enveloped Li-Jared's hands and arms, streaming up his chest. For an instant, they all stood watching in amazement.

The effect quickly subsided—but as Morado released the stones into the Karellian's hands, the wave of light suddenly reversed, and arced across to Morado's hands. He grunted harshly, but looked even more surprised when the two stones flew up and sank glowing into his neck.

─────────

Antares felt a flash of confusion, and then understood. The stones had been waiting to see if Morado would willingly give them up.

Once he had passed that test, *they* went willingly to *him*. But the surprise of the transfer had shaken him; she could feel it. She focused, trying to reach out to the Astari leader.

This was a dangerous moment. If Morado felt threatened, he might turn on them. If the other Astari thought he was threatened—or worse, that his integrity was compromised—they might turn on him as they had on Harding. She focused her powers on just one thing: projecting calm, projecting fearlessness. Fearlessness and calm.

She felt the tension in Morado's thoughts and emotions as he struggled to cope with this new force in his body and his mind. He had to come quickly to some understanding or accommodation; he had to decide whether he was facing friends or foes. She could not sense his leaning; she guessed that he was teetering on the edge—infuriated by the intrusion into his privacy, the privacy of his own mind, and at the same time astonished by the new-found sense of power and knowledge, or the possibility of knowledge.

Fearlessness, she thought. *Calm.*

Something twinged in the Astari's emotional aura: a determination being made. A decision. Morado looked at her, looked at the others. "I . . . see . . ." he said, forcing his words. "I see. There is . . . much need. But you have given this to me, yes? These stones? They have so much . . . I cannot see it all, but I sense . . ." He blinked, and gave up trying to put it into words.

For a moment, there was only silence. Then Li-Jared said, "They are yours. To use, to keep. As long as they themselves approve." Li-Jared's words, too, seemed halting. Antares suddenly realized that he was also trying to assimilate something new. The wave of light that had enveloped him: had that been a massive contact between his stones and the stones that had shared Harding's thoughts?

The deck shook with a sharper rumble from below. Antares glanced out over the sea in alarm. The greenish light deep beneath the waves was growing in intensity. What was the Maw doing? What was happening on the seabed, and in the Neri city?

"We must get our divers up," Morado said suddenly, his lips pulled back from his teeth in a grimace. "Our salvage operation—and *your* people—" he looked at L'Kell as he said that "—may be in danger." He called to an aide. "Find out what's happening below! And get a message off to port: *Eruption worsening. Prepare for extremely high seas.*"

"I must contact our people," L'Kell said urgently, breaking out of the group into a sudden pacing walk. He held up his hands and spread his webbed fingers for emphasis. "They will almost certainly need our help, if this grows worse." He strode to the rail and gazed out worriedly over the sea, then strode back.

Morado gazed at him. "I understand," he said. "You may go whenever you wish." L'Kell made a clucking sound and waved S'Cali and Jontil toward the subs. "But wait a moment, please. You came to ask our cooperation."

L'Kell paused, turning his large Neri eyes upon the Astari. "Yes," he said.

Morado closed his eyes, opened them. "Ordinarily, I would have to seek—" *haaa* "—approval from my superiors ashore. But there is no time. I will try to help you, for now at least. Perhaps these—" he touched the stones in his neck "—may serve as payment for what you wish to remove from our ship."

Antares felt Bandicut's heart leap a little, and she let her own breath sigh out in hope.

"But I must know," Morado continued, "just what it is that you need for your effort. The stones have some understanding, but it is incomplete. It may be possible—if we survive this eruption—to supply some of the materials you need without having to destroy valuable machinery to extract them. But I must ask that you consider the safety of *our* people in your efforts to master this thing."

Morado turned to look out at the pulsating light in the sea. "But if you can find a way to subdue this terrible thing, then we might well find a way to work together, your people and mine."

CHAPTER 30

The Regathering

AS L'KELL'S SUB descended back through the depths, the light dwindled and finally faded altogether. Bandicut and his companions were quiet, but L'Kell was quietest of all. Perhaps he was worrying about S'Cali and Jontil, who had stopped at the salvage site to contact the Neri still inside—this time with Astari cooperation. But Bandicut guessed that L'Kell was mostly trying to absorb the connection he had made with Morado before their departure. The two had talked briefly but intensely, their stones flickering and flaring, just before the Neri and his companions had climbed into the sub.

L'Kell muttered something that Bandicut didn't quite catch, and he had to ask the Neri to repeat it. "I said I'd like for our cities to rise into the sun again one day," L'Kell said, adjusting the exterior lights.

"Eh?" said Bandicut.

L'Kell suddenly looked at him as if they were having a casual, late-night conversation under one of the big domes. Maybe, with all that was weighing on him, he needed casual conversation. "Parts of our cities used to rise and fall, you know, on long anchor tethers, moving much closer to the surface than they do now. Our people used to see the sunlight now and again, and weren't so shy of the surface. We also benefited from much larger populations of fishes around us."

"Was this in the recent past? What happened?"

"No, it was before my time. Our people grew wary of the landers—wary and frightened, I think—even before there was conflict." L'Kell looked slightly embarrassed; his eyes shifted back and forth from Bandicut to the seascape gliding beneath the sub. "We began to work harder to hide ourselves, to be unknown to the landers. The Astari, I mean. I think we felt more protected, hunkered close to the seafloor—and I suppose closer to the factory."

"Even with the factory not working?"

L'Kell did not answer at once. When he finally did, he seemed to change the subject. "You know, we Neri are a part of the sea, and the sea a part of us. Not just in life. When we die, our spirits return to the sea—are rejoined to it, and become a part of it forever." He paused, adjusting the sub's course. "It has seemed to me that the greater our danger and desperation, the more we want to be not just *in* the sea, but *with* the sea. In some strange way, I think, the deeper we have moved our cities, the more closely connected we have felt with our—" *Krrrlll.* The stones seemed to have trouble, and he tried rephrasing. *Khhresst.* "With our God," Bandicut heard finally. "Factory or no. This was before the factory had finally failed, but it doesn't really matter. We might be in greater danger now, with all that threatens us, but we are closer to something we long for and need." He turned his dark gaze toward Bandicut. "I do not claim that any of this is completely logical."

Bandicut nodded without answering. He wasn't about to criticize the Neri. But it did seem a terrible shame that in seeking safety in the depths, or even some mystical connection, they had cut themselves off from the world of sunlight. Then again, of course, if the undersea cities had been detectable by the Astari diving forces . . .

The threat of the Maw was bad enough, he supposed.

The rumblings from below had subsided again, but L'Kell had been unable to establish contact with the city. In the absence of information, they were trying not to speculate too much on what that might mean. It was possible that the comm failure was simply due to acoustic interference from the Maw's muttering stomach.

"On your world," L'Kell said, breaking Bandicut's reverie, "where do your spirits go when you die?"

Bandicut grunted, taken by surprise. "Well, I—don't really know. I don't know if they go anywhere. There are lots of . . . beliefs . . . among my people. About God, and Heaven, and so on. They vary pretty widely."

"Yes? And your own beliefs?"

"Well, I . . . never really decided which I thought was right," he confessed, suddenly embarrassed by such indecision, or ignorance.

/// I have wondered myself
why you seemed so unsure. ///

/Why?/ Bandicut asked in surprise. /Do you know the answer?/

/// Not in the sense you mean.
I of course believe in
the immortality of the spirit.
But I suspect that holds a somewhat
different meaning for me. ///

Bandicut frowned. /Yes, I suppose it might./

"Well," said Li-Jared from farther back in the cockpit, "we know where *our* spirits go. We see it in the sky every night, at home."

"Yes?" asked L'Kell.

"We call our world *Home with Green, Beautiful, Perilous Sky*— among other names. It is not like your night sky, L'Kell. It is filled with highly energetic, nearby stars and gas clouds. It is indeed perilous, and beautiful."

Bandicut looked back at him. "And?"

"It is the belief of most Karellians that our spirits ascend into certain of the clouds or energy pathways that coil through the sky of Karellia. Some of those energetic clouds contain extremely complex holographic patterns." Li-Jared made a soft, thoughtful, gonging sound and added, "The Astari are not too different in their beliefs. I spoke with Harding on our journey to the surface."

"What did Harding say?" Antares asked. She was hunkered in the back of the compartment with Li-Jared.

"Well," said the Karellian, "the Astari know they came here from the stars. That they are exiles here. Many of them are certain that their spirits return to the stars at the end of life. Harding believed this, also."

Bandicut thought of Harding's death, and wished that they could have found a way to pay greater respects. But would it have made any difference to Harding? Was his spirit now floating among the stars somewhere, exploring the galaxy? Or riding the great wheel of existence, waiting to step off on the next plane? Or awaiting his entry through the gates of Heaven?

/// An interesting question. ///

/Interesting, yes. But I haven't a clue to the answer./

*/// Or rather, you have many clues.
You just haven't figured out
how to read them. ///*

/Maybe that's it./

"They return to the stars as we return to the sea," said L'Kell, and he somehow seemed satisfied with that notion. He reached to try the comm again.

This time he got an answer, scratchy and indistinct. Bandicut couldn't understand a word of it, and neither could L'Kell. But someone was still down there, transmitting. L'Kell tried again. This time he got no answer at all.

They finally got a signal, abruptly clearer, just as the lights of the undersea city were beginning to appear out of the night-gloom of the depths. ". . . Send Tandu and the other sub to the nursery complex . . . need tools and patching equipment . . ." And then it faded, just as abruptly, to a hiss.

L'Kell focused intently on his piloting. "That wasn't for us," he said, but there was satisfaction in his voice. "It was local communications, scattered through the water. The sound-carrying channels must be scrambled by the turbulence and aftershocks."

Soon they were in sight of the outer habitats. They were relieved to find that the city was still there. Even so, Bandicut was shocked by the sight of several habitat bubbles partially broken from their moorings—swinging alarmingly, or jammed up hard against other habitats. L'Kell finally got through on the comm and was asked to make best speed to the main hangar. No time to make a survey sweep of the damage.

As they surfaced in the hangar pool, Bandicut had the feeling that they had returned to a city that had just survived a typhoon.

"No contact at all from the factory?" Bandicut asked Ik. He looked around at Neri hurrying about on various missions of damage control. Their resources were strained, and everyone in the city was hard at work.

Ik, who had met them at the first level above the hangar, rubbed his chest with his fingertips. "We received a single transmission from Nabeck, saying that there was a lot of bottom instability. Then the transmission was lost—not cut off sharply, but gradually blocked, perhaps by interference."

"That's encouraging, then."

"Yes. But we also heard from Kailan and Elbeth that they had picked up signs of crustal movement close to the factory—which is not." When Bandicut winced, Ik tipped his sculpted blue-white head. "But they weren't sure enough of their readings to know how bad it really was."

Antares spoke up. "Is there any way to find out, short of going down there?"

"I don't think so. Unless they transmit, somehow."

Bandicut saw L'Kell returning from a quick trip to report to Askelanda. "What did he say?" Then Bandicut saw the Neri behind L'Kell, and he drew a sharp breath. "Lako, is that you?"

L'Kell stepped out of the way to let the second Neri move in front. "I am feeling much better now," said Lako, bowing his head slightly before Bandicut. "I have come to offer whatever help I can." As he raised his head, Bandicut could see some scarring on Lako's face where the blisters had healed. Lako's eyes looked clear, and while he seemed to be moving with some difficulty, it was a miracle that he was moving at all. "And to say thank you," Lako added.

"You're welcome. You're our first success story."

"But not," said Lako, "your last. When you have time, I know Corono would like you to come visit the ward—to see how many are recovering. Ik has been continuing your work, in your absence."

"I would love to," Bandicut said.

"Askelanda will want to talk with you first, I think," said L'Kell. "He was pleased to hear that we were back. But damage to the city is barely under control right now; he can't even spare a sub immediately for the factory. But as soon as he can, he'll approve a scouting and rescue expedition." L'Kell paused, taking note of Bandicut's troubled expression. "We're all worried, John. Let's just hope your robots *and* our people *and* our subs are okay. We can't afford to lose any of them."

Bandicut nodded agreement. And from Antares, he sensed, *Patience. Have patience, and faith.* And he knew that she was just as worried as he was.

"John, we just heard from S'Cali," Ik said. "He's on his way back here, but there are still Neri needing help inside the shipwreck. And also injured Astari. I believe that's a place where I might be of help."

Li-Jared spoke for the first time, bonging softly. "You want to return to the starship?"

Ik's black eyes gleamed with inner light. "S'Cali is going to go back with the cargo sub, to load whatever materials the Astari can provide, as well as the remaining injured. I would like to assist him. By the time we return, perhaps you will have your answers about the factory, and how to make contact with the Maw.

And with luck, we will have the materials you need." Ik cocked his head. "Lako intends to go, too."

Bandicut was startled.

"To help the Neri *and* the Astari," said Lako.

Bandicut saw L'Kell's silent approval, and thought, Lako might make a fine good-will ambassador, as one sorely hurt who now wished to help build bridges. Bandicut knew it made sense to divide up their energy and resources; and yet, something made him wish that he could keep his company together right now. He had a feeling that that could be important, in the near future. But he could hardly object to the plan. "Be careful," he said.

"Indeed," Ik murmured. "But come. Let's not keep Askelanda waiting."

Askelanda listened intently as they described their meeting with Morado. He seemed genuinely saddened to hear of Harding's death. But he responded with surprising grace to the agreement with Morado: the Astari would help the Neri gather materials needed by the factory, but the Neri would otherwise refrain from further salvage efforts on the ship. "Fair enough, if they are true to their word," Askelanda said. Apparently some of Harding's peacemaking efforts had had their effect on the Neri ahktah.

Their discussion was interrupted at that point by word that a sub had returned from the factory—not the sub carrying Nabeck and the robots, but the one that had been stationed to assist them. The sub's young pilot, Gilleum, was brought in to give his report. He was so nervous and exhausted that he had to repeat himself several times before everyone understood.

"... yes, that's right. The ledge over Nabeck's sub just seemed to crumble when the quake hit. I backed away, but Nabeck couldn't. We were able to stay in voice contact for a while, and he seemed okay. But then when the silt cleared—" Gilleum looked around in apparent confusion.

"The sub was just gone?" L'Kell asked. "Or buried?"

"Buried, I thought at first. Except that there wasn't really that much debris piled up. And a lot of it had fallen *away* from the spot, not onto it. The only thing we could guess was that Nabeck's sub had gotten *swallowed up by the factory*. But that seemed crazy."

"But you still had voice contact?" Askelanda repeated.

"Just for a few seconds. It was very scratchy and hard to understand. He said he was all right, but blind. I thought he said his lights worked, but he couldn't see anything. Or say what had happened. But I *thought* he said, 'There's no seawater outside the sub. There's a yellow fluid.' " Gilleum raised his hands in bewilderment.

Bandicut looked at L'Kell. "Is that possible? Could he have been taken into the factory itself? You've got all of these amazing membranes—"

"I have never seen it happen," said L'Kell. "But the factory certainly had docking ports, and various ways of loading cargo submarines, when it was functioning."

"But did it take subs right inside?"

L'Kell looked at Askelanda, who said, "Long ago, I believe it did. But in my lifetime, it has only allowed subs to dock with it." Askelanda spread his finger webs in uncertainty. "It may be that the obliq has information on this."

"So really we need to go down and see, yes?" Bandicut looked at L'Kell, thinking of the unspoken part of the question: if Nabeck and the robots weren't inside the factory, then they must have been swept over the ledge and into the abyss.

Askelanda conferred with L'Kell. "The subs are all being recharged. When one is ready, we'll go."

Bandicut sighed with impatience, despite his own bone-weariness. "How long can Nabeck last, if he's really trapped in the factory? Don't your subs extract their air from the water?"

"Yes, of course," L'Kell said. "But—oh, I see. If the sub is no longer in water, he'll be on reserve air . . ."

The elder Neri said, "He's alone, so he can last awhile. Maybe two days, maybe three. But it is no good going before the sub is ready. Or you are ready. Now, you must rest while you can. We will get you when it is time . . ."

Bandicut tried to sleep, but couldn't get over a feeling of cold and loneliness. His friends were all elsewhere, planning their next activities. Antares and Li-Jared would be going to help Kailan. Ik would be leaving shortly with S'Cali; the Neri had reported that many of those still in the sunken ship needed help, and soon.

Bandicut tossed and turned under the Neri blankets, even after Char tried to help him relax. After a while, Li-Jared came in and sat in a corner of the room, staring silently into the night of the sea. He seemed troubled, and didn't engage Bandicut in conversation; but his presence was like a storm cloud, silent and brooding. A little later, Antares came in, carrying her blankets from the room where she had slept previously. She spoke softly for a moment to Li-Jared, then spread her blankets out near Bandicut and lay down.

He looked at her questioningly. "He's thinking about Harding," Antares murmured. Bandicut nodded, and after a minute closed his eyes, blanket pulled around his neck.

This time he went to sleep almost instantly.

When he awoke, it was to the sound of urgent conversation. He focused on the sounds before he opened his eyes. It was Antares and L'Kell—Antares telling the Neri that she could *feel* that Bandicut needed more sleep. "Is it urgent enough to wake him? I know it's important, but will it make any difference if he learns just a little later?"

" 'S okay," Bandicut mumbled, rolling over. "What is it?"

"Contact from your robots!" L'Kell cried, his voice rasping with excitement. "A recorded message."

"*What?* Where? How?"

"On the comm. Askelanda sent a scout-sub down, and they're picking up transmissions and relaying them. Do you want to hear what they're saying?"

"What do you think?" Bandicut got to his feet with a groan. Antares had been right; he definitely needed more sleep. He realized that she felt chagrined for trying to stop L'Kell, and he reached out to touch her arm. "Thank you, really. You were right. But I wouldn't miss this for anything."

As the three walked together to the communications room, he asked, "Why'd Askelanda send someone else?"

L'Kell looked at him as if he'd asked a stupid question. "You were sleeping quite soundly, my friend. As Askelanda pointed out, there are many here who are capable of undertaking a deep-water search, and summoning you if they found anything." L'Kell paused as Antares made a sound of a hissing chuckle. "He sent Targus and two others."

"And have they found the robots and Nabeck?"

L'Kell's breathing slits flared in excitement. "Not precisely, but they've located the area. Somehow the robots are getting their signal out from below the seafloor. Here's the comm room." They crowded in, and the Neri at the panel made the necessary connections to play the recording. The room was filled with a hiss of watery static . . . and then a robot's voice, in halting Neri:

"This is Copernicus. We are unharmed, and inside the factory space. Nabeck reports he is well, and finds sufficient oxygen in the fluid surrounding the submersible to maintain his breathing needs. He estimates power will last four more days at his present low rate of use, with reserve for return. Napoleon is presently in contact with the factory head, and is attempting to restart production of nano-assemblers and self-repair devices. Initial restart should be possible with materials on hand. However, the previously requested materials are needed as soon as possible. They need not be refined. Refining can be accomplished here, once self-repair is underway . . ."

The Neri operator cut off the playback. "Something new is coming in on the relay."

It was a Neri voice. "This is Nabeck. I hope you can hear me. I am well, and hopeful that the robots will arrange a way for us to leave the factory when they are done. It is very strange in here.

We appear to be inside a large, flexible chamber. Ambient pressure is normal for this depth. I do not know the nature of the fluid surrounding us, but it is a clear fluid, with occasional swirls of a milky liquid. The robots believe that it is a transport medium for the invisible assemblers that make the factory work. I hope it is not harming the hull of the sub."

Nabeck's voice stopped, and Copernicus's came on again, in English. "We do not know if you are receiving this signal, which we are broadcasting acoustically through the wall of the factory. If you can hear us, you may be able to reply by inserting a probe through the outer membrane where we originally made contact. We will continue to broadcast at intervals, to assist you in locating the spot. We do not know present conditions outside the factory. During the last seismic disturbance, we moved approximately ten meters forward, drawn by a mechanism from inside the factory. We have had no further information from the outside.

"A special note. The factory head's core programming contains numerous operating limitations. Certain of these might prevent it from performing nonspecified or abnormal activities, such as contacting the mechanism of the abyss. This core programming is isolated and protected, and cannot be altered by Napoleon. He is still examining this problem; however, it appears that direct interface with a responsible authority may be required to override the factory head's limitations. Nabeck is unaware of any Neri trained in direct interface methods. However, John Bandicut is so trained. You may wish to consider this question.

"If anyone is receiving this message, please respond . . ."

The message began again, this time in the Neri tongue.

The Neri turned down the volume slightly. "That will probably repeat several times. When the robot pauses, we can transmit back to Targus in the sub. Would you like to send a reply?"

"Tell Targus, 'Message received,'" said L'Kell. "Ask if they've located the entry point, and if they have attempted to establish two-way contact." L'Kell looked at Bandicut and Antares. "Anything you want to add?"

"Yes," said Bandicut. "As soon as you can get a message through to the robots, tell them, 'Well done, be careful, and come back out soon.'"

"Amen," said Antares.

L'Kell led them in search of Askelanda. The Neri leader was in an upper room pacing in conference with several others. When he saw L'Kell and his friends, he motioned to them to join in. L'Kell told Askelanda about the most recent message from Copernicus. "You have heard this transmission from your robots?" Askelanda asked Bandicut.

"Yes."

Askelanda peered at him with eyes that seemed dusty with age, and yet sharp. "And are you capable of making a 'direct connection' with the factory head, such as your robot spoke of?"

Bandicut felt a flashback welling up in him, taking him back to Triton, to the time when he'd just *lost* his neurolink ability, to the time of silence-fugues, to the time when a new individual in his life, the quarx, had made it possible to regain those kinds of connections. He reeled with the memory, and realized that Char was watching intently, learning, understanding.

/// So you can do this, yes? ///

/I can if you reach out and make the connection. You're my neurolink pathway./

/// That's no problem. ///

/And of course, if the factory head's language is even remotely comprehensible to me. I'll have to count on the stones, and maybe the robots, to sort that out./

"John?" L'Kell asked.

He blinked. "Yes. Yes, I might be able to make that connection—at least in principle. But—" he hesitated "—how the hell are you going to put me physically in contact with the thing? Do you have any ideas about that?"

L'Kell and Askelanda looked at each other.

"Don't even think about asking me to go out in the water at that depth. It would kill me."

"I expect it would," Askelanda rasped dryly. "It's not so healthy for us, either. We can do it, at need, but there are better ways to die."

Bandicut shivered.

"Could you use a cable connection similar to the one the robots used?" asked L'Kell.

Bandicut thought for a moment, then shook his head. "No, we don't have the interface."

/// *Say, why couldn't you—?* ///

Bandicut blinked, suddenly anticipating what the quarx was about to say. /Yes, of course! It might—/ He opened his mouth to speak, then thought, /But I don't even know how the damn thing works. Submarines, at least, I understand./ Nevertheless, he swallowed and said, "Our star-spanner bubble. I wonder if it might serve . . ."

L'Kell hissed. "The robots were well protected when we found them trapped down there in it. But how would that permit you to make contact?"

Bandicut described the way he and his companions had been able to stretch through the star-spanner bubble's membrane as though it were a rubber sheet. That had been in water much shallower than the depth of the factory, but perhaps it wasn't depth-dependent.

/// *The stones think it might work.*
It's worth a try, anyway. ///

The Neri listened to his description without comment. They were accustomed to membranes that did things Bandicut regarded as miraculous. Askelanda finally said, "I will ask, then, that you prepare to try this, when the time comes."

"When the time comes?"

"At the moment, it seems that your robots are doing all that can be done. It is best that you wait here until we receive word that the factory requires your presence."

"But—" Bandicut began, thinking how badly he wanted to get back down there and make contact, and put his hands on his robots. But he knew Askelanda was right.

Askelanda seemed to sense his thoughts. "John Bandicut, we have already asked more of you than any stranger—or visitor—should be asked to give. This might be our most dangerous request yet."

Bandicut frowned. "I guess we're not strangers anymore, are we? But it is absolutely necessary that this be done, yes?"

"Oh, yes," said Askelanda. "Without the factory—with the Maw threatening to destroy us, and I suppose the Astari too—who knows what would become of us?" Askelanda blinked his great, dusty eyes and readjusted his stole. "But John Bandicut, I must ask this: Why do these things matter to you? Why do you risk your life for *us?*" Askelanda cocked his head, gazing at him.

Bandicut's mouth opened, and froze. He struggled to find words.

"I've wondered, too," L'Kell said. "I have been happy to accept your actions, and your friendship, but—" The Neri's voice faltered, and his gaze seemed to furrow inward, as though he were listening to his own stones. Were they starting to give L'Kell hints of their purpose? Would they be any clearer with him than Bandicut's had been?

Bandicut let his breath out slowly. "I can't tell you, exactly," he said at last. "All I can say is, I guess when I find myself in a situation when I *can* do something to help—"

/// Or in a situation when you have to help— ///

/Yes./ He cleared his throat. "I—well, I try to."

"And," said L'Kell, eyes refocusing, "you are put by your stones . . . in the position of having to do these things, aren't you?"

Bandicut nodded uncomfortably. "But Askelanda—remember, too, I might be spending the rest of my life here under this sea with you." He swallowed hard. "I'm not acting completely selflessly. Even if you weren't my friends, I'd have reason to want your people to survive."

Askelanda gazed at him for a moment without speaking. Finally he cupped his hand-webs in a gesture of approval. "Then you'll abide by my wishes, and rest here and prepare properly? I do not want to lose you in vain—by sending you off too soon, or too tired to do what you have to do."

Bandicut drew a breath. "Yes." And he let the breath out, and wondered how in the world he could stand the wait.

Copernicus ... Napoleon ...

INTERLUDE

Julie Stone

JULIE STONE CHECKED her suit monitors one last time, and stepped cautiously around the barricades that blocked off the inner cavern. The ice floor gleamed in her suit headlight. Ahead of her, the translator squirmed and twisted in its own faint radiance. "All systems normal," she murmured into her helmet comm.

"Telemetry looks good," said Georgia Patwell. Julie's friend's voice could have been coming from light-years away, or inches. She was stationed across the cavern floor, monitoring remote sensors and comm, ready to send in assistance if necessary. Realistically, of course, if the translator did anything that would require her to need help, what were any of them going to be able to do?

"Mass readings are unchanged," Julie reported. "I feel nothing unusual."

"No? Then why the hell is your heart pounding so loud I can hear it without the comm?"

Julie chuckled. "Just trying to keep you folks interested, is all."

The translator was a stark shape against the blue-white frozen nitrogen walls of the cavern. Its black and iridescent globes spun ceaselessly, like turbulent soap bubbles clustered together in the shape of a large top, passing through one another in endless motion, the whole array balanced upon a single black globe.

Julie wondered if it had ever tipped over, and what would happen if it did.

Why had the translator ignored all efforts at communication by the exoarch and technology transfer teams? And why had it resisted being moved? One month and twenty million dollars worth of ruined equipment later, Julie Stone had been sent to find out.

So far it was showing no sign of noticing her presence.

"Okay, Jul'—Kim says you're cleared to approach the translator." Georgia's voice was calm but dead serious.

Making a conscious effort to breathe slowly and evenly, Julie stepped closer to the translator, until she could almost have reached out and touched the thing. She began to raise a hand but stopped, fearful. She knew what had happened to all those pieces of equipment, melted and vaporized. She stood gazing at the translator, thinking, Who are you really, and what are you doing here? Then she felt it tingling at the edges of her mind. Hello? she thought. Are you there?

We are here.

Startled, she cleared her throat, trying to quell a tremble that was beginning somewhere in the middle of her spine, and radiating outward. You are here. Where? In my head?

Please focus your thoughts.

Focus my thoughts? Julie hesitated, trying to decide what that meant. Then she recalled a neurolink technique that John had described to her once, and she frowned, trying to produce the kind of inward direction of her thoughts that people used in the neuro. /Is this what you mean?/ she asked silently.

Better.

She waited, wondering if the translator would say more.

Instead, it silently reached into her mind and began to blow her thoughts around, like a rising autumn wind stirring up dry leaves. Within moments, her mind was filled with a whirlwind of activity. She froze in place, bewildered, as the wind grew to a cyclone. She felt no pain. She teetered, but did not lose her balance, or consciousness. /What are you doing?/ she whispered. And it answered:

Preparing.

She blinked. /Yes . . . but preparing what?/

Preparing to give you . . . the tools that you will need.

And then her consciousness did flicker, just for an instant, as if she'd nodded off and caught herself. And when she blinked back from it, she had the oddest sense that an array of glittering points of light had danced around her in the ghostly cavern, speaking to her, and then had vanished before she could ask them who or what they were.

———

"Jul', are you okay? Talk to me, hon'." Georgia was calling insistently—not in a panicky or distraught way, but over and over so as to get her attention.

"Huh? Yeah. Yeah, I'm fine," she murmured, stepping back a little from the translator. Wait a minute—wasn't she supposed to be approaching the thing? What had just happened here?

"What are you doing now, Julie? Tell us what you saw. Did you hear anything? Talk to me, Julie, talk to me."

"Uh, yeah. I . . . sensed it. I felt its presence. I know it was aware of me." She felt as if she had *dozed off* there for a second. That seemed impossible, with the adrenaline she had rushing through her veins.

"What, exactly, did you sense, Julie? Are you stepping away from it now? Keep talking. Don't drift out on me."

"What do you mean?" She shook her head. Something was happening in her mind; she couldn't quite tell what.

"Your heart-rate spiked, then took a big drop for a couple of seconds. Now it's climbing again. Did you lose consciousness?"

"I'm . . . not sure."

"Well, I think you did. And I think maybe you should come on out," Georgia said, her voice tinged with worry. "And I think you should tell me everything you remember, and everything that even crosses your mind, before you lose it."

"Okay."

"What happened when you first sensed it?"

Julie blinked hard. Looking at the translator she felt that there was some kind of impenetrable barrier between her and it now. It didn't want her to approach.

Take time for acclimation, said a voice, soft but deep in her mind.

"Okay," she murmured, half to the voice and half to Georgia. "It spoke. But it's not as if I understand exactly . . ." Her voice faltered. There was still a voice in her head. She thought she had broken contact with the translator. John had spoken in his letter of an alien intelligence that had somehow come to reside with him, in his mind. Was this one of those?

We are not the quarx. There is only one quarx, and it lives with John.

Lives with John? She blinked, wondering if she had heard that right. *Lives?* She shook her head. /If you are not a . . . quarx, then who are you? If you are not the translator . . ./

We are the daughter-stones. We are of the translator.

/Daughter-stones?/ She shook her head, peering out through her suit helmet at all the lights glaring off the translucent cavern walls, glaring in her eyes. Was she imagining all this? She felt a sudden slight sting, like an electrical tingle, in both of her wrists. She raised her gloved hands—and her arms, encased in the tough, insulated fabric of the pressure suit. For an instant, she had the illusion that she could look right through her suited arms and see her bare wrists—and what she saw, embedded in each wrist, was a pulsing bead of light. *Daughter-stones . . .*

The voice spoke again, as she drew a frightened breath.

There is no need to fear us. There is much that we must tell you.
/Tell me—?/

"Julie?" called Georgia. "Julie, keep talking, girl. Kim, I think you'd better get in there right away—"

You must decide for yourself whether to trust us. But we have a journey to take together. And the first place we must travel is to your homeworld . . .

CHAPTER 31

The Hardest Part

BANDICUT FOUND THE enforced waiting almost intolerable. When Antares asked him if he would like to accompany her to Kailan's lab, he readily agreed. He had spent the better part of two days resting, and didn't know how much longer he could stand to do nothing but stare out into the misty world of perpetual night. All of the reports were promising, but no more than that. The robots reported progress with the factory; S'Cali reported progress at the Astari wreck helping the sick there, repairing the damaged sub, and gathering materials for the factory. They were waiting for some supplies to arrive on an Astari surface craft. Everything added up to the fact that they were just going to have to keep waiting a while longer.

"How's Li-Jared doing?" Bandicut asked Antares, as they rode in the back of a small sub toward Kailan's habitat.

"He's grieving for Harding," Antares murmured, "and working very hard to keep from thinking about it. He didn't want to return to our quarters last night. I think he wanted to keep working all night."

"He is a passionate—" Bandicut almost said *man*, and instead said, "companion."

Antares placed a long-fingered hand on Bandicut's. "Yes," she said. "And he's someone who cares deeply about his friends." Antares was gazing at Bandicut with wide-pupiled eyes. "You might not have realized, because you were in such distress—but he gave his daughter-stones to Harding in no small part because he was afraid for you."

Bandicut's breath caught. Had he been aware of that? He hadn't thought about it much; but then, that episode was pretty blurred in his mind. But now he could almost feel Li-Jared's concern, and *fear*, and shame for being afraid—and his hope that perhaps he could do something.

/// Antares is replaying the emotions for you.
Or at least remembering them vividly. ///

He nodded slowly to Antares. "Do you think there's anything we can do for him?"

"I think, just staying with him is all we can do. I do not know his Karellian emotions well enough to do more than guess."

Antares blinked. "And you—you are worried for your robots, and maybe for everything that is to come. Please tell me if there is any way I can help you."

Bandicut caught her hand for a moment in his, and finally smiled gratefully.

The sub rumbled, turned, and approached Kailan's habitat.

Bandicut worked a long day with the others, without much success—trying to help Kailan uncover useful and relevant information about the Astari, about the factory, the Maw, anything they could find. They couldn't find much. It was not, Kailan was sure, that there was nothing there in the Neri records. But what they had was broken up, lost in a knowledge-base whose design was too confusing, and whose instructions and signposts had gotten lost in the passage of time, or with the appearance of the Maw.

Li-Jared determinedly kept at it, in the belief that *anything* they might find could be useful. That was Kailan's philosophy, too, and Bandicut agreed; it made good sense to try to learn all they could. But he was tiring; he couldn't keep his thoughts on what he was doing.

/// You've been here a long time.
Do you think maybe you should
take a break? ///

Bandicut sighed. /Maybe so./ Antares had gone off to take a walk a while ago, and Kailan was deep in conversation with Li-Jared. He rose from the console where he'd been crouching, stretched, and wandered out of the chamber.

He ended up in a big lounge where the Neri—mostly females here—liked to relax while eating and drinking, or playing with the young. But it was deserted at this hour; he was startled to realize how long they had been working. Almost everyone in the habitat was probably asleep. He walked to the window and peered out into the water where lamps illuminated a fish corral, apparently constructed of partial enclosures of netting, without any visible means of keeping the fish in. Several small schools of half-clear, half-silver fish were gathered in the enclosures, despite the fact that they could leave anytime.

"It's something about the currents, I think."

Bandicut glanced up, startled, to find Antares standing beside him. She pointed to the end of the nearest half-cage, where a slow current was carrying suspended debris, including bits of food, through the enclosure where the fish hovered. "They just seem to like it there."

Bandicut nodded silently. Now it was relaxing to be standing here, looking out into the emerald and white world of the artificially lit ocean. Two Neri swimmers came into view, tending the farm, and a solitary sub moved around like a somnolent fish with headlights, performing slow pirouettes in the night as it performed whatever maintenance chores it was out there for.

"There's a nice little dome room upstairs, where we can have some privacy, if you feel like sitting and talking." Antares held up a basket of fruit. "I just came from the storeroom. We could—how do you describe it?—have a picnic."

Bandicut stared at her, astounded by the thought of a picnic at the bottom of the sea. He began to laugh.

"Is this not a good idea?" Antares asked, with a Thespi grin of uncertainty.

"No, no—I mean, yes," he said. "It's a wonderful idea. Thank you." He grinned a human grin, then turned with a gesture and let her lead the way.

It was a small residence room, with a half dome looking out. "This is where I stay, when I don't return to the other habitat. Come sit." Antares pulled a large pillow to the center of the room, and he pulled another, and they sat with the basket between them, passing out food. There were small, yeasty nuggets that tasted like a bitter bread, and orange, waxy fruits shaped like pears, and twisted dried seaweed. They ate for a while in companionable silence.

After a time, Antares said, "Do you think we were sent to this world deliberately, to try to help these people? Could someone on Shipworld have *known* about the Neri's struggle with the Astari, and the Maw, and the broken factory?"

Bandicut eyed a nugget of bread-fruit, thinking of the normalization that made it possible for him to sit here under—what?—maybe twenty-five or thirty atmospheres of pressure, breathing uncertain gas mixtures, and eating alien plants that would probably kill him under other circumstances. "It's hard to see it any other way," he said. "I guess what I wonder isn't whether they sent us here deliberately, which I'm sure they did—whoever *they* are—but whether they intend to bring us back again. Or will we be spending the rest of our lives here on this world, under this ocean?"

"Or maybe up with the Astari," Antares said.

"Or up with the Astari," he agreed. "It's not a bad place. It's quite beautiful, in many ways. And our friends . . . L'Kell and Kailan and the others. But it's not home, is it?"

She blew through puckered lips. "No. It's not home." She chewed a bread-nugget thoughtfully, then said, "You miss your home a lot, don't you? And the ones you loved. I can feel it in you."

He grunted. He had not spent a lot of time consciously grieving over his past life, and yet, now that she mentioned it, he felt a renewed pang.

"Yes?" she asked.

He nodded. "I've hardly had time to think about it. But yes. Yes, I do." He gazed at Antares, and allowed himself a confused smile, suddenly thinking about Julie Stone—and then, abruptly, about Antares. She was watching him with great interest. "But there's so much I don't know about *you*," he said. "And your world."

"Such as—?"

"I don't know. What was it that took you from your world, and brought you to Shipworld? Was your world saved, the way mine was? The way Ik's wasn't? What can you tell me about your world?"

Her lips turned up in a frown that seemed like a smile. "I do not know what became of my world. As far as I know, it was never in any danger."

"No danger?"

"But *I* was in danger. I was in prison, awaiting execution."

He remembered the image from the joining of their stones. "The forbidden love."

Antares nodded. Definitely a human gesture, this time. She had been studying him.

Bandicut felt a pressure in his throat, as he remembered the wall that had fallen between them, defining limits in the midst of their joining. "And now you feel as though you cannot know love again. Or . . . make love . . . to another. Yes?"

For a moment, she did not speak, though he felt her conflicted emotions pulling one way and another. She touched his hand, and he turned it palm-up and held her hand for a dozen heartbeats. And he knew, as he squeezed her hand, that she knew what he meant by making love. Close enough, anyway. He wondered suddenly how Thespi females made love, and what it felt like to them. Was it an empathic rush of free-flowing emotion? Was it like human coupling, with rising and crescendoing physical urges? Was it sex at all? He thought he had felt inklings of this, when they'd joined stones, but now he could not remember.

Antares raised his hand and pressed it to her throat, just above her upper breasts. He felt the stones come alive, touching hers . . .
. . . *differently*, this time. Almost disturbingly so. But not just disturbing: there was a sharpness, and excitement. As though all the images that before had whirled around them, gathering pieces of their past lives, had been stripped away . . . leaving only the emotions, and the inner sensations of the body. And then new images. Touching. Gently stroking. Fingers on skin. Stroking. Arms gliding together, fingertips brushing. Sensations and emotions mingling, before any physical arousal had begun. Then later came the physical, the flickering of fire in the loins. Dance of electricity in the arms, along the neck. Blossoming into the breasts, sparkling out into the top nipples first. Then the bottom pair slowly brightening, joining.

Bodies slowly coiling around each other, searching for best fit. Hands here, there. Arms enclosing. Mouths touching shoulders, one to the other. Fingers moving through hair. And then bodies pressing close, skin to skin, nipples to smooth chest. Legs opening and closing around each other, bellies rubbing softly. And with an eruptive sparkle, the tiny probe emerging from his stomach and embedding itself in the soft depression in hers . . .

And the two minds, two psyches, coiling around each other and joining

joining

joining who? Antares and

Who? The forbidden lover? Ensendor.

And then a curious shifting. For a moment a wall of grieving. Then the grieving dissolved into a different time, a different place, and the physical joining faded away. Emotions did not fade, but reformed, and bodies reappeared transformed, and he was joined, moving slowly. Slowly. Deeply penetrating. Prolonging. Entangled with, joined with Julie, his sensations inside and outside, the heat of her swallowing him. And the shuddering, and eruptive bursts. And slow dissolve . . .

He blinked, realized Antares' head was cradled on his shoulder, her hair falling against his neck. His hand, and wrist, slipping a little from the front of her throat, to the top of her upper breasts. He sensed her desire, uncertain and confused. He lowered his hand very slowly, and cupped her upper left breast. Then brushed with his fingertips. Felt nipple through soft fabric. Felt it grow warm to the touch.

> This was wrong
>
> no
>
> why would it be
>
> not wrong
>
> different

Her hand covered his and held it there. Cradling the warm nipple. Hard. Feeling the spark, the tiniest electric tingle.

And her thought: *Yes. There. Just that.*

And he cradled her shoulder with the other arm, her head rocking slightly on his shoulder, and felt the wave of sorrow at what was and might have been, and fearful pleasure at what might be. And he held her, held her sorrow and pleasure in his arms, felt her trembling as it coursed through her . . .

Finally she raised her eyes, and peered into his, probing, searching for memories. She silently opened the front of her pant-suit and pressed his hand over her bared breast. Her nipple was hot and hard under his palm. Her hand moved along his arm. Lightly touching his chest, through the jumpsuit. And then lower. Lower. She touched, then tentatively closed her hand over him, holding the bulge of his erection through the fabric. His breath shuddered out.

Her breath sighed in and out, with excitement. But also surprise. Perplexity. Curiosity. "You're *huge*," she whispered. "How can you be?"

He groaned with pleasure, and despite all of his instincts and desires, began to laugh.

"Why are you—am I hurting you?" She started to remove her hand.

"No—no, don't stop—"

"Then—" Eyes large, bright, gold.

"It's just—" he whispered, barely able to speak "—how did you know—exactly the right thing to say?"

She did not answer, but parted her lips in a Thespi smile, and moved her hand very gently, slowly, following the undulating waves of pleasure. Thinking, or perhaps whispering, *show me,* and then finding the opening in the fabric and releasing him into the warmth of her hand and the softness of her belly . . .

---

*/// That was amazing . . .
really amazing . . . quite wonderful . . . ///*

He swallowed, focusing on everything, and nothing. A hundred thoughts flickered through his mind, and fled. He breathed slowly and deeply, letting his eyes come back into focus on Antares. /I didn't know you were there./

*/// Oh yes—watching, experiencing.
Joining.
I hope I didn't interfere. ///*

/No. Thank you./

/// You seem very . . . foggy . . . ///

/Happy./ He touched Antares' hair.

*/// . . . and yet in a strange way, very clear.
But I sense now, she is beginning to
draw away again. ///*

He stroked Antares' cheek. /You don't have to analyze, or explain—don't—/

*/// She is holding you, fulfilled,
in a certain way— ///*

/Please./

*/// And yet she is sad, frightened,
afraid to hold on. ///*

He caressed her face with his fingertips, then drew her close into the comfort of his neck and shoulder, kissed the top of her head, her hair. She smelled of pine and musk. /Let us enjoy it now, please, while it lasts. Ask whatever you want later. Not now./

/// *Yes. Of course.*
Sorry. ///

They went to sleep loosely dressed, but curled together in spoon fashion, or as nearly so as their not-quite-matched bodies would fit. Bandicut kept an arm around her, aware that whatever they had just shared might be a thing of the moment; and yet wishing not to let the intimacy evaporate if he could help it, or disappear behind a veil of caution and isolation. And knowing, even as he slipped off to sleep, that it was mostly beyond his power to control.

They woke much later—slowly, comfortably, but then with a certain amount of awkwardness, when they realized that Li-Jared was asleep in a corner of the room. Antares turned to receive his embrace, then sat up, pushing her hair back from her face. She began sorting through the leftover fruit. Li-Jared woke up, and joined them sleepily in quiet conversation and food.

Word came early in the day that S'Cali and the cargo sub had arrived from the Astari wreck, and Bandicut was wanted for a conference with L'Kell. He took the first sub that Kailan could arrange, leaving Antares and Li-Jared at work with the obliq.

Askelanda was the first to greet him, even before L'Kell. "We have a load of materials—not in great quantity, but perhaps enough to satisfy the factory, for a start."

Bandicut looked from Askelanda to Ik, who had returned with S'Cali, along with most of the remaining Neri. "And is it the raw material the factory asked for—or machines, or what?"

Ik answered, "Raw materials, mostly. Some was ferried out from the land; apparently the Astari ashore are honoring Morado's agreement. Some of it came from storage compartments on the wreck that the Neri hadn't even begun to explore yet. We think it covers most of what the factory asked for, but we have no real way of testing. The copper I'm pretty sure of; it's in thick coils. The rest is the Astari's best guess. I suppose the factory itself will have to make the determination."

"And the factory may be ready for us," L'Kell said, coming in from another room.

"Word from the robots?" Bandicut asked.

"A new transmission. They said that the reprogramming was going well, but complete self-repair and production restart now awaits the arrival of materials."

"How are you doing at getting a message back in to the robots?"

"That's the other news. Delent'l went down this morning to relieve Targus, and he finally located the entry membrane through the silt, and got a probe in. We're not sure about the transmission, though. Possibly the robots couldn't understand Delent'l's speech very well. Delent'l said he tried to explain that you would be coming in your star-spanner bubble, and he got a reply that sounded like—" L'Kell's voice deepened as he tried to sound human "—'Tally-ho, Captain.' "

Bandicut burst into laughter.

"Is this meaningful to you?" Askelanda demanded.

"Yes. I think you can take that as a yes," he reassured the ahktah.

"Then the time has come to prepare for your departure," Askelanda said. He turned to the other Neri. "Please begin attachment of our guests' bubble to the sub." Then he asked Bandicut, "Do you wish to have anyone in the bubble with you?"

Bandicut thought about that for a moment. "Ik, would you like to come with me? It might be risky, but I sure could use your advice and wisdom."

Bring all.

Bandicut blinked, startled by the sudden voice of the translator-stone. His first thought was worry. /Charlie? Char, you there? You okay?/

/// Yes, I'm here. ///

/Why'd it speak directly like that? It never does that when you're here./

/// I think . . . they really wanted
to make their point. ///

/They want me to bring everyone? Just like that? Do you have any idea why?/

/// I think they see this mission as
the crucial determinant. ///

He raised his palms mentally, trying to comprehend.

/// No one expects you to be able
to put things aright here all by yourself.
Nor should you.
What they want is
for you to change the spin, the direction,
the way things are heading. ///

/So?/

/// So that's what we're after
on this trip, and maybe on this world.
John, I'm not really sure . . .
that we'll be coming back this way again.
Don't ask me why I think that. ///

Bandicut swallowed hard. He looked again at Ik and L'Kell and Askelanda, and said, "I think, actually, it would be best if we all went. Ik, Li-Jared, Antares. This is going to be a big mission. And I think I might need . . . all of your help. I would like for us—" he hesitated "—to stick together."

Ik gazed at him with glittering Hraachee'an eyes. "Then I should call the others. Should I not?"

Bandicut nodded, not trusting himself to speak.

CHAPTER 32

The Factory Head

THE FACTORY AREA looked even more desolate than before. There was a haze of suspended silt, like low ground fog, close to the bottom. Rocks and parts of the factory structure poked up like hump-backed ghosts, silent and grey. Bandicut rubbed his eyes, uncertain for a moment whether it was fatigue or water-borne haze that was obscuring the view. He glanced back through the rear viewports, for maybe the hundredth time, to make sure the star-spanner bubble was still attached to the back of the sub. It was, and behind it were the headlights of the cargo sub. His eye caught Antares, and her lips crinkled for a moment in a calming smile. Her emotions seemed cloudy, but she was trying to be reassuring.

"Are you worried?" asked Ik.

"Nervous as a bridegroom," Bandicut said, peering forward again to see if he could spot the entry point to the factory.

He needn't have bothered; Delent'l had left an echoing sonar marker. L'Kell quickly located the marker and brought them to the spot. "Let's insert the probe," he said.

"All right." Bandicut took the manipulator arm controls and began to extend the probe, which was tipped with a bulbous speakerphone. His action was interrupted by a voice on the external hydrophone, speaking in Neri.

"This is Copernicus. We are detecting vibrations suggesting the presence of a submersible. If this is correct, please ping three times."

L'Kell pinged. The sounds reverberated in the sub's cabin like a plucked piano string.

"Thank you. If John Bandicut is with you, ping three times."

Ping. Ping. Ping.

"Thank you." The robot switched to English. "Welcome, Cap'n. We are prepared to initiate contact. Please back away to a distance of at least twenty meters while we clear the area."

L'Kell backed the sub away. A moment later, a great cloud of silt billowed up in front of the sub, white and impenetrable in the headlight glare. It slowly drifted toward the sub, obscuring the pilot's window, and then gradually cleared. Where they previously had seen only a hump of murky sediment, they now saw a membrane pulsing rhythmically outward like a balloon, knocking away the last of the silt residue on its surface.

Bandicut glanced at L'Kell. "Let's try the outside speakers and see if Copernicus can hear us through the membrane." L'Kell touched the switch. "Coppy, this is Bandicut. Can you read me? The entry point is much clearer now."

"Excellent, Cap'n. Are you in the star-spanner bubble?"

"Not yet. What do you want us to do?"

"Let's take care of the materials first. Have you brought what we requested?"

"It's right behind us, in a cargo sub. They can drop it wherever you want it."

The robot's voice seemed to reverberate across the ocean floor. "Then let us proceed with the transfer. Please observe, and report what you see, on the area thirty meters upslope from this entry membrane. About ten meters shy of the large black smoker."

L'Kell pointed out the spot, alerted S'Cali in the cargo sub, and turned his own sub for a better view. There was another massive puff of silt, which drifted clear, revealing a horizontal membrane on the bottom. It looked like a large, metallized tarp stretched over . . . what? Bandicut wondered. He described it to Copernicus.

"At the pilot's discretion, he may approach the membrane," said the robot. "If the cargo is solid and sufficiently dense, he may simply drop it over the membrane."

"Preparing for the drop," came S'Cali's voice. "It'll take a minute to get ready. L'Kell and Bandicut watched as the larger sub maneuvered over the membrane, like a great hen settling into its nest. A few minutes later, S'Cali reported his cargo hatch opened, and the drop completed.

"Cargo received," Copernicus replied. "Contents are being analyzed and broken down. The copper and other elements are being dissolved and placed into the raw material stream. Thank you. John Bandicut, while that procedure is taking place, would you like to attempt contact with the factory head?"

Bandicut drew a deep breath before answering. "All right. I'm going to move into the bubble now." He glanced at his Neri friend.

L'Kell took the remote manipulator controls and began winding in the forwardmost cables securing the bubble. Bandicut peered back to see the bubble rising behind them and moving forward over the sub. L'Kell crouched to peer up through a small porthole, and carefully reeled the cables until the bubble was positioned directly overhead. Then he drew all the cables taut, fore and aft—securing the bubble against the hatch.

They had rehearsed this in relatively shallow water—in the middle of the Neri city, with swimmers standing by to aid him. They had established that it was possible to pass from the sub to the bubble and back, while keeping the internal pressure of both lower than that of the surrounding water. But that differential was small stuff compared to what they faced here. Thousands of pounds per square inch were squeezing against the sub, ready to burst through any structural weakness. Would the seal hold? And if it failed, would he kill just himself, or all of his friends, too?

It was time to find out.

He turned around in the cramped space. As he squeezed between Antares and Li-Jared in the back of the compartment, Antares caught his hand—and his gaze. He managed a smile. Then he climbed up into the conning tower airlock.

As he reached for the metal hatch, Ik called up, "Are you sure you don't want someone with you?"

He glanced back down into the compartment. "Later. Let me check it out first. Now, help me secure this, okay?"

He swung the hatch shut and tightened the latches. He was in a tight cylinder now, lit only by a tiny Neri lantern. He'd been through the tower many times, but it felt a lot smaller with both top and bottom hatches closed. Reaching overhead, he began to loosen the latches on the top hatch, working quickly before he could lose his nerve.

/// If there's sea-pressure against the hatch,
you probably won't be able to open it. ///

He wiped sweat from his eyes. /True./ And it was also true that if the bubble didn't have a remarkable ability to withstand pressure on one side, and allow penetration on the other, he wouldn't be able to open the hatch. He pushed upward. There was resistance for a moment, then a slight give. The stone in his left wrist flickered, and the hatch swung open. A cupful of trapped water splashed down. He poked his head up through the Neri membrane, and the star-spanner membrane, and caught a breath of air that smelled . . . different . . . almost with a hint of ozone to it. But it was air, blessed air.

He climbed up out of the airlock into a dark, dry space. Dark, that is, except for the glow of the sub's headlights and sternlights shining into the abyssal gloom. For a moment, he was nearly overcome with vertigo, and claustrophobia, and sheer quaking terror, as he absorbed the fact that he was sitting in a bubble made of *nothing*, energy maybe, at the bottom of the ocean.

/// It's pretty strong, I think. ///

/Yah./ He climbed the rest of the way into the bubble.

It was eerily quiet. He could hear his heartbeat, and his breath, and some mutters and groans coming from the sub right below him. But there was an overpowering sense of stillness. It reminded him of the other-dimensional realm of the magellan-fish, back on Shipworld; that experience felt as if it had been a training ground for what he was doing now.

/// Perhaps it would be best for now
to focus— ///

/Right. Yes. Jesus./ He drew a sharp breath and secured the hatch on the sub, then crept forward to where he might become visible to L'Kell and the others, through the sub's nose window.

He heard a click and hiss, and suddenly the words, quite loudly, "Can you hear me, John Bandicut?" It was jarring, and seemed to come from everywhere at once; but he knew it was L'Kell.

"Loud and clear! Can you pull the bubble forward?"

With a whine from the winches, the bubble began to move. He glanced back and saw it separate from the hatch, and his heart began to pound again. The front of the sub was coming under the bubble now, and he crouched down to wave to his friends as they peered up through the nose window. He pointed forward. "Let's dock." With the star-spanner bubble resting on the sub's nose, L'Kell began to move them with great care toward the entry membrane of the factory. As the light grew stronger upon the membrane, it turned from grey to shimmering silver. Bandicut guided L'Kell with hand gestures, until the bubble drew very close, then touched the membrane with a quicksilver ripple—and a soft *boom*, like a kettle drum.

He heard the voice of Copernicus, hollow but clear: "Cap'n, is that you? Are you at the entry point?"

"I'm here. I'm in the bubble." With the bubble pressed against the membrane, both surfaces had flattened and formed a quivering mirror. "What now?"

"Can you reach through?" asked the robot.

"We'll find out." The pressure differential was enormous here: the robots at the ambient pressure of maybe four hundred atmospheres, the bubble at maybe forty or fifty atmospheres. How much could this star-spanner technology handle? Could it protect him? He drew a breath, reached out a hand, and pushed against the bubble. It felt like the resilient, but resistant, nothingness of a forcefield. He pushed harder. The interface dimpled suddenly, and his hand passed slowly though the factory membrane.

376 | Jeffrey A. Carver

He wiggled his fingers. It felt like air on the other side, not liquid. How could that be?

"Captain, we can see your hand. Are you all right?" called Copernicus through the membrane.

"Yes, I'm fine."

At that moment, something cold touched his hand, and he nearly jumped out of his skin. *"Jesus! What's that?"* He jerked his hand back.

"It's just me," said Copernicus.

His heart pounded frantically. He gasped for breath. *"Don't do that without warning me!"*

"I apologize. Cap'n—are you okay? Did I hurt you?"

He gasped, collecting himself. He looked at his hand, which he had reflexively pulled all the way out. With a little shiver, he reached back through the membrane. "No, you just scared me, that's all. Okay, where are you? You can touch my hand again."

This time, the metal touch felt reassuring. He took a deep breath, squeezing the robot's hand. "Should I try . . . pushing my face through?"

"If it seems safe to you," said the robot.

Safe? he thought, and almost laughed.

"Are you all right?" boomed another voice. L'Kell, in the sub. Or was it Ik? It was so distorted, it was hard to tell.

Without removing his hand, Bandicut turned his head to look down, over his shoulder. Ik, Antares, and L'Kell were peering out the nose window at him. "I'm fine!" he called. "I'm holding Copernicus's hand." Which raised another question: what was Copernicus doing outside the sub, anyway? "I'm going to try sticking my head through." Then, before he could have second thoughts, he leaned his forehead into the membrane. He felt only a slight resistance, then popped through.

It was like peering into a tent through a fish-eye lens. The first thing he saw was Copernicus, staring at him with dark camera eyes. And behind the robot, the Neri submarine and Napoleon. It was an incongruous sight. He wasn't sure what he'd expected: some very strange alien vista, a seafloor factory, maybe something like the star-spanner factory run by the shadow-people of Shipworld, but of course different because of where it was. Instead, what he saw was the inside of a huge bladder, translucent and glowing just enough to provide illumination, and containing nothing but those three objects: the sub and the two robots. He wondered what *he* looked like, with his hands and head extruded through the silvery membrane.

"Coppy," he said, his voice resonating into the space with a twang. He tried to draw a breath, and felt resistance. He suddenly realized that with his face pressed directly into the membrane, it was going to be very hard to breathe here.

/// Wait. ///

He waited, holding his breath, and sensed that the stones were in contact with the bubble or whatever controlled it, and were doing something to the permeability of the membrane.

"Cap'n," said Copernicus, "the factory has injected approximately one-tenth of one percent of oxygen into the atmosphere here. If the spanner bubble can accommodate selective movement of gases through the membrane, you should be able to breathe. At least I hope so."

/// Try it now.
We've adjusted the star-spanner bubble,
but have no control over the factory membrane. ///

He tried again to draw a breath, and to his surprise, was able to inhale slowly through the membrane. It was like breathing from a scuba cylinder that was nearly empty. He exhaled slowly, inhaled slowly. He didn't keel over. But he was going to become short of breath if this went on for very long.

/// We're going to adjust a few things
in your metabolism to let you stretch
your CO_2 tolerance and oxygen demand. ///

The difference was perceptible within seconds. He took a closer look at the smoothly curved walls that enclosed the Neri sub and the robots. There was perhaps a meter's width of clearance around the sub, just enough room for the robots to move. But within the surface of the bladder walls he saw sparkling flecks of something: maybe just refractions of light through the shimmer of the membrane interface, or maybe something else—say, tiny emitters or control points for nanoassemblers. Bandicut noticed that Napoleon, standing near the nose of the sub at the far end of the chamber, seemed to have several probes embedded in the wall of the chamber. He didn't recall Napoleon's having had those probes before.

"Is the breathing arrangement satisfactory?" Copernicus asked.

"Okay so far," Bandicut said. Raising his voice, he called, "Can you still hear me out there?"

He was startled to hear two different voices answer. "Quite well." "Yes, but faintly."

It took him a moment to realize that the first voice had been that of Nabeck, the robot's Neri companion in the sub in front of him. "Nabeck," he said, "are you well?"

"I am quite well, but weary of the confinement," the Neri answered. "Greetings to you and to L'Kell."

"Thank you. I hope we can give you reason to leave soon," Bandicut said. "And Copernicus, just out of curiosity, what are you and Napoleon doing outside the sub?"

"We locked out after the factory established a dry atmosphere in anticipation of your arrival," Copernicus said. "We thought we could be more useful to you here, on the outside, where you were going to be."

"Oh. Then thank you. I assume Nappy is tied up in conversation with the factory?"

"Yes, Cap'n. I am in close contact with him, however. I am pleased to report that the factory head functions on a considerably higher cogitative level than we had originally thought. The connection is in some respects difficult—"

Difficult. Yes, it would be, Bandicut thought—two AI mechanisms from entirely different worlds, meeting on an abyssal ledge kilometers deep in the ocean.

"—but we seem to have worked through the major communications issues. There are still some areas of uncertainty regarding operations and intentionality."

"I see. Well, is it ready to resume production? That's what the Neri want to know."

"Many of the internal repairs are far enough along for the most urgent tasks to be undertaken. Cap'n, the factory head is extremely eager to speak with you directly."

"That's what I'm here for." Bandicut gestured. He felt, peering through the shimmer of the interface, as if he were operating hand puppets. He glanced down; his hands appeared to be made of watery silver.

Copernicus tapped quietly, probably conferring with Napoleon. Copernicus's upper sensor swiveled away from Bandicut. The robot pointed with a mechanical hand toward the far end of the chamber, over Napoleon's head. "In that case, Cap'n, if you would fix your gaze in that direction, and be ready to receive the laser image—"

Laser image?

He blinked that way, and before he could even draw a breath, there was a light dancing in his eyes. A reflex to shut his eyes was suppressed, somewhere along the neural pathway.

/// It's okay, John.
We're watching for tissue damage,
but it's within safe limits so far. ///

Within safe limits . . . he supposed that was better than having his eyes fried straightaway. But was this how the thing was going to make contact—?

The play of light blossomed into something like a holo, but a holo playing directly inside his skull. The first image was a slow-motion fireworks burst, which turned from sparks of fire into raindrops of crimson and gold and emerald and silver. From out of that rain there emerged a face—a sculpture in chrome-silver, turning in space. It was a Neri face, or something like a Neri face. It was hard to see exactly, because it was strobe-lighted, with pulses of light here, there, filling Bandicut's skull. After a few moments the face was gone, and there was a sudden flickering of textured space that reminded him of human neurolink, with twisted topographies shot through with sparks of light. It produced a jittery sensation, like being overwrought and sleepless in the dark of night, with synapses firing at random. He had the sense that some kind of translation and analysis was taking place, perhaps involving the stones or perhaps just the factory head. The near-Neri face came back, rotating as if weightless; but now it was olive-green, and he could see that the eyes were smaller than a Neri's, and the neck was smooth, with no gills. It seemed to make eye contact, but only a fleeting, empty contact.

/// I have a feeling about that face— ///

/One of the Neri's creators?/

/// Yeah. ///

And then it was gone, leaving only a feeling of strobing images out of memory, and a voice:

You are John Bandicut? Species Human?

The answer—Yes!—seemed to come from somewhere within, and not through his conscious mind. Out of the strobing flashes, he thought he glimpsed an image that looked like Napoleon, spinning in and out of the frame of view. Would Napoleon speak? Not yet, apparently; the next voice was the same as the last:

Do you speak on behalf of the Neri?

/I do. And you are?/

Factory head. Iteration sssssshh— There was an instant of static as the translation through the stones broke down. Then: *—late revision. Communication restored after ... sssssshh ... interruption. Much demands attention. Repairs.* A sudden, flickering image of intricate patterns being changed blindingly fast; circuits maybe, or programming. *Production.* Strobelike images of subs, bubbles, membranes, diving equipment, electronics being spun into existence as though sketched by an invisible pen: nanoassembly. *Threats to the well-being of the Neri.*

Instead of images, there was sudden stillness, and Bandicut thought he heard Napoleon's voice, very distant, addressing the factory head. Abruptly there was darkness all around, with bursts of urgent blood-red heat lightning flashing in a moving pattern around him. *There is need. Urgent need.* And now an image, pulsing: a ghostly light burning out of the darkness of the abyssal valley, and quakes shaking loose rocks and ledges and habitats. After a few heartbeats, the image darkened back into the chaos of the crimson heat lightning.

Bandicut reeled at the intensity of the display. /Very urgent need,/ he agreed in a whisper, trying not to succumb to vertigo.

You wish assistance?

/In stopping that thing?/ He hardly dared hope. /By making contact?/

By making contact. Even now it trembles.

A new image, like a weird fish-eye shot from the back of Bandicut's head, with an overlay of semimirror rippling: the star-spanner bubble, and behind and under it, the sub, and behind that the spectral glow of the Devourer, awakening from its nap in the abyss over which the sub's stern hung like a rock climber's tailbone.

And again: the face of the near-Neri, or pre-Neri, surrounded by billowing concentric haloes of light. And about it, the voice of the factory saying . . .

Those who made us. Formed us. Instructed us.

Bandicut hardly breathed. /Yes?/

They are no more.

He exhaled. /No./

They were my authority. They are no more.

Pulse pounded in his head. /No more,/ he agreed.

Sparks, in a blizzard. A flash of consuming fire, like a great cosmic event, taking all in its wake. And darkness. And . . .

The Neri are therefore my authority. Or their—sssshh—surrogate.

Bandicut drew a difficult breath. /Yes—/

They cannot join in communication this way?

Bandicut hesitated. /Perhaps in time they can learn. They have no experience./

And you do.
/Yes./
And they have asked you to represent them?
/Yes./
Then I must show you my thoughts concerning the thing you call the Devourer, the Demon, the Maw of the Abyss. There are things I can do, but I must be released from my strictures of action.
/Show me, then./

———————

It was a dizzying stream of information.

For so many years the factory head had lain broken and unable to repair itself; and yet it was not wholly broken, not unconscious in all of its capacities. It was directly aware of certain devastations caused by the arrival of the abyss-thing, including damage to itself, and indirectly aware of others. Many comm-links with the pre-Neri on the land, and the Neri in their undersea habitats, were severed—but not before it had perceived indications of serious emergency conditions ashore. And after that . . . nothing, except the occasional visit from Neri of the undersea city, with broken communications which it could not properly integrate and answer.

But elsewhere in its processing stacks, an analysis was undertaken, and grew over the years, and came to occupy a larger part of the working subsections of the intelligence. Though unable to repair its own broken inner pathways, and suffering from the scattering of critical knowledge-bases, it nonetheless had the capacity for extensive use of background processors. (Was it like a person in a coma, Bandicut wondered—one whose unconscious processes continue apace even in the absence of outward awareness?)

And in those silent ruminations, the factory head paid close attention to what its remaining sensors told it about the abyss-thing that had caused so much damage. And it began to assemble patterns of perception that, in synthesis, could have been said to constitute understanding. Understanding of what the thing was, and was capable of, and what it might be trying to do.

The biggest clue came later, when the abyss-thing brought a ship from the sky crashing into the sea—its motive system hopelessly ensnared by the gravity/density/EM-spectrum/time-altering effects generated by the thing of the abyss. The specifics were unclear, but the factory head recognized similarities between the abyss-thing and the motive system of the wrecked ship. A connection remained between them, even after the crash; and the factory head discovered that certain of its comm-circuits resonated inexplicably whenever the two interacted.

Were they communicating? It seemed so, though only a small fraction of the signal was decipherable. But interaction between the two often preceded traumatic eruptions in the local area— which threatened not just the factory but the Neri, and even the crash-survivors on their perilous perch at the edge of the sea. But why?

/It seems to be a space-time-altering device, almost like a stardrive,/ Bandicut offered, following which the factory paused for several microseconds of thought.

It had not understood it in quite that way before, and did not quite know what Bandicut meant. But there were areas of knowledge previously inaccessible to it, now being made available through the help of the robots, or from the robots' own datastores. Many things were becoming clearer. And one of them was that the Neri's survival utterly depended upon making contact with the Maw of the Abyss.

And another was that the Maw itself might be silently desperate for such contact . . .

———————

/Why do you say desperate? Does it think? Feel?/

His question was answered by cascading raindrops of light. Uncertainty. Affirmation. It was the robots who had first noticed that such cognitive patterns might be present. The robots seemed to understand confusion and other emotion better than the factory. *Communications indicate the presence of confusion in the Maw. Confusion of purpose—and need for clarification.*

/That doesn't mean it's going to welcome contact./

No. Just that it is desperate.

Bandicut waited. The factory had raised this issue, and it seemed to have an opinion it wanted to express regarding course of action.

To assist you would require authorization to exceed my original mandate and limitations. Reason: factory involvement in the chain of contact could jeopardize primary factory operations. However, I can point out that analysis suggests that an instrument of communication can be fabricated. If you have your own design for such a—

/No./

Then I can offer my own design, which I could manufacture and deploy, if authorized to do so. Do you instruct me to attempt this?

Swirling mists of uncertainty, anxiety, anticipation . . .

/Mokin' foke yes, I instruct you—/

Unclarity. *Please restate.*

/Yes. Yes—I instruct you to do this thing./

You authorize, on behalf of the Neri?

/Yes! On behalf of the Neri./

Firing synapses. Lightheadedness. A snowstorm of sparkling plankton against a dark sea, like stars of the galaxy against the night. *Program is now activated.*

Bandicut drew a breath. /That's it? You were just waiting for authorization?/

Rapidly flickering checks and rechecks, configurations established. *Raw materials sufficient; energy sufficient; assemblers being programmed.* Spiraling orbits, wheels spinning in darkness. *Yes. And materials.*

Strobing views, too fast to be assimilated: fluid-filled chambers / plumes of chemicals / nano-assemblers riding the streams / skeletons rippling in laserlight / clouds of piranhas tearing apart and putting back together, at furious speed . . .

/How long?/

Zigzag pattern of shooting stars, electric arcs. *Nearly ready. Time grows short. Eruption is imminent. Are you prepared to descend into the abyss?*

/WHAT?/ His heart nearly jumped out of his chest. /What do you mean?/

Are you prepared to descend into the abyss?

/I heard that. But—/

Spiraling clouds of light, funneling toward a black hole, toward nothingness, toward—

This contact must be face to face, in person.

Bandicut stared dumbfounded at the images, and suddenly saw in them the swirling winds of chaos that had brought him here, and the deliberate machinations of the powers of Shipworld, as well. And he thought of the time not that long ago when he and his friends had had to face down a thing called the boojum in the terrible emptiness of a reality that only the magellan-fish understood, and he thought, No, God damn no, it's happening again, it's happening again . . . just like when the translator called me out of that godforsaken cavern on Triton . . .

And he knew there was no choice, really no choice, if he wanted to help the Neri survive; and in those spiraling clouds of the factory's images, he saw the currents of chaos rising and falling finally into place, like an interlocking puzzle, an intersecting tangle of currents that had brought him inexorably to this last great trial in the depths of the sea. And he thought, /Damn you, stones, if you know what this is *really* all about, you had better give me some answers, and give them to me now./

And came an answering whisper:

We will. When we know. Soon.

He shuddered in helpless fury and said, /I will do this for my friends, for the Neri. And I will await your answers soon. Damn it. Soon./

The laserlight faded abruptly from his eyes and he blinked in stunned silence at the two robots.

"Cap'n," said Copernicus. "If you're ready, permission for the two of us to join you in the bubble?"

CHAPTER 33

Into the Abyss

IT WAS ALL happening so fast . . .

The robots had joined Bandicut in the star-spanner bubble, Napoleon carrying a strange object like a silver starfish—part of the communications device, apparently. Even as Bandicut looked around, dazed to find himself back in the undersea realm, he heard an audible voice from the device Napoleon was holding.

"*Back away from the entry port . . .*"

It was the voice of the factory. He recognized it, though he had never before heard it outside the direct link.

Back away . . .

L'Kell had heard the instruction and was already powering up to move the sub. The reason for the instruction became obvious a moment later, when the stern of Nabeck's sub poked through the membrane. The rest of the sub followed, as Nabeck also powered up and backed his sub out. As soon as he had enough clearance to turn, he swung his vessel around to face L'Kell's and S'Cali's, and Nabeck himself became visible, peering out into the sea. The view of his friends was no doubt welcome. But what Nabeck thought of the sight of Bandicut and the robots in the star-spanner bubble, Bandicut could not even guess.

/// What's that? ///

/Eh?/

Something else had just appeared through the factory membrane—something very thin and silver and sparkling. It looked like a living thread, snaking out along the silty bottom; it was moving *fast*. It remained attached to the factory, as it grew outward, stretching longer and thinner. The leading end slipped toward the edge of the abyss, and then dropped away into darkness. Bandicut shivered a little as he watched it disappear.

"We need to talk," he called down to L'Kell.

The Neri winched the star-spanner bubble back into place over the sub's hatch. As he was waiting for the chance to return to the sub, Bandicut slowly became aware of a soft glow in the water that was not from the headlights. It was coming from the emptiness of the abyss. The Demon was stirring, perhaps awakened by whatever the factory had just sent down toward it.

As quickly as he could, Bandicut opened the hatch and, leaving Napoleon and Copernicus on watch in the bubble, climbed down to rejoin his friends in the sub. As he tumbled into their midst, he practically wept with joy. "How much did you hear?" he asked, through a tangle of welcoming arms. He looked around into each of their faces. It was clear they'd had a lot more time to be afraid for him than he had had. He reassured them that he was completely unhurt.

"Did you speak with it?" demanded L'Kell. "What happened? Did you speak with the factory?"

They hadn't heard a word of it. He filled them in as best he could, but parts of it were hard to explain.

"Dive to *meet* the Maw of the Abyss?" Li-Jared cried. "You can't be serious!"

"I'm afraid I am. And you know something—I think my stones knew this was going to happen." The memory of the link was roiling in his mind like a bubbling pot—the memory of the stones promising to give him answers when they had them, but as if they knew most of the answers already and were just waiting to fill in the last details. "Most of it, anyway. And I think that's why they told me to bring all of you along on this expedition."

"I, hrrm, have the same feeling about my own stones," Ik said, and peered thoughtfully out the viewport as if there were something else he wasn't ready to say yet.

Li-Jared let out a twanging groan. Clearly the thought of diving into the deepest abyss, and confronting a machine of cataclysmic power on top of it, was almost more than he could take. Bandicut hardly blamed him; he was terrified, too.

/// But don't you think it's the right thing to do? ///

/How the hell would I know? The factory wants us to go; the stones want us to go; but for all I know, it's our death sentence. If it doesn't kill us outright, it'll scare us to death./

*/// I have a feeling, John,
that the stones have more in mind
than just contacting the Maw
and stopping the eruptions. ///*

/What do you mean?/

*/// Well, they definitely have suspicions
about the Maw, and its origins. ///*

/So—/

*/// So I'm not sure what it all means.
But they want to find out more about it.
And about who or what put it here.
This is of great interest to them. ///*

/As much interest to them as saving the Neri?/ Bandicut thought, wondering suddenly if he'd been crediting the stones with the wrong motivation.

/// Maybe as much. Maybe more. ///

/And what do they want to do with this information once they get it?/

/// I'm not sure.

But I think it might mean moving on.
Going elsewhere. ///

Bandicut shivered.

"John? Are you okay?" asked Antares, touching his arm. Her eyes were dark and round and full of worry.

He blinked. "Yeah. Charlie thinks we should go ahead and make the dive. In case the extra opinion helps."

Antares' eyes seemed to take a silent poll within the gloomy cockpit of the sub. It was evident that everyone was willing to go—even Li-Jared, who simply closed his eyes and said nothing. Ik touched the stones in the sides of his sculpted head and murmured his affirmation. As though to confirm the decision, there was a brighter flicker outside the sub, and a soft rumble. The comm squawked, and Nabeck—who at the moment was hovering closest to the drop-off—reported an increase in light activity over the ledge.

S'Cali's voice came into the cockpit, asking L'Kell what they were going to do next. L'Kell told him to stand by, and faced his companions.

"Can your sub go that deep?" Bandicut asked.

"Risky, but it could be done," the Neri answered. "Power reserves could be a problem. And I would have to pressurize the compartment to a much deeper level. Can your bodies tolerate that?"

"Probably not. But we could all ride in the star-spanner bubble, while you pilot the sub." Even as he said that, a tickle from the stones suggested that they agreed.

The suggestion brought a fresh shudder from Li-Jared. At least inside the sub, he didn't have to look out unless he wanted to. In the star-spanner bubble, he would feel completely naked.

"Can your bubble withstand such pressure?" L'Kell asked doubtfully.

Before Bandicut could ask, Char responded,

/// We think so.
And it is capable of pressurizing
if it detects the need. ///

Bandicut nodded. "If our nerves can stand it, I think the bubble can."

/// *And if it does fail,*
at least it'll be over fast . . . ///

———————————

The descent into the abyss was like nothing Ik had ever imagined. They were alone now, crowded into the bubble; S'Cali and Nabeck had been sent homeward with the news of what they were attempting.

It was like falling endlessly, following the path of a fine silver thread into darkness, into light. It was like falling into an aurora-filled night sky. The demon-fire flared with erratic intensity, sometimes seeming to shine up through all of the water below. That was impossible; the entire water column must be aglow. Ik half expected to see the bottom looming out of the depths, but he knew it was still far, far below.

Some moments, it seemed to Ik that they were floating in space, or in one of the shadow-people's fractal-dimensional folds, where no harm could possibly befall them; the star-spanner bubble was made for precisely this sort of environment. At other times, he was aware only of the incredible crushing pressure of the ocean, squeezing squeezing, doing everything in nature's power to crush them out of existence—almost a sentient will to destroy, and them with only an invisible air bubble surrounding them. It made him wonder about the life after, and whether he was about to get a firsthand look.

His companions were crowded around him in various positions: Bandicut standing silent in thought, Li-Jared crouched protectively, eyes squinting, trying to hold onto his sanity. Antares stood just behind Bandicut, not quite touching him, but clearly focusing her thoughts upon him and the support he would need. Something had transpired between them; there was a connection, an intimacy that had not existed before. Ik was glad for that, though he was aware that that, too, could bring problems. The robots clicked and muttered, gathering data.

Three meters below, in the sub, L'Kell was probably wondering if he was piloting his friends to their deaths, and perhaps wondering too if he would ever return to his beloved city and its people. The odds certainly seemed against it.

Ik, for his part, felt a strange calm. He wondered at his voice-stones, which were tickling in his temples, and clearly making preparation for something. He had a strong sense that he had an important role in what was to come.

Through the shifting rays and curtains of light, he occasionally caught sight of the chasm wall, off to their left, where the thread of silver was still visible, dropping downward from the factory. Occasionally he saw small creatures moving along the wall. Some were fish, darting in and out of view; some were floating creatures of jelly and glass, sparkling out of the night like jewels, then vanishing abruptly. They seemed like tiny voyeurs, peeking at him and his mission.

My mission? he thought suddenly, startled by the thought. Just what was his mission—or John Bandicut's, or Li-Jared's? They had been sent to this place from Shipworld, by someone who must have known that there was a crisis requiring intervention, by someone who thought there was at least a chance of the company succeeding in that intervention. But to what ultimate end?

Ik found at the moment that he didn't care greatly, as long as he knew his immediate purpose: to do what they could to save L'Kell's people, and the Astari. And then perhaps to learn of what else was at stake.

Could this job be accomplished by any one of them alone?

The answer to that was clear. Ik sat on his haunches, his stones throbbing in his temples.

———

Time seemed almost frozen, moving in slow, erratic surges as they floated downward. Bandicut stared at the wall off to one side until he could stand it no longer, then stared down into the flashing darkness, his eye caught by the shadowy form of L'Kell's sub, alternately invisible in the dark and then silhouetted against the ghostly rays shining upward, from the Maw. Hairs prickled at the back of his neck, reminding him that every moment the bubble held against the crushing depth was a new miracle.

The sea began to rumble audibly around them.

Surely they were almost there. Surely.

It was like a flare in the night, a fusion burst. Bandicut peered, hoping for a better view. A diamond-shaped *something* of white light blossomed into a halo of radiance. And in its heart was a new kind of darkness, a darkness filled with myriad sparkles, splinters of brightness, pulsing and fading. Streaking down into the darkness, the silver thread from the factory was alive with fire. What was happening? Bandicut had only begun to wonder, when a strange and powerful outcry began to reverberate around him, shaking his thoughts like the cry of a terrified animal—or a short-circuiting machine, arcing into his thoughts and demanding demanding demanding that he set right the wrong and go through go through go through . . .

The robots were clamoring at him—was it Napoleon?—he couldn't tell, but a voice was calling, "John Bandicut, John Bandicut—"

And he was able at last to summon the presence of mind to answer, in a hoarse voice that surely was inaudible against the crashing sounds that filled his head, though maybe not the bubble itself, "Yes I'm here, Nappy, I'm here."

"We have contact, contact—"

"That is good—"

"The antenna and interface are working—" the silver starfish was flickering in Napoleon's hands "—but we have no translation, no understanding. The signal is confounding our analytical circuitry. I cannot even tell you what kind of signal it is."

"Translation—you need translation—"

That was not Bandicut's voice, even though he felt as though it were; it was Ik, staggering forward to crouch beside him, and together they peered over the nose of the submarine and saw sparkling, coruscating fire in the depths below. "What do you think?" Bandicut whispered, not looking at his friend.

"I am ready."

The bubble shook, as a tremor passed through it.

Bandicut turned to gaze at his friend. Ik's eyes were clear, but filled with an inner Hraachee'an fire. The stone in his right temple was pulsating with light. "Ik?" Bandicut said, suddenly understanding. "Are you going to *share your stones with that?*" He pointed down into the fire of the Maw.

"Hrrll. Is it not what we need?" Ik's voice sounded distracted, as though some other conversation were vying for his attention.

"Yes, but—" Was it possible to do this, to share stones with a thing like that?

/// We think so. ///

Stunned, Bandicut thought, /Then . . . it *is* what we need. Exactly what we need. And that's why the stones wanted Ik here, isn't it?/

/// One reason . . . ///

Bandicut nodded slowly to Ik. "I think you're right. I'll help if I can," he murmured. "Are your stones ready?"

"Hrrm, they have been waiting for this, I think." Ik nodded as though some understanding were falling into place for him. He stood in the front of the bubble and stretched out his arms.

"Napoleon, can you transmit that something is coming, something to help translate?"

The robot clicked. "I do not seem able—"

The bubble shook again with another tremor. The sub's maneuvering seemed sluggish. Through the confusion, Bandicut heard a distorted communication from L'Kell. "Having difficulty here. Conserving power . . ."

/Damn. He said it'd be tight. We'll never make it back up, will we?/

/// Weren't we all prepared
for a one-way trip? ///

/Yeah, I guess./ Bandicut drew a tight breath and called back, "We understand, L'Kell. You can turn off your lights, at least."

"I've already done that," L'Kell answered.

The Maw was putting out so much light now, Bandicut hadn't even noticed.

"Urrr, attempting to make contact," Ik reported. There was a sudden twinkle, dazzling—and two sparks streaked out from his head, flashing through the star-spanner bubble as if it didn't exist. They flared downward, vanished into the ghost-lighted depths. Vanished. Nothing else happened.

Had it failed? Had Ik's daughter-stones split for nothing?

Bandicut held his breath. Finally: "Ik? Do you feel anything?"

The Hraachee'an remained silent, but slowly lowered his arms. Something brightened below the bubble. Like an explosion, half masked by clouds. It darkened, then brightened again. This time it stayed bright.

And Bandicut felt something in a front corner of his mind. It was a tickle, mystifying and elusive, and then grew louder, echoing, until it seemed to shoot from one corner of his thoughts to another . . .

is
　is
　　is
　　　is
　　　is
　　　is
　　　is
　　this
　this
　this
this

this

this

this

this

to

to

to speak

speak

speak

speak

speak-k-k-k

-k-k-k

-k-k-k

-k-k-k

-k-k-k-k-k

and then paused, as though trying to analyze what had just happened.

Bandicut sensed Ik standing more erect. The Hraachee'an had heard the voice, too. Softly, Bandicut called, "Ik, do you have contact? Should I shut up and stay out of the way?"

"Hrrrl, I can feel its presence. But it is not clear, I do not understand it. It senses me, senses all of us—but this is something you know how to do better than I."

That's what I was afraid of, Bandicut thought, gazing down into the ghostly fire.

/// I will do what I can to help. ///

/It's so alien—I don't know if I can—/

*/// It's a machine, I think.
It reminds me a little of the robots. ///*

/Is that good? What do the stones—/

/// They want you to try. ///

Bandicut caught his breath and spoke silently but forcefully: /We wish to communicate. Can you understand my words?/

His thoughts were interrupted by a stuttering . . .

cannot

cannot

cannot

cannot

follow your statements

what is good

what is biological

what is neurolink

what is afraid

A pale circlet of fire was rising toward them.

stones parse

robots parse

words parse

communicate parses

The circlet of light twisted oddly and vanished, as if into a strange phase shift.

"Napoleon!" Bandicut yelled. "Do you have contact?" *Robots parse.* /THESE TWO ARE ROBOTS. THEY CAN HELP COMMUNI-CATE./ "Napoleon!"

Bandicut glanced away from the Maw and saw that Napoleon's sensors were flicking madly from Bandicut to Ik to the silver-thread antenna to the silver starfish to the fire of the Maw, as though he could not find the right place to focus.

"Nappy! Coppy! Tell me what's happening! Report!"

He was answered with a loud tapping—Copernicus—and then that robot's voice, garbled as though speaking through water. "It is . . . a machine . . . disabled . . . attempting to regain . . . or reconstruct . . . its design capabilities . . ."

A concussion like a thunderclap knocked Bandicut to his knees. A halo of light surrounded the bubble, then began closing inward, giving Bandicut a moment of panic as it seemed to squeeze the bubble, as though to crush it. But instead of collapsing the bubble, the light drew inward through its walls, until Bandicut and all of his friends were floating in a sparkling glow. And then voices filled Bandicut's head, the inner voices of his friends, and he found himself struggling to connect voices with owners.

Antares: *It is fearful . . . confused . . . we must not be fearful . . .*

Trying to kill us, to destroy us—whispered Li-Jared.

Thing of terrible power, hrahh . . . but has a purpose. I can sense that much, cannot quite comprehend . . .

From another age, another place in space-time . . . displaced, lost . . . whispered the quarx in thought.

And L'Kell: *What are they doing . . . they must do what is needed, and not think of me . . .*

Bandicut struggled to force his own thoughts into clear channels, to separate them from his friends'. Maybe the thing out there could listen to all of them at once, but *he* couldn't. My name is John Bandicut, I am human, I am lost, as my companions are lost. Why do you do this, why do you cause such destruction, what is it you are trying to do—?

And suddenly he felt a strange curling of forces around him, responding to his effort to sort it all out, to focus inward on his thoughts. And he recognized the forces; he had felt them before, in another place . . . in a long tunnel stretching to infinity . . .

He had touched these forces, this *thing*, in the stardrive of the lander's ship.

And the thing touching him now remembered, too . . .

that which was injured

    in distress

        you took away

/Yes. *Yes.* A living being. Harding was his name. You helped me, or the other helped me . . ./

    yes, now we begin to recognize you . . .

        and these others . . . ?

/My friends. All. We work together. Trying to help. Please, what is the purpose of the eruptions—?/

broken, broken, trying to correct . . .

error in previous contact

trying to correct

correct

Error in previous contact? With him? With the Neri? The Astari? Or—

/// The Astari ship.
The Maw caused it to crash,
and it wants to correct for it! ///

Bandicut's head swam. /Is that what you mean? Is that the error? The crash of the starship, all those years ago?/

correct error . . .

boost it through

Dizzily, Bandicut tried to follow the sea of information that was coalescing around him. The connection with the stardrive had caused disaster . . . but he already knew that, it was why the Astari were on this world, why the wrecked ship was there . . .

For an instant he glimpsed the stardrive-room of the Astari ship around him, and he blinked and tried to clear his eyes. But it was not his eyes; what he was seeing was the distorted space-time field of the stardrive; it was bound to the Maw, their alterations of the continuum interlaced and entwined, coiled around each other like a tangle of serpents. And it was wrong, it was an error; and the Maw was trying to untangle, to unsnake itself, to correct the error. But how could it correct an error that had already caused the ship to crash?

There was no explanation now, there was only awareness. Awareness of someone else, someone *not here*, and yet so close it seemed he might touch the other . . . and voices, familiar and un-familiar . . . Astari voices . . .

"Do not . . . we fear what is in that room."

"I fear it, too ... but something is in there, I can feel it pulling, something that needs to speak—"

"Leader, wait—"

But it was too late; he was already inside, and the field was coiled around him, and there was no turning back . . . exactly as Bandicut had felt it once before . . . happening all over . . .

/// It's not you, John!
It's not your memory.
Someone is in the stardrive . . . right now . . . ///

/Yes?/ he whispered dizzily. /But who? *Morado?*/ Drawn in by his stones, Harding's stones? /Why would the Maw want—?/

/// It's the connection between them.
It's still trying to pull the Astari ship through.
It's not letting go. ///

/But I don't—/

The words were swept away by the coiling strains of the field, and it felt much worse than when he had been in the stardrive room himself. He was helpless now in the movement of information and memory. Memory . . .

His breath went out as he caught a piece of memory. But whose, the stardrive's? No, not the stardrive's, the Maw's . . .

It moved through the infinity of space like a panther through woods, like salmon returning from the sea, in search of the connection it had been established to make, in search of its home. It lived for, was created for movement through the light-years. But not its own movement, not once it had found its nesting place; no, it was made to move others.

It was a stargate, a stationary portal through space-time; and it had been given existence, life, so that it might move vessels through the infinite sea of the galaxy and beyond. As soon as it found the place where it was to take up its station . . .

/Given existence, life,/ thought Bandicut. /Is it from Shipworld, is this thing from Shipworld?/

He felt a shudder, and a reply, from Charlie or from the stones, he couldn't tell which. *No, no ... not from Shipworld, or its hidden masters. Not from the translators.* Then from whom? That was what the translators had wanted to know, too. Who had the power to make such things and send them out into the galaxy?

The Others ... as we suspected, feared ...

The Others—?

And what had gone wrong?

A burst of imagery flooded the connection, touching Bandicut and Ik and Morado and all who bore stones of knowing:

Streaming through space, using transformational powers from its own space-time fields, caroming from star to star, drawing energy from the stars and leaving them lifeless in its wake, shrunken and cool. (*Stars supporting life?* Ik cried in silent horror.) Pressing onward, ever onward toward its assignment, snaking outward through the galaxy (*not from Shipworld, from another direction*, whispered the quarx) ... until a stellar encounter that was somehow misread, miscalculated, too many unexpectedly chaotic variables. Instead of providing the needed measure of energy, the star flared up in a nova, engulfing the passing star-gate and nearly destroying it ...

Damaged but still determined, limping onward, it realized the impossibility of reaching its assigned station. And so, equipped with a certain measure of self-determination, it began searching, probing for an alternate site, examining the space-time fabric of the surrounding region in hopes of finding a spot that would allow it to perform useful, if altered, service.

/Then why did you—and how—?/

What happened next was jumbled in memory. There was a malfunction in approaching the selected region. Incorrect data? Broken sensors? Unclear. It focused on a planet (Why? An anchor point? A nest?) and bent space to make an attachment to the gravity well of the planet, intending to spiral in and slowly devour the planet's mass for energy ...

Miscalculation ... malfunction ... errors multiplied in the

orbit, until finally it made a botched forced landing, coiling space inward and materializing once in the atmosphere (*killing my ancestors*, whispered L'Kell) and once again deep in the crust beneath the sea . . .

And then endless reverberations, seismic shockwaves, and a window opening out through the crust into the deep-sea abyss, from the bottom of the world looking up . . .

CHAPTER 34

The Eternal Night

VOICES CLAMORED IN the connection like echoes in a canyon . . .
robot, Hraachee'an, Thespi, Karellian, quarx, human . . .

Bandicut struggled to gather the images like butterflies into
a net, trying to discover what lay beneath the memories, the who
and the why. /You did not intend to destroy the civilization on the
planet?/ he asked the stargate.

> *did*
>> *not*
>>> *come*
>>> *to*
>>>> *destroy . . . . .*
>>>>> *no . . . . .*
>>>> *came*
>>> *only*
>>> *to*
>> *serve*

/Nevertheless, you *did* destroy . . ./

Like a holo of an explosion in reverse, a million bits of memory
coalesced into fragments of history . . .

—sailing proudly into the eternal night, one of a thousand
such, dispersing into the galaxy, long before the failure that

brought it to this place—

—struggling to function in spite of damage—

—trying and failing to stop earthquakes and violent atmospheric storms from destroying fragile constructions on the edges of the continents—

—*a civilization dying*—

—the stargate itself slowly dying—

—frantic attempts to restore itself, to feed matter through interspatial channels, to reestablish normal function, to *correct error*—

—and coiling its fields outward to connect with another intelligent machine passing close by, bringing in this first who might pass through and be boosted onward, as intended—

—*error error*—

—starship struggling to maintain its own course through the tortured paths of altered space-time, but caught helplessly in the web of this other *thing* . . . and finally brought planetward in a cataclysmic entry, grinding into the seafloor—

—while the two minds, struggling to comprehend each other, remained entangled, able neither to mesh nor to separate, and both of them slowly dying—

—but determined to send the starship on its way, to boost it as the stargate had been designed to do—

—trying to do its job—

—before death—

—to correct its error, terrible error—

—must correct—

—must correct—

The Maw was dying. And it was determined to do whatever it could to complete its unfinished task before its strength failed . . . sometime, perhaps, in the next several hundred years.

/You cannot change what has been done—/ Bandicut whispered.

Must

/—it can no longer fly—/

must fly

/—you have destroyed those lives, can only go on with what is—/

what lives?

what lives?

And a furious cry like a fist of darkness rising into the halo of light. "*Our lives! Ours!*"

who—?

"*Our ship and lives that you destroyed—!*"

The voice came from the twisted, tortuous connection with the shipwreck, and Li-Jared's voice rose to meet it with a sharp twang. /Morado! Can you hear me? I feel the stones; can you hear me? Why are you here?/

"*Drew me, the stardrive called me . . . drew me through these stones, there is so much they know, so much . . .*"

/Then you've heard, and you know—/

wait

    do

        not

            know

                the

                    meaning

In answer to the skittering cry, Bandicut called, /What meaning don't you understand?/

Lack of comprehension: lives.

/Life itself? Do you understand life?/

Describe life.

/Do you not know your own life—?/

Before he could say more, there came a howling wind of images from the stardrive, from Morado: Astari struggling to gain a foothold on a hostile seacoast, facing earthquake, unpredictable

seas and storms, failing technologies, dangerous salvage operations in an ocean they didn't understand . . . and sea creatures
who came and vanished . . . until alien stones flickered and blazed
into union with Morado . . .

. . . as they had into the stargate itself . . .

these

> **stones**

> > **from**

> > > **creators**

> > > > **like**

> > > > > **mine**

There was a flash of imagery, like a lightning bolt, too
fast to frame and hold. A glimpse of a world . . . or a collection
of worlds . . . a race of beings, the makers of the stargate . . .
and a need, a responsibility . . . Bandicut couldn't focus; it was
gone.

Different, answered the stones, someone's stones. And
Bandicut realized there was something in the stones' voice that
was ominous.

The stargate didn't seem to notice; but it understood something now that it hadn't. These entities were similar to its makers
in one crucial respect: their machine intelligence. It understood
the stones, and their connection to life, even if it didn't understand the life itself. But could it understand harm? Could it be
persuaded to stop what it was doing?

*/// It believes, to correct its mistake, it needs to
send something winging into infinity. ///*

/Send something winging into infinity—?/ Bandicut said, and
then stopped, caught by a half-formed thought.

"Do you see now?" asked Napoleon, of the stargate. The robot
was trying to explain something to the Maw, trying to explain
that its corrective efforts were harming both organic and machine
intelligences. "But there may be alternatives—"

The Maw rumbled through the sea, and then for a few frightening moments was utterly still. And in the dead silence, Bandicut faintly heard L'Kell's voice: "Motive power is gone. I cannot control our movement. We are descending, and will continue to descend until we strike bottom."

Bandicut shivered. How much farther down was the bottom? Or *was* there a bottom? He felt a sudden pang for L'Kell, who was protected only by the sub's pressure-hull; Bandicut, perhaps absurdly, felt safer in the star-spanner bubble.

The Maw suddenly spoke:

please

   state

      alternative

Bandicut's breath caught, as Napoleon spun out a suggested plan of action . . .

"The starship is no longer flight worthy. However—"

There was a sudden rush of emotion from Antares, or rather through her, *focused* by her. Puzzlement. Desperation. Need. Almost those things; not quite any of them. But it was the stargate's sensation, its near-desperation, as palpable as any emotion from a living, organic being.

Bandicut was so focused on it, he almost missed the final beat of Napoleon's proposal:

/—if you accept a substitute for the Astari ship, your chances of success will be greatly increased. We are flight worthy; you could boost us—/

What? Bandicut thought. And realized that this was precisely the thought that had almost crystallized in his mind earlier. Char had figured it out, and Napoleon. The stargate, more than anything else, was desperate to report a successful transport. Nothing else mattered except that act of completion of its mission . . . its purpose in being . . . before its own life came to an end.

/// *It was programmed to cross the galaxy,*
maybe more than the galaxy,
solely to do this thing and keep doing it.

And if it could do it just once,
and be able to report success,
even to itself . . . ///

Bandicut held his breath, waiting to see what it would say. And if it said yes, what then? Had they just volunteered to be flung somewhere across the galaxy again—only this time not under the control even of the Shipworld Masters, but of some completely different alien intelligence? /Going where?/ he whispered softly. It seemed like madness.

But if it saved the Neri and the Astari from ruin? Wasn't it worth it, for them?

/// The stones are willing. ///

Willing. Because they'd planned it all along and knew what was happening, or because they too saw a thread they could hang onto through the crazy, chaotic winds of this journey? And what of the others?

He dared a glance. From Antares, fear and longing both; and from Ik, determination. And then the stargate replied:

Are

you

starship?

"We are starship," said Napoleon. "Our purpose and nature are as brethren to the ship that has crashed. We seek to find a new world. It is in our nature."

And

your

nature

is

"Intelligence," said Napoleon. "Joined to machine."

Then

said the Maw, and with its words there was a flickering of light against the darkness that enveloped them, *substitution*

is acceptable

"Yes," said Napoleon. But the Maw was not finished speaking.

if approved by

command authority of Astari ship

have you such authority?

"I believe so. John Bandicut?" asked Napoleon.

Bandicut blinked, uncertain; and then from far off, through the link with the stardrive of the sunken ship, came Morado's voice: *"I am commander of this ship, and I have such authority. I approve, provided those before you are willing . . ."*

Bandicut caught Ik's glance, which was fiery. Yes. And he could feel Antares' affirmation.

And Li-Jared? The Karellian was gazing, half-entranced, not into the Maw, but up into a kind of tunnel, where the figure of Morado, encased in an Astari diving suit, was silhouetted against the coiling light of the stardrive chamber. Bandicut could almost read Li-Jared's thoughts from his face: *Let us do this for Harding, to make good his life and his death . . .*

"We are willing," Bandicut said aloud. "But—"

There was a quiet rumble.

"Will you agree, when this task is done—when your triumph is finished—to cease trying to move the Astari ship? To cease creating earthquakes and disruptions?"

it is agreed

this task is our purpose

you will all

take this journey

together?

"Together," Bandicut said. But looking around suddenly, he had a panicky thought. "Except—"

/// L'Kell. ///

The quarx's voice was quiet, but stark.

Bandicut peered down through the bottom of the star-spanner bubble, into the viewport of the sub. He could just make out L'Kell's face, staring up at them—helpless, without maneuvering power for his sub, which was still descending. Could L'Kell hear any of this? Did he know the agreement that had just been reached? Bandicut shifted his gaze, looking for the heart of the Maw's light, but it was impossible to localize now. They were surrounded by an almost celestial glow. "We are willing," he called to the Maw, "except for the one in the submarine, the vessel beneath us. Can you send him back up through the ocean above, to the city in the sea? His home is there, his purpose, his mission. We can move on, but he should not. Can you do this before sending us through?"

Silence. Or not quite silence, but a low hum that grew very slowly until it seemed to fill this glowing abyssal place. And then the stargate replied:

it

   can

      be

         done

if

you

release

the

submarine

Bandicut knelt. His voice caught as he called out to L'Kell. "Can you release the bubble?" He made chopping gestures toward the cables that secured the bubble to the top of the sub. L'Kell peered up in obvious bewilderment. Had he lost power even for the comm? *"We have an agreement with the Maw! Release the bubble!"* Bandicut shouted.

L'Kell's voice came back very thinly: "What do you intend?"

"We're sending you home!"

"But you can't! What about you?"

Bandicut gestured broadly, then cupped his hands to his mouth. *"We're going back to the stars!"*

L'Kell's expression was unreadable, but he suddenly moved away from the viewport. The hum in the ocean was growing louder. Something was opening below them, and the bubble was beginning to vibrate. L'Kell returned to the window. He was doing something with the controls. There was a jarring sensation in the floor of the bubble, and the line at the front of the bubble went slack and floated free of the sub. The bubble rocked alarmingly. The lines at the rear followed a moment later, and the net holding the bubble floated loose. The bubble jostled in the current, not quite lifting from the top of the sub.

L'Kell's face was pressed to the viewport now. His expression was clear: fear for his friends, and grief. Where must he think they were going?

Bandicut raised his hands in salute. The hum had grown too loud for him to speak to L'Kell. /Can the stones make any contact at all with him?/

/// Feelings, sensations . . . ///

/Then send him joy and hope. For him. For us. For his people./

are

> *you*

>> *ready*

asked the stargate.

/Yes./

There was a perceptible surge, as an unseen current lifted the bubble and jostled it away from the sub. A pellucid, horizontal ring of light encircled the bubble now, separating it from the submarine. The bubble stopped rising, but the sub did not. A powerful upwelling current had developed beneath it, made visible now by the movement of suspended silt. Beneath it stretched a glowing tunnel that appeared to reach down into the very depths of the planet. In fact, Bandicut knew, it reached through some twisted bit of space-time to another part of the sea, on the far side of the planet. This time, instead of drawing seawater down in a vain attempt to tug on the shipwreck, the Maw was pumping water upward.

The sub turned as it rose. Its nose came around and, for a few heartbeats, L'Kell gazed straight out at them, his eyes dark and wide with fear and wonder. In that moment, Bandicut thought of all the unspoken things he wished he could say, wishing he could shake L'Kell's hand, join stones with him, spend a night in conversation and learn all there was to know about the Neri. An electric current seemed to join them, and not just Bandicut but all in the bubble. "Hrah, farewell!" called Ik. Li-Jared and Antares both shouted good-byes, and Bandicut cried, *"Godspeed, L'Kell!"* and somehow sensed that L'Kell, through his stones if no other way, had heard them. The Neri's eyes seemed to soften for an instant, and then the upwelling current lifted the sub away from them.

The stargate held the bubble solidly, as the sub dwindled overhead. In the last moments it looked like a toy riding the spout of a fountain, against a haze of spectacular night-lighting. It moved with startling speed, and in another eyeblink was gone.

Bandicut's heart was pounding with excitement and fear and sorrow. Around him, his friends crowded close, encircling him with their presence. He felt Antares' hand on his shoulder, then Ik's. He cleared his throat, not knowing what to say to his friends. "Stargate!" he cried. "The sub has no power of its own left. Can you guide it to the region where there are others like it, near the city?"

this

is being done

prepare now

"It will be all right, I think," Antares whispered.

Bandicut sighed. "Yes. I only wish I could—"

"Rakh, we understand, John Bandicut. We understand." Ik peered downward. "I wonder, where is this thing going to send us?"

Bandicut closed his eyes. /Where are we bound? Where will you send us?/

There was no answer from the Maw. Perhaps it did not even know.

Bong. "Wherever, is better than here," Li-Jared said with a blaze of electric-blue fire in his eyes. He clearly preferred making a getaway to the stars over the risk of dying a piece of flotsam at the bottom of an alien sea.

"Cap'n, I believe we are beginning to be underway," said Copernicus, tapping.

Bandicut swallowed and looked at his friends, and wondered if the star-spanner bubble could exert any influence over where they were about to go.

/// *We shall soon see* ... ///

When it came, it was swift and silent as a dream. The tunnel of light darkened and closed. All the brightness below faded to blackness, and if there was a current still flowing, it was no longer visible. They were surrounded now by a ring of cool, emerald-sapphire light, contracting and hardening.

From out of the darkness at the bottom of the abyss came a flickering of energy ...

fleeting sparks of light, ruby then gold

strobing pulses of color, scaling up and down through the spectrum

and finally the diamond-studded blackness of space, and a sudden awareness that they were falling, *had been* falling. The ring of light around them was gone. The ocean over their heads was gone. The abyss ... the stargate ...

Nothing at all surrounded them now except stars, a heart-stopping panoply of stars.

CHAPTER 35

Chaos Unbounded

FOR A TIME, Bandicut felt as if his heart really had stopped. There
was no sense of motion, no sound; not even the quarx seemed to
stir. Was he suspended in some pocket of reality where everything
would remain frozen for eternity? But no . . . that could not be, if
he was aware of his own thought.

And now he felt something, not outward but inward, as though
his body were undergoing change. Decompression? Renormalization? He couldn't tell, but he felt comforted by the thought, and
clung to it like a child's security blanket.

In time he noticed a slight movement nearby. Ik, just within
his peripheral vision beside him, moving his head ever so slowly.
And now he noticed his own chest expanding in glacially slow
movement, breathing.

And some time later, he noticed that the stars, so pointlike in
their diamond iciness, had blurred. Smudged.

And then Char spoke.

/// We're all . . . here . . . I think . . . ///

/That is good. All here./

Except L'Kell, their dear friend L'Kell. They had not even been
able to say a proper farewell. What of the Neri people? And what
of the Astari? And the undersea factory? And the Maw? They would
probably never know, he thought. Never know.

It saddened him, and yet he felt curiously uplifted—reminded of those images that certain of the quarx incarnations had been fond of showing him as they described chaotic attractors to him: tiny forces kicking spinning, dynamic systems in unpredictable ways, their kicks resonating into the future like the reverberations of a plucked string. Had this company kicked some useful reverberations into the future of the Neri world? He wondered if the translators, or the Shipworld Masters, would keep tabs and find out.

The quarx's thoughts still came haltingly, from the time distortion.

/// Don't forget . . . you left . . .
four sets of stones . . . and an intelligent
stargate. ///

/A stargate,/ he whispered. /A dying stargate./

/// Dying, yes.
But perhaps not . . . for a few
hundred years. ///

/But belonging to someone else. Someone not of Shipworld./

/// Indeed, someone . . .
about whom the stones are . . . deeply concerned.
The Others. ///

/Is this what the stones promised to tell me about?/

/// Indeed.
The Others are a race
whose home lies far across the galaxy.
A race whose goals are inimical to Shipworld's.
To the stones'.
To your own peoples'. ///

/Humanity's? Earth's? Why do you say that?/

/// Remember the stars the Maw put out,
getting to where it was going?

Remember the comet that almost
put out the Earth? ///

Bandicut was silent for a moment. /Jesus./

/// Exactly.
But of details, the stones know little.
That's why it took them so long
to be sure of the origin of the Maw. ///

Bandicut absorbed that. /I wonder where the Maw has sent us. Not toward its creators, I hope./ To that, Char had no answer. He began to turn his head. It was like stirring molasses, but a little less so than before.

In time he managed to bring his head around to where he could see his friends. He discovered that Antares was closer to him than anyone, even Ik. She was looking his way. Almost at his eyes, but not quite, as though she had just begun to glance away from him to gaze into the mysterious infinity of space, wondering also where they were bound. He began to raise his left hand. It felt as though it were floating on a slow-rising bubble, not requiring great effort, but incapable of moving fast, regardless of the force he might apply.

He noticed that her hand was moving, too.

By the time their hands met, her lips had parted in a Thespi smile. Her eyes shone with puzzlement and uncertainty. As their hands touched, and their fingers slowly clasped, he felt her presence within him, in a way that reminded him of their joining through the stones. He felt in her a stalwart companionship, and intimacy, as if they had traveled through danger together for years; and yet also an electrifying alienness. And she touched not just him, but Charlie, too. Char. What connection had they made? He was startled to realize he didn't know, and perhaps couldn't really fathom it if he did know.

What *was* Antares to him now? Friend? Lover? Stranger?

It was still being worked out, he knew, not just in his mind but also in hers. And as he slowly, slowly squeezed her hand, he felt the memory of Julie rising in him, and with it a tide of sadness. And yet, he thought, she would be glad; she would want me to take the chance. I think. I hope.

/// You, John Bandicut,
are a complicated . . . person, ///

the quarx said slowly, in a tone that he thought was approval.

He started to think of an answer to that, but was interrupted by a feeling, almost a verbal thought, from Antares. *You are, and I am, and we shall see. In time we shall see.*

But before he could answer, he became aware of something changing around them.

———————————

There was a faint *crinkling* of the starfield, as though it were embedded in cellophane. An instant later, a shock wave hit the bubble, and it shone blazing golden around them, and for a moment it seemed as if their own bodies were filled with an interior light. Bandicut felt a quivering sense of *release*, and realized that the molasses was gone; he was left in near-shock, but he could move and breathe normally again. Had they arrived, were they arriving somewhere?

Star-spanner beam intercept.

He blinked. /Huh?/

"John Bandicut," said Antares, "I—"

/// The stargate's transport effect
had been interrupted. ///

/By what?/

/// By a star-spanner beam. ///

/From Shipworld?/

/// Presumably. ///

/I'll be . . ./ He peered at Antares, who appeared to be listening to her own inner voices—and then at Ik, whose eyes were alight with inner fire, and at Li-Jared, whose head was snapping back and forth as he tried to take in everything at once. The stars were no longer visible through the bubble, though whether it was because they were gone, or just because the inside of the bubble was bathed in light, he couldn't tell.

"Did you all hear that?" Bandicut asked hoarsely of the others. "We've been grabbed by Shipworld, from wherever the stargate was sending us. I think—I *hope* we're out of the Maw's sphere of knowledge and influence—"

Affirmative. Course alteration in progress

He cocked his head, waiting—and thinking, /Course alteration back to Shipworld? Or to somewhere else?/

He heard a clicking and tapping from the robots, and Napoleon chirped, "Cap'n, I believe we have a transmission coming in. I'm attempting to translate to audio."

"*Transmission coming in?*" Bandicut asked in disbelief. "Coming in from where?"

"Uncertain, Cap'n. Shipworld, I assume. Here it is—"

A voice was speaking to them in English. *English!* And it was in a slightly metallic tone, as if coming from an artificial source. Like a robot . . .

"*Congratulations on your successful departure. I look forward to your return, and to meeting you. My name is Jeaves. If you can hear me, then you know that the intercept by the star-spanner beam has been successful. Godspeed, and drive safely.*"

And with that, the voice fell silent. Around them, the bubble began to change to flickering rainbow hues, and the stars became barely visible again, stretched and blurred into short, angled, moving streaks of light.

Bandicut looked in amazement at Ik, Li-Jared, Antares. "Was that voice speaking in your language?" she whispered. He nodded.

In time we shall see.

In time. Indeed.

—Continued in Book 4 of
The Chaos Chronicles:
SUNBORN—

Afterword

NOT AGAIN! IK thought, as the story opened for our intrepid band. Did *I* know why Ik thought that, when I wrote it? I did not. And that was probably the first sign that *The Infinite Sea* was going to be like *Strange Attractors* at least insofar as I would be writing out on the edge, on a wing and a prayer. There was a reason my subconscious had decided to call this series *The Chaos Chronicles*.

One thing was clearly different in this book, though. I would be drawing more on personal experience than I had in any previous book. How's that? Have I swum in alien seas? Nope. And I've never flown in space, or traveled to other stars. But I *have* logged a great many hours underwater as a sport diver, and some as a working diver—and for a brief period I even worked as a scuba diving instructor. While I didn't know about oceans of alien worlds firsthand, I did know what it felt like to be in the deep and the dark, enveloped by the squeezing pressure of depth, the world transformed into another place and time, measured out by the hiss and bubble of compressed air in water. I'd even done some night diving (my favorite), and had a visceral sense of the strangeness of it, of lights flashing in weightless darkness, of sparkling plankton, of the briny taste and sea smell, of the near-total dependence on technology to maintain existence.

Translating that earthbound experience to an alien world was a challenge, but it was one I felt I could meet. I'd written a couple of undersea stories before, the most realistic one being a near-future eco-short called "Seastate Zero," published in *The Magazine of Fantasy and Science Fiction*. I knew what worked and didn't work in the undersea environment, and I had a pretty clear feel for the sensory details that might bring the experience to life for the reader.

To carry that into an offworld setting, I needed to combine elements of realism with an even greater sense of the inhuman.

Dangers like decompression sickness and nitrogen narcosis still loomed—indeed, the bends would prove fatal to someone at a crucial part of the story. At the same time, this was an *alien* ocean, and unearthly elements pressed in on our people in unpredictable ways. I had a toolbox—to be used cautiously!—that included normalization and translator-stones and other alien technologies sufficiently advanced to be indistinguishable from magic (to quote Arthur C. Clarke). Perhaps those tools could help our band adapt to life under this alien sea. My goal was to write a plausible and compelling story, justifiable in terms of known science but with plenty of latitude for extrapolation. My biggest concern wasn't to persuade you that this is how it *would* be in an alien sea, but to convince you that this is how it *could* be.

As in the previous book, I left the storyline largely up to the characters: I turned them loose to see where they would go. God knows *I* didn't know where it was headed, except in the most general terms. The original proposal as I look at it now seems like an interesting premise for a *different* set of novels.

In an earlier afterword, I wrote about differences in the way writers handle the development of a storyline—some planning everything out ahead of time, and some discovering it as they go. That same principle applies to the characters who live in a story. Some writers excel at getting to know their characters in great detail before they ever let them step on the stage; these writers often have extensive biographies of their characters all written out and organized, for easy reference. It's a fine way to work—*if* your muse works that way. Others learn about their characters as need and opportunity arise. It requires interaction with other characters, with setting and plot, to ignite the synapses in the brain that make you realize, *Oh yes, of course. He was a loner who worked on physics problems, and he was feeling keenly and morosely aware of his aloneness on the night that the aliens came.* That's how it works for me, most of the time.

There is one character in this story about whom I knew a lot before I even began *The Chaos Chronicles*. That's the one who spends the least time on stage: Jeaves, the robot who makes his appearance on the final page. Readers of my Starstream novels (*From a Changeling Star* and *Down the Stream of Stars*, both available in multiple formats) may have recognized Jeaves, who played a key role in both stories. We'll be seeing more of him in the books to come; and if you think this is the first clue that the Chaos universe is the same as the Starstream universe: Bingo, you're right.

I'd like to close with a few words about *The Chaos Chronicles* as a whole—and about the next few episodes in our company's journey. The series has taken far longer to write than I'd ever imagined. Life is like that sometimes. I'm grateful to the longtime readers of the Chaos books who have stayed with me.

There was a long, unplanned gap in publication between this third book, *The Infinite Sea*, and the fourth, *Sunborn*. For contractual reasons and because I needed a break from the world of chaos, I undertook an unrelated novel after this one—*Eternity's End*, set in my Star Rigger universe. Maybe I should have guessed: *Eternity's End* took years longer to write than I'd projected. It all worked out well in the end, but by the time I got back to Bandicut and his friends, the chaos engine had churned things in my head to a fine murk. It took me years longer to sort things out before I would finish *Sunborn*, which was finally published in 2008.

The fifth book, *The Reefs of Time*, took until 2019 to complete and publish; and by the time it was done, it had grown into two volumes, the second being *Crucible of Time*, also published in 2019. I've learned my lesson; I'm not going to predict a publication date for the seventh and final book, *Masters of Shipworld*.

You've been with me, and with Bandicut and company, for quite a journey so far. I hope you'll stick around for the rest of the ride.

Next up, *Sunborn*.

Thank you for reading *The Infinite Sea*. If you enjoyed it, please help others discover it by posting a review in the store where you bought it, or your favorite social networking site. Word of mouth is the best appreciation you can offer to any author whose work you enjoy. Thanks in advance!

—Jeffrey A. Carver

About the Author

JEFFREY A. CARVER was a Nebula Award finalist for his novel *Eternity's End*. He also authored *Battlestar Galactica*, a novelization of the critically acclaimed television miniseries. His novels combine thought-provoking characters with engaging storytelling, and range from the adventures of the Star Rigger universe (*Star Rigger's Way, Dragons in the Stars*, and others) to the ongoing, character-driven hard SF of *The Chaos Chronicles*—which begins with *Neptune Crossing* and continues with *Strange Attractors, The Infinite Sea, Sunborn*, and now *The Reefs of Time* and its conclusion, *Crucible of Time*.

A native of Huron, Ohio, Carver lives with his family in the Boston area. He has taught writing in a variety of settings, from educational television to conferences for young writers to MIT, as well as his own workshops. He has created a free website for aspiring authors of all ages at *www.writesf.com*. Learn more about the author and his work, follow his blog, sign up for his occasional newsletter, and see all of his books at:

www.starrigger.net

About Starstream Publications and Book View Café

Starstream Publications is the publishing imprint of Jeffrey A. Carver.

Book View Café Publishing Cooperative (BVC) is an author-owned cooperative of about fifty professional writers, publishing in a variety of genres, including fantasy, romance, mystery, and science fiction.

BVC authors include New York Times and USA Today bestsellers. Our authors have won and been nominated for numerous awards, including: the Agatha, Campbell, Hugo, Lambda Literary, Locus, Nebula, PEN/Malamud Award, Philip K. Dick, RITA, World Fantasy, and Writers of the Future awards, and the Academy Nicholl Fellowship.

Since its debut in 2008, BVC has gained a reputation for producing high-quality ebooks, and now brings that same quality to its print editions. Find out more and sign up for our newsletter at:

bookviewcafe.com